THE CHASE LIMO
WAS BURNING

Four agents were half dragging a hideously injured body into the lobby. Another agent was pulling the young Air Force officer carrying the "football"—the nondescript case that carried the codes required for the president to initiate a nuclear release—away from the room. The agent heeded the officer's command and pulled a small lever on the case. An audible *pop* came from the case, then fine streams of black smoke.

Bud cringed visibly. The Air Force officer had just given command of the nation's nuclear arsenal to another officer, an Air Force general, high above the plains of middle America in one of the *Looking Glass* command aircraft.

It was an act authorized by only one occurrence: the death of the president.

THUNDER ONE

RYNE DOUGLAS PEARSON

(Originally published in hardcover as *CLOUDBURST*)

AVON BOOKS  NEW YORK

AVON BOOKS
A division of
The Hearst Corporation
1350 Avenue of the Americas
New York, New York 10019

Published in hardcover by William Morrow and Company, Inc.; for information address Permissions Department, William Morrow and Company, Inc., 1350 Avenue of the Americas, New York, New York 10019.

First Avon Books Printing: July 1994

FOR
MOM AND DAD

ACKNOWLEDGMENTS

PUTTING IDEAS INTO words, and words to paper, is rarely a solitary endeavor. Thanks are due.

First, before all, to my wife, Irene, for the encouragement and the love

To Gordon Covey, who helped a neophyte to better understand the fascinating culture of the Arabs

To a certain SEAL, who did "strange things" with dolphins

To R.H., S.H., and M.G., who may never know what they started with their encouragement, but I hope they do

To Tom Colgan, editor and just plain nice guy, for making it better

To Clyde Taylor, my agent, a very special thanks, which these words only begin to convey, for the chance, the belief, and the guidance

And, finally, to those police and military units who work in the shadows, as they must, a thank-you for that which we know of, and that which we don't

PROLOGUE
··············
COMES A STORM

Los Angeles

THE CALF-HIGH, BLACK leather boots hit the carpet with a
muffled thud.

His features were dark, both hair and skin, and in the darkened room his form was specterlike. His eyes surveyed the
area. It was devoid of life, as he knew it would be. To his left
the slender beams of morning light which pierced the adjust-
able window shades were glinting off the polished table tops.

A few words were said to his comrade and then the equipment was passed down, followed by the second man, shorter
than his partner. The tall one gathered his things and went to
the window, carefully parting the thin metal blinds to scan
the area below. The other moved to the center of the room.
He put the satchel at his feet and looked up.

The first movement was visible on the street sixty feet
below. The tall one let the blinds close with a metallic snap.
"It is time."

The shorter man simply nodded and pulled the loading
lever back on his rifle, chambering the first round. Next,
he picked up the green tube and extended the two sections.
Finally, he said a silent prayer and prepared to ready the last
weapon, waiting for the final word from his brother.

After a quarter century of service in the Bureau, Art Jefferson
had learned to stay out of the way when the president came
to town. If he had to serve as FBI liaison, the best place for
him was away from the action, yet close enough to be found
if any Secret Service type needed a Bureau man to answer
a question. The quiet, shady spot on the north side of the
pricey hotel was as far away as he could realistically be,

1

yet it provided what he needed most at the moment: relief from the ninety-five-degree weather, which hadn't abated in daytime for a week. A few steps behind, inside the Los Angeles Hilton, it was comfortably air-conditioned. But it was also teeming with bureaucratic bodyguards carrying Uzis in black briefcases and wearing tiny earphones at the ends of coiled wires that disappeared beneath their collars.

Art instinctively reached into his side jacket pocket, but the cigarettes weren't there.

"Shit!" He hated the idea that he *had* to go without something. It wasn't in him to admit to mortal frailties like high blood pressure and reduced lung capacity. The doctors—three of them—had told him to drop fifteen pounds and kick the habit, or he might end up like a lot of black men pushing fifty . . . lying in his backyard next to the lawn mower and clutching his chest. *What the hell do they know*? he thought.

The sun was just about to peak over the baby skyscraper to Art's right. Even in the building-shaded downtown area the heat was already oppressive in the late morning, and the direct sunlight soon to come would only add to the discomfort. At least Art could be grateful that the hubbub of activity that always accompanied a presidential visit brought with it the disappearance of the normal Sunday traffic. It would have been light for the weekend, but that was a relative term. Light only in comparison to the weekday lines of cars on Wilshire Boulevard, a thoroughfare on the Hilton's north side that stretched west a number of miles to the beaches of Santa Monica, but east for only another three blocks to its end at the base of the One Wilshire Building. The cars filling the street with noise and exhaust fumes on a normal day of rest would have been, at the least, annoying. On a weekday . . .

Art left his leaning post, one of the covered drive's pillars, making sure to put on his mirrored sunglasses. He also nonchalantly ran his right hand up the side of his jacket. It was there. He knew it would be, but checking was a habit developed from a single incident, many years before, that had almost cost him his life. The feel of his gun was reassuring. If he never had to use it again, that was fine; if he did, he was damn sure going to be certain it was there. It was a compulsion, one he was joked about—*Stroked Mr. Smith and Wesson today*?—but so what?

Across Wilshire sat the Secret Service war wagons, identical black Chevy Suburbans, their windows tinted to the point of reflectiveness. In each were five armed-to-the-teeth Service agents, the Counter Assault Teams, who would respond to any call for assistance from the presidential detail leader with authorization to fire as needed to protect the chief executive. The CAT agents would just as eagerly empty their automatics into any perceived threat as they would place themselves between harm and the "man."

Good work by the Secret Service and other agencies had prevented the need for using force to protect the president in the past ten years, but they knew their luck could not hold out. Terrorism had come to the States long ago, though to some it was seen only as a more violent criminal element exposing itself. The truth was more frightening. Violence was not the greatest weapon of the terrorist: Intelligence was. Brains multiplied the effect of bullets by a factor of ten. It was only a matter of time before the Service adage "Innocents be damned, save the man" came to be.

Art rolled up a stick of Big Red, his cigarette surrogate, and pushed it into his mouth, getting an immediate taste of the hot cinnamon flavor. Standing curbside he looked east, to his right. Every building in the vicinity of Seventh and Figueroa, the intersection nearest where the president would exit the hotel, would have a Secret Service countersniper team atop or in the structure, some two. Each pair, distinctive in their mottled gray-black-white urban cammies, was a true team: one spotter with his own M-16A2 assault rifle, and one long-rifleman, master of the PSG-1, a highly accurate and hideously expensive German-made .308 sniping weapon. These teams had an extraordinary degree of latitude when it came to "fire or forget it" situations, even more so than the immediate presidential detail, to the point that they alone made the decision to drop a threat. There was no waiting for the proverbial green light as in SWAT-style operations. They did not take the awesome responsibilities of their job lightly. They would do what had to be done, and God be with the bad guy on the wrong side of the cross hairs.

Art strolled easily, his hands in his pockets. His FBI shield, clipped to his black belt, was the only official ID he needed, being a ranking and easily recognizable special agent of the

Bureau's L.A. field office. His speciality was OC, organized crime investigations, an area he had worked mostly in for fifteen years, and exclusively in for the last ten in the City of Angels. In rank he was fourth in L.A., under Lou Hidalgo, Jerry Donovan, and Special Agent in Charge William Kileen. Art liked to think that the Irish blood at the top was a sign of luck, at least for himself and his fellow agents, but he also knew there was a long tradition of Irishmen in the Bureau, dating back to its beginning. There was an abundance of the people from across the sea back then, almost all sturdy, patriotic individuals who took to their new home quite well. Art's ancestors had had no such luck in the early 1900s. Just avoiding the lynch mobs his grandmother had told him about seemed to have occupied much of their time in Alabama. He didn't put much stock in the belief that something was owed the black man, though, instead believing that one's true grit could be measured by exploiting his own abilities. Some called it pulling yourself up by your bootstraps. Art called it having balls . . . and using them.

He stopped at the corner of Wilshire and Figueroa, the northeast corner of the Hilton's block-square complex. There were a number of uniformed officers of the Los Angeles Police Department standing at several points in the intersection, some near the open-doored squad cars that blocked the streets for two blocks in all directions. Art could see, south on Figueroa, the more heavily guarded area near the presidential limousine, which was hidden from view under the south side covered drive. Numerous black and some white chase-and-lead vehicles were visible lined up through the intersection of Figueroa and Seventh. The short covered drive, with both its entrance and exit on Seventh, was totally hidden from Art's line of sight, but he had seen it many times. It was similar to the one on the north side, though not as ornate, for lack of a better word. Anything other than his beloved, comfortable TraveLodge was ornate to Art.

Catercorner from the Hilton was a Los Angeles landmark, the 818 building, called the "eight one eight" by the natives. Its light red masonry façade had been refurbished ten years before, when Art was beginning his tour with the L.A. office, and the interior was restored as faithfully as modern civilization would allow to its early-1900s decor, save the large, glass-encased show windows on its street sides. The old architecture of the city was a check in the pro column when Art was considering a move from the Chicago office to the West Coast. It reminded him of the beautiful antiquity showcased in his native Alabama, though scholars of design would tell him that the two styles were products of totally different influences. Art didn't look at the subject that deeply. His was a simple appreciation: The buildings looked nice to him.

Atop the 818 a single two-man countersniper team was visible, the spotter's head a foot or so above the tiny circular silhouette of his partner's. Art knew the routine: The spotter would scan a sector, his slice of the pie, with the naked eye, using his binoculars only to take a closer look at what was seen with unaided vision. It might have seemed strange not to use the magnification of the powerful Bushnells. Not so. The unaided eye was the perfect tool of the spotter, able to detect motion over a wide area, which was the basis of his training. See movement where it should not be. The rest, following an instantaneous decision, would be up to the rifleman.

The engines of the war wagons behind Art started, signaling that the president would be leaving soon. He stretched out his left arm to uncover his simple, black Casio digital. Ten-thirty. With any luck he might make it home by one after accompanying the motorcade to the airport. His Bureau Chevy Caprice was only a few feet away, nosed south on Figueroa. He spit the wad of gum into the gutter—the flavor never seemed to last too long, or be very satisfying—and started for his car.

James "Bud" DiContino, the Deputy Adviser for National Security Affairs, commonly known as Deputy NSA, labored down the stairs of the Hilton with his stainless-steel-edged Anvil briefcase in his right hand. He could have given it to an aide to carry, but the contents were sensitive and ripe from the meeting between his boss, NSA Jeremy Paley, the president, and the visiting British foreign secretary. His late wife had given him the case after some subtle comments about how distinctive yet practical it was. At the moment it was neither, feeling simply like a ton of weight, and making him wish there had been room in the elevator.

He didn't really mind, though. This job beat the prospective future of his last one. An Air Force colonel working on defensive penetration systems for the Stealth bomber program in a time of budget slashing did not feel totally secure in his position. The challenges were gone, for him, in the military. Thirty years had been enough. Now he was invigorated by public service. It was exciting and ever-changing, and, most prominently, worthwhile, even with the political BS that came with the territory.

Lugging twenty pounds of material in his shiny briefcase, however, was anything but exciting. Bud looked at his watch as he reached the bottom of the stairs. Ten thirty-one. His wife would slap him if she were there. His lifelong habit of unconsciously checking the time every few minutes had grated on her nerves to the point that he had been required to remove his watch whenever he was at home. *"We have clocks, sweetie"* was her explanation. He missed her.

The heavy fire door moved against Bud's weight, opening into the hallway off the south lobby. He turned left at the direction of a Secret Service agent and walked quickly to meet the presidential entourage, which had already reached the ground floor and headed out to the covered drive. Bud stopped upon reaching the expansive lobby. The desk was to his left, and to the front he could see through the glass walls, watching as the president, his chief of staff, and Jeremy bade farewell to Foreign Secretary Smith with double-grip handshakes. Again Bud checked the time. Ten thirty-three. He looked back up, waiting for the president and his two advisers to get into the first limousine. That would be his cue to exit and hop into the follow-up car.

The handshakes ended and the president, a tall, snowy-haired man, stepped back toward his limo with a toothy smile stretched across his deeply—he would say distinctively—lined face. Then Sam Buck, the president's personal Secret Service bodyguard, reached for the chief executive. His hand had barely touched the president's sleeve when all hell broke loose.

The sight reminded Art of his short stay in Vietnam, all played in slow motion through the windshield. He first saw one streak of fire come from a hidden part of the 818 building and dive down to an area at the south end of the Hilton, followed quickly by a thunderous crack and flash. A second streak followed from the same unseen point, shooting through the smoke trail left by its predecessor and exploding closer to Figueroa in what looked to be a much fierier blast.

Art's cop instincts instantly took over his actions, throwing his body out of the driver's door into the street. His Smith & Wesson 1076 was already in his right hand when he rolled to his feet, pointing in the direction of the 818. There was no cover where he stood. For some reason the door of the Chevy had closed, leaving him crouched a few feet away in the open.

Then came the gunfire. A shitload of it, he thought. Mostly from where the rockets—*they had to be rockets*—came from, steady bursts from familiar-sounding weapons. M-16s! Then the distinctive cracks of repeated rounds from the countersniper teams atop the hotel. The others must have been blocked out, but *they* had a target. Art crouched and ran to the east side of the street for cover against a building and moved swiftly along its wall toward Figueroa and Seventh, looking alternately up to see where the countersniper team was firing and then back to his front. Automatic fire from the bad guys was kicking up dust and fragments as the .223 rounds impacted the street and sidewalk. For the first time Art could see the impact area in the covered drive, though most of the scene was obscured by smoke from a burning black limo. *Damnit!* He looked behind. Three LAPD officers were crouched almost on his ass, following his lead, and, in the background, Art saw the war wagons disappear east on Wilshire, obviously going around the block. It was the 818!

Across the street two Service agents, one with an Uzi, and the other with a pistol and clearly injured, emerged from the drive and ran to the intersection's center, finding cover behind a disabled chase vehicle. They immediately began returning fire and, almost as quickly, the injured agent caught some rounds in the head, which exploded as he crumpled into a ball at the side of the bronze government sedan. The instinct to go to the aid of a fallen brother lawman was suppressed by the reality that they had to get to the source of the fire.

Art peeked around the corner. About halfway down the already bullet-scarred Seventh Street face and five stories up, the fire was coming in steady streams from two windows. One of the war wagons came tearing around the corner of Seventh and Flower, one block east, and skidded to a stop over the curb at the main entrance. Its doors and tailgate swung open, disgorging the black-clad Secret Service CAT team. Two of the agents on the Chevy's street side, one lying on his back, returned fire almost straight up as their three comrades raced into the building. A burst of fire stitched up the sidewalk to the cover of the building's corner, catching Art with some shards of concrete kicked up by the ricochets, most hitting his jacket. One caught him on the right jawline and a trickle of blood began to flow from the half-inch wound. He recoiled around the corner, cursing in pain. One of the cops covered the cut with a white handkerchief, which rapidly turned to red.

"Fuck! This shit hurts!"

"Hold on, pal," the senior cop, a three-striper, said. "It looks like it hit a vein." He pulled back the stained cloth and probed the wound, feeling the dime-size fragment under the flesh.

"To hell with it," Art shouted, pulling away. The handkerchief fell to the sidewalk.

The amount of fire from above dropped off. Art looked around again and could see muzzle flashes from only one weapon, but the rapid *crack-crack* of the long guns high above picked up, peppering the window where the lone source of fire was coming from. Puffs of reddish dust spurted from each impact on the brick frame.

"You guys game?" Art asked, seeing that they were. "Let's lay some fire on."

"Gotcha," the sergeant answered, looking back at his two subordinates and motioning to a white Caprice behind the bronze sedan. Its roof had been opened like a sieve, and its windows spiderwebbed. "On my go."

Art brought his gun up. "Ready cover."

"Go!"

The two patrolmen, one still in his peaked cap, sprinted low the forty feet to the cover of the big car. Art and the sergeant stepped from the corner and fired up into the window. It was a long shot for a pistol, but the rounds were meant mainly to discourage. "Out!"

Both men returned to cover, ejected their spent magazines, and inserted fresh ones. The two cops were holding their guns above the trunk in two-handed grips, but not firing. Then it was clear why.

"It's quiet," the sergeant observed. He wasn't exactly right. A lone Service rifleman was squeezing off rounds into the windows, which were all shattered, leaving only frames between the stone columns.

Art looked around the corner's edge carefully. He saw two blacksuited Service men moving along the sidewalk against the wall of the 818, their guns trained upward. They weren't the two who had rolled out of the Suburban. Those two were still at the vehicle's edge, aiming up, one apparently trying to clear a jam.

For a few seconds it was quiet, almost silent except for the crackling of the burning car in the Hilton's drive.

Then it seemed like the lights went out.

The blast threw Art back, though it was mostly a reflexive act. He landed on the sergeant as the thunder of the explosion rumbled in the street and shattered what appeared to be every window in the nearby buildings. He didn't know how he ended up lying facedown very close to the wall—the sergeant must have rolled him there—but it surely saved his life, considering the shower of glass that rained down from above. Smoke and dust were everywhere, turning day to near night, and the sound of debris impacting the obscured area reminded Art of marbles falling into a cardboard box.

He pulled himself up and was joined by the sergeant. Both saw the pair of patrolmen and the Service agent prone in the intersection, raising their arm-covered heads to see what had happened. They were okay. Art came to a crouch and peered around the corner, rising to full upright at the sight before him. A full four floors of the 818 had been blown out onto the street below, two above and one below the fifth, covering and crushing the Suburban and both men near it. He couldn't see either man, or the two who were about to enter the building, but they could only be under the massive pile of rubble, made up of both the building and its contents. The cop behind him said something into his radio, but Art couldn't tell what. The smoky, foglike haze that filled the space between the buildings on each side of Seventh glowed with light from the flames that were licking slowly from the gaping wound on the face of the 818.

Slowly, the police officers with Art began to converge on the piles of rubble, some trying in vain to find a sign of life. They worked without fear. Nothing on the fifth floor could have survived the massive blast.

"Goddamnit!" Art swore aloud, safing and holstering his gun before turning to walk back to his car. Along the way, without even knowing it, he stepped on his mirrored aviator sunglasses, which lay in the street, crushing them to bits.

Bud DiContino brought his head up and was nearly trampled. Four Secret Service agents hurdled him where he lay on his Anvil. *My ribs!*

Outside, or inside—he couldn't tell which—was mayhem. There was no glass wall where one had been, and no dull metal window frames. Only the heavy support columns, stripped of their decorative covering, were intact. The presidential limo was nosed into one directly in front of Bud, twenty feet away. Its roof seemed strangely ballooned upward and there were no doors on the passenger side, or any windshield, or any windows at all. Everywhere, though, there was glass: tiny blocks of the shattered shatter-resistant panes that had been walls. And there was smoke. Bud saw, cocking his head to the left as he came to his knees, that the chase limo—*I was supposed to ride in that car!*—was burning furiously, sending a chute of black smoke along the roof of the covered drive. Only a little entered what had been the lobby, but it was enough to make the Deputy NSA cough for fresher air.

The four agents who had passed him only seconds earlier were half carrying, half dragging a hideously injured body into the lobby. Another agent was pulling the young Air Force officer carrying the "football"—the nondescript case that carried the codes required for the president to initiate a nuclear release—away from the front of the room. His arm was injured, and he was furiously trying to pull a small lever on the case just beneath the handle. The agent, also injured, heeded the officer's command and pulled the lever. An audible *pop* came from the case, and then fine streams of black smoke, as the codes were destroyed.

Bud cringed visibly. The Air Force officer had just given command of the nation's nuclear arsenal to another officer, an Air Force general, high above the plains of middle America in one of the *Looking Glass* command aircraft. It was an act authorized by only one occurrence: the death of the president.

Bud got to his feet, wanting to see if anyone was left alive, but his endeavor was cut short by an anxious pair of Secret Service agents, both of whom had carried the body in.

"Mr. DiContino, we have to get out of here."

"Is that . . . ?" Bud couldn't finish the question.

"Yes, sir . . . dead. The chief of staff, too. And General Paley. Now let's move!" It was not a choice, Bud knew, as the burly agent spun him around and practically carried him down the hallway by the collar. Ahead was another agent, gun drawn, clearing the way, and behind, though Bud could not see them, were the other two carrying the body of the president.

Paris

Praise Allah!

He prayed silently, thanking the Great One for bringing success to his operation, though it was only the beginning. There was much yet to be accomplished, much that could still go awry. But he had faith, as his mentor had in him, and worry would do no good. As it was, his comrades had penetrated the den of the Great Satan and exacted the first taste of revenge. The television news showed the scene over and over, obviously taken by a very lucky cameraman outside the hotel—lucky not because he got the pictures, but to be alive, as evidenced by the shrapnel-caused crack in the lens and his close proximity to the explosions. Many had been killed, some innocents, and that was expected. Many more would die before all was done.

The name he was known by was Mohammed Hadad, a combination of names he had taken from two long since departed fighters. His given name was part of his past, a life destroyed by the Americans, much in the same way his mentor's life had been forever altered. The past was the past, not forgotten, only put aside so as not to interfere with the purpose. The purpose was all that remained to live for. Exacting a toll on the murderers of so many, a mighty toll, would avenge the spilled blood.

The TV picture faded at the touch of the remote control. Mohammed walked to the dresser near the window. The traffic sounds were audible through the glass as a dull rumble. Five or six floors higher up, where the *very* wealthy stayed, there would have been near silence. Mohammed's room, though, four floors above the bustling Paris thoroughfare, did give a decent view of the city's lights after dark. He was not accustomed to the luxuries, however slight in comparison to many of Paris' hotels, but he admitted they were nice . . . for now.

A quick call to the desk settled his account. *The convenience of American Express.* Mohammed missed the irony of his thought.

His two bags were already packed and waiting on the fold-up luggage tray by the door. One last look in the mirror convinced him he was ready. He looked the part of any number of Egyptian businessmen, which was exactly what his passport identified him as. Mohammed missed the beard, having grown fond of its soft, furry feel when he lay down to sleep, just as his father had missed his after it was so degradingly shaved from his unflinching face by the Zionist vigilantes on the West Bank.

So long ago, Mohammed thought. He stood still and turned to the window and stared out upon the city, though the picture in his mind was that of a small wood-and-stone dwelling a scant mile from the Jordan River. The land around it was hot and arid, and the few people near the Jordan lived similarly. It was a simple life. No, he corrected himself, it *had been* a simple life.

He came back from the daydream, looking again at the mirror. A smile came to his face. His neatly trimmed black mustache and hair gave him an air of professionalism and went perfectly with the clothes chosen carefully for him, and, as always, his smile was affecting. He reached into his inside jacket pocket and removed the clear-lensed glasses, putting them on. It was a look Mohammed wasn't really fond of, but if it worked, so much the better.

The room key was on the bureau. Nothing was left to do. His flight from Charles de Gaulle was scheduled to depart in three hours. He gathered his bags, left the room, and headed to the stairs: elevators in this hotel were unreliable, he had been told. Along the way he thought of his brothers, martyred in the attack on the Americans, and of the words of his mentor, another Arab brother: *"The wind is rising. Soon there will come a storm."*

1

....

ARTICLE XXV

The White House

THE PRESIDENT NODDED to a group of White House servants as he walked past with his entourage, consisting of his COS, Chief of Staff Ellis Gonzales, and four Secret Service agents. The returned smiles from the cook and kitchen help weren't forced, just strained. It was an effort this early after such a long night to put on a friendly face. Seventeen hours before, those at 1600 Pennsylvania Avenue had been answerable to another man, one whom everyone had loved. He was a good man, a grandfather to the nation, and doubly as endearing because of his gentle Southern manner.

The new president was a West Coast native, and, more important, a political maverick who had found his way on to the Democratic ticket a year and half before by dint of his youth and fervor. He, as vice president, had provided a balance with the chief executive, a comfortable symbiosis that necessitated his being relegated to the unseen areas of government. But then that wasn't uncommon for VPs in the latter half of the twentieth century. The position had, like it or not, become largely a training ground for likely electoral winners after a four- to eight-year grooming period. State funerals and "policy reinforcement" trips to wavering third world governments were the norms of the agenda. It was all very proper, and very safe. What had happened seventeen hours before was not supposed to. It was a variable planned for only in Article Twenty-five of the United States Constitution.

Out the windows on his left he could see three helicopters. They were squat and dark, unlike the presidential chopper, *Marine One*. "The lawn looks crowded."

Gonzales looked past his boss as they walked. "Granger came in on one of them. The others . . ." He shrugged.

They turned right at the end of the connecting hallway to the East Wing, heading away from the north lawn. The pace was set by the president, who found himself walking faster than he normally did and slowed, the four agents in tow adjusting their cadence and stride.

"Everybody here?"

"Yes, sir," the COS answered without looking up from his folio. He could do that, walk without looking, the same way he had back in high school with the president. There had been many a memorable backpack trip where Ellis had been walking along some backcountry trail in the Sierras with his eyes closed restfully. He called it peace walking, the president remembered.

There was one more turn, to the left, then the entourage entered one of the three elevators to the White House's lower level, thirty feet below the dew-covered earth. This one opened into a room where a lone Secret Service agent sat behind a wooden desk. He stood when the president exited and returned the nod given him by the nation's new leader.

The room itself was small, barely twelve by twelve, but its purpose was hidden by the simplicity of design. It was more of a passway than a room. Overhead and at the upper sections of each side wall were sensors meant to detect everything from metal to high-density plastic, a necessity in the age of strong, composite materials that were suited to the manufacture of weapons as easily as to aircraft structures. The agents called it the radar room, as there were several millimeter-wave radars used within to detect the exotic plastics. Before anyone entered the room, the air in the elevator was passed twice through a "sniffer" element that could sense the smallest amount of explosive materials.

The security had to be unobtrusive, and effective, since the door opposite the elevator led to the situation room, the working nerve center of the White House during times of crisis.

One of the agents opened the door, pulling it outward then stepping aside.

"Good morning, Mr. President." The chorus from the standing men was new to the president. He had rated only a very courteous "Yes, sir" in his previous capacity. This would take some getting used to.

"Morning." The president moved to his seat at the peak of the half-oval wooden table.

The situation room, as designed, was a functional area for working, much more so than the Cabinet room almost directly above. Mostly that was because of the reduced number of people that were required to be in attendance. That group was usually made up of the National Security Council and, rarely, a few aides. Through a door to the right of three projection screens there were two other working spaces for added personnel, the National Security Planning Groups, deputies and appointed analysts who could be called upon for information and clarification if needed. There was one group working presently, just five people. Assassination was a crisis, though more bodies could do little to aid the situation. As it was, the NSPG was linked directly to the State Department, CIA, DOD, and, quite routinely, to the four major news networks. If they needed something, it was theirs.

Four coffee tureens were arranged within reach of the seven participants, and pitchers of ice water were also present, though, not surprisingly, they were full. The coffee was half gone.

Bud DiContino was there, two seats from the president. The circumstances might have prevented him from attending as acting national security adviser, but the death of the only other deputy NSA two days previously in a boating accident on the Chesapeake left little in the way of alternatives.

The president had immediately noticed the acting NSA upon entering. "Bud, glad you could be with us. I hear you're a bit bruised up."

"A bit, sir," he answered, forcing a slight smile. "And I'm glad to be here."

Secretary of State James Coventry, sitting between Bud and the president, put a hand on the acting NSA's shoulder. "From what I saw you were damn lucky. Damn lucky."

Being in the *inner* circle was new to Bud. Deputies, though close to the power center, were never closer than the second ring of chairs in any official meeting. They would sit behind their principal, sometimes two or three of them, and wait until cued to pass forward some needed bit of paper. It was usually a brief of some sort or, if it was a congressional committee hearing, some piece of documentation or evidence. Necessary bullshit, mostly, Bud believed. Politics. It was the nature of the beast.

"They tell me I started down just before the explosions, but I don't remember that. I think adrenaline wipes out short-term memory. There was enough of it in my veins right then to make an elephant stupid."

Coventry flexed his jaw muscles as the scene rolled again through his mind. The whole front of the hotel and lobby had been demolished and Bud hadn't even been cut. Just some bruises.

The president straightened himself against the back of his gray leather chair. He felt tired, and wondered how he looked. If it was like the others in the room, probably like shit. Fifteen of his last seventeen hours had been sleepless and filled with a somber swearing-in ceremony in the Oval Office, an emergency Cabinet meeting as the clock tolled midnight, and several other official meetings with the chairman of this committee and the majority leader of that house. It was a blur, literally, and that couldn't continue, for him or his Cabinet and close aides. They were human, after all.

"All right, let's get going." He slid a stack of his schedule for the day to both sides of the table. "Today's busy, as you can see, but I want to make something clear," he said, his tone bringing eyes up from the paper, "I want each of you to schedule some sack time. You all have deputies . . ." The president caught his mistake as his look passed over Bud. " . . . or others who can hold down the fort for a while." He'd make sure that his acting NSA got some assistance. "Capishe?"

A staggered recital of "Yes, sir"s acknowledged the request. Or was it a directive? A presidential directive to sleep? Coventry mused.

"Ellis, do you want to start?"

"Certainly, Mr. President," the chief of staff said. His black hair, however well he might have combed it, never seemed quite right. It had always looked just a little unkempt, even back in their younger days. "I talked to Jeff at Protocol about an hour ago. He says the funeral arrangements should be completed by this evening. It's tentatively set for Thursday at Mrs. Bitteredge's request. She wants to wait until the family can all get here."

"He had kids . . . how many? Nine . . . all over the place." FBI director Gordon Jones shook his head. "Two are in Africa with the Peace Corps."

Bud leaned in. "What about Jeremy's, Ellis?"

"Thursday or Friday. The family wants a private ceremony. They're going to fly him back to Montana today." The COS saw Bud nod acknowledgment and went on. "There's no official word from the British embassy on the foreign secretary's funeral yet, but I wouldn't expect anything on that until later today. We will need to notify them of our representation, sir."

"Right. I'll touch on that later. Anything else?" Gonzales shook his head. "Secretary Meyerson."

"Sir. Mm-uhm. Excuse me. I just can't shake this flu," the secretary of defense apologized. As much as he hated to admit it, he did resemble a graying Clark Kent. "General Granger can cover any specifics if need be," he said, gesturing to the Chairman of the Joint Chiefs of Staff. "As for generalities, we're maintaining a slightly increased state of readiness worldwide—the military jargon is condition Bravo—as a matter of prudence. Some of our higher-risk outposts, like Guantánamo and South Korea, are taking some further precautions. This is standard procedure following any unforeseen event, especially when the upper-echelon chain of command is affected.

"That aspect of the situation went very well. Our system of control over the strategic forces is intact, and the transfer went quite well, considering."

"How long was an elected official out of control?" the

president asked, obvious to point out his concern with thinly
veiled words.

"About twenty minutes."

"And in the interim?"

Meyerson looked to Granger. The smooth-headed soldier—
Chrome Dome to his adversaries on the Hill—cleared his
throat. "Mr. President," the four-star Army general began,
in his well-known slow-cadenced voice, "our Top Hat commander aboard *Looking Glass* passed the ball, so to speak, to
you as soon as you were confirmed in position. It went damn
smooth considering Naycap was off cycle at the time."

"What is Naycap, and what is off cycle?" the president
asked. "Something doesn't sound right about that."

You're right, Granger thought. Maybe he could score some
points for the service here. "I'm sure you know what it is. We
get used to acrospeak, sometimes. Speaking in our language
of military hyphenations and what have you. It's actually the
NAACP. You can see why we modify it. There ain't much
about civil rights to do with it, and we don't want to offend.
It stands for National Alternate Airborne Command Post. It's
the pure military equivalent of your Kneecap, or NEACP—
National Emergency Airborne Command Post." Kneecap was
in a hangar at Andrews Air Force Base, ready to leave on
two minutes' notice. Its purpose, like its military counterpart,
was to provide a safe aerial command post to direct U.S.
forces in the event of a nuclear attack or serious threat. "Up
until eighty-seven we had one *Looking Glass* aircraft up at
all times, usually just flying randomly over mid-America.
They'd stay up for sixteen hours at a time, sometimes longer
if need be. There are two complete crews on each—we have
four aircraft—and tanker support can keep them flying until
something critical gives out."

"The routine shifted in eighty-seven, sir," Meyerson added.
The president looked his way, then back to the general.

"The administration at that time, sir, well . . . if you'll par-
don the critique, they fell into the tunnel-vision syndrome.
Since the Russians were starting to play Mr. Friendly it
didn't seem all that necessary to have a *Looking Glass* bird
up around the clock. They decided that just having one on
the runway at ready five—ready to take off with only five
minutes' warning—would do. But, as this shows, we don't

have to have a major threat pointing a gun at us to see our triple C get all screwed up." Granger saw the puzzled look in the president's eyes, but not on his face. "Command. Control. Communication. In a war, or a near-war situation, those abilities are paramount."

The general looked at each man. "The scary thing about this is that there was a window of vulnerability for us, and a goddamn big window of opportunity for someone who might just decide to take advantage of the situation."

"I agree." The president's words stopped the exchange cold. Granger turned to face his commander in chief. "The general is absolutely correct. Now don't sully my hard-earned reputation by granting me hawk status," he prefaced, hoping the humor would lighten the moment, "but I don't believe we can afford to be caught with our pants down . . . ever. Not for a second. Drew, I want around-the-clock readiness of the National Command Authority ensured. If that means flying those Looking Glass planes twenty-four hours a day again, then do it."

"Yes, sir," Secretary Meyerson acknowledged the order, calmly but with satisfaction welling inside.

"Anything else, General?"

"No, sir."

Secretary Coventry caught the visual cue that it was his turn. "Sir, there is nothing out of the ordinary from our embassies. We have, however, received a number of inquiries from governments concerning the timing of the services. Is there any time frame for putting the word out?"

"ASAP," the president answered. "If that would be proper. Ellis?"

"I'll draft a statement for you. Noon okay, Jim?"

"Fine. Nothing else, Mr. President."

"Okay. Gordy?"

The FBI director passed a two-page brief to the other participants. The president had received the same report earlier. "This is a preliminary report from the Los Angeles field office. They're handling the investigation. It's still in its infancy, but we are getting some good information, though it's just about all physical evidence from the lab at this point. We were fortunate, however, to have a senior agent on the scene as the assassination happened. He even got a piece of the action and caught some shrapnel. Anyway, he's heading up the investigative team out there, which gives us a good start." Jones noticed that each man was about done with the first page of the report, and moving on to the second. "You can see, I take it, that there are a couple of interesting questions raised by what's come to light thus far."

"To say the least," Granger commented. "But some of this is damn thin."

Herb Landau, the director of Central Intelligence, agreed with the Chairman of the Joint Chiefs, but for different reasons. Granger thought in his own terms; invariably, Landau knew from experience. His appraisal came from black-and-white logic, whereas the DCI's doubts came from more of a personal, secret knowledge. Unconfirmed, yes, but the supposition had hit him immediately upon hearing of the assassination. The report, which he had seen even before the president had—thanks to the close relationship between the Bureau and the CIA—added credibility, if not confirmation, to his . . . guess?

Landau's guess, if verbalized, would carry weight. He had been a fixture in the government mechanism for forty-seven of his seventy-seven years, though DCI was his first high-level post, one that the late president felt he been too long overlooked for. That was the nation's loss. His crotchety exterior was as unlike his real self as appearance could be. "The general has a point, though I can't speak for his thinking on it. I see the information as interesting. Maybe even a little worrisome. But how it can affect our impact on the probe I'm not sure."

"It's just preliminary, Herb." Jones's tone was agreeable. "But this is the way an investigation starts. A little conjecture has to be the lead after any hard evidence. That's the natural investigative process."

"M-16s. LAWs." Granger scoffed noticeably. "Do you know how easy those are to get on the arms market?"

"Outside the United States, yes, very easy. But internally there's a pretty tight grip on any missing stock," the FBI director pointed out.

Bud jumped in. "Wait. That doesn't fit. How does the Bureau keep track of a *missing* bunch of weapons. That's contradictory. If these guys were able to utilize assault rifles and anti-armor weapons to kill the president, then something didn't work. Somewhere they were able to get the stuff to do all this with." Bud was a little heated. He had seen the effects. "Tell me—is it easier to smuggle those types of weapons in, or to get them right here? I'd really like to know."

Jones felt the animosity to his line of reason, but he was a reasonable man and could easily understand the acting NSA's motivation. "It's all a matter of circumstance. Sure, there are some military weapons floating around out there, on our own streets, but holders of those stocks tend to try to sell them en masse. That keeps their distribution and storage problems to a minimum. Bringing them in from outside the States is just as easy sometimes, and much harder others. It's all situational. What my real gist is that once a weapon shows up we have a good chance of identifying the source. That's tracking. Once we track and pin that person or persons down, then we have a bust." Jones still talked like a street agent at times. That was natural, considering his twenty-eight years in the FBI. That a street agent had risen to the post of director was highly uncommon in the days of political appointees. "Now, the other side of it: Why and how? It's pretty clear that there's a conspiracy of some sort. Two killers just don't penetrate a security perimeter with the weapons they had unless there was some pretty decent assistance. The mere number of killers—two—indicates the lowest form of conspiracy." Jones hinted some frustration. "Unfortunately this kind of thing doesn't lend itself to a quick solution. Every hour past twenty-four it's going to be tougher to zero in on any other players."

It was quiet for a few seconds.

"Hell of a security perimeter," Granger observed sarcastically.

"The Service is working overtime to figure it out," Jones said. "And no excuses. Somebody screwed up royally."

Royally. Bud thought that was an understatement. His emotions were running rampant inside, and finally it clicked in him. *Sink or swim, Bud*. This wasn't the time for petty emotions to cloud his professionalism. "Somebody on the wrong side was good."

Landau noted the change in Bud's tone. He scanned his

memory for specifics on the man. Early fifties. Retired Air
Force, and a graduate of Colorado Springs. Left as a colonel, wasn't it? There was more but the director's once fine
memory didn't retain as well the past few years. His wife
told him he was getting foggy. Other factors were affecting
it, too, though he wouldn't admit to that.

"Good may be an understatement," Landau said. "To pull
that off they had to have good intelligence on their target, or
targets. Like the director said, they didn't decide to do this
overnight. There was a leak somewhere. Maybe innocent, I
don't know. But this meeting wasn't even set until a month
ago. That's a short amount of time in the real world to
pull off this sort of thing. Hell, I don't even know if the
location of the meeting was publicized much before last
week."

The implications of that were unspoken, but fully understood. Somewhere, someone had access to schedules and
the like, and the transfer of that information had cost men
their lives.

"Herb, what did you mean by targets?" the president asked.
He poured a first cup of coffee before the answer.

"We're only assuming that the president was the intended
target."

"Who else?" Jones posited. Then an alternative flashed.
"The foreign secretary?"

"A possibility," the DCI agreed, though only in words. It
was possible, but not likely. Possibilities had to be explored,
though. "We know the IRA has access to the firepower and
their networks in this country aren't bad. It's mostly prevalent out here, in the East, but . . ."

Jones wondered if L.A. was looking at that angle. He'd
mention it to them.

Landau continued, "And the money end of it." The balding CIA chief held his hand out and rubbed his thumb
back and forth across his outstretched forefingers. "They
needed moola, and lots of it." He sat back in the chair. His
snow-rimmed, gaunt skull made him look sickly, though he
had always been a wiry-framed man.

"Exactly," Jones confirmed. "This wasn't a couple of
Hinckleys. We're more than likely dealing with some major
players here."

"That could influence our response to this," Bud added, carefully avoiding the word *reaction*.

The president knew the eyes were upon him. At thirty-nine he had a lot to prove, or so some would say. He wasn't above admitting that he had a great deal to learn. "Bud, I'd like you to put together a list of options we have if this turns out to be what I'm afraid it might, considering what I've heard so far. Tomorrow's good."

"In the morning, sir." Bud quickly jotted a few ideas that were fresh in his mind.

"Now, shifting gears a little," the president began, closing his folio. "I'm meeting with the congressional leaders at eleven. Hopefully that'll go smoothly. I don't anticipate anything out of left field. I'm going to ask for some assistance, butt kicking if necessary, to get my nomination for vice president through the Senate. I've decided to ask Nate Harmon to accept the job." He waited, letting the choice settle in. "Any comments?"

"He'll fly through the process," the secretary of state noted. "I don't think there will be much need for 'butt kicking' to get the nomination confirmed." He looked around knowing that there wouldn't be any disagreements.

"Definitely," Bud said. "Four Senate terms. He's squeaky clean and—"

"And old enough to be your father, Mr. President," Gonzales finished the sentence with a grin.

"As is three quarters of the membership of both houses," the president responded. There was a unified chuckle.

"His antiabortion stand conflicts with your view on the subject," Meyerson pointed out, raising the first possible concern. Granger, sitting to his left, knew this wasn't his area to input. He was a soldier. The vagaries of bureaucratic goings-on were uninteresting to him, and he often found himself cynical when allowed to observe. This wasn't his place.

"I was no clone of President Bitteredge, if you remember. But he knew that." *He knew a lot.* "It was a strength to him to have a . . . I don't know . . . maybe a counterweight of sorts on the other side of the fulcrum. I think Nate Harmon will be a good addition to the administration."

There was no further discussion on the decision. It was

a wise choice. Nathan Hale Harmon had been a constant player in government since the early fifties when he began his long career as a public servant with the State Department. He could have opted to continue as a paid appointee, but allowed himself to be chosen instead for office by his home state of Louisiana. The president expected him to accept and felt that he would be the proper representative at the services in Britain. The others concurred.

With the meeting over, the president rose, as did the others in the accepted show of respect, and exited through the heavy oak-covered steel door. His augmented security detail met him and escorted him and the COS to the Oval Office.

The other participants gathered their things and filtered out, Director Jones leading off to his waiting car. He seemed to be in the most hurry. Granger and Meyerson quietly exchanged critiques of their new boss. There was nothing improper about that, Bud thought. He was doing the same thing silently.

Herb Landau strained against the armrests to push himself up. The doctors had said it would be a matter of months. Spinal cancer was a hideous thing and unfortunately not as painless as some forms of the disease. He walked over to the acting NSA in steps that he forced to appear normal.

"It may not be appropriate," the DCI began, "but congrats, Bud."

He took the director's hand. The old man still had a hearty grip and shake, which Bud especially felt in his right side. "Thank you, sir, but it's not official." The grimace was obvious.

"It will be. Like it or not, he's going to ask you to be his national security adviser." The director's expression changed. "Bad, son?" Landau was genuinely concerned.

"Three broken ribs. Landed on my briefcase." Bud tapped his Anvil, which he had lifted to the tabletop.

The director, who stood a head shorter than the NSA, brought a closed fist to his own stomach with a *thump*.

"I broke every rib and both legs on the *Lexington* back in the big one. It hurt like a son of a bitch for a year, every time I breathed. They can't tell you how to stop breathing, can they?"

Bud smiled. "No, sir. The tape doesn't help much either. Just seems to squeeze tighter every time I take a deep one."

"Stick it out, Bud." The DCI almost made a comment about making sure the wife took care of him, then remembered that the man's wife had died a few years back. Heart attack, or something. "Listen, son, could you come by my office later today? Say one o'clock?"

"Urgent?"

Landau didn't want to telegraph the genuine concern he felt. "I'm not quite sure, but I'd feel better if you would look something over for me."

Bud mentally checked his schedule. He could push back the meeting with the German ambassador a couple of hours or so. "Sure. One's fine. Is this quiet?"

"I'd appreciate it." The DCI pulled out his small pocket calendar and made a note to himself. "I'll have a bird here for you at about half past twelve."

"Fine."

A parting handshake, gentler than the first, and the DCI was slowly on his way. As he walked away his gait appeared somewhat shuffling. His own detachment of plainclothes Agency security was waiting in an anteroom near the elevator upstairs. They formed up and escorted their chief to his helicopter.

Bud finished stowing his papers in the case. The lid closed with a sharp slap. Lifting his eyes he saw that he was alone in the room. He hurried out, passing the guard outside without a look.

Los Angeles

There were twelve round tables arranged in one corner of the banquet room. Each had at least one phone, one had four, and duct-taped wires snaked along the floor to a temporary junction box just inside the only open door. Contrary to the fire regulations the other four doors that led out of the room were secured, chains and padlocks around their panic bars. But then the hotel was empty, much to the displeasure of its manager.

The makeshift office was temporary home to the FBI's

investigative team, which exceeded two hundred agents, though most were in the field following the scant few leads there were or just arriving in the city. Offices from as far away as New York were sending agents to augment the resources on hand, and that was fine with Art Jefferson. He knew he would need a lot of manpower to sort this one out.

Other government agencies were working with the Bureau, each having a senior representative who reported to Art. Alcohol, Tobacco, and Firearms, the government apparatus whose name, when compared to others, most accurately conveyed the scope of its mission, had agents sifting through the debris-strewn street below the 818 and inside the damaged areas of the building. ATF's work had paid off so far with an identification of the types of weapons used. Now they were trying to find evidence that would aid in identifying the source of the weapons, and, working with the Bureau's explosive experts, trying to determine the maker of the explosives used in the blast.

Art read over a brief summary of findings prepared by his second, Special Agent Eddie Toronassi, affectionately known as Joker by those fortunate enough to have avoided being a victim of his near legendary practical jokes. Art called him Eddie.

"The shooters weren't born on the fifth floor," Art said, sipping from his convenience store cup of coffee. The Hilton's kitchen was closed. "They came from somewhere." He looked up. "Where?"

"You got me, boss." The fourth-generation Italian-American agent had spent an hour putting the report together. He wanted answers as much as Art. "You know what: These guys were stupid. They did things all wrong."

Art coughed up a swallow of coffee. "You might find some different opinions on that one."

"Sure." Eddie's eyes, crystal blue like cheap marbles, lit up. "They killed a whole slew of people—"

"*A whole slew of people?*" Art responded, flipping to the last page of the report: the casualty list. "The president, his national security adviser, the British foreign secretary, *fifteen* Secret Service agents, six local cops, six government aides—four American and two British—and two bystanders.

Twenty-two injured. Shit, Ed. I'd call that a fucking accomplishment."

"Yeah, but they were sloppy in some ways, and smart in others. Kinda cocky, yet paranoid." Eddie's face expressed mild bewilderment.

"What do you mean?" Art leaned back in the swivel chair he had borrowed from the front desk.

"Take the rifle we found—the parts, anyway. The stamp markings were bored out. I talked to one of the ATF techs, and he said that it must've been taken apart and sanitized. And from what he said it's not easy. It's not the same as filing down some serial numbers like they did on the receiver. That's solid steel, so a file does the trick. All that's there is a shallow gouge. The numbers that are stamped on are a whole different story. When they make the guns there's a lot of sheet metal used. He says it's easier to manufacture and—"

"I'm up on how they're made, Ed."

"Okay." Eddie had a tendency to get excited when detail work was needed. It was his forte, and a small embarrassment at times. He continued, "So the stamp in the sheet metal is another identifier. When you file it down you end up with a hole. You've gotta practically cut out the stamped part and weld on a patch flush with the rest of the metal. To me that sounds like someone who wants to cover his trail."

Art continued to listen attentively as Eddie reached across the table and took the bag which forensics had delivered earlier. "Then they're stupid. Kinda like they don't care if it helps us ID 'em. I'm not talking about flaunting anything. Just carelessness . . . no, indifference. It just didn't matter." Eddie shook the contents of the clear plastic evidence bag. Inside was a blackened, melted lump of plastic whose previous form had been narrowed down to some type of credit card, though any further specifications were impossible to obtain. "And that . . ." He motioned to another of the Ziplock bags. A single wallet-size picture shielded by the body was the only contents, showing a young man and an even younger female child, each dark-haired with obvious Mediterranean features. "I mean, we don't know who the people in the picture are, but it's a clue. If I were gonna do this, I'd wanna ditch this stuff before I did any shooting."

"Ed, these guys were suicidal. They didn't have to hide their identity."

"Then why clean the weapons? Huh? Why the trouble?"

Art thought for a moment. "Apparently the shooters didn't give a damn if they were fingered, but they wanted the trail to stop with them."

Eddie nodded. "That's what I'm thinking." He tossed the evidence bag containing the plastic lump on the table. The other one he held up. "You've seen the picture?"

"Yeah." Art took the bag and studied the faces through the plastic. "But I'm trying not to jump to any conclusions."

"You think it, too."

"What? That the shooters might have been Arabs? Just because of this." He slid the bag across the table. "Come on."

Eddie sniffed a laugh and pulled out a handkerchief. *Damn cold!* "How's your jaw?"

The stitches were hard to the touch. "I guess I'm going to have a macho scar."

"You were lucky."

Art remembered having been ready to dash across to the 818 just before it blew. "More than you think, Ed."

Another agent brought in a box of coffees. Eddie took one and slid a chair around. "We're gonna run dry here in not too long. What's next?"

"Like always. Who? Who were the shooters and where were they from? How? They got inside the security zone; that is not supposed to happen. How did they do it, and what help did they get?"

"Another 'Who?' " Eddie said.

"Correct. And why? Suicide is something you think about. What pushed them to do this?" The inevitable assumption of some kind of fanatical terrorist bent on death, or glory, or whatever they called it, flashed in Art's mind. *Remember Beirut.* Those people were crazy. And the picture. He couldn't let a snapshot of two Arab-looking kids influence him right now. It could help, though.

Art exhaled heavily through his nose. "We have to start with 'Who?' The other stuff is going to all come from that."

"So we've got two guys, almost surely male." Eddie

pulled the flimsy lid off the cup. He never could stand drinking through those flip-up openings. "We have nothing on a physical makeup yet."

"Who has the bodies?"

"You mean the pieces," Eddie corrected. "The county coroner. Stan is with him. You know he told me the only way they could tell right away that there were two bodies was the arm count. They found parts of three." He laughed. "Maybe it was one guy and he was a Medusa or something."

"You're sick, Toronassi."

The conversation was interrupted by another agent. "Sir, they want you outside."

A minute later Art and Eddie were standing at the base of what had been the original rubble pile, which was now divided into several smaller mounds of debris as the sifting progressed. They looked up at the gaping hole in the front of the 818. Floodlights, still providing illumination in the early-morning din, outlined the damage. A full four floors were literally gone, blown out both front and back of the tall structure. Art wondered what times out here were like when the 818 was *really* a tall building. Now it was dwarfed in the shadows of its steel-and-glass successors to the east, and barely rose above some of the buildings along the Wilshire corridor to the west.

"Best guess so far is fifty pounds of C-4," Eddie said, referring to a military-use explosive. "Hellish."

Art didn't respond. He just turned away, amazed that anything had survived as evidence.

"Sir," an overall-clad agent said.

"Jefferson." Art extended his hand, not recognizing the agent.

"Agent Mike Stafford" came the reply, very formal and businesslike. "San Diego forensics."

"Right. You work with Dan LaVerne."

"That's right."

"He's a good guy. Has he still got that enormous dog?"

"Irish wolfhound, sir. He calls him Sir Galahad. I met the mutt at a barbecue he threw out at his ranch near Fallbrook."

"What do ya know. Small world. What have you got for us?"

"This." He reached into his breast pocket.

Eddie smiled. "Bingo!"

Art took the bag, smaller than the evidence holders. It held a single key, which appeared to be untouched by the blast. "Where did it come from?"

"Embedded in a piece of buttock we found a little while ago," he answered matter-of-factly. "Over there. The location makes me think it was one of the bad guys. We found some other parts there earlier. This was deeper."

"In his ass. Can you beat that." Art held it up to the light cast by the floods. "Awfully clean."

Stafford shrugged. "It was probably in his back pocket. We were able to pull some fibers out with it. Those might help us, but that . . . not with body oils and the like. We couldn't pull a print, or even a partial off of it in a million years. I thought you guys might be able to use it."

They could. Art turned to his second. "There's no marking on it."

"We could tell what model from the book," Eddie said. "Hell, there's probably a locksmith around here who could tell us quicker than that."

"In a while. We can move on it now. This means they drove here."

That was almost a surety, Eddie thought. "I'd bet on it. And if they drove here . . ."

"Right!"

Minutes later they had twenty agents redirected to several locations within walking distance of the 818.

London

The young Irishman set the one Samsonite down on his right and knocked four times as he had been instructed. *They said four, didn't they?* After pausing thirty seconds he knocked again, three times. There was no answer, which meant he could proceed. He inserted the key and opened the door to the modest second-floor flat. The front room was furnished comfortably, he noticed, but he did not linger to enjoy the decor. An easy kick closed the door behind him. The hall ahead led to the bedroom, or so it should if his instructions were correct.

They were. He laid the one Samsonite at the head of the

single bed, and the other at the foot. The key to the flat was left on the one at the head.

He gave the room a look from where he stood. It was nice. Nicer than anything he'd ever lived in. The colors were peach and blue, and the only window was catching the afternoon light. Back to his duty. He opened the second suitcase and removed its contents: a leather shoulder bag and a cloth sack which held the valued contents. As per his instructions he put the sack into the shoulder bag and closed the case. On his way out he noticed that the flat lacked some of the small things that came only with occupancy. Pictures and the like. This piqued his curiosity but did not break his discipline. He resisted the urge to explore, which was natural, having never been far from Belfast before.

With the brown leather bag slung on his right he exited the flat, locking the door before closing it behind. He could feel the other key in his shirt pocket without having to touch it. But he was nervous and ran a hand up just in case. *In case what, you fool? You already locked the bloody door!* To himself he shook his head. Iain *would* have to pass this one on to him.

The other flat was a half a kilometer away. He would leave the shoulder bag there and drop the key in the WC. Then, he would be on his way. The underground would be near, as would a bus stop. He would try the underground, he thought. It would be fun. Just a phone call left to place in a few hours. It wasn't really work, then, was it, lifting up a telephone? It was all the better, though. He understood the need for a routine.

It's not too bloody bad, this job.

Fort Bragg, N.C.

He looked little like a soldier at the moment. He was, in actuality, much more. The shorts *were* military-issue swim trunks, but the T-shirt, emblazoned with a neon Nishiki logo on both the front and back, was nonregulation. That was excused, even expected, at the Stockade, the former military jail, which at present, and for the past decade and a half, housed the world's most elite counterterrorist force: Delta.

"Gotcha!" Captain Sean Graber blurted out. He had been

at *Demon Ninja* for over an hour already and had, as yet, made it through only two of the twelve known levels. There would be more, he knew. New computer games from the *Demon* series had never disappointed him.

"Slay a nuclear robot or something?" Buxton asked. He was a lieutenant, right below Graber in team seniority, and he dressed equally as comfortably.

"A dark lord," Graber answered without looking. "You want a try next, Chris?"

"Yeah, right." Buxton snickered and went back to his book.

The eight men of Charlie Squad, Special Operations Detachment Delta, had been on alert since 1330 the previous day. That was a precaution and basically it required the team to be near their barracks—the unit rec room in this case— and have their gear ready. The latter was accomplished soon after the alert in the indoor firing range. They all checked the sighting and performance of their three standard weapons. Any special needs would be taken care of as required.

"Captain." It was Major McAffee.

Graber paused the game and came to a relaxed attention, as did Buxton. "Sir."

"The rest of your squad, Captain—where are they?" McAffee looked all business. He wore the old-style olive drab BDU—Battle Dress Uniform—but not the favored baseball-style cap.

"Back of the building. I think it's a game of three on three."

Blackjack, as the major was informally known, eased his stance. It was his job to ensure instantaneous readiness of the team on alert, and it was doubly important to him since he would lead any team that went into action. He was second in command of the ground forces of JSOC—Joint Special Operations Command.

The major noticed the computer was on, the image of a sword-wielding white knight frozen on the twenty-six-inch screen. "A good guy, I presume."

Graber looked over his shoulder, smiling away from his superior. "A good guy, sir, of course." The smile now was obvious to the major. "Good guys are always in white."

McAffee wouldn't allow a smile, though he wanted to.

"I'm sure you mean clothing, Captain." The major's skin was a dark chocolate brown, and there was a rumor among the team that his nickname was race-related, though they couldn't figure out how or why. "Or are you referring to my tan?"

"Clothing, sir. Naturally."

"Good." The major heaved his chest out exaggeratedly and cocked his head to the side, pretending to examine the blond-haired captain. "You're looking pale, Captain. Kinda pasty I must say." His head shook, then he turned and walked out. "That boy's gotta see the doc," he said just outside the door, then he was gone.

"That's one for the maj, Sean," Buxton said, his own face covered with a wide grin. "Pasty! That's a good one."

Graber shook it off and laughed at the exchange. Mock verbal battles could be a hell of a good time. It was the real kind that scared you shitless.

"Okay, level three . . . watch out!"

Langley, Va.

On the seventh floor of the Central Intelligence Agency's headquarters, DCI Herb Landau was at work behind his light oak desk, which jutted out from a wall unit of bookcases and framed the director with the scene of the damp Virginia country behind him. Lines of rainwater trickled along the double window, which ran half the length of the wood-paneled wall and was more a transparent continuation of the wall than a true window. It did not open and its lay-ered, tinted surface made the inclement weather seem more ominous than it truly was. It was the first good rain after summer. Landau had his chair swiveled and was watching the storm.

A knock at the door was a courtesy as Deputy Director, Intelligence Greg Drummond strolled in carrying his soft briefcase, one that he used only inside the Agency's secure building. It made transferring sensitive files easier and less cumbersome than using the pyro-lock leather-oversteel attaché case required when transporting such material outside the confines of Langley. The DDI's office was three doors down from the DCI's, but he was a stickler for security procedures, and dutifully put the copy of the requested file in his case.

His boss smiled when he entered, stretching his hand across the nearly barren desk. Those were two of the things that made working for Herb Landau pleasant: He always greeted you with a handshake when first seeing you for the day, and he was impeccably organized. Work on his desk was in neat, square-edged folders, which found their way back to the file cabinet when he was through with them. Personal items were few. A picture of his wife of fifty-two years, Adella, and one of the entire family: six children, seventeen grandchildren, and three great-grandchildren. And there was the clock. It was a gift from his longtime friend, the late president, upon his confirmation by the Senate as the Director of Central Intelligence, and it was as indicative of Landau's thoughts on decor as anything could be. A simple wooden-cased timepiece, no bigger than a normal windup alarm clock, with two hands and a crescent moon which turned bright at night and dark in the daytime.

"Morning, Herb."

The DCI glanced at the clock. Its sleeping moon face stared back. "Hardly, Greg. Is he here yet?"

The DDI nodded and pulled two chairs close to the desk and sat down, wondering why the director's chairs were more comfortable. His domain in the Agency was the Intelligence Directorate, whose role and territory were all those things that collected, gathered, or generated intelligence data for the nation. Analysis of the data was also his turf, and, surprisingly to some, he had no idea how many people actually worked for him. Often the other major directorates—Science & Technology and Operations—overlapped with Intelligence and each other, but their primary roles were what their names indicated. Intelligence calls were his.

"Did you bring your copy?" Herb motioned to the case.

"Sure did."

A security officer knocked, then opened the door for the guest. Bud DiContino entered. His hands were free, having left his briefcase on the Executive UH-60 Blackhawk helicopter, which would wait for him on one of Langley's five marked pads. Another seven were routinely used some distance away from the official ones.

The DDI stood to greet the acting NSA. "Mr. DiContino, I'm Greg Drummond."

"How are you doing?" Bud shook his hand, then the seated DCI's. "I met you at the assessment conference at Meade a month ago, right?"

"That's right," Drummond answered. He liked the acting NSA, but had no overt reasoning for his feelings. He just seemed to be, at least, not a bastard, like so many appointees could be. "You did a good job. That was nice stuff on the low-grade-warfare concept."

"That was my area of so-called expertise in the Air Force. Stealth technology and the like. Hell, that's going to be the way of the next war." Bud took the seat offered by the DDI, who sat down also.

"Next war." Landau grunted, shaking his head. "Why do we always seem to be able to look *forward* to those instead of away? Hell, we're supposed to be benefiting from the greatest thaw in superpower relations in fifty years, and we can still see ourselves at war! Oh . . . don't mind me, Bud. I'm just an old fart who's seen too many *last* wars, big ones and small ones. Believe me"—he brought a finger down on the desk for emphasis—"men die in any war, and one is too many, at least from what I've seen."

"Yes, sir . . ." Bud began.

"No, please. I'm old enough without the 'sir.' It's Herb."

"Certainly," Bud agreed, though calling the DCI Herb would take some getting used to. "What I mean by 'next war' is the probability of small, contained regional conflicts. If we get involved in those conflicts we're going to need technology that will minimize our risks. The country won't be ready to accept heavy casualties from any of these small actions. The Gulf War proved that it can be done, and damn decisively. Stealth and other technologies played a big part. I mean, if we can place a conventional and powerful smart weapon on a target from five or six hundred miles away, or hundreds of these weapons, then we can effectively fight the most dangerous part of any action—the beginning—from a safe distance. There are many, many uses for this kind of technology. But then that point is moot when you look at the cutbacks in R&D. That's the one war the Congress usually wins."

"You're a convincing speaker, Bud, and you know the limits of rhetoric. I like that."

Bud smiled at the DCI's compliment. "Thanks, Herb."

"How was the helo ride?" Drummond asked.

"Fine. I'm not used to a decked-out Blackhawk."

It was Landau's turn to smile. "Get used to it. This time tomorrow you'll be official."

"That's not definite," Bud said, knowing that it probably was.

The DDI reached for his wallet. "I'll lay money on it."

"Damn right," Landau said. "Like I told you this morning, do yourself a favor and get up to speed on the idea of it."

Bud was flattered but didn't show it. Couldn't show it. He didn't want to seem cocky. At fifty-two he felt younger than the DDI, who was a babyish forty-three, a result of the new-kid-on-the-block syndrome. He was a newcomer, and he could deal with that. As the DCI said, he was almost certain to be the new NSA, which went against conventional wisdom. That didn't bother him because it obviously didn't concern the president, who had requested him to arrive a half hour before the two P.M. NSC meeting. He would then be "official" for that meeting. The position was officially known as Adviser to the President for National Security Affairs, and had fortunately been condensed to the more widely known designation of National Security Adviser—NSA to the "in crowd." Press were the only ones to use official and full titles.

"Herb tells me you're from Colorado. Snowmass, wasn't it?" The skier in Drummond believed he had found another person with whom he could swap downhill stories.

"Born and raised," Bud proudly affirmed. "I never got back there enough after Colorado Springs."

"Air Force Academy—do any flying?" Drummond was probing for another of his passions. The DCI watched the two men with little knowledge of their apparent shared interests. He hated snow, and his experience with aircraft was limited to his duties as squadron painter aboard the old Lady Lex back in World War II.

"Four years in F-105s, mostly Wild Weasels."

"Nam?"

"Yep. Two years of that was enough for my lifetime. I

did not, repeat *not,* enjoy flying suppression for 52s. Down on the deck is definitely not the way to gain a love for the beauty of flight, especially when the guys you're supposedly covering are forty thousand feet above you." Bud didn't go into the link he saw between his early career and Stealth technology. *B-2s don't need Wild Weasels.*

"Sorry to interrupt, boys, but are either of you hungry?" The DCI's illness hadn't taken away his appetite. "Bud?"

He looked at his watch.

"Don't mind the time," the DDI reassured him. "Our mess is good and fast."

"Sure, then." Bud was hungry, not having eaten since a late dinner the previous night.

Herb nodded and took the phone. The sandwiches arrived five minutes later with a large pitcher of water and a smaller one of iced tea. Bud took a corned beef on rye, with a smile from the other men who chose the ham and Swiss on wheat. His first bite gave away the reason for their mild amusement.

"The executive cook has a thing for hot mustard," Drummond shared with a chuckle.

Bud finished his bite and washed it down with a gulp of iced tea. "Obviously."

The men finished the light meal in ten minutes as the cordial conversation was interrupted by the food and frequent drinks to quench the fire in Bud's mouth. As the steward removed the tray and dishes, leaving the drinks on a separate tray, the atmosphere echoed the seriousness of the coming conversation. Bud could feel it.

The DDI opened his case and removed a single file. It was not unusual, except for the red-and-green label in the upper right-hand corner, under which was an acronym, MSRD, which Bud had become familiar with during his work on the Stealth program. It stood for Most Secret, Restricted Distribution. The red-and-green markings identified its "owner" as the CIA. Each government agency with sensitive material was issued a color code. The CIA had this one, the Defense Intelligence agency was red and blue, the State Department was yellow and orange, and so on. This was intended mainly to prevent the mixing of files, and each page was also color-coded the same as its folder. Bud knew that the MSRD designation meant that fewer than ten pairs of eyes were authorized to view the material. Actually, he was to become only the fourth living human to have the right to know the contents of the manila folder.

"I don't need to remind you about security, Bud," the DCI began, signaling for Drummond to hand the file to the newcomer, "so we'll just get to it. There are only two copies of this: I have one and Greg the other. They have never left either of our offices except in our own possession, and when they have it's only been between our offices. When we aren't in our offices they are kept in our personal safes. We know each other's combinations, as does the Deputy Director of Operations Mike Healy, but he is not privileged to this information. Bud, the president is not privileged to it."

Something was up, Bud thought. The president was cleared for everything. Or maybe . . .

Landau continued, "Now, to my point. First, you better read what's in the file."

Bud opened the folder, looking to both men before he began reading. There were only four double-spaced pages, which he finished in less than three minutes. He spent another two minutes reading over the second page.

His eyes came up from the paper, though not to meet the others'. "Did Jeremy know about this?"

The DCI nodded.

"Jesus! This was dated to last December, and this last part just a month ago. Was the president informed?"

"He was, yes, about the last part, but he vetoed any measures that would have compromised the source," Landau answered. He knew Bud wouldn't ask about the source. "Jeremy didn't even want him informed because it would take away presidential deniability. We convinced him to at least inform him of the risk to himself."

Bud was incensed. "Who the hell authorized this operation?"

"We don't know," Drummond replied. "There was no finding or authorization; no hard copy other than the Eyes Only brief that you're looking at. Somehow it missed the shredder and ended up in a case file. The officer who the file belonged to—he was stationed in Sicily—left the Agency after the inauguration." He carefully avoided letting on to the officer's role in Italy. "There's no way to tie him to this since it was a stateside report, probably dictated. It ended up in his file . . ." Drummond shrugged. " . . . mistake, maybe. A stupid oversight. It's even conceivable that it was intentionally left unshredded for future purposes, but that's a paranoid's view. It's among the possibilities.

"The best we've been able to do is run the trail back here, to this office." Drummond saw Bud's lips part slightly as the enormity of the situation continued to sink in. "The typewriter used for the first three pages is right there." The DDI pointed to the DCI's machine on the oak rollaway behind and to the right of the desk.

"That's a photocopy you're looking at," Landau informed him. "The original is in my copy of the file."

"So, what you're saying, and what this information describes, is that the former director—"

"Correction, Bud," the DCI interrupted, "the former upper apparatus of the Agency, probably including the DDI at least, and probably the DDO."

Many had been surprised when the entire executive structure of the Agency had left after the new administration won the election. Now Bud knew why. "Okay. So they initiated a covert operation upon their own authority, without presidential approval or congressional knowledge. And this! Christ, were they totally oblivious to the possible ramifications?"

"Not anymore," Landau responded. "Unfortunately they're no longer with the Agency and even if they were, the trail they left is nonexistent, except for my predecessor."

"Doing anything now would be counterproductive," Drummond said, shifting in his seat. The whole damn thing made him uncomfortable.

"Counterproductive?" Bud raised his voice. "The action initiated by that . . . that man more than likely was the direct cause of the president's death, not to mention the others."

"Whoa there"—the DCI raised his hand to his front—"as much as you and I and Greg here find this distasteful, we can no more bring this into the open than the president could have taken precautions to safeguard his own life. If we do, a very important asset of ours would likely be compromised, and *that* would be counterproductive. This asset has given us a hell of a lot of vital intelligence on terrorist movements and intentions, including what just happened. But that is not confirmed—officially."

"Unofficially?" Bud asked.

The DCI thought for a second before answering. "My predecessor apparently didn't buy the colonel's feigned humanism. Neither did I, for that matter, but the solution proved to be more of a catalyst than an end-all. Hell, he got us back. Grammar school–style revenge. Tit for tat. We wagged his tail and he pulled ours clean off."

"And we take it. Damn! Has there been any confirmation on the success of our . . ." Bud hated to even imply ownership in the rogue operation. " . . . endeavor?"

"Nothing definitive," Drummond replied. "But the colonel has been lying low. Very low."

"There *has* been a resurgence of activity at the old training camps," Landau noted.

That figures, Bud thought. "It appears we convinced the colonel that change was futile."

There was a quiet in the room as Bud again looked down at the open file on his lap. He flipped the pages quickly, wondering who exactly had thought of the plan, and beyond that, what genius had decided to carry it out. This was precisely the reason for controls on covert operations, the process of which was supposed to begin with the president and move quickly to Congress, or at least to the small number of congressional leaders known as the "gang of eight." It was required by law as spelled out in the Intelligence Oversight Act. Sometimes Congress wanted too much control over executive actions, Bud believed, but this would have been a perfect time for some knowledge of the operation.

"So," Bud began, "you want me to decide whether the president is to be informed of this. Am I correct?"

The DCI's answer was silent, but obvious. He detested having to be the custodian for his predecessor's dirty work. *Damn them!*

"Your recommendation, Herb?"

"If you inform him there is no deniability. His lack of action against a former government official who has violated several federal statutes can be construed as obstruction of justice. If he does decide to take action then we open up a new can of worms."

"It'd make Iran-Contra look like *The Peoples' Court*," Drummond added.

Bud was angry. "Damnit! Is it just because I spent twenty-five years of my life as an honorable military officer that that word—*deniability*—has a decidedly sinister ring to it? Or has it become a concept, something our political leaders must have? A fallback tool instead of that old standby: responsibility? I tell you, gentlemen, this kind of garbage . . . I don't know." There was a long pause. "I imagine we'll be dealing with this for a period of time to come."

"Who knows," the DCI said, lifting his hands in a gesture of wonder or futility. Bud couldn't tell which.

Bud closed the folder and ran the long edge between his thumb and forefinger. It felt slick, almost wet, and the rough edge, neat and straight from its limited handling, was sharp enough to cut skin. He handed it to the DDI, who looked to the director before returning it to his case.

There was a curse that came with knowledge. If Bud were to let it stop here, with him, it might be over, and any crucifixion for nondisclosure could be absorbed by him. But that held as much appeal as his old days in Wild Weasels. Soaking up the heat for someone else went against his grain, and that was what would be truly counterproductive. The truth was that it was just too risky to inform the president. Bud could take the rap if it ever did come out, but suspicion would always lead to the president. The damage would be done—and severe. But then it might just bury itself.

"It's a no-win situation," Bud observed. "A shitty no-win situation. All in all I'm glad you filled me in, but I didn't expect it to start like this."

"D.C. is no Disneyland," the DDI pointed out. "This is not a fairy tale."

"Yeah. Yeah." Bud's sarcasm was directed to no one. "I guess I should have expected less from the brochures." He rubbed his smooth upper lip while thinking, but the decision was already made. He was just trying to reconcile it with his conscience. "Okay . . . this stays in this room. If it ever becomes necessary I will inform the president myself. My gut tells me otherwise, but this seems like the best course." Bud stood, as did the DDI. "I just hope it is.

"Well, I've got to get going." He didn't but he had to get out of that room. Out of that building.

"Bud, thanks for coming over." The DCI offered his hand. Bud accepted it, shaking the DDI's next.

"Thank you, Herb . . . Greg. Maybe next time it'll be something mild, like an increase in Chinese SSBN deployment."

The DCI laughed. "Okay. We'll see if we can arrange that for you."

The acting NSA left and was airborne a few minutes later, heading back to the White House through an early-autumn storm. Drummond returned to his office, leaving the director of Central Intelligence alone at his desk. He turned again toward the window and thought for some time of the topic at hand. It made him mad as hell that someone with his authority could go off like a loose cannon and leave the mess for others to clean up. But that was the reality of government. That drew a private smile. His predecessor was enjoying a lucrative slot on the lecture circuit, reportedly pulling down twenty grand a speech. A *couple of engagements would buy a lot of coffins*.

Maybe, though, it would be over now. Who could pay? No one, he believed, so what was the point in looking back. It was over. Done.

He could not have been more wrong.

2

. . . .

ABOVE AND BELOW

East of Athens

THE DEEP SHADOWS of the coming summer evening stretched out from the Greek coast to cover the Aegean Sea in an eerie blue incandescence as the light danced rapidly from the earth below. Andros, a larger island in the chain of many smaller ones, was directly beneath the *Clipper Atlantic Maiden* as she descended gracefully toward Athens, her stop for the night. She floated downward, the sun low on the horizon but still gleaming brightly off her shiny surfaces. Her sister ship, the *Clipper Angelic Pride*, was some forty nautical miles behind on a flight from New Delhi, though she would be doing a quick turnaround and flying on to the States overnight, New York being her final destination. The *Atlantic Maiden*, inbound from Beijing, would continue on across her namesake ocean the next morning on her somewhat special flight.

Captain Bart Hendrickson, the picture of a sturdy Nordic American, loved his job and especially the *Maiden*, as he called his plane. It was not just *his* plane. Other pilots flew her, as was the norm in the scheduling of flight crews in the operations of the larger carriers, but he had been very fortunate to rotate into the Maiden two times out of every three over the last nine months.

She was a new—in aircraft life—Boeing 747–400, one of the more recent generation of jet airliners that relied on new technologies to enhance their performance and extend their useful life. The bulk of the advancements were on the flight deck, the cockpit, which now required a crew of just two: the pilot and a first officer. Use of video display–type screens for nearly all of the instrumentation and the condensation and restructuring of information presentation had allowed for a reduction in the crew size from the old four. The move was fought tooth and nail by the pilots' unions, who claimed that it would be a safety risk. Captain Hendrickson knew that claim for what it was: a complaint that jobs would be sacrificed and the ladder to reach the pinnacle of flying, a captaincy, would have a discouragingly large number of rungs added to it. In the major airlines a pilot could wait up to thirty years to command a jumbo jet. Elimination of the flight engineer position on the flight deck would reduce the number of entry slots and the need for pilots. It was a wise economic move for the carriers to appropriate planes such as the 747–400 and its older and smaller cousin, the 767. Profit margins were shrinking in the industry, making every penny count. Bart Hendrickson, fifty-eight, blond with no hint of gray, and a wearer of the coveted bird wings for thirty-two years didn't care much for the financial or economic reasons for the changes. The main thing was that he felt flying was safer and, as important, more fun.

"Bart, number three is showing that four percent drop in compression again," First Officer Adam "Buzz" Elkins announced. He was an old Marine—one was never an ex-Marine—as his taut upper body and the now graying crewcut attested. There hadn't been a day since his first at Parris Island twenty-two years before that he had let his hair grow beyond the half-inch needles that they were. His brown eyes, set into a tanned face, were passionless, but read like a novel when emotion spurred them.

The captain looked at the engine performance indicator. In earlier days he might have thumped the glass-covered gauge with a finger, but now the needle was represented by a slim video image on the display, and that was merely for quick reference; the digital readout above each engine's indicator rendered an exact measurement. "It's probably the compressor."

"Again. Oh well." Buzz was not surprised with the problem. The *Maiden* had needed the primary compressor replaced twice before in the number three engine, the last time less than five months earlier. "Athens doesn't have the facilities for us."

"Yeah." That was one problem, the captain thought. Not every airport could service some of the newer jets. "What was the max flux in compression?"

"Just four percent," Buzz answered. "Passing one-two-thousand."

"Roger." Hendrickson pressed the mike switch, opting for manual operation instead of "hot mike," which continuously transmitted everything said. Most crews did the same, except in busy times. The ground didn't need to hear all that was said upstairs. "Athens approach—Four-Two-Two heavy passing one-two-thousand."

"*Roger, Four-Two-Two heavy. Maintain descent to four thousand. Enter pattern on eastern leg at six thousand. Maintain heading until coastal VOR intersect.*"

"Roger, Athens. Descending to four thousand. Maintaining two-eight-zero to VOR intersect."

"Inbound, five-zero miles." Buzz called out the distance to "wheels down."

Hendrickson acknowledged the announcement, smiling at the half-oval glow where earth met sky. Even glitches couldn't dampen his spirit, nor the growing sense of nostalgia he was experiencing. The big, beautiful 747–400 could just as easily have been an old Lockheed Constellation, his first command in the Air Force. That moment flashed back in his mind. God! Had it been *that* long?

"I hope three doesn't drop anymore," Buzz commented, his attention focused on the instruments.

"If it does we're going to have to have a spare feathered in."

"That'd be a bitch!" The sight of a spare engine attached to a perfectly good 747 was unnatural. The spare, slung beneath a wing like a normal, functioning engine, made the bird look lopsided and perform sluggishly. Buzz didn't want to wish that upon any other pilot. He had previously been *fortunate* enough to crew on a big jet that had brought one into Karachi, Pakistan, and it had not been fun. "Specs say one to two constant is nominal. Three to uh . . ." The first officer scanned the specification and performance lap book for the 747's power plants. " . . . three to six is acceptable."

"Yep. It fluxed to twelve that last time before they replaced it. We can call ahead and have one waiting at Heathrow tomorrow."

Buzz hated delays, but a delay in London was better than a delay in Athens. For all its supposed beauty, he hated the city. It was dirty everyplace he looked. "Sounds like a plan."

Hendrickson gave it a subtle nod, and Buzz called the ground maintenance station in Athens on the company frequency. They would notify Heathrow.

The bustling British airport would be a welcome destination for the captain. His last stop before arriving home . . . for good. Thirty-two years in the air had been good to him. Never again, though, would he have to leave Anita. Yes, thirty-two years of good-byes had been difficult, but she had never, ever complained. She knew that her husband loved to fly, almost as a child would look wide-eyed at the big and pretty planes as they landed. He had wished as a child to fly someday, a wish that became reality in the Air Force. Anita remembered his excitement the day of his first solo in a Lockheed Constellation. Nothing could shut him up. He told her every detail of the two-hour flight, and most of it was Latin to her. His outward excitement had softened over the years, but not the inner rush.

"Passing ten thousand," Buzz announced. He could see the slight smile on the captain's face and the reflection of the day's last light in his dark aviator glasses.

"Roger." Hendrickson pressed the seat belt sign activator. "Three's back up to nominal."

"Good. Maybe we won't have to delay in England."

"Anxious to get home, Bart?"

"I'm always anxious. This time I get to stay."

Al-'Adiyat, Libya

It was a place shown only on the maps of some intelligence services, but it did exist, just south of Benghazi. There were buildings, some modern, but none larger than would be found elsewhere in the desert, and there was space. That was the need. Space for those who came to Al-'Adiyat to become proficient at their craft. To help them, there was a teacher.

Did they not receive my warning? Did they not believe me?

Captain Muhadesh Algar felt the warmth fading from his back as he pondered what had happened. He swiveled his chair around to face the open window. There was a glow on the horizon from the sun, and to the north the lights of Benghazi would soon start to overcome the approaching desert night. Very far away something was happening in America. He wondered what. He had tried to warn them.

"Captain Algar."

Muhadesh swung around. It was Indar. "Lieutenant."

"I knocked, sir, but you did not answer."

The wormlike lieutenant may have knocked, Muhadesh thought, but probably not. A father on the Revolutionary Council could get you any job, and protect you from losing it, even if you were a tactless incompetent. "What is it, Indar?"

"Sir, the new group scheduled to arrive tomorrow has been canceled."

"On whose authority?"

"Colonel Hajin," Indar answered, swallowing hard. His job was safe, but Captain Algar's wrath was legendary, especially of late he was told.

Muhadesh pulled himself up to the desk. The lieutenant stood at perfect attention before his commander, his hands folded left over right behind his back, just as prescribed in the regulations. In appearance he was a fine officer. Every crease in his green uniform was straight and crisp, his hair was trimmed in the fashion of a recruit, close to the skull, and his face was shaved as close as close could be. He was attentive to detail, as expected, and followed every order exactly. *But the orders are not always mine, Indar. You listen too well to others.*

"I see," Muhadesh replied calmly. He opened the top center drawer of his metal desk and removed his writing paper.

"Sir?" Indar was at a loss. His commander was accepting this too easily.

"Do not worry, Lieutenant," Muhadesh said, looking up at his young assistant. *Twenty-five and a lieutenant in the Training Battalion. My battalion!* "Colonel Hajin must have his reasons. Good reasons. You show too much concern for an executive lieutenant, Indar. Others better equipped than we to understand situations make these decisions, and we obey. Of course I am not happy with the loss of a group, but it has happened before. Maybe the Americans are in an excited state after the death of their president and are thinking, once again, of taking vengeance upon us. Colonel Hajin would surely not want a group of our revolutionary brothers caught in a raid by the devil Americans. We are a target, after all." Indar began to smile with understanding. That was the *one* nice thing about the lieutenant: He bought the revolutionary hogwash without question. "So go about your duties. I will deal with the developments."

"Yes, sir!" Indar saluted enthusiastically, a smile spreading across his narrow face. The commander would surely let Colonel Hajin know what he thought about the cancellation of this month's class. Captain Algar was a master of the venomous pen. Indar could only imagine what his commander would write in his message to the high-and-mighty Hajin in Tripoli.

He did imagine, but he was wrong. Hajin, Colonel
Muhammar Qaddafi's personal aide and a man of considerable power, would receive no letter from Muhadesh—
he would receive a visit. The written message was going
elsewhere.

Benina Airport, Benghazi

The last of the daylight had touched the ceiling of the hangar through the slightly parted sliding doors a few minutes
before. The three men who were in the hangar did not notice
this, as the powerful overhead lights created their own sense
of day and night as they were turned on or off. They were all
ready and waiting to begin what they had prepared for. There
had been many months of training in a place near where all
three had grown up, though it was not their home. It could
not be. Only one place could be their home. One day it would
be. All there was to do now was continue with the minor last-
minute details that were important preparations for success,
but at this stage more so for usefully occupying time.

One of the three stood, taking his weapon in hand from
the small square table, where two others were disassembled
for cleaning. The Israeli-made Uzi felt good, but still a bit
slick from the penetrating oil used to clean the desert dust
from its exterior. He took it by the sling, wiping his palm on
his pants. It never occurred to him that his choice of weapons
was somewhat ironic, yet a man could be easily killed by his
own handiwork. That might have pleased him, if his limited
intellect were to allow its comprehension.

"I am going to rest," the man spoke, his voice soft and
steady with a slight nasal pitch. It was mild in comparison
to his size, which was massive, both in height and width.

"We will wake you, Wael," Abu assured him.

Wael walked toward the small office on the opposite side
of the hangar, passing the four large boxes that sat on wheeled
aircraft cargo pallets. They were connected in a short train as
ordinary ones were, but the five-foot green cubes were not
the usual metallic containers. They had the appearance of
oversized wooden boxes with two-by-fours for edge supports
and diagonal braces from corner to corner. Without breaking
stride he let his free hand go to the boxes and glide along

their surfaces. He wondered what was in them. What was it that they now sat with that would help them succeed in their mission?

The thought left him when he entered the small office, separated from the hangar by glass. A cot had been moved in there, and a second later his body disappeared below the window line.

3
....

A CERTAIN MR. JACKSON

Los Angeles

THE MAROON FORD Taurus sat idle among a sea of cars whose engines were coming to life as FBI agents and employees of the impound yard worked methodically to move the other vehicles surrounding it. There normally would be a steady roar as cars passed the Harbor Tow Company on the 110 freeway as noon approached, but the air was silent except for the noise in the yard itself and the background sounds of police radios. At the request of the Bureau, the California Highway Patrol had closed the old freeway, so aged and dangerously curved that trucks were forbidden to travel it from downtown to Pasadena.

A senior agent of the Bureau's bomb unit approached Art, who was standing behind the only protective barrier available, just fifty feet from the car.

"Art. How's it going?" Agent Larry Purnell asked.

"You tell me in about a half an hour," Art answered.

"Ha." Purnell laughed. "You think this'll save your ass?" He patted the cinder block wall.

"Thanks." Art knew that Purnell's triple-layered Kevlar and Nomex "moon suit" would do little to protect him if the car was booby-trapped.

Another member of the bomb unit came up. "Nothing obvious."

"You check the wheel wells?" Purnell inquired, pulling on his Kevlar-covered bubble helmet.

"Yes, sir."

Larry Purnell smiled a wide smile through the clear Lexan faceplate. "Good. We'll sweep it again."

"Right."

"Larry." Art put his hand on the man's padded shoulder. "The manager said they slim-jimmed it when it came in. Still, no heroes. Okay?"

"Me?" His smile hinted of the devious. "C'mon."

Minutes later the area around the Ford was clear and the preliminary sweeps of the vehicle's underside for explosive triggers was done. The fact that the vehicle came in on the hook of a tow truck pretty much ruled out any motion sensors to trigger a device, and a door- or domelight-activated switch was not likely since the driver's door had been opened in the yard. But was there a key switch? Purnell would be the first to know.

First would be the trunk. Every person in the yard cringed or ducked behind cover as the agent inserted and turned the key. There was an immediate click as the trunk lid popped up a few inches. Purnell was careful not to touch anything as he gave the rear of the vehicle a cursory inspection. He next moved counterclockwise around the vehicle, opening each door. The hood was last. He released it from inside, then inspected the engine compartment carefully, taking extra time to look for any additional wires or parts. Once a car he was checking was equipped with two batteries, the second one having four sticks of dynamite inside.

There was no explosion or hint of any booby trap. It wasn't "tricked." Art breathed now, not only because of the lack of explosion, but because the key fit. It was the car. Confirmed. He was just damn glad that a young agent had had the gray matter to put two and two together when no one else could see the numbers. After striking out on her first check of one of the many parking garages downtown, a rather clever thought had struck her. The belief was that the shooters had parked nearby in one of the public pay lots and walked to the 818. It made sense. But Special Agent Francine Aguirre had come up with a different idea: What if the shooters just had parked the car on the street? The nearest lot was on the back side of the 818, which would have required them to walk around to the front. Two M-16s and LAW rockets would not have been the easiest things to hide on the downtown street. Aguirre's theory also made sense, and more of it. If the shooters were on a one-way mission, why garage their car? Just street-parking it would ensure its proper disposal by the parking enforcement unit of the city, whose contracted tow trucks swept the congested downtown streets clear of illegally parked vehicles. Her quick thinking earned a personal commendation from Art, and a bump up on the investigative team. She and her partner were already at the LAX-based rental company whose license plate frame identified the car as one of theirs. Eddie was coordinating this new aspect of the investigation from the Hilton.

Art would wait with the car as the forensic teams poured over it. He doubted they would find much. That was the way this thing was going. Eddie was right. The shooters were damn stupid to leave the car where it could be found, but it protected their backsides. There was a trail that Art could imagine already. It stunk.

The car was a solid lead, though. That was satisfying. Art popped a stick of cinnamon gum in his mouth and pulled off his jacket. He leaned back, half sitting on the wall. The sun was beating down as it had for so many days. The weatherman said it would be cooler than the day before. Art wasn't sure about that. It felt like another hot one coming on.

The White House

The president stood alone in the Oval Office, touching the front of his desk lightly as he gazed through the windows to the outside. On the credenza, along with the recently placed pictures of his wife and parents, was the gumball machine that had belonged to the late president. His widow had insisted that it should stay there, with her husband's successor. And the chair. It was a bright, fire-engine-red rocker that was known as the Santa Claus chair. *He never even had the chance to be Santa for his grandkids in the White House*. She wanted the chair to stay too. *Damn*.

An early-autumn storm was falling outside, though it felt

more like one of late summer. It was humid and warm, an uncomfortable combination, but one not uncommon in Washington this time of year. Even the rain was warm. The president, however, was not aware of the climate beyond the glass. It was a comfortable sixty-eight degrees where he stood.

The car and driver were perks of his new position. Prior to the meeting, as expected, the president had asked Bud to take the position officially. He had readily accepted it. It would be a challenge. His biggest challenge.

His first dilemma in the position was the one in the past. Or was it? He could have informed the president of the revelations told him by the DCI, but he didn't. That went against his better judgment, against his core feeling of duty and integrity. For whatever reason, things were different the further one progressed in government. *So this is it*? Bud wondered if it would happen to him. And the past. Was it really behind them? He would have given anything to be psychic just for a while.

Beltway traffic was picking up as the Secret Service Lincoln joined the throngs of other government workers leaving early. There was a pall over the city, and it had nothing to do with the weather. People were on autopilot, just performing. Only the stonehearted were unaffected by the killing of the nation's leader.

Tomorrow would be a new day. The beginning of the fledgling president's administration. Bud would be rested, as the president had insisted. Already he was feeling the lack of restful sleep catch up with him, but lying down in the backseat wouldn't do. He would be home soon, anyway, which was all the better since his side was really starting to throb again. Fortunately there was a full bottle of Tylenol in the medicine cabinet.

Los Angeles

"Bingo!"

Art was pleased, as Eddie could see. "And that's not all, boss. We'll have a list of charges on that card in a few hours."

The photocopy of the charge slip and driver's license was the next step in the trail. Art was happy, and thankful as hell that Aguirre had had her brainstorm. Otherwise the car would still be buried among hundreds of others and the trail would be dead. He reminded himself that it wasn't the end. Just a little closer.

"Harry Obed . . . hmmm. This isn't the same guy in the picture with the kid." Art compared the two again. The photocopy was grainy, but it would do.

"Nope. New York is sending a copy of the license info. We'll have a better photo then."

Art studied the face. It was Arab. And the name added credibility to his guess. This wasn't looking like an easy one to deal with. Solving it might bring even more problems, considering the way of the world. "I think tonight is going to be busy. How about you?"

"Shoulda brought my jammies," Eddie joked. He was good for some comic relief when needed. Things were liable to get stressful now that they had a suspect, or a knowing accomplice.

"So, what's our next move?" Art mused.

"I think we should wait until the American Express records get here. That'll give us a trail."

"If they used it."

Eddie became serious. "They used it once. Why not again?"

"What if they used the other card? Forensics found that blue tint in the melted card. Amex is green."

"Right."

"It was dark blue," Art added. "Visa and Diner's Club both have blue in them. Maybe they were trying to spread their trail around."

Eddie got up from the table and walked to the two-pot coffee machine someone had brought from the office. It was saving trips to the 7-Eleven already. "You want some?"

It was placed close to Art's area, and his fill for the past hour or so had been achieved. "No thanks."

"You know, boss, it still all comes back to their carelessness." Two sugars were emptied into the cup. "We'll have their bio before long, but what about whoever was in the background? How do we find them?"

Art knew that was supposing there was an accomplice, or accomplices. It was becoming more apparent that there was considerable help given. "It's not going to be a direct link, that's for sure. We've got possible assistance with the car. Maybe it was rented for them in advance."

"The records don't show that," Eddie said.

"Then check back to the reservation, and the credit card. Who's paying the bills?" That was already in progress, a task made easier by the proliferation of credit and computers. "Someone who dealt with the transaction might remember something."

Eddie returned to his chair. "Slim, but worth it." He didn't really think so. His hunch was that the car end of things would be cold soon.

Art had a thought. He stared away from Eddie as the concept formed. "Ed, these guys were sacrificed. They were willing, at least I'd think they'd have to be, but they were used. Whether they knew or not . . . I doubt it."

"What's your track?"

"Obed. Picture. Name. It's a good bet he's Arab, and probably his partner. If there's a connection here with any terrorist groups, then we might want to get with some people who have experience with Arab terrorists."

Eddie agreed. "That's one possibility. Israeli Intelligence." It wasn't a question.

"Right. Do you have copies of the license info and picture?"

"Plenty."

The senior agent scribbled a note onto his legal pad, then tore it off and folded it down. "Here. Give this guy a call. Meir Shari. He was with the embassy in D.C., if I remember right, but he's back home now. I was at a seminar he spoke at in Frisco. Smart, realistic thinking sort. No politico thought there."

"Connections?" Eddie asked.

"He was it. Military liaison with a full portfolio." Art remembered another bit of information. "He's the guy who cuffed Eichmann."

"Who?"

He was young, Art realized. "Adolf Eichmann. He was a Nazi war criminal hiding out in Brazil back in the sixties.

Mossad sent a team in to bring him home. He had a date with the gallows."

"And Shari was in on it? Sheee-it!"

"His connections go back. Way back. He might be able to help us. Hell, he may already be looking into it. The Israelis get nervous when any Arab kills someone."

"But how would they know the killer might be an Arab?"

Art smiled. "I'll give you a book to read. It's called *The Guys*. It's on the restricted list, but we're cleared. The topic is intelligence appraisal, Mossad style. The way they get some of their stuff is spooky."

He wasn't an avid reader—his last book had been *The Hunt for Red October*—but this one sounded worth the effort. Eddie figured he'd take Art up on it.

"We better keep this quiet." Art knew that would require a secure line. There were plenty at the office, but secure sometimes meant "away from colleagues." "The Israeli consulate will have a direct line to Tel Aviv. Head-on—"

Their attention shifted to Dan Jacobs. He entered the Hilton's nearly empty banquet room carrying something wrapped in a white towel. "Dan," Art said.

"Hell. When are they going to get you a desk." Jacobs unwrapped the item. It was a two-by-four with fractured pieces of drywall nailed to its shorter edges, one side of which was singed an uneven black. "This might interest you, Art."

"What do you have?"

"Just a wall member with a story to tell. Look." He pointed to the top, exposed part of the wood. Eddie and Art came close, leaning over the piece. "They're faint, but we can print them. We already did."

"Scuff marks," Eddie offered.

"Actually from a black sole, we think. This is virgin wood. It was above a doorjamb, so it was clean as a whistle. Not even dust. There was an acoustical hanging ceiling to about here." Jacobs traced along an obvious line where paint on the drywall had faded from exposure to light.

"Where was this originally?" Art asked.

"Do you have those floor plans—fifth floor?"

Eddie retrieved them from a nearby table.

"Okay," Jacobs began, "here's the room where the fire

came from. We figure that the charge was about here, in the center of the room. The blast went every which way, but less so to the left and right, or east and west in this orientation. Everything, streetside, shooters, walls, and all, was blown out onto Seventh, while the interior south wall blew straight across the back side of the building."

"We know all this, Dan." Art was impatient.

"I know. Bear with me. So, we had most of the blast go north and south, plus up and down, more up though. This wall"—his finger pointed to the blue line—"was an interior support structure. You see it runs from the exterior north to almost the interior south. There's this little indentation here; it kind of makes the room look like a lopsided *L*."

"That was the east wall," Eddie observed.

"Right. This little alcove—it measured about seven by seven—used to be an open area to the room, just like these prints show. But we found this piece of wood strapped to the northwest corner junction of the alcove's walls. That's code. It's for earthquake safety. See, these prints are from the late sixties, but there was a major remodeling done in the late seventies when an art school moved into the fourth, fifth, and sixth floors. This room where the shooters did their dirty work was an AV class—audiovisual. The little alcove was walled in a year after the remodeling to create a small room to store equipment in. VCRs, cameras—stuff like that. It had a single door"—Jacobs sketched the location's most recent appearance—"right here. And it was padlocked. Only the teacher and dean had keys because there was about two hundred grand's worth of stuff in there. Anyway, this piece was from right here." The pencil point came down. "Right above the door."

"I'm not clear on this," Art said. "What's the significance?"

"Lifelong cop, right?" Jacobs inquired. Art nodded. "Do you know how I put myself through school? I was a draftsman. Learned it in high school, three years of it. It paid damn good. All my meager knowledge told me that a wall went from floor to ceiling."

"Right. So?"

"So why, or better, how did the scuff marks get there? I'll tell you how—the new wall did not go all the way to the *true* ceiling. It went about three inches above the suspended ceiling. That gave maybe twenty-seven inches of clearance to the true ceiling." There was still no light of revelation. "Shall I expand?"

"Please." Art didn't let on that an image was forming in his mind. It both intrigued and angered him.

"The wall that closed off the alcove was weaker structurally than the rest of the east wall, so it folded back against the north side of the small room when the blast went off. Strapping kept some of it intact, including this part and the doorframe. A lot of debris was blown into this seven-by-seven area, and the stuff in there was buried by it. Layers of debris. The outer layer was stuff from the room— bits of chairs, etcetera. Next were the actual parts of the blown-in wall and door, including the padlock, still closed on the hasp." He raised an eyebrow. "Then the electronic equipment, all smashed to pieces. Finally, along with little parts of all kinds, were twelve empty soda cans and cookie and candy wrappers. The bottom of the pile."

Eddie looked at Art. He was staring down at the wood, his jaw muscles flexing. The Joker had never seen his boss this pissed.

"So," Art said, the air coming from his lungs like steam passing from a pipe, "we suspected they hid out for a day or two." His body straightened up, hands in pockets, the right one squeezing his key ring for all it was worth. "The tow date on the car was Friday. That means they spent two nights in the Eight One Eight, in a locked room."

"Correct," Dan affirmed. "They went into the building, maybe that evening, and somehow got into that classroom. From there, just move a couple ceiling panels and climb over."

"The scuff marks," Eddie said. Jacobs nodded agreement.

"A few snacks and forty hours later they climbed back over and . . ."

"Goddamn it!" Art cursed loud and slow, each word distinct and filled with the anger his body was trying to suppress. His hands came to his hips as he turned away, looking up to the ballroom's patterned ceiling. The lines crisscrossed and twisted, interconnecting each design with the eight to all sides of it. *Go easy, Art. Breathe. Breathe.* The compressed feeling in his chest abated slightly with the last of the three breaths, and he turned back. "That building was swept by the Secret Service on Saturday, and again on Sunday before it was secured. For Christ's sake, how did they miss this?"

"It's just a guess, but the Service was working off of floor plans only as recent as the remodeling." Jacobs had thought that one out. It pissed him off royally.

"Which didn't have the new room on it."

"Right, Eddie."

Art was shaking his head. *Idiots!* "That's a bullshit excuse! There was a door. They had to see it, and they should have checked it. Damnit!" His heart rate rose again. "Why didn't they just stick the key in the lock? What the hell was so hard with that?"

"No excuses, Art." Dan wouldn't try to make any for the Service. "The maintenance super for the building was supposed to meet the Service security detail on Sunday morning for the lockdown of the area. The one Saturday wasn't real thorough. That was supposed to be the one on Sunday. Anyway, the maintenance guy didn't show, so they contacted his assistant. Apparently, though, they didn't wait for him. By the time he got there the detail was already to the sixth floor."

"How the hell did you get all this?" Art had calmed somewhat. He sat down, his hand massaging one corner of his growing forehead.

"The assistant super was over at the building with some people from the management company that oversees the place."

"When?" Something clicked in Art. A quick look to Eddie confirmed that he had caught it also.

"This morning. They're pretty worried about the structure, you know. They want to get some engineers in there as soon as we'll let them."

Dan Jacobs was an agent who specialized in the scrutiny of physical, inanimate evidence, not the oddities and nuances of human behavior. That was the street agent's territory. Art's and Eddie's. They had worked the street, knocked on doors, and asked thousands of questions during their years in the Bureau. The potentially important clue Dan had unknowingly brought to their attention might have been discovered later—maybe too late.

"Do you think that's funny?" Art asked.

"I think it is." Eddie smiled, his expensive and perfect dental work open for viewing.

Just as the two senior agents had failed to comprehend Dan's analysis of the physical data without extended explanation, he did not follow what they had deduced. "What's up?"

Art took a pen in hand. "What's that assistant's name, Dan?"

Within twenty minutes Eddie was en route to the Israeli consulate, and Art, with six other agents, was heading for address on La Cienega Boulevard, less than thirty minutes away.

It was a small house on the east side of the street, set on a small lot like those on either side for several blocks. The peeling yellow trim and dirty white clapboard siding were just one of the many signs of decay indicative of the neighborhood, and of many of the urban areas around the downtown area. Of course there were corridors of wealth, the high- and lowrise glass towers that were the main scenery visible from the freeways. Art wondered sometimes if it was planned that way, considering that most visitors to Los Angeles never left the freeway between their touristy destinations.

Art checked his watch. Three fifty-five. "Where the hell is the call?"

Agents Omar Espinosa and Hal Lightman did not answer. The question was to himself. The bulky Latino agent sat in the back, behind the driver, with the Atchisson shotgun resting on his lap. It was an ugly weapon, brand-new in the Bureau's arsenal, looking like a puffed-up assault rifle less the stock. The twelve 00 buck rounds in the box magazine had only one purpose. Hal was driving, with Art to his right clutching the mike. From where they were parked the house was in view continuously, and the gas station lot afforded some protection from being seen.

"*Seven Sam.*" The dispatcher's voice brought the radio to life.

"Seven Sam," Art acknowledged his call sign.

"Be advised, LAPD units are on standby two blocks north of your location."

"Ten-four." *Good.* The local cops were in position, just in case. He was hoping they wouldn't be needed and was fairly certain that they wouldn't be. If *he* were Marcus Jackson he'd be long gone. Jackson was the maintenance superinten-dent for the 818, and there were more than a few questions the Bureau wanted to ask him. Thanks to Jacobs's innocent discovery of Jackson's absence the day of the assassina-tion—a time when he was expected to be there—and early this day, Art and Eddie were able to find a possible link in the conspiracy. The shooters would have needed inside help, particularly if Jacobs's theory was correct. Marcus Jackson had worked for the management group that owned the build-ing for just six months, and he would have knowledge of the relatively easy access to the storage room.

A blue Ford Thunderbird rolled past the three agents, going north on La Cienega. Art saw the passenger crane his neck, looking down the driveway as the car passed the house.

"Deans and Harriman," Hal said, identifying the two agents in the T-Bird.

Art figured that they could all hit the house within thirty seconds. He, Omar, and Hal, along with Rob Deans and Andy Harriman, would come from the front. Shelly Murdock and Drew Smith were on the opposite street and would come over the back wall. All they were waiting for was a signed search warrant. Judge Gallanter was assigned to the investi-gation full-time to provide for quick and easy processing of warrants. He had, however, taken it upon himself to take a late lunch, and had further complicated matters by leaving his pager in the office. He was being "hunted" as everyone waited.

"Seven Sam."

"Seven Sam."

"Possible suspect is identified from DMV as male, black, five eight, one sixty, black and brown. DOB of four twelve sixty. Justice shows arrest on five-oh-two; conviction on nine eight eighty-eight. Time served: one month in county. License status: valid. Possible suspect is registered owner

of nineteen ninety-one Jeep Cherokee four-door, blue; license of four-Charlie-Frank-Mary-two-eight-one. Registration expires three one ninety-four. Copy?"

"Ten-four, copy," Art replied. The information was written on the notebook stuck to the windshield on a suction mount. LAPD cars had computer terminals that displayed such data. No such luck in unmarked Bureau cars.

"Seven Sam, stand by."

They waited. Art checked the time again. It was one minute past four.

"Seven Sam."

"Seven Sam."

"Be advised, the warrant is approved and en route. Copy?"

"Ten-four, copy. Dispatch, clear the channel and stand by." The time was close. Art felt for his gun. *Good.*

"Channel Charlie is in priority use. Seven Sam is senior. All other units stand by. David and Edward channels are clear. Dispatch by."

"King One and Two," Art called.

"King One, by."

"King Two, by and ready."

Everyone was ready. Hal started the engine.

"Seven Sam to King One and King Two—move in!" The Chevy lurched forward, its tires screeching only slightly until the rubber grabbed. It wasn't like the movies, Art had realized long ago. "Dispatch. Notify the LAPD units."

"Tenfour." The answer was quick and condensed.

Art was focused on the house. Down the street King Two—the T-Bird—came around in a U-turn and approached the house from the north. Neither Bureau car bothered to activate its small red strobes, but the local cops were coming hell-bent with their racks flashing a block behind King Two.

Seven Sam came across the street diagonally from the gas station and into the house's driveway. The three doors came open and the agents jumped out. Deans and Harriman pulled up in front, facing traffic on the wrong side of the street.

Art went right up the porch steps, taking a position on the knob side of the door. There was no screen. Hal was hinge side, his back flat against the house. Omar ran to the south side of the house to cut off any escape route there. Deans and Harriman placed themselves on the north side, in the driveway, with Rob moving along the structure toward the rear, keeping well below the high window lines every step of the way.

"*Seven Sam, King One in position,*" Shelly reported from the back. The house was completely surrounded.

Agent Harriman directed the four LAPD officers to cover the garage and the windows overlooking the driveway. Two of them had shotguns from the patrol car racks. They all moved to the safe side of a stone wall between Jackson's house and his neighbor's, three of them working their way back to the single-car garage.

Hal looked to Art and got the nod. "FBI! Open up! We have a warrant!" Lightman's voice boomed. Anyone in the house would have heard it.

They listened for a few seconds. It was quiet. Not just in a lack of response to the entry demand, but hushed. Deserted. Art had thought as much. Jackson was gone. But they had to do it by the book.

"FBI! Open up, *now*!" Hal added decibels to the last word.

There was still no response.

"Hal," Art said, holding his Smith & Wesson two-handed and pointed low. "Kick it."

Hal warned the other units by radio that they were moving in. He looked back to the street while putting the radio in his back pocket. Traffic was stopped. He couldn't see south, toward the freeway, but a hundred feet north there was an LAPD unit blocking the street in both directions. "I'm ready," he said, getting the go from Art.

The lock was flimsy, as most single locks were, and the door swung violently inward under the force of Hal's flat-footed kick. There must have been a table with something glass on it near the door as the breaking sound indicated.

Hal went in first, with Art right behind. Harriman followed them. They moved quickly, their guns pointed forward and to one side—Art left and Hal right. Andy also swept the right side, double-checking entryways as the trio passed them. Room after room was checked. The house was empty. For good measure Hal stuck his head through the covered opening to the attic. It was also empty.

Two of the uniformed cops entered as Hal hopped off the kitchen chair. They saw the dark hole to the attic above his head. "Damn brave, mister," one of them commented. Its meaning was more "damn stupid."

Art's head turned sharply to the lawmen. "Secure the outside, please." The words were not a request. Having jurisdiction did have advantages. Both of the cops retreated out in silence. Art turned to Hal. "Let them handle perimeter, but I don't want them in here. This is Bureau territory."

"Got it, Art," Hal said. "Gladly."

Outside, the senior LAPD officer—a sergeant—instructed his men, more of whom had arrived, to secure the scene. That meant stringing a line of yellow perimeter tape all around. It also meant closing the right northbound lane of traffic. The FBI vans belonging to the forensic teams would need the parking space very soon. The downside was obvious; this close to the Santa Monica freeway there was bound to be a hell of a traffic jam on La Cienega, especially at four in the afternoon—the height of rush hour.

"Hal, you're front," Art said. The agent moved to block the front door. Only those with a suit and a shield would get past him. Andy opened the back door, letting Shelly and Drew in.

"Shelly, check the back. Drew, you secure it. Watch the back wall. We don't want any busybodies getting over. Andy, you're with me—let's take a look." Art lifted the hand-held Motorola to his mouth. "Seven Sam to dispatch."

"*Seven Sam.*"

"Notify forensics that we're going to need two teams at this location. Roll six more teams out here, ASAP. Copy?"

"*Ten-four, copy.*"

The two men first took stock of the front room. An older TV stood on a wobbly looking stand. And no VCR. Stone age, Andy thought. The rest was sparsely furnished. Nothing extravagant. Art led off to the back of the house, to the lone bedroom. Andy detoured back to the kitchen. Their inspection wasn't detailed, just designed to pick up any obvious clues. Forensics would tear the place apart.

Their first look at the bedroom had been past the barrel of

their guns, with hearts pounding and senses tuned to detect threats. They hadn't seen the obvious. Art saw it now. Maybe people who knew they weren't returning to a place were predisposed to leaving it disheveled as a defense against their loss. *Horseshit*. The drawers were open, as was the closet. Art walked to it. It was half empty, he estimated. Mr. Jackson must be doing some traveling.

"Sir." Shelly stepped in.

"Yeah." Art was scanning the room, outwardly not acknowledging the agent's presence.

"There's a car in the garage. It matches with the suspect's vehicle—license and everything."

"Huh!" Art's eyes were wide when he turned to Shelly. "Well, imagine that. A new-looking car, right?"

"I wouldn't mind driving it."

"It looks like our friend is getting guiltier by the minute." And he wasn't going to make himself simple to find. "He may be using some other transportation. Oh well. Go ahead and call it in, Shell. I want an APB out on this guy." Art looked around the room from its center, then down. The bed was made. *Didn't sleep here, did you, Marcus*? Something happened here, though. Art could feel it.

The all-points bulletin went out immediately. Mr. Marcus Jackson, whose present whereabouts was unknown, was a wanted man. The official reason was for questioning in relation to the assassination. Unofficially, the reason that often carried the most weight in the legally constrained world of police work, he was a suspect in the conspiracy and a person who had the capacity to kill. Twenty-five minutes after the broadcast went out nearly every law enforcement agency south of Sacramento had at least the verbal information. The larger ones had photos spitting out of their teleprinters. The California Highway Patrol field offices were the first to get them, and soon after, their fleet of patrol vehicles had them as well.

The newly arrived teams of agents were pounding on doors in the neighborhood. People saw things—that was a fact of human nature. The presence of the police and serious-looking men in suits made the resident of the house on La Cienega an instant celebrity up and down the block. Soon everyone would remember something about Jackson.

Most of it would be useless, but something helpful was bound to be sifted from the whole.

Art left the house by the back door just as the second forensic team was arriving through the front. They would start on the house. Art's interest was now on Jackson's Jeep, which the first forensic team to arrive had already begun working on.

He recognized only one of them. "Bobby. You're among strangers."

"I'm the guide," Agent Bobby Valenzuela explained. "This is the team from Denver." He went on to introduce the three visitors. "No one thought about getting all these guys around once they were here."

No one *had* thought of that, Art now saw. You couldn't just hand the van keys to out-of-town assistance and expect them to find their way around a city like L.A. "Where are our guys?"

Valenzuela slid the elastic-strapped dust mask over his head, letting it hang at the neck. It was meant to keep the moist breath of the forensic agent off any prints he might be examining on the vehicle. "They're all tied up with evidence back at the site."

Even with the incoming help they were still stretched thin. Art motioned to the vehicle. "What do you think?"

"We'll get prints for sure. I can see some with just my eyes."

"I want to know if there are any besides Jackson's. If there are we're going to need a rush match with any we found on the suspect debris."

Valenzuela shook his head. "I don't know about that. Dan said there isn't much, if anything, that we can use. A couple partial prints at best."

"Still, let's do it," Art persisted. "Do your best."

The mask came up, covering the agent's mouth, and he turned to do his magic on the Jeep. Art stood silently at the open side door to the garage. The big double doors that opened to the driveway were still closed to the dismay of the crowd gathering across the street.

Art didn't see Jerry Donovan come up from behind. A tap on his shoulder alerted him. "Jerry. How the hell did you get here? I mean, *in town*?"

Donovan had been on a backpack fishing trip in the Maroon Bells area of Aspen, Colorado. "Let me tell you, it's a damn shame when an Army chopper plucks you out of a spot that God Himself made for the fisherman. What've we got going here?"

It took five minutes to update his boss. "He's got some relatives, according to some lady two doors down. But that'll take some time to confirm."

Donovan took it all in. He had obviously come straight from a quick change of clothes and a shave. His balding head of black hair was longer than he usually wore it. "A smart one, it seems."

"Maybe." Art wasn't sure about that. Fortunate, possibly, and well directed more likely. He felt it in his gut that there was a further player in this, someone behind Jackson.

The second agent felt his top collar button pop. "Damn fast dressing!" He left it undone. "Hey. What say you and me head on back to the barn." The barn was the office, and Art hadn't been there since the morning of the shooting. Donovan bent forward and down, examining Art's chin. "If that's the worst you ever get . . ."

"I know. I'm lucky."

"Who's senior here?"

"Hal Lightman." Art looked to the front.

"Good. Ready?"

The drive to the FBI office was slow in the lingering Los Angeles rush-hour traffic, taking nearly forty-five minutes.

"I went a little out of channels, Jerry," Art admitted as the car exited the freeway. Donovan's silence meant "go on." "Eddie's over at the Israeli consulate. I wanted to contact someone I knew from their embassy—a terrorism expert."

"I don't know, Art." Donovan could see how that might backfire. "Picture the media if they get a hold of it. 'FBI and Israelis investigate the Arab connection in the assassination.' " His gaze emphasized the words. "You get my drift? Especially if this Jackson connection pans out. The press would read that as a homegrown job, even if it's not."

Art wanted to tell his superior that his line of thought was bullshit, but wisely toned down his tongue. "I understand, but one of the shooters is—"

"Alleged shooter, Art." Again, Donovan spoke louder with his eyes. "Remember that."

"Are you telling me to back off on that?" Art asked, with no love of the idea in his voice.

Donovan paused. "No. It's your call."

There hadn't been any doubt in Art's mind. His boss was just doing his job, and in a small way, he was right. But then he thought in political terms, not those of a cop. He had come up through the ranks from the financial investigations section, a path that was safe and deskbound from beginning to end. That, Art believed, made him a candidate for something, somewhere, someday. Fortunately, though, he didn't impose his own skittishness on those he supervised. And there was that small bit of truth in Donovan's words. The whole thing could be taken wrong, and that could lead to even more problems. International incident? Maybe. But the detrimental effect it could have on the investigation was what worried Art the most. The Israelis certainly wouldn't be happy to share any information if their role were disclosed and twisted. He had to make sure it was kept quiet, and he had to get a good, solid link. Evidence that Obed was one of the shooters, and that there was something substantive in any relation he or the other assassin had to any terrorist backing.

From the underground parking garage at FBI headquarters Art went up six floors, directly to his office. The guard sitting at the reception area near the elevators paid little attention to the senior agent.

Art opened the door to the outer office. Carol, his secretary—administrative aide, he corrected himself—was gone. He checked his watch. It was almost six. *Shit! Eddie.* He picked up the phone.

Eddie answered on the first ring as it echoed in the Hilton's banquet room. "Toronassi."

"Ed. How'd it go?"

"Jeez, boss. I hear you've been kickin' doors."

"It keeps me young. What happened at the consulate?"

"It went good. They were helpful, to say the least. Damn nice people. I guess they've had enough experience with this crap too. Anyway, I spoke with Meir. He said he would personally work this through and call back as soon as he has anything."

"Ed. I want you to take the call. No one else."

"Okay." Eddie wondered what the problem was. "Something up?"

There was no need to burden Eddie, or anyone else, with the trivial crap that had trickled down. "No. I just want to keep this under wraps."

"No problem." Someone was laying something on the boss. Eddie figured that had to be it. The boss didn't let little things show, but he couldn't hide those things very well that really bothered him.

"Great. Thanks for handling all that." Art pulled off his tie with a tug and stuffed it into his jacket pocket. Then the jacket came off and landed on the couch. "Jackson was clean gone. No suitcases or anything like that left in the house, and lots of his clothes were gone, so I think we can safely say he wanted to get out of town before the—" Art's phone buzzed. "Hold on, Ed." He pushed the intercom button. "Jefferson . . . Okay." Art pressed another line. "Hal, what's up?"

It took only a minute for Hal Lightman to explain the development.

"All right. Okay, get that out as a supplemental. Good work." He returned to Ed. "Good news."

"Jackson?"

"One of his neighbors got home from work a while ago and had some very interesting info for us. It seems our friend pulled into his driveway early Saturday in a brand-spanking-new Cadillac DeVille, white with that gaudy gold trim—her words. She said it looked like a pimp's car. He threw a few suitcases in the trunk and took off. She didn't remember any plates on the car, just a dealer frame. She couldn't remember where from."

"It looks like he came into some money," Eddie said.

"But from where? Or who?" Art fumbled with his sleeve buttons before rolling them up. He dropped his body into the high-back leather chair. "God, this feels good. Ed," he said, leaning forward on the desk, "get everything you can on Jackson. Personnel records and everything. One of the neighbors mentioned something about him having relatives back East, but not much more than that. There might be something in his records somewhere. Check that against his five-oh-two arrest. Maybe his mother or brother or someone bailed him out then."

"Okay. We've already got his file from the building manager, but they don't keep very good records. There's nothing there about family."

That was a little strange. "Was there a place for it?"

"Yeah. It was just blank."

Oh, well, Art thought. Nothing was going to be direct or easy in any of this. "Who was his last employer?"

"RTD. He drove buses for them starting about ten years back. We should have that file in an hour."

Art nodded, looking at the coffeepot. It was off and empty. Carol usually had a pot waiting for him, but then he usually walked into the office at six A.M. "Okay. Let me know if the Israelis call, and call me if you get anything on Jackson. Jerry said the director wants an update in the morning, so I'll be here for a while. It's longhand tonight."

Eddie chuckled. "Carol's gonna love you tomorrow. Good luck."

Art hung up and pulled his top drawer out. He set the legal pad there, then got up to make a much needed pot of coffee. Again the guard paid Art no mind as he filled the glass pot at the water cooler. Back in the office he put a prepacked filter in the drip drawer and switched on the machine. Three minutes later the first smell of fresh coffee reached him behind the desk.

Two cups and four pages into the report he felt the uneasiness again. First he found himself focusing on his hand gripping the pen. It wouldn't move. *Damn!* Two weeks had passed since his last . . . *She's gone, damnit! You blew it.*

The pen slid out of his hand. Art stretched the fingers from both hands out, examining the palms and his quivering fingers. They steadied after a few breaths.

Art rose from his seat and went to the couch, sitting at the end uncluttered by his shed clothing. He wondered if anyone in the office knew how many nights he had slept here. The apartment just wasn't the right place. It didn't feel like a home. Home was the house in Monrovia, and Lois had gotten that as part of the divorce settlement. *You drove her away.* Hell, she deserved the house, and a lot more. Art was sure of that. It had been a good fifteen years, or so he thought, that had ended less than a year ago. Now she was in the house alone . . . or was she? He decided he was beating himself up enough without throwing in the "new lover" factor.

He took the jacket from his left and balled it into a pillow, adding that to the cushioned arm of the couch, then lay down, his eyes looking straight up. The doctor said these relaxation exercises were important as part of his overall program to better his health—and save his life. *Overall program! Quit smoking and do visualization exercises.* It was supposed to do good. He would do them as promised.

First, he found a point on the dim ceiling as he closed his eyes . . .

Georgetown

As morning passed to afternoon, and afternoon to evening across the nation, people dealt with the shock of the previous day's events in whatever way they could. Some were indifferent. Some were in disbelief. Some were openly grieving.

Bud DiContino was quiet in his contemplation of his feelings. President Bitteredge had been a man of integrity and high morals. He only wished he had been given the opportunity to know him better and work more closely with him. Deputies did not have the privilege of easy access to the president.

But what about the new president? Would he be as rocksteady in his beliefs as his predecessor? Could he handle the job? Bud didn't know. No one did. He had done well so far. But the adrenaline rush of the day and the motivation to get the job done would wear off of everyone, including the president. What then? Bud decided that waiting was the best cure for his questioning.

It had been a long day and his side hurt like hell as he lay on the bed in his jogging shorts. With these ribs he wouldn't do any running for a while. Next time, he thought, to hell with the Tylenol. Pure codeine, as the E.R. doctor had suggested. The shower had felt good, standing under the hot stream for twenty straight minutes. Bud glanced at his watch and let both arms rise in the air and fall to the bed above his head. His eyes were closed. The two Secret Service agents assigned to him had been asked to wake him at five A.M., just in case he found his way to the snooze button. They would pass it on to the twelve-to-eight detail shortly.

Sleep came easily. He could feel it enveloping him as his mind drifted off to a place where yesterday never happened.

4

· · · · · · · · · · · · ·

DEMONS

Georgetown

BUD ROLLED OVER at the sound of the phone. *God, it can't be five already.* He felt cold with just shorts on and pulled the sheets up to cover his shoulders as he picked up the receiver.

"DiContino."

"Sir," the male voice began, sounding much like one of the many government subordinates, secretaries, and deputies who came on a line in advance of their superior. "This is the NSC watch officer. I have a priority-one message from the FAA."

Bud pushed himself up to a sitting position on the bed's edge and shook the last of the sleepiness from his head. "Go ahead." It took only a minute for the situation to be explained. "Jesus! You better get the coffee going. I'll be there shortly."

He released the line and dialed the White House communications center. It rang only once.

"Com center." The operator was female and all business.

"This is NSA DiContino. Secure this line and connect me with Secretary Meyerson." There was a hollow hum as the connection was switched and then the ringing at the other end, sounding like an alarm bell in a tunnel. There hadn't been time since his ascension in government to install one of

the newer UltraCrypt telecommunications security systems
on his phone, an older, still compatible system having been
placed in a rush.

"Hello," an abruptly roused Meyerson answered.

"Drew, this is Bud."

"What time is it?"

Bud checked. "Almost three." He switched the receiver to
the other ear and flipped on the bedside lamp. "There's a
situation."

The secretary noticed the sound of the secure line.
"What?"

Bud took a little longer explaining to the secretary than the
NSC watch officer had giving him the information. Meyerson
was already half dressed when he hung up, and only his tie was
left to put on by the time he made the call he had to make.

Flight 422

Captain Bart Hendrickson leveled the *Clipper Atlantic
Maiden* off at three thousand feet above the shimmering
Mediterranean Sea. Normally he would be flying at an altitude of thirty-one thousand on a heading of three-zero-zero
degrees, but this was obviously no ordinary flight plan, and
certainly not normal conditions. It had been nearly a year
since he had commanded with a third man in the cockpit,
thanks to the advances of the 747–400, and never had he
flown with that third person wearing what he said was a
bomb and pointing a submachine gun at the back of his
head. He figured it was going to be a day for firsts.

"Any other instructions?" the captain asked.

The young man, looking like a Middle Eastern business-
man traveling on the Athens-to-London leg of the flight,
pressed the muzzle of the 9mm Mini-Uzi harder into the
captain's neck. "Two-five-zero . . . just fly," he repeated the
earlier orders.

The first officer had to grit his teeth in an effort to restrain
himself. An old Marine, Buzz would always retain the habits
instilled in him by the Corps—like keeping his crewcut. And
there were other more valuable ones: like respect, and pride.
To some they were clichés. To a Marine they were part of the
soul. Which was why his stomach was turning at the sound

of the pirate ordering his captain around. *You fuckhead.*

The hijacker stepped back and sat in the observer's jump seat, a fold-down chair behind the captain's seat, facing forward, which was often used by pilots hitching a ride between airports. He kept the compact black Uzi in his left hand, pointing at the console between the pilots, and the trigger switch in his right. Both pilots were stubborn, he noticed. They were probably soldiers. Arrogant American Marines. Killers! Yes, they would expect that the whole world should bow to them and their mighty numbers, caring nothing for those they crushed on their unholy crusades. Oh yes! They were a powerful force, but they answered to an infidel. The armies of Allah fought a just cause. They were blessed by their purity and devotion to the Great One, the Almighty Protector of the faithful legions that would march into battle with souls cleansed by His grace. The power of Allah gave strength to even the smallest of His armies, and that strength would now be used by the smallest of those many armies—a single man—to deal a crushing blow to the Great Satan.

Buzz turned his head to face the hijacker, disregarding his tendency toward a lack of self-control. His stare was met by dark, flared eyes, and a swivel of the gun, which now pointed directly at his face. The hijacker raised both eyebrows as if to ask, "Do you want to be shot?" The time would come, Buzz knew. He turned back to the instruments. Next to him Captain Hendrickson guided the *Maiden* on the ordered course. It was "his stick." He wanted his first officer well rested to back him up, remembering the prolonged ordeal the crews of other hijacked aircraft had gone through. That would be difficult, knowing Buzz. He was probably pissed as hell and ready to snap the hijacker's neck, if it weren't for that suicide vest and its deadman's switch.

The captain was angry himself. Angry at the animal that would play God and threaten the lives of the 342 people aboard his aircraft, but angrier still at the unseen person or persons who made this act of barbarism possible. The hijacker could not have carried his weapons on board under any circumstances. No, someone had done the job for him ... the tools of terror had been waiting for him when he boarded and took his first-class seat.

Fort Bragg, N.C.

He was up, showered, and dressed in his olive drab BDUs twelve minutes after receiving the warning order. Showering included shaving. The creases were perfect and as straight as an arrow, as they always were, except when he was doing what he loved most: being a soldier. William "Bill" Cadler had begun his military career as a private in 1959, a foot soldier who had slogged through his share of mud. He was a colonel now, the ground forces commander of the Joint Special Operations Command, an entity encompassing the much touted and maligned Delta Force—his unit. They were a formidable group, the GFC believed, but rarely were they allowed to show their mettle, and never had they been ordered in to actually perform their prime assignment: the rescuing of hostages.

Now another "stand to" order. They came regularly, usually followed by a "stand down" order. Occasionally there was an assignment. Protecting high-risk dignitaries was common, though that simply relegated Delta to the role of a reactionary force. Someday, though, it would come. The right circumstances and place and time would all come together, and the green light would be given. They would be ready.

The phone in his private quarters buzzed. "Cadler . . . Right. Good, Major. Hit the buzzer."

The claxon would have woken the dead. Eight pairs of legs swung over the bedsides in the barracks of the "hot squad." In a separate barracks the "slack squad" was still sleeping, but they, too, would be called if additional manpower was needed. Other men besides the eight had also been roused. Two three-man crews were running to their Blackhawk helicopters less than two hundred yards from the barracks. Farther to the east, at the adjacent Pope Air Force Base, a C-141B lifter assigned to the somewhat secret Twenty-third Air Force and dedicated to Delta would soon be fully crewed, her engines ready to crank.

The men were dressed in their mottled green camouflage BDUs in three minutes and running with their gear bags in hand to the nearby briefing center a minute later. Delta's headquarters, the Stockade, even after extensive modifications, from the air still resembled its former self. Getting from point A to point B was not the easiest of things in the Stockade's periphery corridors and rooms which all snaked off the central building complex. The Delta troopers had long since learned that the quickest way from their barracks to the briefing center was outside: a jog out the side exit, then a half-oval course past the building's main entrance and its somewhat out-of-place rose garden, and finally to the green door that led in.

A bright sodium light illuminated the area outside the briefing center, and the figure standing next to the door. He was there as he always was when the unit was called out, his face as black as the darkness farther away. Major McAffee stood solidly as the men approached. He made "at ease" look overpostured.

Captain Sean Graber hit the door first. Inside he dropped his bag at the back and took his seat. Colonel Cadler was already at the room's lectern. Lieutenants Buxton and Antonelli followed their squad leader in and were in turn followed by the rest of the team, all sergeants of various grades. Quimpo, the Filipino weapons specialist and senior NCO leadoff, with Jones, Makowski, Lewis, and the unit's chief medic, Goldfarb, following. McAffee followed the last trooper in. Behind, in the distance, one of the two helicopter's engines started. The closed door failed to muffle the sound completely.

Colonel Cadler waited for the major to join him at the front before beginning.

"Morning, boys," he said, his thick Texan accent dripping from each word. They all looked eager, as they did each time they entered this room. Cadler noted that it was Graber's squad. They had the highest number of call-outs per rotation. Just lucky, he guessed. "Major McAffee, would you read the orders, please."

The colonel handed the red-striped envelope to his XO, who had already read the orders. McAffee stood next to Cadler, who leaned on the podium.

" 'From: Chairman, Joint Special Operations Command. To: Special Operations Detachment, Delta. At oh-seven-forty Zulu, an American passenger aircraft was hijacked by an unknown person or persons. You are to immediately begin preparations for extraction of the hostages. More to follow. General Burkhardt sends thumbs-up and fingers crossed.' " The major looked up and handed the orders back to the colonel. The troops had received the same type of order before— many times. General Burkhardt knew this when issuing the warning order. "Fingers crossed" was not a wish for luck; it was a hope that the mission would get a go.

Cadler stepped to the side of the podium. "I want you on the helos in two minutes. We've got a hangar reserved for us at Pope. Major McAffee will lead the planning. Major, make the slack squad hot, and get a senior NCO in on the liaison group just in case we need to sweeten our force." McAffee nodded acknowledgment. "Any questions? Good. The birds are turning, so don't keep them waiting. Major McAffee and I will follow in the second bird. Fingers crossed. Dismiss the squad, Major."

The eight troopers stood automatically. "Dismissed."

They were gone from the room in seconds. Cadler and McAffee walked out behind them into the chilly early-morning air. There wasn't a cloud in the sky, evidenced by the countless specks of light visible in the area of the base with its lack of civilian lighting. The colonel looked up. "Mike, someone up there knows if this is the one."

"When it's right, sir," McAffee said, exposing his non-fatalistic streak.

"Right my ass! These boys are as ready as they'll ever be. They've got combat experience, they're pumped. Hell, we've trained and trained and trained, Mike. You know that as well as I do. These boys need some honest-to-God experience taking down some bad guys. Hell, only you and the captain have any actual trigger time."

"You, too, Colonel."

"My sorry old ass? That was a ground action, and it was a cluster fuck," Cadler answered, referring to his part as the unit XO in the failed Iranian rescue mission. Blackjack had also been there.

"I hear you. It's not our worry, though."

"Oh hell, Mike. There you go again with that crap. Washington and the briefcase brigades make the decisions, but do you have to accept it so easily?" Cadler smiled, putting his arm on the taller man's shoulder. "Jesus. Someone might think you graduated from Harvard instead of our beloved West Point."

McAffee feigned surprise. "Go Army!"

"Spirit, man!" Cadler let out a deep chuckle, a true belly laugh. The Blackhawk was directly ahead.

"What's our status, Colonel?"

Cadler didn't look hopeful. "Our end of it's up and running. The liaison group is set up; they'll plug in with the intel services and pass it along to planning. You have the force. The planning is yours. If we get a go, you lead. I'm gonna try and get something hard on whatever's going on."

"What's the best we have?" McAffee asked. He would need something in order to start the wheels of a plan in motion.

"Diddily. It's a 747, that's it. The pilot squawked the hijack code and dove for the deck. I'd assume we'll have somebody keeping an eye on that bird pretty soon."

"Okay," the major responded with some exasperation. "It looks like nothing ever changes. Minimum intelligence at best." He was silent for a few steps. "What about something similar to rehearse on?"

Cadler punched the major in the arm, then pointed a strong finger at his nose. "You've got it."

The two officers walked slowly toward the sound of the turning rotors. Lights were coming on in the distance, illuminating the side-by-side dark green helicopters. They sat long and squat under their idling rotors. The eight men of the hot squad trotted, heads ducked, to the side door of the near Blackhawk and jumped in without breaking stride.

"Colonel, I want a go as much as you . . . as much as they do." McAffee motioned to the helicopter. It was a hundred yards away as the engines revved and lifted it skyward, its nose slightly down, and moved forward away from the lights. Its own anticollision lights colored the underside a pulsing red. The noise was oppressive, and it passed almost directly above Cadler and McAffee on its six-minute flight to Pope. A group of soldiers ran up to the second Blackhawk and loaded several boxes and duffels under the direction of the dark-helmeted crew chief.

"It ain't any different," Cadler said, his head shaking and eyes downcast before coming up. The noise of the departing helo waned as it moved off into the night. "We train and drill. Every time we think it's *this* time, it's not. So, Mike, we do it all over. You know why? 'Cause we've got some demons to exorcise."

Demons, indeed, McAffee thought. Delta was still associated with the fiery debacle in the Iranian desert back in 1980, something that they had no culpability for as a unit. Again it was "brass fever" that had fucked things up. It was a reputation, though undeserved, that they had to overcome.

Both officers stepped into the dark cabin of the Blackhawk, returning the salutes of the crew chief and ground crew as they did. Colonel Cadler put on his headset and immediately got to work contacting the mobile headquarters now operating out of hangar 9 at Pope. Blackjack closed his eyes and crossed his fingers, hoping for a go, but wondering if anyone really knew what a green light would mean.

Four miles ahead, Captain Sean Graber was entertaining much the same thought.

Benina

Captain Muhadesh Algar was cold. He regretted having brought the topless jeep, wishing he had driven his Range Rover instead. His one small bag was on the seat beside him.

What? Benina Airport, eighteen miles from the center of Benghazi, was a civil and military airfield familiar to Muhadesh. He had often met his students there as they arrived from the many countries of their origin. But never had he seen this.

He slowed the jeep. A soldier of the regular army stood mid-road with a hand held out to his front. On both sides of the two-lane road were T-80 tanks, their 125mm cannons pointing down the length of the road. A group of twenty or so soldiers became very serious, taking their AK-74s in both hands as the jeep came to a stop. One of the crewmen protruding from a tank swung the 12.7mm heavy machine gun right at the small brown vehicle. The soldier blocking its path did not move as an officer walked hurriedly past to the driver side of the jeep.

"What do you . . ." The tall, thin lieutenant let his hand slip from where it rested on the top of his holster to his side with red-faced embarrassment. "Captain Algar!" He came to attention. "Sir, I did not know it was you. Lieutenant Ashad Hamshari, sir! Can I help you?"

Muhadesh looked around from his seat. "I am going to the airport. A flight to Tripoli."

The lieutenant swallowed hard. "Sir, my orders are to allow no one into the airport perimeter. Did you not pass the roadblock at the highway? They should have told you of this. I will—"

"Lieutenant Hamshari, I am commander of the Third Training Battalion, fifteen miles east of here. I traveled on the entrance road to our compound." *You idiot. Incompetence and ignorance seem to be required for promotion.* "As you must know, it intersects this road between here and the main highway."

"Yes, of course."

"So, Lieutenant, can you tell me why I must miss my flight? There is a reason?"

"Sir . . . yes, I am certain there is, but . . ." The Lieutenant stared, mouth open, at Muhadesh.

"I see. Following orders." Muhadesh snickered. "Who, may I ask, issued the orders?"

"Colonel Hajin, sir."

I should have . . . "Very well. I expect that Colonel Hajin has made it clear that only those with his permission may pass."

"Exactly," the answer came, almost apologetically. "Do you have such authorization, Captain?"

"Would I be sitting on this road if that were the case? Lieutenant Hamshari, you are responsible for notifying me, or my executive officer, Lieutenant Indar, immediately once the airport is open. Is that very, very clear?"

"Yes, sir. You will know the moment I do."

Muhadesh returned a salute and turned the jeep sharply around, putting one wheel on the soft side of the road before heading back the way he had come. Already he was trying to figure out what was going on. Something was, that was certain. He wasn't a good analyst of inferences or subtle intelligence tidbits—that was not his way. But he couldn't shake the feeling that something was terribly wrong. *Hajin . . . what are you up to?*

Flight 422

Mohammed Hadad felt at peace and in control. All had gone so well. The attack by the martyrs in America had dealt a crushing blow, the beginning of a greater deed that would teach not only the Americans, but also their unholy allies and puppets, the power of Allah. And they would be powerless to stop it. The blessing of the Great One brought strength and determination to the righteousness of his purpose. His own life was meaningless when compared with the purpose. It was what drove him now. It was his reason to go on. The only reason. The power was awesome. None could resist it. The Greek infidel could not. He had placed the weapons on the plane for a simple, meager bribe, and he would surely be discovered. And soon, Hadad knew, the final dagger would be unsheathed.

Hadad looked ahead. The pilots were intent on their flying, almost as if the concentration could mask their fear. Oh yes! They feared him, even in their arrogance. That was why he made them fly so low. He saw that they feared that too. They were comfortable in their routines and familiar procedures, precisely why he commanded them to do what *he* wanted. He was in control. At one point he had ordered them to fly just three hundred feet above the water. They were very nervous then. *I am in control. They fear me.*

He looked at his watch. It was time to begin the taunting. Now he would captivate not only these people, but the entire world. Hadad reached into his pocket while holding the Uzi under his arm.

"Broadcast this," he commanded, handing the message—typed in perfect English—to the pilot.

Captain Hendrickson took the paper in hand and scanned it. The message was short. He half turned in his seat, a task made difficult by the harness and semi form-fitting cushions, and faced the hijacker. He was young, very handsome, and neat-looking with his nicely cut dark hair. There were tan lines along his temples where glasses had been. Odd, the captain thought. The hijacker looked like he had spent some time at the beach. And what could cause a young man like this to do what he was doing? He didn't fit the terrorist profile: nervous, loud, violent. He could have been fresh out of some corporate training program by appearance. The man was calm, almost serene, though his eyes bore no doubt that he would use his weapon. But the bomb? Was he suicidal? Would he release the switch and kill everybody, or was it a bluff?

"Buzz, send this," the captain said, handing the paper over. "My stick."

"Roger, your st—"

"No!" Hadad shouted, displaying agitation for the first time. "*You* send the message! *You* do it as I ordered!"

The captain turned again. "Listen," he began, his voice raised noticeably. "*I* am flying this aircraft. If you want to get wherever it is you're planning to go, then I suggest you let me do my job."

Hadad glared into the pilot's wide eyes. *Yes, I need you to fly, infidel. It is all right that you think you have won.* He shifted his look to the copilot and stepped back, sitting down in the jump seat. "Go ahead."

Buzz took the paper and, after a quick look over it, pressed the column-mounted mike switch.

Hammer Two-Seven

One hundred and twelve miles to the west the Frisbee-topped E-2C Hawkeye from the USS *Carl Vinson* had just finished topping off its tanks from its tanker. Two F-14 Tomcats, with their own tanker support, were loitering seven thousand feet below the Hawkeye, designated Hammer Two-Seven. The Tomcats were just a precaution. Flight 422 was paralleling the North African coast some three hundred miles offshore, and Hammer Two-Seven was equally close, following the 747's westerly course.

The crew of the Hawkeye, an early-warning aircraft with a powerful radar in its top-mounted rotating dome, were mostly young, but highly trained and vigilant. Not only were they monitoring the hijacked aircraft, a task they performed with great seriousness, they were also keeping an eye open for any of Qaddafi's "aerial submarines," as they called the hopelessly ill-manned Libyan fighters. The colonel had been crazy enough to send his warplanes after U.S. forces in the area before, hence the derogatory nickname as the jets became proficient at subsurface maneuvers. The crew of the unarmed radar plane were nonetheless pleased that the two F-14s were nearby.

On the radar officer's screen the 747 was a clearly painted target. The altitude of the target—nonhostile aircraft were targets, hostile ones were bandits—was fuzzy, but certainly below two thousand. That was an altitude quite uncomfortable for the pilots of large aircraft, as it left little room for error or recovery in the event of a power loss. The radar officer tried to picture it, lumbering over the ocean, its four turbofans leaving a trail of thunder on the water. The altitude readout had actually ceased at one point, a sign that the target had dropped below five hundred feet. *Crazy fuckers*!

"Sir! Target is transmitting!" the communications officer, a lieutenant, announced. Both hands were pressing the black headphones against his ears.

Commander Jack Polhill, Hammer Two-Seven's commanding officer, ordered Com to put it on speaker. *On speaker* meant through the intercom feed to the other crew members. It was a term that had stuck, though it was something of a misnomer, like Polhill's title; he commanded the aircraft, but didn't fly it.

"*Four-Two-Two heavy to any station.*" The broadcast was on the international civilian aircraft emergency frequency.

"Com, don't reply," Polhill instructed. "Let's ride it out and see what's up."

"Aye, sir."

"*Four-Two-Two heavy to any station.*"

The commander knew that several stations would be listening to the transmission. "Everyone is hesitant. That figures." Contact could be more than its worth to any uninvolved government.

"*Four-Two-Two heavy . . . this is Cairo Tracon . . . go, uh, go ahead.*"

"Not a popular conversation partner, sir," Com observed.

"Never are."

"*Four-Two-Two heavy to station responding . . . you are faint . . . repeat.*"

The commander turned to Radar. "Plot."

The information was instantly available. "Target bearing

zero-one-eight, relative; one-zero-eight, true; angels three; speed four-zero-zero knots; course, two-five-zero, true."

The air traffic controller in Cairo did not respond immediately to the call. Flight 422 was a scant three thousand feet above sea level and having difficulty reading the transmission from the land-based station. It was a simple matter of radio line of sight.

"Coming up, sir," Radar said excitedly. "Angels three and a half. Bearing and course steady. Distance one-one-zero miles."

"Keep it coming, Radar." An uneasy feeling materialized in Commander Polhill's stomach, like something wasn't quite right. Why was Cairo answering instead of . . . ? "Com. Move the Tomcats twenty miles south . . . fast!"

"Aye, sir."

"Sir, target climbing from angels three and a half."

"*Cairo Tracon . . . this is Four-Two-Two heavy.*"

"Sir, angels four. Everything looks steady."

"*Four-Two-Two heavy,*" the controller acknowledged in non-native English, the international air traffic language, "*this is Cairo Tracon. You are coming in clear. Go ahead.*"

"*Cairo, this airplane is under the control of the Avengers of the Islamic Brotherhood. The lives of the hostages are meaningless. They will live or die depending on the actions of the godless American government. We have no hatred of the oppressed peoples who must live in the homeland of the Great Satan, but we can not ignore the deeds of their leaders. Our brothers have been killed by the soldiers of the Great Satan and their Zionist lackeys for too many years. The victims of this unwarranted barbarism have been unable to defend themselves. They have no weapons. But now they do in us. The Americans will be made to pay. If they do not cooperate, the hostages will die. In the name of Allah, the compassionate, the merciful, tell the Americans we are coming.*" The air went dead.

Cairo tried to raise the aircraft several times, unsuccessfully.

Polhill's face was contorted in thought. "Com, what'd you hear?"

The redheaded lieutenant brought the boom mike closer to his lips. "He sounded pissed—just like a pilot would."

"Pilots don't call their rides 'airplanes'; it's 'aircraft.' But you're right, he was not a happy camper having to read that." The commander noted the time and other observations of the message. "Hijacked out of Athens, a crackpot message . . . another A-rab terrorist."

"Aye on that, sir." The lieutenant leaned way back in his seat. There was another damn animal playing a game with the lives of hundreds of people, and not a thing they could do about it.

"Go ahead and get that off," Polhill ordered. Within a minute the message was encrypted and sent by burst transmission up twenty-three thousand miles to a Navy communication satellite which would relay the message, condensed to less than half a second's duration, back down to a Pentagon receiving station. Polhill wasn't brass, nor did he have much intelligence experience behind him. He could tell, however, that this situation was probably going to develop into a first-class pain in the ass.

"Aircraft sets!" Radar shouted. At petty officer's rank he was the juniormost member of the five-man crew. "I've got two . . . yeah, two sets at one-seven-nine. Search stuff. Wait . . . two more!"

The commander turned to his own screen, which duplicated the radar officer's readout. The emissions gave only a bearing to their platforms—aircraft in this case—but little else. "Radar, do you have them on active?"

"Negative, sir," Radar answered, adjusting his controls for sensitivity. "They've got to be on the deck. Checking bands now. Jesus! Their strength just came *way up*. They must be burning like there ain't no . . . Got 'em!"

"Plot!"

"Two . . . three . . . four. All of 'em!"

"True bearings only, Radar." Polhill switched his radio selector to the *Vinson's* CAG frequency. "Rowboat, this is Hammer Two-Seven. I have four bandits. Stand by." Four obviously military aircraft popping out of nowhere weren't considered even remotely friendly.

The radar officer scribbled furiously on his console's notebook. "Sir, I have Bandit One, two MiG-31s it looks like, bearing one-five-zero; speed nine-zero-zero; course zero-zero-zero. Bandit Two, looks like Foxhound emissions, too, bearing one-four-nine; speed nine-zero-zero; course . . . shit! . . . three-five-zero; distance one-three-zero miles."

"Rowboat, I have four Libyan MiG-31s inbound. Two on me, two on the big bird." He switched all his channel selectors to open. "Com, get the Tomcats on Bandit One. They're heading for the 747." The com officer acknowledged the order and sent the F-14s flying.

"Hammer Two-Seven, this is Rowboat . . . Two 'Cats are on the way, and the ready-fives will be up in two."

"Roger, Rowboat." The commander saw that the two Tomcats nearest him were now racing at full afterburning speed directly at the two MiG-31 Foxhound interceptors directed against Flight 422. The other two just shot from the carrier were gaining altitude and speed as they moved to intercept the other pair of MiGs. It was not a comfortable feeling knowing that the F-14s assigned to protect him were going to cover another aircraft—a civilian one—while Libyan Foxhounds with their Amos air-to-air missiles were coming right at him. But he had no choice. He had to keep them off that airliner. Lord knew what they'd do.

"Sir, CIC designates our 'Cats as Viper One, the new 'Cats as Viper Two," Com reported.

"Radar, distance to Bandit Two."

"Sir, one-one-five miles to us; eight-two miles to Viper One."

It was too damn close. The Amos missiles had a range of sixty miles, roughly forty miles less than the Phoenix missiles on the F-14s, and weren't as accurate. Russian-trained pilots didn't have a habit of popping missiles off at extreme ranges, or so the intel boys said. The Tomcats weren't likely to fire their Phoenixes at similar ranges either. It wouldn't matter much, though, with the MiGs moving at a mile every four seconds. Practical range would come in under two minutes. And Viper One. Polhill knew he'd have to order them to literally fly by the MiGs to get to Bandit One. The passing distance would be under ten miles. With a closing speed of over twenty-one hundred knots, the seconds of indecision were a precious commodity, one he couldn't afford to waste.

"Com, order Viper One to paint Bandit Two."

"Aye, sir."

The commander gave his neck a quick roll to shake some of the tension. He was hoping that the Libyans racing toward him would find it unsettling to hear their radar-warning receivers go off as the F-14s "painted" them with their powerful AWG-9 fire control radars. The same tactic had worked in most other confrontations with Qaddafi's fighters.

"Com, does Viper One have Bandit Two?"

"That's an affirm, sir. They have lock-ons. Viper One leader reports a red light on one of his Phoenixes."

Damn! That meant they had only three of the long-range Phoenixes and eight of the shorter-range Sparrows between them.

"Rowboat, this is Hammer Two-Seven . . . request permission to order weapons-free rules of engagement to Viper One." The CAG didn't need to be told who the targets might be. He could see the same radar picture via data link that the Hawkeye was privy to.

"*Permission granted.*"

"Com, send it."

The message was relayed to the Tomcats. They now had the authority to fire if they perceived a threat to be real. It was an order with a great deal of latitude. Polhill had been in the Navy for going on twenty-three years, and he knew fighter jocks; they were cocky, and arrogant, and above all, disciplined. Their job was to protect the Hawkeye and, by the nature of the mission, the 747. Two MiGs aimed directly at the radar aircraft could only be perceived as one thing: a threat. It wouldn't be long.

"Sir, target . . . uh, the target is turning. Coming south." The radar officer leaned closer to his screen. "Around. There. Steadying." It was a few seconds before the call-out continued. "New course is one-seven-five . . . no. Still turning. Make that one-eight-zero. He must've hauled that baby over on her wingtips to turn that fast."

"Radar, what's Bandit One doing?"

"Slowing. Same course, and speed's down to five-zero-zero knots. Distance to the 747 is nine-zero-miles."

"Hmm," Polhill grunted. *Setting up a shot, maybe?*

"Viper Two is six minutes out," Com said. "Whoa! Fox three! Fox three! I have two fox threes. Viper one just fired." Two Phoenixes—"fox threes"—were on their way.

"There go—" Radar's words stopped abruptly. "Bandit Two is firing! I've got two missiles inbound! Looks like they're going for the 'Cats."

Smart! Polhill had seen this before. The MiGs were gambling that the Phoenixes' own guidance radars hadn't picked them up on active yet, and that the Tomcats would turn away to avoid the missiles targeted on them. That would take away the beam of radiated energy painting the target and cause the Phoenixes to miss. It was a gutsy move.

But the Tomcat drivers were no stranger to the ploy either, and with their defensive jamming systems on, they slowed to four hundred knots and watched their missiles streak toward Bandit Two.

"Viper One . . . shut down! Disengage!"

What? The radar officer turned to the commander, who returned his quizzical look. Viper One was already heeding the order from the CAG aboard the *Vinson*. The two F-14s rolled into a tight right, diving turn and shut down their fire control radars, coming around a full three hundred and sixty degrees to face the MiGs again. They were both visible on the Tomcats' search radars, and to the Hawkeye, heading on a reciprocal course back to Benghazi.

Viper Two took up station thirty miles to the east of Hammer TwoSeven, while Viper One remained at its present location to track the retreating MiGs. The weapons officer aboard the Tomcat with a remaining good Phoenix kept his finger on the radar transmit switch, ready to power up the AWG-9 if need be.

Aboard Hammer Two-Seven Commander Polhill questioned the order from the CAG. The Tomcats had two certain kills, courtesy of the overly confident Libyan pilots. Why order them off? It was a clear case of provocation. Hell, MiG-31 Foxhounds closing at nine hundred knots didn't warrant just a "hello."

"Sir, look." Radar was pointing to his display.

Polhill took the suggestion. His heart stopped pounding. Directing planes in battle was stressful. An airborne controller was not at all removed from the fight: He was an integral part of it. Missiles streaking toward one of his aircraft might just as well have been aimed at him. Looking at the screen, however, Polhill brought his mind back to the here and now, and an answer to his questioning was apparent. The CAG had the luxury of watching Bandit One as the near battle erupted around the Hawkeye. Bandit One's two MiGs had formed up on the 747, one mile off of each wing, and were escorting it toward the Libyan coast at four hundred knots.

It never had been necessary to send his Tomcats to protect the hijacked aircraft, the commander realized. Flight 422 was not an intruder . . . it was a guest.

The White House

"Good, thank you." The chief of staff hung up the phone. "Bud, Meyerson just arrived."

The NSA poured himself a cup of coffee. Gonzales waved off the offer. The cups were white stoneware mugs with the presidential seal emblazoned on opposite sides. The hot liquid felt good as Bud wrapped both hands around the mug. "It's cold in here."

Gonzales joined Bud, taking one of the seats around the antique coffee table. It sat near the Oval Office fireplace and closer to the president's desk than the main door. "Mary said the building engineer is going to check on the AC in the morning." He laughed. "The *real* morning."

Really. Bud sipped his cup of caffeine. It was giving him the necessary jolt. He hadn't wanted to wake the president, hoping that the NSC could get things under control. That wasn't to be. The report from the Sixth Fleet required that, the need for sleep notwithstanding, he be roused.

"It's amazing, Bud," the COS began. "Two days ago we were really only functionaries. Second-string. Look at us now." His voice trailed off in a melancholic tone. "Damned if I ever wanted to move up this way."

The Oval Office was a lonely place. There were two men in the room, but each felt alone in many ways. It was an aura of solitude. Bud decided he wouldn't trade places with the man for anything.

"What do you think's up?"

Gonzales shrugged, running a hand over his quickly shaven face. "I don't know, and he may not know, but he sure as hell is going to want a good estimate of what's happening."

What was happening? It was Bud's question of the day.

He had at his disposal every military and civilian intelligence service, their analysts, and all the technological gadgetry available to them. They would already be working to identify the perpetrators and their intentions. But it was *he* who would have to make an intelligent assessment of the information and present recommendations to the president. It was the challenge he wanted, though a little more time to settle into the job before having this dumped on him would have been welcome.

Gonzales heard the clock's minute hand click forward. It was that quiet. The president would be down any minute.

Both men rose as the door opened. It was a new reflex.

"Bud. Ellis." The president wore a gray sweatsuit and dirty white tennies—his comfies. The Secret Service hadn't given him much time to dress. He took a seat across from his advisers. "What do we have?"

Bud pushed the mug away from the edge of the table and brought both hands together. "Mr. President, I've called in the NSC. They're assembled in the situation room and the deputies group is also working. About an hour and a half ago an American carrier passenger flight, numbered 422, was hijacked out of Athens. Then, not very long ago, some of our naval aircraft tracking the jet near the North African coast had a confrontation with several Libyan fighters."

The president was instantly awake. "Were there any casualties?"

"No, thankfully." Bud wished he had written a brief, but there hadn't been time. "There was fire exchanged, but the commander on the *Vinson*—that was the carrier involved— ordered his fighters to disengage."

"Why?"

"Flight 422 was in the middle of the whole thing. Our fighters were trying to protect it as the Libyans approached in two groups. Our pilots believed the fighters were going to attack the 747, and their own command aircraft, so they fired. The Libyans returned fire."

"And there were no casualties?" The president was a bit perplexed, and his face showed it.

"None. While the action was taking place the hijacked aircraft made a turn and headed toward the Libyan coast."

"Could he have been maneuvering to avoid fire, or a missile?" the president asked.

Bud shook his head. "There were no missiles directed at the 747, and they wouldn't have known if there were; commercial aircraft don't carry the types of sensors that would indicate if they were targeted, and the Libyans were well out of their visual range."

"My God," the president said. "How many people on board?"

"Over three hundred," Bud answered.

"Including the crew," Gonzales added.

The president was silent for a moment. "Am I reading this the way it sounds?"

"I'm afraid so," Bud affirmed. He couldn't read the president's mind, but the man was smart. "The aircraft made no radio calls indicating a course change, nor did it receive any; our command aircraft would have detected that. Plus, the two Libyan fighters that appeared to be in a position to attack flight 422 formed up to *escort* it." Bud paused. "You can understand why the air group commander called off our fighters."

"I can now." The president was visibly upset. His mouth formed into a pout of seriousness. "So, Colonel Qaddafi has decided to become involved."

"In a very large way, sir," Bud added.

"The good colonel didn't hold to his promises very long, did he? Well, we've got two incidents to deal with now." The president made a point to keep the two happenings separate, though his mind was putting that which was obvious together. "I can't keep Nate here. We need him over in Britain. They're pretty pissed off, I understand. Not at us, just in general. He can do a lot to keep things calm. Bud, you'll have to chair the NSC on this, and I want to be kept up-to-date. Every four hours, and more if you think it's warranted." He turned to his COS. "I remember the media circus some of the past hijackings have generated. You talk to Herman and set some guidelines for press contact on this. It could get messy. That's just a feeling.

"Bud, what have we done so far?"

"Delta has been activated to start preparations for any contingency. The necessary agencies are working on why, how, and who. That's the tough stuff to figure out in this kind of situation. After the council takes a look at it we may have more, but for now . . ." Bud threw his hands apart.

"I don't like the fact that these people always seem to be controlling us," the president said. "We're always reacting. And with the rest going on, jeez! So, an American aircraft is going to be landing in Libya. When?"

"About thirty minutes," Bud replied.

The chief executive sat back into a thinking pose with one finger tracing circles on his chin. "This will not turn into another flight 847," he said, referring to the seventeen-day ordeal on the ground in Beirut.

Bud had one final thing to inform the president of. "Sir, there was a message from the aircraft just before the confrontation with the fighters."

"We can't take everything they say as truthful, sir," the COS pointed out.

The president took his friend's words, then looked back to Bud. "What was said?"

"They said they're coming here."

"Here?"

The NSA nodded. "To America."

Flight 422

The coast was approaching fast. Mohammed Hadad crouched behind and between the pilots, his hand resting on the top of the arrogant copilot's seat back. The man was nervous. Every few seconds he would cock his eyes to the left to see the trigger switch just four inches away. Hadad sensed more than saw this. Soon this man would be more frightened.

"You are a soldier," Hadad stated. The barrel of his Uzi rested on the co-pilot's shoulder.

Buzz's jaw muscles spasmed at the tone. *Fuck you!* "Marine," he said softly.

"Marine. Ahhh!" Hadad smiled, his head nodding. "Were you in Beirut, Marine? Did you murder the children of Beirut, Marine?"

Buzz tried to ignore the taunting, unsuccessfully, and the rising burning sensation in his neck tingled on the surface as hot met cold. *Raghead asshole!* He would have bitten his lip to control the anger . . . no, hatred welling up in him, but that would have given something away to the pirate. Anyway, snapping his neck would have been a better use of adrenaline.

"You." Hadad stepped back to his seat. "You do not know or care what happens to the many children of those you oppress . . . do you?" There was no answer. "You will know. You will know."

Captain Hendrickson tried to block out the conversation. He knew that Buzz would kill this guy given the chance. He wanted to smile, but resisted when Buzz practically prayed the word *Marine* in response to the hijacker's verbal jab. It was a fitting answer. His first officer was a gung ho jarhead if ever there was one. He had probably eaten guts and farted bullets at one time in his life. Marines did that for fun, he had heard.

As the *Clipper Atlantic Maiden* neared the coast the captain increased power in the four big engines. The warming air above the desert floor was thinner than that over the water and thus required more thrust from the turbofans to maintain lift. A slight pull back on the control column added a little more nose-up attitude to the aircraft, and additional upward force. There was an immediate rise in the whine of the engines as their RPMs increased.

They were going to land. Captain Hendrickson had the stick, leaving Buzz to handle the minor duties required to set the huge aircraft down. The first officer keyed his mike to raise the tower.

Hadad jumped forward, striking Buzz with the Uzi's barrel behind the left ear. A shallow gouge opened and filled with blood.

"No radio!"

Buzz's hand came down bloodied from the left side of his face. He felt a cool trickle of blood on his neck. "You fucking—"

"Buzz!" The captain reached across the center console, grabbing his co-pilot. "Another time." His eyes bored into those in the seat opposite him, into those of his friend. Buzz was more than his first officer. They had flown together too many times over the years to be just co-workers. "We have to fly her, Buzz. Another time. Okay? Another time."

Hadad pulled back and smiled. "Listen to your cap-tan, Number Two. He is wise with his words." *But there will not be another time.*

The old Marine swallowed his contempt and again wiped his reddened ear and neck. Rivulets of blood ran down and stained his collar a dark crimson. He shifted his stare to the pirate, whose face was lit with an unnatural glow from the sunlight filtering through the thick windscreen. He was half turned, facing the grinning pirate, whose eyes showed no fear, only power: the power that came with the gun and a planeload of unarmed innocents.

"If you wish to be first to die, Number Two, that would please me." The smile left Hadad's face.

Buzz turned back to the front and the attention of the aircraft. He scanned the instruments—they were all nominal. The captain was right. Now was the time to fly, to keep the *Maiden* flying. There *would* be another time. He touched his ear again. The blood flow seemed to be minor and slowing as clots formed at the source. At the same instant the *Clipper Atlantic Maiden* crossed the coastline.

Michael Alton held his wife's hand as it lay across the armrest and touched his knee. Sandra's fingers ran gentle, yet nervous figure eights on his jeans. He could sense her fear, though she would not show it. They had both seen the man, but Michael was one of the few passengers to recognize what he was carrying pressed against his side as a weapon. The couple looked at each other incredulously after the captain announced that they had been hijacked. This sort of thing happened only on the news, or in the movies—not to them.

Several of the flight attendants were doing their best to calm the upset passengers. The number of them was amazingly small. Michael figured it was because most people, like him, half believed it would all just suddenly end, like a dream when one wakes up. Probably the most unsettling thing was the very young stewardess who was beyond hysterical. Two of her co-workers had escorted her down from the upper deck with a group of passengers just before the captain's announcement. One of them had her in the forward galley.

The other stood at the base of the stairs, glancing at the passengers with a feeble smile at times, but mostly her eyes were fixed upward.

Michael felt his wife squeeze his fingers in her palm. Sandy was his life, his reason for living. Their children were precious and more important to him than anything, except her. At least they were home safe with her parents. If they didn't make it home the kids would be taken care of. If they did make it out of this, Michael swore that he would listen to his wife the next time they planned a vacation. She had wanted to go to Maui.

The aircraft circled once at his direction and was now entering the empty landing pattern for a visual approach. Hadad checked his watch. It would be happening now, he knew, and the smile again came to his face.

London

The noise from the traffic two blocks away was momentarily masked by the sharp crack of an explosion. There was little flash visible on Winslow—the blast originated farther back in the second-floor flat—but the sound and visible effect at the front of the three-story stone-faced structure were pronounced. Shards of wood, stone, and glass rained down upon the empty street and sidewalk. A groaning came from the building as the initial roar of the blast subsided. The horizontal support members between the first and second, and second and third, floors were breached, and the upper stories settled downward, pushing the ground floor into the basement. Surprisingly, there was no fire following the collapse, only a panicked scream from someone inside the devastated structure.

Less than four hundred meters away a young Irishman dialed the Scotland Yard operator and delivered a message that he recited verbatim from memory. The operator passed the information to the inspector on duty at the Domestic Terrorism desk. He received it at the same time the first calls came in on the explosion. He immediately notified the explosive ordnance detail and left for number 316 Chatham, where the caller said another bomb would be found.

5
··············

SAINTS AND SINNERS

Los Angeles

THE DOOR SLAMMED. It must have. He heard the sound of wood on wood and the rattle of the latch, but it should have been louder. Shouldn't it? Who was it? Who? Who?

"Art," the familiar female voice called to him.

Art's eyes flickered open. He reached up, rubbing the sleepiness away as best he could. There was a heavy aroma of fresh coffee . . . and vanilla. But . . . "Carol?"

She was there, with the coffee only she could brew. Not that packaged foofoo crap that smelled like cake. It was her recipe. Art used to laugh at that: She had a *recipe* for coffee. "*Your* pot was cold, Arthur. Jerry tells me there's a report to get ready."

He pulled himself up, first on his elbows and then to a head-hanging sitting position. His shirt back was wet and his mouth was heavy with a filmy taste. "Guess I dozed off for a while."

"A while?" Carol set the glass pot on the desk blotter. "You, young man, did more than doze off—it's almost two A.M."

"What?"

Her hands found their familiar position on her hips, which, along with the twisted look, signaled her displeasure. She was gruff and caring, much like Art's grandma. "Listen." A single finger aimed at his nose. "You were asleep. Jerry looked in and saw you and decided to call me. He thought you might need some help, so don't start fussing."

"Jesus, Carol."

"Don't 'Jesus' me, young man."

Young man, hah! Only in comparison, though her sixty-

95

three years had been kind to her. He would tell her, and she thought jokingly, that she didn't look an hour past fifty.

"Now drink your coffee." She poured the first cup and handed it to him. "Jerry's already gone home and Eddie's taking a nap at the Hilton. I spoke to him about ten and he said he'd call and wake you if the information came in. I typed up what you already had—*and* corrected your spelling—so you can just pick up where you left off."

"Ehh!" Art coughed. The vanilla coffee was hot. And it did give him that kick he needed. Getting to his feet was easy after four sips.

"I'll be at my desk—awake—when you need me," she said, giving Art a wink as she pulled the door.

Art took stock of himself. "I must look like shit," he mumbled aloud. A quick check of the pedestal mirror behind his desk confirmed the suspicion. He had left the file drawer half open before pausing. Why change shirts now, he wondered. Before him, neatly arranged, were the typed pages of the report and a fresh legal pad. He smiled and softly chuckled.

"Okay, Arthur," he said aloud, "from the top."

Fort Belvoir, Va.

Number 8601 had raced across the sky at eight thousand miles per hour to a point over the North African coast where the Gulf of Sidra reached its farthest point inland, roughly above the town of Al-Uqaylah. Along its path it gradually dove from its previous altitude of 450 miles to a position in near earth orbit—108 miles above sea level. The position was practically perfect for photoreconnaissance, weather permitting, but uncomfortably close to the dense atmosphere closer to the earth. Already sensors on the surface of the KH-12 ENCAP—Enhanced Capability—had detected a rise in temperature as the huge satellite skirted the upper reaches of significantly measurable atmosphere. The friction with the heavy—compared to the vacuum of space—gases created heat. Several pumps were alerted to the buildup of heat and began sending additional amounts of cryogenic coolant to the heat-sensitive photoreceptors—the infrared eyes of the spacecraft.

When it reached its destination it was slowed, then stabilized, by tiny but powerful hydrazine rockets that aligned the "barrel" of the satellite at a predetermined reference point. Controllers at the Consolidated Space Operations Center in Colorado Springs then passed control of the KH-12 ENCAP, the first in its series, to the technicians at Fort Belvoir. In one relatively small room in the windowless cube-shaped structure that was the Keyhole ground station, two technicians sat at their control consoles. They were in control of the "bird," as they called it, though any maneuvering would still need to be done from CSOC.

"How long?" one of the National Security Agency officials asked. He was actually an Army colonel. His companion was a civilian officer of the NSA.

The senior technician did not look at the two "suits" who sat behind. He was moving a computer mouse, directing a cursor as it danced across a secondary CRT, which was dwarfed by the wall-mounted seventy-inch monitor. "A minute, sir." *Sir!* These guys expected a bird to do a speed run, slam on the brakes, and start transmitting wedding portraits! And *they* wore the suits!

A tunnel view of atmospheric haze and distant ground clutter filled the high-resolution monitor. The two NSA officials sat slightly higher than the technicians, bleacher style, giving them a comparable view. The room was much like a large closet in size. One wall was covered by the large viewing screen, below which was the instrumentation that controlled the sensors aboard the satellite. The walls, ceiling, and the single door to the room were covered with an indigo-colored fabric paper to eliminate glare and reflected light, enemies in a room where visual acuity was required for proper analysis.

"Okay, Chief," the junior technician said. "I show a pos on the RPL. That's a catch!"

"Stability?"

A look at another section of his display. "Set."

The chief let out a breath. This rushed shit, especially the altitude dives, made him nervous, considering the bird was one of a kind. There were three of the originally planned four KH-12s in orbit, the fourth having suffered a rocket motor explosion as it climbed to its 550-mile area observation altitude. Right now it was tumbling away from earth. An expensive piece of space junk. One KH-12 ENCAP, three standard KH-12s, plus a handful of the older, less capable KH-11s in orbit was stretching the thin minimum needed. And none of the 11s or 12s had the capabilities of the 12 ENCAP, whose most important feature was its ability to "hover" over the same point in low earth orbit, giving continuous surveillance of that spot.

"Hmm," the bearded suit grunted. "Fuzzy."

Just hang on. "It'll clear up. We're focusing down slowly. Got to, otherwise the lens motor might cause gyrorotation."

"I see," the suit lied. He had no idea what it meant. *Hurry.*

"Chet, start VDI and half inch. Do you guys need one tape or two?" the chief asked, turning to see the single finger in response from the colonel.

"VDI up and nominal. Half inch is nominal. Running . . . now." The junior technician engaged the two recording devices. The half inch was, quite simply, an improved VCR with a higher-resolution recording capability. The Video Data Interface was another story. As the signal came down from a Milstar relay satellite in geosynchronous orbit it was broken down into microseconds of digitized information. These bits of imagery were then stored on computer disk for later enhancement and retrieval. It was basically a high-tech file cabinet, though the pictures could be pulled up on the data terminals, in their original form, at will.

The picture began to twist and roll as the optics oriented themselves and began to focus down. The "target" was Benina International Airport, miles outside of Benghazi. It would be a low oblique shot from the south, approximately forty-three degrees above the horizon—not an ideal angle of view, but one necessitated by the moist air directly over the target.

"We have visual definition," the junior tech announced. The picture became clearer. Objects took on a somewhat familiar appearance, at least to the techs: They were accustomed to overhead views.

"Okay, Chet, float the op-pac and sync with a three-point burst. Do you reconfirm reference lock with VDI?"

"Yep. Ready to synchronize."

"Do it." The chief saw the picture flutter, then appear to lock down solid. The optical package, a fancy name for the lens array, was "floating" in a gel-encased bearing ring and was stabilized against minor shaking by a short burst of narrow radar beams directed at three points around the airport. The beams, fired every two seconds, gave precise information as to the satellite's position in relation to the target, allowing the gyrostabilizer to precisely calibrate itself with the optics and compensate for unwanted motion.

"We have capture. Solid." The young tech, thirty years the junior of his chief, always got excited at this point. "Ready for focus down."

"Good. Take it down to a three-mile start."

Now the NSA men were able to make out details, the most prominent being the ten-thousand-foot east/west runway. At the extreme west end, on the picture's left, were the buildings and spacious surrounding tarmac. But . . .

The chief saw it, too, or rather didn't see it. He shifted the glasses on his nose, scrunching his face in a conscious effort to better his vision. "Simple grid."

A white line grid system overlay appeared on the screen, angled to the perspective of the lens and parallel with the ground features. Letters denoted columns; numbers were rows.

"Center on G-twelve," the chief directed.

The junior tech placed a light dot on the grid and the lens moved smoothly, centering on that area.

"Grid off." It disappeared. "Zoom down three-oh. No more."

"Right." The picture grew, and for the first time the aircraft they were looking for was visible, roughly in the screen's center. "Strange, Chief. No other planes . . . anywhere."

There was no response. The chief didn't analyze like his young partner. It had been too many times early on that he'd spoken out of turn, or the wrong thing. Times were different then. Openness was supposedly promoted now, from what he'd heard.

"Okay, let's move on in." He was all business now. "Align west, Chet, say, point-five, and take it down another ten."

"Right." The picture went down farther. Now the aircraft filled half the screen, the tail at the left (west) and the nose at the right (east). A hundred feet or so to the front of the 747 was a building. Shadows from it were becoming shorter as the sun rose higher in the sky.

"Chet, what's that structure?"

"Just a sec." He typed something on his keyboard, calling up the data catalog on Benina from the VDI. The airfield had received a great deal of attention before the 1986 raid, resulting in over ten thousand stored views. The junior tech scrolled through the data, cross-referencing the known landmarks with the view before him. "Warehouse. Spares and stuff."

The civilian NSA man scratched his beard. "Damn, that's clear."

"This? This is a wide view, mister. Snapshot stuff." The junior tech was beaming. "Hell, we can take it down and look in a window, especially at this angle. We might get some glare, but that's no prob. Minor adjustments."

"Label those buildings," the colonel said. "But don't obscure anything."

"Right." *Like I'm an idiot, suit.*

The hint of sarcasm was apparent to the chief, who flashed his partner a warning look.

"Movement," the junior tech announced. "We have movement."

They watched for nearly two hours before the senior NSA official left with a videocassette of the events and two Marine guards. Their destination was the White House.

Benina

A rough thud signaled the connection of a passenger ramp to the forward port cabin door.

Captain Hendrickson loosened his tie and sat ramrod straight in the seat to stretch his back. It was aching like hell. He couldn't stand the lumbar supports, and the stress of the situation wasn't helping. That was all right. He would make it home, and when he did the overstuffed armchair, neglected for so long, would find itself with a permanent user. He could fish and hunt in the stream and hills of his beloved Maine, and spend the rest of his quiet retirement with his even more beloved Anita. For now, though, he would endure the nightmare that was unfolding around him through the cockpit windows. Endure and conquer.

"Tell them to open the door," Hadad commanded from behind.

Buzz chewed on his lip. The captain saw this, knowing that it was hard for his first officer to accept what was happening. He was not a man who accepted the thought of captivity with glee, having evaded the Vietcong for weeks after his F-4 was downed.

"Cap-tan . . . The door. Now!"

Hendrickson lifted the cabin phone and waited for the buzz to be answered. "Who is . . . Millie? Open the port number one. I know. I know. Just go ahead. It'll be okay." He hung up.

Seconds later there was a minor vibration and an annunciator signal as the door was opened. Other than that it was quiet. The four engines were idle, the aircraft receiving system power from a GPU—Ground Power Unit—whose distant hum was negligible.

Michael Alton craned his neck to see over the seat before him. The occupant of that seat was also trying to see.

"Michael . . . what is it?" Sandy Alton's voice was hushed.

He didn't answer right away, but what he could see made his neck hairs stand on end. *Why?* he asked himself. Unconsciously, he squeezed his wife's hand.

"Sweetheart . . ." Her tone was now almost pleading.

He lowered his body back into the seat. "Men with guns."

"Oh God."

He eased his touch on her hand. Her voice was almost a whimper, very soft and breathy. He wanted to say something, but what? There was nothing he could do.

Wael was first in. The two flight attendants recoiled at the sight of him. Arabic men were small, at least those that they had seen. Not so Wael. His build was that of a tank and reached six feet five inches. In green fatigues, replete with black infantry boots, he looked especially menacing, the Uzi in his hand completing the picture. His most terrifying trait, though, was yet to be made apparent.

The barrel of his weapon directed the two attendants back

toward the galley. One of them said something, but Wael spoke only Arabic. He continued to wave them back.

Abu followed Wael in and went directly to the stairs, giving the passengers to the rear only a quick look. They were surprised, he thought, not frightened. The eyes of one woman near the door caught his, asking a question without words. She was older, yet pretty in the way American women were. He could have communicated well with her, if he had wished, thanks to his three years at the American University in Cairo.

At the top of the stairway he found an empty lounge. Each of them had flown on identical aircraft as part of their training for the mission. The Americans, like most Westerners, were fascinated with their own comfort. Huge planes with two levels! And the furnishings! Spacious chairs and tables between them with holders for the glasses of alcohol they always seemed to need. Abu wondered if there was a bath or—what did the Americans call them?—a hot tub. It would not surprise him.

Abdul must be downstairs now. The shouts were echoing up the staircase in his throaty voice. Abu smiled, but it faded quickly. It was really happening.

He went to the cockpit door, its face similar to the wall around the frame. He knocked gently, as if on a friend's door.

Hadad opened it. Abu stepped in, crowding the cockpit. He flashed a look at the two pilots, the one on the right not turning to face him. The other, a blond man, met his look.

"Soldiers, Hadad?" Abu asked in Arabic.

"Yes, of course," the answer came in rapid Arabic. "Old soldiers," Hadad finished in pronounced English.

Abu, impressed by the size and opulence of the aircraft, was not so affected by its electronic gadgetry. It was a jumble of things which he did not understand. Flashing lights and . . . televisions? Abu found himself shaking his head.

"I am glad you are here, my friend," Hadad said, reaching into one of the Velcro-closed pockets on the vest. There was an audible click, and he released the thumb switch, letting it drop and hang by its short connecting wire.

"Cap-tan, Number Two . . . stay in your seats." The Uzi

was trained on them as a warning as the hijackers left the cockpit. The door made a metallic sound as it closed.

Hadad unfastened the two hook closures on the front of the vest and leaned back. The weight of it made it slide easily off. He set it on one of the lounge seats near the cockpit door.

"Is it heavy?" Abu's brown eyes were fixed on his comrade.

"Very." Hadad let the mini Uzi drop awkwardly on its strap to his elbow as he reached up to rub his neck and shoulder. The muscles were not sore, but the skin was. "The loading went well?"

"Perfectly." Abu waved his friend's hand away and reached, straight-armed, to massage both of his shoulders. Hadad let his head fall back and roll in a circular motion. The kneading felt good on his aching flesh. It had been less than three hours and already the weight was a bother. That angered him. He realized that he should have been more physically prepared for the mission. He could relax now, though. He was among friends.

"Thank you."

"Is it better?" Abu pulled away and slung his own Uzi, a full-size model, on his left shoulder.

"Yes, much."

Abu motioned to the cockpit. "Will they cooperate?"

"They will. The number two is arrogant . . . a Marine. But he will do as I say." Hadad swept his hand before them, looking around. "Look at the power we have over them. All of the pitiful souls below are ours." He almost laughed. "And, my friend, the Great Satan will do as we wish." His confidence in his performance was high. Not only his enemies required convincing.

A scream was heard from below, and shouts in rapid-fire Arabic.

"Abdul and Wael are moving the passengers back, out of the first-class section," Abu explained.

A thin smile formed on Hadad's face. "It sounds as though Wael is himself."

"He is motivated," Abu commented, knowing that Wael's massive frame was matched by his sometimes maniacal demeanor. "How long will we stay?"

The men had not been together for a month. "We will leave here tomorrow afternoon."

"Is there any word on the colonel?"

Hadad wiggled his shoulders, bringing his weapon back up. "I have not heard anything."

"So, it has begun," Abu declared.

"Yes, my friend, and there is much to be done." Hadad went to the stairs, then turned. "Remember, we have a funeral to attend."

Abu nodded. *Indeed we do.*

Los Angeles

Not quite two days ago.

So much had happened in such a short time. Art knew his agents were working their asses off to keep the answers coming in. The picture they had painted so far was an accurate representation of the assassination, and Art's report was faithful to their efforts.

The two shooters, Harry Obed and his still unidentified co-conspirator, had come in on separate flights to LAX from New York early Thursday past, and before that from Paris. Passenger records identified the partner as Benny Obed, but that was slim. Harry was fingered by the use of his American Express card to rent the car, and confirmed by the clerk who had rented it to him. She remembered him as friendly, comfortably well dressed, and Arab-looking. Fortunately she was good at labeling accurately. His friend was Arab, too, she had recalled. He was quieter, but still seemed nice.

From the airport they went to a motel in Pasadena, the Squire Inn. It was a nice place; Art had checked. No hourly rates or fresh sheets at check-in. Apparently the men had left Friday and made a stop somewhere before heading downtown. It was this trip that puzzled Art, warranting a "reasons unknown" tag where it was mentioned in the report. Mileage records from the rental agency and the car's odometer narrowed the trip's distance down to within a five-mile corridor from LAX to Pasadena. The side trip might have been to pick up the weapons, or they might have been waiting for them at the motel. The latter was unlikely, though. It would have provided too direct a connection since someone, presumably Marcus Jackson, would have needed to rent the room in advance and place the weapons there. The charge slip itself negated part of that supposition, showing that Obed had rented the room. Art silently thanked his maker for credit cards and the ease of tracking their use.

The rest was educated conjecture, supported by the available physical evidence and eyewitness accounts. The shooters had obliterated most of the evidence with themselves. Forensics and ATF had determined the type of explosive and the presence of a timing device. A one-centimeter piece of metal was all they needed to prove that. Art thought those guys were witch doctors.

"You guys were bold little bastards," he said aloud. The report was finished. He drove the last period on the paper with purpose. Carol would pick that up, as she always could. His anger or frustration always manifested itself with deeply embedded punctuations in his writing. She would tell him to stop stressing himself out, then pinch a fleshy cheek. Carol reminded him of his grandmother, who had died many years before. She was a sweet and gentle old woman, originally from Boston, who had moved south to Alabama early in life. Later she raised Art when his mother left. He was only three at the time, hardly old enough to remember what she looked like. That was a step up on his father, who hadn't even stuck around for his birth. By all rights he should be in prison, or himself an absentee father. But he wasn't. His grandma taught him fairness, and right from wrong. Some people might take those lessons for granted, figuring that it was a given that all children were taught similar lessons. Maybe most were, but in the South when Art was growing up the lines between these beliefs were sometimes foggy, and often nonexistent. Learning violence and hate by example would have been easy had it not been for her.

He smiled to himself, still staring at his legal pad and remembering. She had pushed him hard. Oh, so hard! Hard with words, and pointed fingers, and sometimes, with a switch. She had made him work hard in school, and play with equal energy with his friends. And when it came time to think about college her words were simple, poetic, and straightforward. "*Arthur,*" she had said, "*I have never told you you were ugly, but you are certainly not pretty. And I have never, ever called you stupid, but most assuredly you are not a genius. No one is going to make your way for you.*"

That old lady! Art thought.

The phone buzzed. "Yes. Thanks, Carol." Art pushed the finished report aside. "Eddie, g'morning."

"Ungodly hour to say something like that. Get some sleep?"

The lack of it reminded Art that he felt like shit. "Not enough. I don't know if there is such a thing as *enough* right now."

"Well, boss, it's my turn. *Bingo!* Shari came through. We've got a whole new barrel of pickles now."

"Lay it out, Ed."

"Harry Obed is one Mamir Khaled, a Palestinian. And we've ID'd his partner: little bro Nahar Khaled. Shari faxed photos of both and we ran the pictures by the rental agency clerk. Let me tell you, boss, she was not a happy camper being roused out of bed at one A.M. Anyway, she confirmed that Nahar was the second guy."

"So that puts them together at the airport."

"And the motel," Eddie added. "The desk clerk was certain it was both of them."

"I guess we can expect confirmations from the airlines in Paris, here, and New York on the second ID. But what about before that?"

"Nothing. Interpol, Brits, Frenchies . . . zippo. Israeli intelligence had to go through their national police."

"Huh?"

"Punks, boss. That's what Shari called them. They were picked up a few years back for throwing stones and shit during the West Bank uprising. Intifada, they called it. They weren't real troublemakers, just followers. Lots of kids were doing it. It just happened the Israelis decided to come down hard on the protests that week, so it was a quick trip across the border to Lebanon."

Art tapped the desk. "Deported. That could piss one off."

"Yep. So we've got two young brothers forcibly removed from their family and their home. Shari says the latter is sometimes more devastating to the West Bank Arabs than having to leave their families. It's the same thing the whole Palestinian culture has been subjected to. You know, that Israeli friend of yours is a smart fella. He looks at reasons for what he's supposed to help prevent."

It was good info, but not enough for a complete picture. "It's more than we had before, but aside from America being responsible for all the world's ills, what was their motive? Hell, there are hundreds of people—whole families—deported every month since the Intifada began. Why attack us? Why not do something against the Israelis? They could have done more damage in a suicide attack there. I saw a tape a while back of a suicide attack in southern Lebanon. The terrorist had his car filled with five hundred pounds of TNT and another hundred pounds of nails. So this guy had his pals film him with a video camera from a rooftop as he drove by an Israeli army truck loaded with troops and blew himself up."

"Boss," Eddie interjected.

Art paused. "Yeah?"

"They had a motive. Remember the picture?"

"Sure." *No!*

"The little girl. About a month after the Khaled brothers were deported there was another protest . . . a big one. An American cruiser made a port call at Haifa and a whole slew of demonstrations broke out. Some were pretty violent, Shari said. American ships have stopped at Israeli ports before, so who knows why it was that one to cause an uproar. The West Bank, Gaza, even Jerusalem. Anyway, the Khaled boys' mother and little five-year-old sister just happened to be near one of the demonstrations near their home when the Army moved in to break it up."

"Oh Jesus," Art said softly.

"The troops used rubber bullets to break up the crowd. One of them hit the little girl right in her mother's arms. She was trying to get out of the middle of the thing, but there were too many people. The bullet caught the kid in the head. Killed instantly. How's that for a motive?"

"In their minds, yeah. Okay, where from here, Ed?"

"Well, like you said before, these guys were the trigger pullers, but someone put them up to it."

Art wasn't sure about that. "Exploited their grief would be a better way to put it. Now we've got to pick up the *hot* trail."

"Jackson," Eddie said.

"Right. He is *the* link. I don't know. Maybe the trail

in Paris can be picked up, but our best shot right now is trying to find Jackson and figure out what he did to help the shooters. Then we can find the head of this monster."

"I better put a push on Jackson's trail."

"Yeah, that's what we've got to do." They were moving, Art knew, but there was a long way to go. "Is there anything new on him yet?"

"Not much," Eddie answered, no discouragement whatsoever in his voice. "His neighbors confirmed that he does have some relatives in Chicago, but the employment records don't jibe. According to them he's an only child or an orphan, but then *he* filled them out. It's not like he had a security clearance."

This end of the investigation, only two days old, was already reaching its peak, a reality that convinced Art that the conspiracy had tentacles of as yet unknown length. There was little left to do in the Los Angeles area without some information from or about Jackson. Or was there? "Ed, I'm going to finish up here and step out for a while. You at the Hilton?"

"Yeah. Where are you going?"

"Out and about."

The White House

It was Herb Landau's turn to visit Bud's office.

The hastily called NSC meeting had just wrapped up after two hours of discussion and analysis of the situation, and fifteen minutes spent viewing excerpts, prompted by a National Security Agency official, of real-time satellite imagery.

"How long until we can get some enhanced stills?" Bud asked.

"An hour . . . maybe," Landau answered.

Bud grimaced. "We'll have to go to the boss before that." He looked at his watch. "Fifteen minutes. So, you thought we should talk alone. I don't know, Herb. You sprang a doozy on me the last time we did this."

"Are you prepared for another?" the DCI asked. After a few minutes he was sure by the look on the NSA's face that he wasn't.

6

•••••••••••••

UNPLEASANTNESS

Los Angeles

THE FREEWAYS AT 4:30 A.M. were a wonderful thing. In an hour they would be packed, which was usual for the weekdays. Art's Bureau Chevy had already made the trip from downtown north on the 110 freeway to Pasadena, and was heading south again, past the western fringe of the L.A. skyline. He could see the Hilton to his left, empty but strangely alight in the predawn darkness.

Art took the gently sweeping transition road from the 110 south to the westbound 10. He wondered if rural types would be surprised by the amount of cars at this time of the morning, and he almost laughed aloud when he realized that at one time many years before *this* traffic would be equivalent to rush hour. It was a problem with few solutions. Mass transit had to take up some of the slack and remove some of the single-occupant cars from the road. But then Art knew he wouldn't ride the bus. Oh well. So much for examples. *Maybe that's why I'm not a parent*, he thought.

He shook the thoughts from his head, realizing that he was wide awake and that it would be a bitch to get back on a normal sleep schedule. So it would take a few days. Who knew how long the hours would be like this? Back to the work at hand.

The Khaled brothers more than likely fell into the category of first-time visitors to Southern California, just two of the thousands who found their way there every day. Some came to visit Disneyland. Some came for business meetings or conventions—the downtown area was perfectly suited for this purpose with its many business hotels and the numerous meeting facilities. But the Khaleds did not come for any of these reasons. They did, however, share one important trait with the flood of tourists: ignorance of the area. The route between their two known destinations, LAX and Pasadena, would have needed to be a simple one. Interstate 405 north to Interstate 10 east to the 110 north to Pasadena. That was the quickest, most direct route, one that could be easily explained in a simple set of directions. Art believed they had made the unknown stop between the airport and the motel on the day they arrived, to pick up the weapons almost certainly. It wouldn't have made sense to make the stop between Pasadena and downtown on the day they hid out in the 818. Too many things could have gone wrong, and one delay had the potential to throw the timing all off. Yes, they had done it as Art thought. It had to be.

But where? Finding a specific location in the city of Los Angeles and its adjacent suburbs would be a major task for a newcomer. The seemingly endless grid system of streets stretching from the freeways was akin to a maze, simple if one was only slightly familiar with them, but potentially an impossible labyrinth where a first-time visitor might lose himself.

Behind him, above the pairs of white dots in his rearview mirror, the predawn horizon was just beginning to show traces of a bluish glow. Soon the yellowish cast that signaled sunrise would spread across the skyline, and with the daylight the crush of cars would come. The traffic . . . the countless streets . . . the unfamiliar language emblazoned on the green highway signs—the Khaleds would have felt bombarded by the newness. Their native land was pristine and rich in history, ancient-looking and simple. Or it had been at one time. The brothers must have reacted with wonder to the abundance of glass, and lights, and billboards . . .

Wait! Art's locked on a billboard. The painted image of a red stone-and-glass tower was lofted fifty feet above and to the right of the freeway. "*A weekend in L.A., just $99 a night.*" Art jerked his eyes back to the road. *It could work!*

He lifted the cellular handset from its cradle by his right knee. It was answered in the Hilton immediately. "Eddie, I've got an idea."

"Shoot," Eddie answered through the burger in his mouth. "It's not even five and you're eating that . . . never mind.

Listen, the shooters had to get their gear somewhere, right? And I figure, more than likely, they had to get it before they got to Pasadena."

"Yeah. They wouldn't have put it off till the last minute, and they wouldn't have risked a face-to-face with Jackson." A swallow followed.

"Or vice versa. He wouldn't have gone for that. Like you said, Ed, the shooters didn't give a damn about themselves, but Jackson—he seems like the kind of guy who didn't want to take any chances before he split. For both of them it would have to be a clean pass, which got me thinking . . . well, I had a spark."

"What hit you?" Another bite.

"A billboard." Art leaned forward, checking his right side mirror as he moved to the exit. "The downtown Hyatt. Right up there to slap me in the face. It would be easy, clean. All Jackson would have needed to do is rent a room somewhere for a day or two and stash the weapons. Then he could have put the key for the place with the directions in a locker at the airport."

"It'd work."

"But it would have to be a place close to the freeway: someplace they couldn't get lost finding. I don't know, maybe no more than five or six blocks from the freeway. Probably off the Ten, or *maybe* the Four-oh-five. Just some cheap motel would do." The red light at the off ramp's bottom only made Art hesitate. Running lights was a perk. "How much manpower can we shift to check out the motels in the area?"

There was silence as Eddie checked the roster. "I show thirty-five teams we can move around."

"Good." Art turned left, back onto the freeway, heading east. "Put out pictures of all three. Someone at one of those places must have seen one of them."

"If they did as you think."

Art moved over three lanes. "There's always an if, Ed."

The White House

It was the second viewing of the tape for Bud and Herb. The president stared intently at the pictures. He had commented early on about the clarity.

"These look as if they were shot from the upper floor of a building nearby," the president commented. "Where did these come from?"

"A modified KH-twelve," Landau replied. "Normally you'd be briefed in a transition period on 'National Technical Means.' "

"Of course. I've heard of the KH-twelve, but not about any modifications."

Bud was the most knowledgeable of the two advisers on the subject. "Basically the KH-twelve ENCAP—enhanced capability—is a hybrid between a standard KH-twelve and the Hubble Space Telescope. Its existence is super secret. It was put up by the shuttle in two flights: One took the bare pieces up, and the other assembled the sections and fueled it. There is nothing in space that even compares."

"From seeing these I can't imagine anything that would."

"These are 'real-time' images—taped, of course—but we should have some enhanced stills in a short while." Bud froze the picture on the Oval Office's normal television, below which sat a pricey VCR. The frozen frame showed just the 747 sitting near a building.

Director Landau noticed the shaky quality of the images put out by the standard VCR. "Given the time, sir, we could have watched the feed directly in the situation room as it happened, but we've found it's usually better for the crew at Belvoir to screen it."

"No opposition to that. This is fine. Shall we?"

Bud touched the remote and the picture began to move. He pulled a small notebook from his jacket. The tape counts where significant events appeared on the tape were written inside. "Watch from the right, sir."

Two vehicles, one a large stake body truck and the other a smaller jeep, entered the frame. The jeep drove directly under the wing to the right rear of the jet, the larger truck swinging wide around.

"Note the men getting off the truck," Bud suggested. "Uniforms."

Each man wore a dark olive drab uniform and carried an assault rifle. They formed a rough oval around the 747, directed by one of the officers from the jeep. About every ten meters the soldiers stood, their rifles at their chests.

"Mr. President," Bud said, freezing the tape once again, "there are three things to take note of here. First, the soldiers are regular army troops—not militia or second-line. General Granger pointed that out to us. They're wearing full uniforms and battle dress, and those are AK74s. Newer rifles. Their second-line troops don't have those yet.

"Second, it appears to be a single unit. Probably a platoon. These"—Bud pointed to a few points on the screen—"are the officers, probably equivalent to our own NCOs, and the platoon commander . . . here. The Libyans are notorious for using hodgepodge formations with a variety of equipment for ground missions. Granted, this is somewhat of a special occasion for them, but it is an indication of the seriousness. Plus, this officer from the jeep is a full colonel. We can tell by the shoulder boards."

"We should be able to identify him and the captain with him in a few hours," the DCI announced. "Luckily they obliged and looked up a few times."

"Amazing," the president said.

"And third, notice which way the troops are facing—toward the aircraft. Not one is faced outward, as you might expect if they were there to protect it."

"Could they be guarding against the hijackers doing something?"

"Another place, another time—maybe." Bud advanced the tape. "But not when you take into account this." The image slowed to a normal rate.

"What are those?" The president leaned in, closer to the screen. From the front of the 747 a squat-looking tug appeared pulling a short train of baggage containers. Or were they? The four dark-colored cubes sat on separate carts in the train, which made a tight half-circle turn behind their tow vehicle and came to a stop near the right rear cargo hatch. Two other vehicles approached from the same direction.

"The one that went to the back is a GPU—Ground Power Unit," Bud explained as he let the tape run on. "It provides power for the aircraft system when the engines are off. Air-conditioning and the like. They'll be running a cable to 'plug it in.' The other one is a heavy lift truck—a sort of forklift."

The president glanced worriedly at the DCI and NSA. "This is not comforting, gentlemen."

"It gets worse," Bud said. He advanced the tape further.

"Here you can see they've opened the cargo hatch at the rear," the DCI commented as the picture sped by at eight times normal speed, "and are unloading the baggage containers. Okay, Bud."

The picture slowed to actual. "Watch carefully, sir," Bud directed.

After the last baggage container was removed by the lift, several soldiers manhandled the first of the four dark boxes onto the lift, though the machine itself did most of the work. Four soldiers looked down from the hold as the box began to rise.

"Sir, that is a *heavy* lift vehicle," Bud pointed out. "You saw that it took two baggage containers off at a time. Those are not light. Now note the trouble it's having with these objects."

Haltingly, the box rose. Its weight visibly affected the lift, whose rear tires bounced as the bulk of the back-mounted counterweights struggled to keep the vehicle planted on the ground. The clarity of the picture allowed the soldiers in the cargo hold to be seen stretching their arms downward, as if willing the box to rise. When the first was raised and pushed in on the rollers, the second was loaded onto the lift. Herb Landau had already made a call to Langley, directing that the analysts working on the tape identify the capacity of that lift vehicle.

Bud pressed the fast-search button. "Whatever they loaded took an hour to complete."

"And they were damn heavy," the DCI added, shifting in his seat to relieve a sudden twinge.

"This is kind of hard to pick up, but watch the shadows." Bud slowed the tape, pointing to the hidden side of the aircraft. "There comes a mobile ramp, just like the old days."

"You don't see those much anymore." *Air-conditioned ramps and elevated lounges for the jumbos these days*, the president thought. *But the president still walks up a set of stairs to board* Air Force One.

When the ramp made contact there was a visible jolt. It had to back off and line up a second, and then a third time to correctly align with the number one door.

"He's a novice, sir," Bud said. His Air Force days gave him the confidence to analyze this. "The driver of that ramp truck is probably a soldier." *Another point.* Bud had never seen the president angry, even in his days as the VP, but he sensed now that the man was. He drew audible breaths through his nose, both nostrils flaring. "There, at the front." Three figures jogged past the nose of the 747, disappearing behind it. "Now watch the bottom of the stairs—here. You can just barely see it." Thin shadows appeared, then faded. "One. There goes number two. And three." A minute later the ramp pulled away and drove out of view, leaving just the aircraft standing alone, ringed by the soldiers and attended by the GPU. The TV went off.

The president stared at the screen for a few more seconds. There was a silence. Only the soft crackling of the static charge dissipating from the screen's surface was heard.

Bud knew it was time. He was reversing a decision he had made the day before. "Sir, there are some obvious questions raised by this." He motioned to the TV. "Before we get to those I need to inform you of something."

"You make it sound ominous."

"It very well could be, Mr. President." Bud's mouth was suddenly very dry. He wanted a drink of water, but there was none close. "Yesterday Director Landau informed me of an . . . operation that was carried out during the last administration. Initially I made the decision not to inform you. The information is extremely sensitive."

The president understood. "Deniability."

Bud nodded.

Director Landau said, "Apparently the operation was conceived at the highest level of the Agency and carried out upon the authority of the previous director."

"What are we talking of?"

"Sir," Bud began, "an asset we have high in the Libyan military responded to a request from us and notified the Agency of a trip Colonel Qaddafi was taking to Rome. We knew he was having health problems—gallbladder ulcerations, I believe—so the trip was anticipated, but the exact time was unknown. Our asset gave us that. The colonel underwent surgery for the problem in Italy."

"I heard nothing of this," the president said, his voice up considerably. "I understood the Italians were distancing themselves from him."

"Exactly, which is why it was so quiet. Another reason being that the Agency didn't want the information out. That might have caused the colonel to cancel his trip. They wanted him there. It's even possible the Agency exerted pressure on the Italians—through which channels we don't know—to let Qaddafi in. We just don't know, and probably never will."

"Why? Can't the CIA trace this, Herb. It was internal, so what is stopping you from finding out?"

"Sir," the DCI said, pushing himself upright. He found himself slowing in chairs more. "Any investigation would invariably lead to our asset in Libya. He very possibly could be compromised. Weighing his value as an intelligence source against the negligible benefit we might gain from getting the 'whole picture,' it is not worth it."

"He was not involved in what happened?"

"No, sir," Bud responded.

"Not at all," the DCI agreed emphatically. "He was used."

"I don't believe I need to know any details about the asset, Herb. Bud?"

"I agree."

The president felt relieved, though he had no idea why. "Good. Go on."

"While Qaddafi was in Rome for the surgery, an agent of ours was ordered to switch the blood supply for the colonel. The agent was employed by the hospital, so it was relatively easy. Again, we don't know if he was a plant specifically for this purpose or if he had been working there for some time. Checking could be detrimental." Bud waited. He knew a question was coming.

"And why was the blood switched?"

"To assassinate Colonel Qaddafi." Again Bud paused. The president did not react. "Our agent replaced the blood designated for the surgery with tainted blood."

"Tainted?" the president asked, coolly.

"Yes. The blood was purposely contaminated with trace

amounts of plutonium chloride. That's plutonium in salt form, and it dissolves rapidly in fluids. It doesn't act as a poison. It does, however, do horrible things to cells, especially blood cells."

"And the effect?"

Bud drew a breath. "Our indications are that the colonel is presently suffering from advanced leukemia."

"Can you explain the Agency's logic behind this?"

"I think so," the DCI said, knowing he would have to choose his words carefully. "I'll ignore the obvious because I have no way of knowing why a few men chose to ignore the law. However, there was considerable intelligence from our asset concerning the colonel's reneging on his promises to end support for terrorism. He may have been gearing up for revenge attacks on Americans. He has never forgiven us for killing his daughter in the eighty-six raid. Plus, there may have been some direct PLO pressure during and after the Gulf War. My predecessors believed this was the best solution. It would provide a reasonable cover, possibly even to the colonel himself, and with a little disinformation—leaks about his 'long-term illness'—there could be a logical explanation. That, though, is where my predecessors screwed up.

"Tracing leaks is not difficult. We usually pass information to European sources first. That gets it into their press fast, and ours pretty soon after that. All intelligence services have usual channels for routine disclosures."

"Routine I can understand," the president said, "but this was not routine. Not by any stretch."

"I know. Why they handled the operation that way . . . I don't know. I'm at a loss, but the fact remains: That aspect of the operation virtually assured that Qaddafi would find out that we were responsible."

"So, this is his revenge. And he's still alive?"

"We don't know for certain," Bud responded. "He hasn't been seen in public for six months. He even missed the Pan Arab Summit in Tunisia four months ago. As for revenge . . . maybe."

"It seems fairly obvious." The president raised his brow. "Or not?"

"There's more, sir." Bud ran through the rest of the information quickly in his head.

A deep, nasal breath. "Yes?"

"As we said before our asset has been giving us valuable intelligence on terrorist networks and activities for some time now, including a warning earlier this year that an attempt on the life of the president was being trained for. He gave specific details that match very closely with the actual assassination."

The president's eyes went wide. "We knew there was a threat before . . . and nothing was done?"

"Yes, sir, and President Bitteredge *was* informed. He refused to allow any overt safety measures to be taken because of the chance it might compromise our asset. It was his decision."

"Damn! So some wild, unauthorized operation carried out years ago has led to this! God!" He stood, shoving both hands deep in his pockets.

The DCI was pleased that the man was angry. Truly angry.

The president looked back to Bud. When their eyes met the anger drained instantly, replaced by a sense of coming disbelief. "Your face tells me there's more, Bud."

At least this is the last surprise—I hope. "Mr. President, just before this meeting Director Landau informed me of some very disturbing news—especially so considering what we've just seen. Herb . . ."

"Mr. President, it is our belief that the Libyans may have the capability to construct a nuclear weapon."

Slowly the president sat down again. "And it may be on that plane." His teeth were clenched. "I do not expect that it's an accident this is all happening at this time. I would like some explanations. One minute." He walked to his desk and picked up the interoffice phone. "Mary, I'd like you to notify my nine o'clock that we'll have to reschedule . . . No, no specific time yet . . . Thank you." He took his seat again and motioned to the DCI.

"Sir, have you heard of Anatoly Vishkov?"

"A vague memory, that's all. Nothing specific."

Herb continued. "He's the thorn in the side of the Russians, and a major reason the Cubans are still at odds with their former big brother over reforms. He was a nuclear physicist, still is, but now he has no real allegiance. Sort of a wunderkind weapons designer, until he took a trip."

The president remembered. It showed on his face. "He was the one who defected."

"Correct," the DCI affirmed. "An act more damaging because it was to a 'brother' country. I know, it seems strange, but the Soviets of old could accept someone like Vishkov coming over to our side. But to defect—*emigrate* may be a more choice word—to a fellow Communist country? And worse yet, the Cubans let him stay . . . and guaranteed his safety. A lot of things have changed in Russia but not so much that their military would let a scientist of his caliber leave their domain. Especially the Strategic Rocket Forces. They keep a tight hold on their people, and they do consider them *their* people. Their own domain. That makes Vishkov a very lucky, and a very shrewd, man. The only reason Castro hasn't given him back is because he is married to the sister of a very high-ranking military officer, General Eduardo Echevarria Ontiveros. He was with Castro during the revolution, even at the attack on the barracks."

"So this general is protecting Vishkov?"

"Correct, again, Mr. President. Our sources indicate that a byproduct of all this business with Vishkov is a strain between Castro and a small faction of the military with ties to Ontiveros."

"Then how does Vishkov fit into the picture? Is he working with, or for, the Libyans?"

Landau shook his head. "Not directly. Let me explain. We assume that he began marketing his designs after his defection. Selling them. Probably for cash, but we're not one hundred percent sure of that. He might not actually need the money, but it's certain he's getting a bundle of it. To date, through intermediaries, he has sold designs for two weapons. Unfortunately, we were unable to acquire only one of the sets—the Libyans got the other one."

"Whoa! Whoa! Hold on. *We* bought one of his designs?"

Landau might have been a subordinate, but not in wisdom. Holding such back was not his way. "If we didn't, someone would have, and I am prepared to keep Vishkov in furs and caviar as long as necessary to keep his designs out of the wrong hands."

The president hadn't experienced a subtle lecture since his college days. It reminded him that being wrong was a variable whenever one made snap judgments. He knew that, as the nation's leader, he couldn't base his decisions on emotions. There was still much to learn. "You're right, Herb. Point well taken, and I'll personally kick in for the next can of beluga."

"Yes, sir," Landau said, chuckling only slightly. "Now we know that Qaddafi purchased a set of designs through his IRA contacts. We've known for many years that he wants nuclear weapons. Just about any leader in the Middle East would. He's tried in the past to buy them whole from India and from the Chinese."

"Herb, I'm not well versed on this issue, but I thought the actual design of a weapon was not extremely complicated, I mean, we've had college students design bombs for their theses and doctorates for over ten years. Some guy did it while I was at UCLA."

"I may be less versed than you." Both men looked to Bud.

"My specialty was defensive penetration. I know a little, and probably as much about Vishkov." Bud mentally reached back to his days as a member of the military "in club." "First, you're partly right about the design aspect of it. The general design is within the abilities of most physics grad students, and a more detailed one could probably be managed by those same students with a little added knowledge and some delving on their part. The problem is that all these designs lack detailed spec sheets. Those are the parts lists: everything you'd actually need to build the thing. The builders of the first A-bomb called it the 'gadget,' and rightly so. Even the stuff we have today—artillery shells, warheads, etcetera—is extremely difficult to construct because of the close tolerances. Some of it's unbelievable. A few microns off and the thing doesn't work. You just end up with a squashed core and a minor radioactive mess."

"But Vishkov made some breakthrough in the design," Landau interjected.

"If there was a breakthrough, why wasn't it bigger news to our intelligence agencies?"

The DCI's silence signaled his non answer.

"Bud?"

He didn't know, either. "I think we need someone more knowledgeable to brief us on that point." The president and DCI agreed.

"Okay. So they may have placed a weapon on the aircraft. Three questions. First: Can they build a nuclear weapon? They have the plans, but what about the material and the technology to actually construct it? Second: What are they going to do with it if there is a nuclear weapon? Third: What can we do to stop this?"

Bud thought the chief executive was remarkably calm. "Sir, trying to answer the first right now will be useless until we get some technical information first. As for what they'll do, I think we need the input of the NSC on that . . ." Bud saw the president nod, signaling him to continue. "My thoughts, well"—Bud brought a hand behind his head, pinching the neck muscles—"this feels like an overall effort. It's entirely possible that both the incidents are related. The assassination could have been meant to embarrass us and prove that we're vulnerable. It also can add a factor of disarray to the transitional period. Your perceived inexperience probably was seen as the perfect target to interject some chaos." Bud hated to say that, but it was reality. The press, fueled by the opposing candidates in the presidential campaign, had had a field day with the then vice presidential candidate. Fortunately it was largely ignored by the voting public, but, knowing the media, Bud was sure it would be hashed up shortly. Doubt was an easy sell in the papers. "The hijacking may be planned to exploit any confusion caused by the assassination. Maybe they'll push for some concessions on who knows what. With the statement they issued anything could be on their wish list."

The president left the trio of questions for a moment. "What does Delta think?"

"They're in the early stages of planning," Bud answered. "Andrew says they need more intelligence—how many hijackers, what weapons, etcetera. And they're going to need to know what *may* be on there. If they go in, they'll have more than the hijackers to deal with."

The president went back to his desk and flipped open his gray schedule book. "Bud, you have overall authority for handling this situation. Any final decisions are mine, but your recommendations will carry weight. Get the ball rolling if you need to, then inform me. I want a report at two this afternoon on progress, and if anything major happens I want to know immediately. Herb, any chance the asset you spoke of can get some information for us about what's on the plane?"

"Possibly," Landau replied. "But it will almost certainly compromise him."

"Which means?"

"We'll have to extract him."

There were ramifications to everything a president or high government official decided or authorized, this event being a good example. The president pondered the decision. *Reaction*! He was forced into reacting to the assassination and the hijacking. The thought irked him, and also reminded him to be prudent. "Go ahead. I'll put it in writing. Is this going to fall under the covert operations reporting requirement?"

"The extraction, yes." The DCI wanted to add a caution, "But . . ."

"We'll report on that after the fact," the president said. Landau smiled and nodded. "I'm going to get Gordy in here. He needs to know about this, but I want the nuke theory kept quiet. Only those that need to know get it. No leaks."

There was no response. It was an order that needed none.

"Let's get to it and hope for the best." The president looked hopeful and confident to Bud. That was good, he thought, but then remembered the president's stone debating face. He brushed that thought aside, which was just as well, because if he had looked closer he might have seen the worry in the chief executive's eyes.

QUESTIONS AND ANSWERS

Washington, D.C

THE D.C. MORNING rush was nearly over. Joe Anderson had barely arrived at his Department of Energy office when a phone call sent him scurrying out to a waiting government car. The driver, seemingly annoyed at his taxi driver status, directed Joe to sit in the front seat next to him. No more was said during the short drive to the White House. Joe had been there before, once, to receive a quiet thanks from the president. There was a citation of sorts, but it was all classified. That came with the territory. He wasn't a war hero, after all.

This *was* a little odd, however. No warning at all. If there had been he might have dressed for the occasion. Maybe his blue three piece, the one his wife picked out to make sure he matched. "You didn't marry me for my fashion sense," he often joked with her. The Park Service guards at the Executive Avenue entrance looked as serious as one could be, and there were more of them. They waved the shiny black Ford through the cement planter barricades.

A few minutes later he entered the comfortable office on the ground floor of the White House. He recognized the two men right away.

"Captain Anderson." Bud stood and walked around his desk, shaking the visitor's hand. "I'm Bud DiContino, the president's national security adviser."

"Yes, I recognize you from the news." Joe turned to the DCI.

"Herb Landau, Joe." He stayed seated in a wing back chair. Joe walked over to greet him.

"Mr. Director."

"Have a seat, Captain." Bud touched the back of a chair. "Director Landau filled me in on your background—it's very impressive. He recommended we contact you."

Joe fidgeted visibly. "I hope I'm of some help."

He looked like a cross between a college professor and a drill instructor. Passionless eyes and tight skin topped by silver-gray hair. He was forty-seven. The hair must have been a family trait, Bud thought. It looked too natural to be caused by aging. And the voice: deliberate and measured. Every word carried maximum impact and was spoken slowly.

"I understand you're cleared for 'Q' material."

Joe shifted in his seat again. "I'm cleared for everything nuclear."

Bud smiled politely, realizing that he'd hit a nerve. "Captain Anderson, we need your expertise. We have a situation . . . a bad one. Potentially disastrous. First, let me ask you about Anatoly Vishkov. What's so special about him?"

Vishkov? "He designs nuclear weapons and offers the plans up for sale to terror groups and nutcakes. His real claim to fame goes back to his days with the SRF. He did a great deal of work on dirty bombs. Those are the old *atomic* bombs that are primarily fission weapons. He was trying to perfect area-denial weapons, ones that would make an area so hot nothing could enter it. It wasn't anything new, just a routine R&D program to improve what they already had. Unfortunately for just about everyone but himself he stumbled onto something. Do you want the technical rundown or the abridged version?"

Bud figured a mix would be proper. "How about something up the middle."

"Okay." Joe slid forward in his chair. "A pad of paper?" The NSA handed him one. He spent a few seconds drawing as Bud leaned in to see. Landau strained through his bifocals to watch the diagram take shape. "This is roughly what Vishkov came up with."

"Little Boy," Bud said. He had seen the thing before, in what book he didn't remember. It was very similar to the "Little Boy" gun bomb weapon that fell on Hiroshima. Simpler than the implosion-type bomb dropped on Nagasaki, the gun bomb was basically a large gun barrel with a uranium target at one end and a smaller uranium "bullet" at the opposite end. Upon detonation the bullet was fired into the target, compressing the uranium to a supercritical state and causing the nuclear explosion.

"Good call," Joe said. He was getting a little irritated. So far this didn't sound like any kind of "situation." It was sounding like a waste of time. Every so often some government official would want to know something related to his unique line of work. Since he was the senior member of NEST, DOE's Nuclear Emergency Search Team, the PR and legislative appeasement duties usually fell to him. "He took the fairly easy to construct gun bomb design and made it easier to build, and increased the low-range relative yield twofold. Taking the reduction in size—compared to the Hiroshima weapon—into consideration, we have an extremely dangerous weapon when in the hands of terrorists. That's his market."

"How did he accomplish this?" Bud asked.

"This." Joe's finger touched the area of the uranium target. "The major problem with the gun bomb was the large amount of fissile material needed to make it work, and the fact that it had to be highly enriched material: usually uranium 235. That isotope occurs only in quantities of less than one percent of mined natural uranium, so you either have to enrich what you have or process enough to 'make' U235. Neither is cheap or easy. What Vishkov did was discover a way to aid the compression of a smaller amount of U235 by placing this uniform explosive band around the center section of the target. When the uranium bullet strikes the target there is usually some deformation of the fissile core as it tries to expand outward, like this." Joe drew several arrows going out from the target. "This 'explosive doughnut' is triggered by the melding of the bullet into the target. The target itself is a section of a cylinder with a portion in the center coned out—that's the bullet. When the bullet is fired and fills this conical hole, the doughnut around the cylinder blows and further compresses the target. Vishkov used a simpler aspect of the implosion method to increase the density of the target while the bullet pushed into it. He also used laser switches to time the firing. You see, all the firings have to be timed right on the money. The bullet has to impact the target perfectly and the compression of the cylinder must, absolutely must occur nanoseconds before impact." Joe noticed the NSA go wide-eyed. "Look, basically what Vishkov did was take the best parts of the implosion and gun bombs and combine them, and somehow it's easier to make than either of them separately."

It was explained as asked. Bud expected that he should have gotten the full gist of it, but he didn't. This nuclear netherworld stuff scared him, more so because he knew too little about the mechanics of weapons. His job had been developing aircraft that could get the bombs to their targets. What went in the bomb bays was someone else's worry.

Anderson felt the silence. "Look, I've given this riga-marole twenty or thirty times to generals, secretaries, and anyone else who wanted a little 'in' knowledge. It's my job to do this, but I also have other, more important things to do. I have a shipment of plutonium from France to Japan leaving in less than a week, and I am supposed to coordinate security with the Japanese. It may not seem like much to you, but there will be enough material on that freighter for a hundred bombs, so if you have no more—"

"Captain Anderson," Bud cut him off, "what we have here is an immediate threat." He was upset at the disregard Anderson was exhibiting and, for the first time in days, felt the stubbornness of his years surface. "Please watch."

The tape was already in the VCR and began to play at the touch of the remote. The men watched a few minutes— Bud and the DCI for the third time in as many hours—as the boxes were loaded on the aircraft. Bud turned off the machine.

"Captain, that happened in Libya, at Benina International Airport. The aircraft is a 747 that was hijacked out of Athens early this morning. Just prior to what you watched, the aft cargo hold was emptied; just after that, the door opened and some probable unfriendlies boarded." Bud took a folder from his desk top. The photos inside had arrived from Fort Belvoir just minutes before Anderson's arrival. "Please take a look at these. They're enhanced."

Joe took the small stack. Fifteen photos. He looked through them quickly a first time, then more closely a second, discarding all but three of the eight-by-tens onto a side table. Two were good angle views of the boxes which could be useful for scale calculations. The third . . .

"I know you can't tell much from these," Bud said, "but we have to ask the obvious: Could the Libyans have constructed a weapon using Vishkov's design?"

"If they had the design it might—"

"They do," Bud interjected.

Joe was quiet for a few seconds. He searched both men's eyes for the truth, not expecting to get it directly from their words. "How?"

"One set got by us," Landau answered. "A few years ago in the Netherlands. The IRA bought it at auction for Qaddafi."

"I don't . . . Don't you guys think I should know this stuff, that my team has a legitimate reason to be informed? For Christ's sake! We don't spend every damn day running around looking for friggin' atom bombs in country! Ninety percent of our job is security—nuclear security." The furrows on his forehead deepened, coming together just between his eyebrows. He scratched his brow with one finger. "So Qaddafi has a set of Vishkov's designs. Is it the same design as the one we have?" *At least they showed me that one.*

"We don't know," the DCI answered.

Bud gathered the discarded photos and put them in the folder, placing it back on his desk. "You said *if* they had the design . . ."

Joe swallowed hard. "Then things would be much simpler for them."

"Could they build it?" Bud pressed.

"Not likely. Not with their resources."

"They have access to the technology, don't they?" Landau inquired.

"Except for the most important part: the fissile material. Or at least the right kind." Joe was unsure, unsettled by this. *The picture.* "Weapons-grade material for this kind of device, like I explained before, would need to be either highly enriched uranium—around ninety percent U235—or plutonium 239. The Libyans have no plutonium."

"None?"

"Absolutely none, Mr. DiContino. Your business may not

allow you to make one hundred percent assured statements, but mine does. Plutonium is not found—it's made. Processed. And damn tightly controlled. The Libyans do not have the capacity to 'cultivate' or refine P239."

"What about uranium?"

Two sets of eyes bored into Joe. "As I said, they have none. Just highly enriched uranium for . . ." *The picture!*

"What?" Bud saw doubt.

Anderson looked again at the third photo. *It is.*

Bud slid his chair closer. It was the enhanced blowup of one of the officers around the plane. *Nice of him to look up.* "What is it?"

"His name is Ibrahim Sadr. Captain's rank. He runs the Libyan research reactor at Tajoura. It's a small ten-megawatt job. The Soviets built it in the late seventies/early eighties. It started up in eighty-one."

Everyone was wondering the obvious. Bud did so aloud. "Could the reactor fuel be used for the weapon?"

"It's not likely."

It wasn't convincing. "That's not good enough. We have to know. Where's the hundred percent assurance?"

Joe had to admit that had been a bad way to characterize the usual certainty with which he could do his job. "No one has ever tested Vishkov's design. It's only theoretical, but it should work. He figured that, and so do I. But it still needs highly enriched uranium."

"You said—"

"—it needs ninety percent or higher concentrations to work." Joe paused. *Could it?*

"Your expression worries me," Bud admitted.

"Me too," the DCI agreed. "Could the weapon work with a lower percentage?"

"I don't know." The face stared up at Joe from the photo. "It shouldn't. The only way to know without a doubt is to test it, and we can't do that. I could make a million sets of calculations and there would always be a plus or minus four percent error, up or down, on either end of the performance scale. That four percent could be the range of error Vishkov made allowances for *if* he calculated for a lower percentage concentration of U235. The fuel for Tajoura is seventy to seventy-five percent enriched uranium. You'd need to implode that concentration to get it to the point of supercriticality, unless Vishkov's bomb increases the artificial density enough. I wish I knew, but I don't."

"Then it is possible, yes?" Bud asked.

Joe hesitated only a second. "Yes."

For Bud the contemplation was over. He had his answer, and with that answer he reaffirmed decisions he had already made. *Dear God.* "Captain Anderson, could you defuse such a weapon?"

"If it's on that plane and you can get me to it, yes. I've done it before."

"We have to assume it is."

"Joe, if you could ask Sadr any questions, what would they be?" Landau inquired, pointing to the tablet of paper. "Be simple and brief."

Anderson allowed a hidden smile inside. "You guys have someone everywhere."

"That's not your concern," Bud reminded him.

Joe grunted. There wasn't much to think about. The questions were simple. He scribbled them on the lined paper, then tore off the sheet and handed it to the DCI.

"You're leaving from Andrews in an hour," Bud informed Joe.

"Only the secretary of Energy can activate my team."

Bud no longer felt like being polite. "We are on the same side, Captain. Now, if you want, I'll get the secretary on the phone and he can tell you personally. Or, I can go upstairs and get the president to sign the order. In either case you will be going—alone."

"What?"

Bud was struggling with the security aspect of the situation. "Do you have to have your team? If not absolutely, then it's solo."

Joe would rather have a five-person team with him, but why protest? The NSA had obviously seen his file—the classified one—which told him that he had worked alone on his biggest job. "Whatever you say."

"Good. Gather up whatever you need. The driver who brought you will see you to the field." Bud thought Anderson looked less than pleased. He left immediately, with no good-bye or parting words.

Herb Landau tucked the sheet of paper in his inside pocket. He stood up with a shove of his arms on the chair. The suit felt baggy. It had to be more noticeable.

Bud stood, too, pinching his lips with two fingers. "He's a little arrogant, Herb. I'm not sure I like him."

"You don't have to like him, son. Get used to it. You'll work with more assholes than a proctologist if you stay in D.C. for a while."

Bud opened the door for the DCI.

"Besides, he's damn good at what he does."

"He must be," Bud replied, thinking a second later, to himself: *He better be.*

London

"Don't worry," the ordnance expert assured the Scotland Yard officer. "Putty."

The inspector assigned to the Domestic Terrorism Desk squeezed the material between his fingers. It felt much like his little girl's PlayDoh after it had sat out for a day or two, but not as flaky. There was a detonator—a mock one—protruding from the block of putty, obviously used to simulate explosives. The ordnance boys had dissected the explosive device, which turned out to be a harmless replica of the one that had all but destroyed a building less than a kilometer from where the fake was found. This was according to a note found with it. Trusting terrorists, the inspector had learned, could be deadly. But this seemed to be different: It was a warning.

"So our friends have a rather clever gadget here, do they?" the inspector commented. He was looking for a more descriptive outline of the explosive-laden vest that lay sliced open on the table. Several of the large pockets were open to view, and certain wires were neatly snipped at the points where they exited the pockets on the front and sides of the canvas garment.

"It seems so, sir. Eight pockets, each containing three pounds of high-explosive plastique. I don't think we need to doubt that they have the real thing." He poked the block of putty which approximated the size and weight of each pocket's contents.

"Any more?"

"Well, the triggering mechanism is quite sophisticated. A deadman's switch—this thumb switch, here." He pressed it down, and released it, demonstrating its use. "If the chap holding this lets go . . . *boom.* Interrupter switches on each separate block of plastique. If a wire or wires are cut . . . *boom.* If the power is lost—*boom.* The only way to deactivate the thing is this." The ordnance man pulled a small metallic box from the top left pocket. It had three red rocker switches on top and a rubbercoated conduit running from the bottom to the other wire bundles. "We cut this conduit and the ones running from pocket to pocket. It's green wire to one terminal, then red to another—no consistency. And in addition there are secondary links to the charges. There are these individual wires from the switch box to each charge, and a loop conduit from the box to number one, from there to number two, and so on. No dice cutting or defusing. Only the proper positioning of these switches will safe it."

"Is it a onetime safe?"

"No. It can be engaged as often as desired. That way the chap doesn't need to worry about getting his thumb tired."

The inspector raised his eyebrows. Behind his back his thumbs were grating against each other. "Damn hideous."

"Right."

"Our friends in America won't be pleased to hear this." *And I have to be the bloody one to tell them!*

Pope AFB

The crew of the huge green-and-black C-141B Starlifter sat in their seats, strapped in and ready to fire up the four turbojets if and when the word came. It hadn't yet. They were no different from the "boys in black" in that a go meant a chance to prove themselves. Their civilian superiors would deny that *their* troops harbored any such feelings, afraid that it might paint an unwanted Rambo image. Shortly another crew would come on station to relieve them, and again they would go to their bunks for another few hours of sleep.

A quarter mile away the boys in black enjoyed no such respite. They sat on the wing of a loaned 747 in a massive hangar at the extreme east end of Pope Air Force Base. The aircraft, politely acquired from the airline, was configured identically to the interior of the *Clipper Atlantic Maiden*. Civilian carriers often lent aircraft to the military for counter-terrorist training. The airline, mindful that it was their aircraft on the ground in Libya, had called first to offer. The *Clipper Angelic Pride* arrived an hour earlier and was immediately moved into hangar 9. Its crew and several engineers familiar with the 747–400 were "quarantined" with the JSOC liaison team in the adjacent command post.

Major McAffee stepped from the port number three door onto the wing. He was dressed in full assault gear, colored black, with a low holster on his right hip and a stubby MP5KA4 stockless submachine gun in hand. A black titanium helmet and attached respirator hung from a rubber hook on his web gear. The rest of the team looked much the same, bathed in an unusual orange glow from the reflection of the overhead lights off the pumpkin-colored walls.

The eight men had just finished their first full-dress run-through of the aircraft, an activity designed to give them a look at the interior as they would see it in a real takedown, but having the added undesired effect of drenching them in their own sweat. No matter how light- or vapor-permeable their gear was supposed to be, it was never enough. Their sustained and rapid movement was part of the cause, but the stress was more of it. Even the mock takedown was stressful. It was supposed to be. The team had to psych up for a go, with no thought that they wouldn't get it.

"That's the first one," Blackjack said. "We'll do at least two more, but first we've got some intel." The men perked up at that. "It looks like at least four bad guys—maybe just that many. They probably have SMGs. We're told they're Uzis, and if they have those you can bet they have frags and pistols. Standard stuff. That's the good news. British Intelligence gave us some stuff through 22 SAS about twenty minutes ago." He didn't mention that the information had been forwarded surreptitiously to Delta from their SAS counterparts *ahead* of the official message. That was probably still in the Pentagon. Not everything had changed. "There was a blast in London earlier today and an inert duplicate of the bomb was left close by." McAffee explained the specifics of the device, as the British had determined, and contents of the note left with it. "So the head bad guy is wearing this thing. All he has to do is release the switch."

Antonelli snorted. "Hell of a deadman."

"Exactly." Blackjack looked at each man. "Tear it apart."

After a few seconds contemplating his knees Graber spoke up, "If this guy is dedicated he'll blow it—no doubt in my mind. Especially if he sees us coming through the door. They know we don't go looking for prisoners."

"What if we do that?" Lieutenant Quimpo suggested. "I mean, if we take out the other bad guys and just, you know, point at him, maybe he'll hesitate. If he does we might be able to get him talking long enough to get the hostages off." Quimpo saw the skeptical looks. "Hey, it's slim. I know."

"Nah," Goldfarb commented. "He's probably a fanatic. He'll blow it. We've gotta make sure he doesn't . . . somehow."

Graber thought about that. "How?"

McAffee sat down. The men were now in a loose circle, discussing the possibilities.

Langley, Va.

"DONNER received and acknowledged the order," DDI Drummond said. He looked out the window past the DCI. He sipped lemonade from a wide ice-filled tumbler. "He got real bold."

"How so?" Landau asked.

"He sent the Rome station a message . . . direct." The ice clinked in the half-empty glass. "Apparently he wasn't too happy we didn't listen to him."

Landau shook his head. "I can understand. What he must think. All in all, though, I'm glad he's coming out. He's getting . . . oh, I don't know . . . not careless, but fearless. We've gotten more of those 'scoldings' lately, just like his previous message."

Drummond finished off the lemonade. "He's been a good asset."

"Better than anyone will ever know," Landau added, his words accompanied by a crack of thunder nearby. "Damn! When's this supposed to let up?"

"I think the paper said the day after tomorrow. Think positive: It's not snow."

He's right about that.

"I'll issue the extraction order at two today. Is that all right by you?" the DDI inquired.

"Of course. We better get Mike in here: It's his department. Is he around?"

"I think he's in a conference with S and T. I'll check." Drummond spun the DCI's phone around and dialed Deputy Director, Operations Mike Healy's office. "Nance, hi. Is Mike in with the brains?" The humor was common and good-natured. "Can you ask him to come up right away. No . . . the director's office. Thanks." He replaced the phone and turned it back to face the DCI.

Herb pointed to the glass. "You want some more?"

"Nope."

A few minutes passed before the DDO entered, preceded by a polite rap. He was a pudgy man, one who had been behind a desk too long. Years of active service "in the field" tended to keep one fit, not primarily for survival reasons, but because of the unbelievable amount of walking field officers often found themselves doing. But he was a lifer: a career Agency man. It was good to have one of those as a deputy, Herb knew, realizing further that he was damn lucky to have three as his chief deputies. And they were good *people*, which was more important to him.

"Boss . . . Drum." He slapped the seated DDI on the shoulder and took the chair next to him. "Long time, no see."

"We're not the ones hiding," Drummond jokingly accused him.

"What's up?" Healy settled back, his hands folded on his lap.

"Mike," Landau began, "we're going to need a pickup."

"Where?"

"Can you manage Benghazi? It's a preset," the DDI pointed out.

"DONNER?"

"You got it," Drummond confirmed.

"Well," Healy exhaled the word, "he's given us some good stuff. Saved some lives, that's for sure. When?"

"Probably tomorrow . . . late. I'm going to notify the

Rome station. Logan's been running him for the last six years." *Administrators come and go*, Drummond thought, *but spooks always hang on.* "DONNER is gathering some final intel before he splits. His transmission of the information will be the signal he's finished things. You have the location."

"Yeah. That's an addendum to the file," Healy said.

"*Vinson's* in the area. With all the ruckus her presence can be expected. Do you know if they've got any special ops people on board?"

"Not offhand," Healy answered, "but I can check. In either case I'd like Logan to go in with the extraction team."

The DCI looked at the DDI, pouting uncertainty and caution. "If you think it's the best course, it's your op."

"Thank you, sir."

"All right." The director felt some sense of relief knowing that DONNER was soon going to come out. "Who's going to receive the last message? Logan will be on the *Vinson* I presume."

"I'll brief the station chief on the whole thing. I think having him receive and relay it to us will be the best."

Herb thought of the time. It was 11:45 on the East Coast. He did some quick addition to figure the time in Italy. "Maybe we should move up the warning to the station. I'd hate to have something happen where DONNER would have to leave sooner than we planned, and Logan not be in position."

"Then let's notify Rome as soon as we're done here," Drummond proposed. The others agreed.

"Good. Anything else?" Landau asked.

The DDI and DDO signaled that there was nothing, and the meeting ended. Everything would now begin. Alone in his office Herb Landau took the DONNER file from his safe. He wanted to read once again about the man who had done so much for a country he knew little about, and would now be called upon to finally turn his back on the land of his birth in one last act of treachery against it.

Los Angeles

It was just a fact of life, Francine Aguirre told herself. Her questioning of the desk clerk and motel manager—

their twenty-seventh so far—had taken nearly twenty minutes because of the language barrier. L.A. being the melting
pot that it was, the agents had to be prepared for communication difficulties. Francine—"Frankie"—could joust in her
native Spanish with the best of them, but Korean was as
foreign to her as any language other than English was to her
partner, Thom Danbrook. She knew it had to be amusing to
any spectator who might have seen the two of them writing
the words out and using hand gestures to get their messages
across.

"Thank God this is the right time for blue jeans," Frankie
said. She had "graduated" out of business suits three years
before and now wore casual street clothes nine days out
of ten. Court days were different. She hated *them*. "Can
you chew quieter?" she asked her partner, rubbing her foot
through the Reeboks.

Thom swung the car around the corner. There was another
motel down the street. "Sorry. I'll smack softer."

Talk about vague! So the director wanted answers fast. No,
the wording was *needed*. There was no elaboration. Art
found that puzzling. The director was *pushing* him from
three thousand miles away. Someone had to be pushing
hard. The boss was a decent guy. His message said more
than its wording implied. Something was up.

The seventy agents had so far struck out, even looking for
just a sighting of any one of the three men. It was early still,
though, Art kept reminding himself.

He looked around his office, forgetting the investigation
for a moment. In a way he wanted to be out of there. Back at
the Hilton there was activity, decreasing though it was, and
thus more to occupy his body. He could *do* things there. That
would occupy his mind. The latter rarely came alone for Art.
Lately he had had to keep his body busy to check the endless
wandering his mind wanted to do.

But self-discipline was a goal of Art's, as suggested by
his shrink. He straightened up in the chair to focus on the
matters at hand. Eddie could handle things at the Hilton.
Art was going to review all that was known . . . from the
top.

Rome

Dick Logan, the economic liaison officer at the United States embassy in Rome, was packed in under ten minutes. As a habit he kept a bag packed except for his everyday essentials. What he felt would be best described as overwhelming apprehension. He didn't consider himself a chicken, but on his best day he knew that he was basically a paper-pushing case officer with a standard cover assignment. He had all the training: surveillance, countersurveillance, personal combat (hah!), and all the other skills, whose mastery was supposed to keep him alive.

Behind a desk. The pay was good and the job was interesting. Those were pluses, he told himself. And DONNER. *His* agent. His man, insofar as one man could control another. As scared as he was about choppering into a hostile country—scenes from *Apocalypse Now* kept flashing through his mind—he was more excited that he was finally going to meet the agent face-to-face. Only the chief of station years ago had met the man. It would be an honor. DONNER was not the mystical agent of spy novels; he didn't reveal top government or military secrets, or give any high-technology items over for security. His traitorous deeds were simple, yet hundreds, perhaps thousands of people, mostly Americans, owed their lives to this man.

And all he did was give us pictures. Logan knew it wasn't as cut and dry as that. There had been a long road, one that DONNER had traveled alone. He wondered what gave a man the strength to live day after day with the knowledge that death at the hands of his countrymen was but a slip of the tongue away. Men, and women, of all nationalities were spies, all with their own reasons. Some were motivated by financial considerations, pure and simple. Others wanted to fight conflicting ideologies and feel the power that came from never being known to those they betrayed. Logan believed that a good number of spies were motivated by a sense of vengeance. He wondered often what motivated DONNER, trying not to classify him in any of the molds. The best he could do was try to keep an open mind, being aware that his agent's motives might be less than honorable. He wasn't sure he wanted to know that.

Logan plopped the native fedora on his head before leaving the office. He left the key with the desk officer before exiting the embassy. His car was in the courtyard and he would drive himself to the airfield. On the way he planned to think through all the questions he would ask DONNER, sure that some would seem rather strange to him. Maybe not. After all, he was a human being, not just a code name, and Logan couldn't care less about the debriefing the agent would surely go through in the months to come. The Agency diehards could handle that. Logan wanted to know the man.

The White House

There are three distinct sections of the White House. What tourists see, at least partly, is the center section, where official receptions and dinners take place. The private living quarters of the first family are also located there, on a higher floor. The west wing houses the power center of the executive branch, namely, the Oval Office. Offices and working spaces for the president's advisers are also in this wing, along with the Cabinet room. At the opposite end, just past the president's private theater, lies the east wing. Here his military advisers maintain offices and a pseudo command post.

The chairman of the Joint Chiefs of Staff kept a desk there, though he felt more at home in the Pentagon. General Granger found it an inconvenience at times that he was tied so closely with the 1600 Pennsylvania Avenue address. He was a soldier, and the nation's top military commander, which complemented and conflicted with each other. In his heart he longed for his turf: the battlefield, or at least where soldiers were. Like most professional soldiers he found the thought of war infuriating. To prevent war was the military's premiere reason for existence. It was that that gave him purpose in the midst of politicians.

His phone buzzed. "Granger . . . Sure, come on over."

Bud walked through the general's door a few minutes later. He sat in one of the high-back colonials that Granger had "transferred" from his old Colorado Springs office, but he couldn't get comfortable and ended up standing behind it.

"I spoke with the president a few minutes ago," Bud said.

"I recommended that we begin the necessary preparations for any military operation that might come. The aircraft's been on the ground for nine hours now. Something's going to happen. Who knows what? It's best that we're ready."

"You're old Air Force, Bud," the general reminded him, aware of the unenthusiastic ring of the NSA's announcement.

Bud brought a hand back over his head, momentarily flattening the gray locks. "That does not exclude me from being damn worried about escalating this."

"We can handle them—conventionally," Granger pointed out calmly. Letting emotion into his words was not an option.

"I have no doubt about that. It doesn't mean it's the best option." Bud finally sat. "My misgivings aside, can you have a report ready by . . . say, seven."

Granger took his pen in hand. The light from the desk lamp shone off his smooth forehead. "The objectives?"

"Ending the Libyan terrorist threat."

"Uh-huh. Minimum collateral damage," the general assumed, correctly.

Bud nodded. His eyes added the emphasis. "And there's something else. I didn't discuss this with the president, but any order to carry it out would come from him. I do want the necessary personnel and equipment in place, ready to go."

Granger's expression asked the next question.

Bud went on. "If there is a nuclear weapon on that 747, we can't allow it . . . I mean, there's no way that—"

"I know," Granger interrupted. "I know."

Somehow it was easier not to verbalize what he was thinking. "It has to be certain. There can't be a mess." Bud let the words sink in for a moment. "Get it moving."

After the NSA was gone Granger called his chief of operations at the Pentagon. The National Military Command Center—the War Room—was now operative. A planning group of senior officers and their deputies would begin work on the contingency plans, sets of which would be modified to fit the situation.

With that done he asked the Pentagon operator to connect him with the commanding officer of the Louisiana Air National Guard. Granger knew the Air Force—"things with wings are my life," he would say—and where certain special abilities could be obtained. The Louisiana ANG had some F-106s left, and if the worst-case scenario happened, at least one would be needed.

Pope AFB

Even military pilots had to defer to the mighty power of thunderstorms. This front of them had delayed Joe's departure from Andrews by thirty minutes and kept the twin-engine executive jet, in which he was the only passenger, circling west of the air base for over an hour. Finally the clearance to land came, without the announcing lighted signs that Joe was accustomed to. The pilot had simply poked his head back, instructing Joe to buckle up. He cinched the belt snug. On his lap was a small, hard case with all the instruments he would need . . . hopefully. Joe held it tight. Inside were sensitive measuring devices so miniature that the fact that they were even built was amazing. There was an easy $2 million worth of gear in the case, something that worried Joe not at all. It could be replaced: The people who might die if the instruments failed could not.

A screech and a thud beneath signaled the landing. When the small jet stopped, Joe emerged to a windy tarmac. The afternoon sun illuminated the cloud bottoms above as they sped across the sky from the south. The ground was wet and slick beneath his feet on this part of the tarmac, and looking around he saw that it must have rained recently. From the look of the clouds more was on the way.

A car approached the jet, whose engines still whined. It stopped a few yards from the left wingtip. In the near distance bright perimeter lights outlined a low row of buildings and several large ones. Joe noticed several soldiers bathed in the light.

"Captain Anderson." The soldier saluted instinctively.

"Mr. Anderson," Joe corrected the soldier. He was a corporal. "Save your salutes for noncivilians. I assume you're taking me somewhere."

"Yes, Mr. Anderson." *Asshole.*

Joe walked around the car to the passenger door as the jet throttled its engine slightly, pushing it forward and kicking up a spray from the wet ground. The drive was short, only a few hundred yards at best, ending outside a hangar opposite the one he could see from the aircraft.

"Wait here," the corporal said curtly. He jumped out and double-timed to a building connected to the hangar, obviously an afterthought addition.

Something struck Joe as strange. *A corporal? This is an Air Force base. What's Army doing here?* The unmistakable sound of boots—more than one pair—came toward the car. A figure stood in front of the car, aglow in the headlights. The driver opened the passenger door for Mr. Anderson.

"Anderson," the voice drawled. Joe could almost smell the cow pies. "I am Colonel William Cadler. Nichols tells me you can be quite an ass." Joe eyed the corporal, who stared back without a flinch. "Well so can I. Understood? Good. Now get your gear inside . . . now that we're done with the introductions."

8

....

A SOUL FOR THE TAKING

Al-'Adiyat

HIS LIFE WAS one of routine. It was both a reminder of his dark side, and a way of retreat from the everyday realities that he had let himself become master of. Only by carving each day up into manageable portions could he hope to make it through, from sunrise when he would run, to sunset when he would finish up his duties as commanding officer of the 3rd Training Battalion. Then he would sleep.

Muhadesh Algar was a man of inward contradictions. To those around him he was a strong, confident leader, a man able to turn idealistic, trigger-happy teenagers into efficient killers in a short time. He was a revolutionary brother, one who would willingly give his own life in battle against those who would destroy his country. Never would a man who knew him question his bravery, or his skill, or his authority.

All those things he was. He was also a man who felt weak and small. Of course those who knew him would attest to his bravery, though few had seen him exhibit it, but he was painfully aware that he had failed the truest test possible of his will. He had *once* been afraid many years before, and that lapse of inner strength had set his life on a course that outwardly he thrived on, but was, day by day, tearing his soul from the very foundation of his being.

He held the rank of captain in the Libyan Peoples Army, a title that, at times, was passed out as a ceremonial reward. Muhadesh, however, had earned his. At twenty-three, after several years studying medicine in Italy, he was commissioned a lieutenant in the army of King Idris, Libya's pre-Qaddafi ruler. It was a good time in his life. His uncle, who raised him after his parents' death, saw to his nephew's education, sending him away to learn to be a doctor. At the time the medical profession was, perhaps, the highest symbol of status in the small North African nation, one that Surtan Algar was determined to give to his brother's only child. The pride Muhadesh felt when he was assigned to a military hospital was matched only by the sadness he felt when his uncle passed away. He vowed to make his uncle proud.

It was then that his life forever changed. The government of King Idris was overthrown by Colonel Muhammar al-Qaddafi, who ordered all of the young officers in the military to undergo reeducation and swear allegiance to the country's new leader. Being a smart young lieutenant, one who was unaware of the enormity of the changes soon to be, Muhadesh did just that.

The hospital near Benghazi to which he was assigned resembled little of the medical facilities he remembered. It had been converted into a facility for the administration of pain. Qaddafi knew that the easiest way to silence any opponents was with a swift and brutal campaign of "eliminations." But the mere execution of someone was not always enough of a deterrent. Muhadesh became one of those who would use his medical expertise to torture those sentenced to that fate, and more often than not he would have an audience.

Mostly they were officers of the military wishing to watch their enemies die a horrifying death. Occasionally the family of the condemned would be forced to watch as their loved one was disemboweled, or tortured in any of the many other ways Muhadesh had mastered.

To refuse his "duty" would have meant death. Muhadesh Algar, the iron fist who could break a man's arm, or leg, or neck with ease, and teach others how, had at one moment been weak, choosing life for himself.

Routine became his escape. Regimentation was his savior. Up at five for a run with a group of commandos stationed nearby. Work from eight to six, one patient/victim per hour. He gave himself only that much time, which motivated him to become even more effective. It usually took much less. The longest—a twelve-year-old boy—had taken an hour and a half. After work came another physical outlet as he ran obstacle courses with his commando friends. Eight o'clock—home. At ten came sleep. The routine repeated itself day after day for seven years. The lapse in the routine came in the form of Commander Salaam al-Dir.

Muhadesh Algar, the methodical doctor of pain, had come to the attention of the commando leader, al-Dir. His daily training with the men and his obvious competence—something not considered as a prerequisite to command—brought him the offer of a new position, one that would remove him from his present duties. It did not matter to him if it was mopping barracks, but that was not to be his job. He was to be al-Dir's assistant, a position that would allow him to use his intellect, though not his medical training. A little more than seven years after Muhadesh began his military career as a man of medicine, his conscience was eased, but not cleansed, with his appointment as executive officer of the 3rd Training Battalion.

Now he worked with men, not animalistic excuses for them. Those that came through the battalion left eventually to join other units, ones specializing in the application of their learned skills. Other countries might have higher-profile special-warfare units with highly specialized weaponry, but few could boast of a more dedicated group of warriors. It was amazing that al-Dir was able to turn out truly talented soldiers of above-average intelligence in a country where fundamentalist ideologies had clouded most realist thought. Al-Dir, like Muhadesh, loved his country. The land. The people. It was a uniquely serene place which he vowed never to abandon, despite the disparities in beliefs. Finding his own way to contribute without compromising what he believed had been supremely difficult. The 3rd was his way.

For Muhadesh it was at last a way to seek his own peace, but one that would last a short three months. Commander al-Dir disappeared with a small group of commandos on what was rumored to be a cross-border operation into Egypt. The true circumstances would probably never be known. The only certainty was that al-Dir was gone, forever, and Muhadesh was the new commander of the 3rd.

Soon after assuming command, Muhadesh found his unit being restructured on the orders of Colonel Qaddafi and given a new mission: to train revolutionary freedom fighters in the craft of terror. The skilled, capable warriors whom he had been proud to serve with were taken from the 3rd, some being sent to other, conventional units, and others off on missions that did not officially exist. It was a waste of fine, devoted patriots, and it left him with little to assist him in his new orders.

Again, though now indirectly, Muhadesh would be charged with causing pain and suffering. The skills of commandoing, which he picked up voluntarily, and the craft of torture, would be the curriculum as he taught others the finer points of savagery. He knew that to refuse or hesitate in carrying out the orders would mean death, and again his weakness forced acceptance of the mandate.

He began turning out skilled killers, and as the ranks of his remaining training officers shrank with their transfers, Muhadesh became more closely involved with the instruction of his pupils. A retreat into routine was an attempt to manage his life as he once had, but it was increasingly difficult to get up each day, knowing what knowledge he would be imparting to others.

It was during a weapons-buying excursion to Rome that a remedy to his guilt presented itself, quite by accident and with no forethought. Muhadesh loved the city, Italy's great capital, especially because of its sounds. He could walk for hours—for days even—without tiring of the constant chatter of the people, whose animated discussions were like staged performances. And the birds. Everywhere they were. Some said they were messy, a nuisance, and good only for shooting, or as food for the cats, but he saw them as armies of aerial beauty and grace. He marveled at their ability to fly, and turn, and dive as a single entity, when there might be hundreds of birds in the flock. The diving flock he was gazing at that day drew his attention to a building: the United States embassy.

Everything came to him very quickly. The thought surprised him at first, then it calmed him. He wouldn't be betraying his country, after all. Really, he didn't know what he would be doing.

The simplicity of making contact amazed him. He just entered the embassy and asked to speak to an American intelligence officer, something the Marine guards had become accustomed to. Someone always wanted to sell something. Not Muhadesh. He hadn't thought that far ahead. Even the thought that he could be killed for his bold move didn't occur to him immediately. In fact, it really wasn't that dangerous, considering the ineffectiveness of Libyan counterintelligence.

An unimpressed CIA station chief, after seeing the military ID and hearing of his position in the Libyan army, gave Muhadesh a phone number. It was that of an electronic component supply company in Rome. He was told to call it on a certain day, at a specific time, and when asked, he was to place an order for some equipment. At the time he didn't know it, but that simple order would cause his call to be transferred to the embassy.

At first he was tested. Only simple information was requested, more to verify his authority than for true intelligence needs. It was "safe" stuff, which had a low probability of compromising him. Muhadesh's position and viability were confirmed to the extent that it was possible to use him as a low-risk source, but to exploit his use the Agency had to take a chance. On a second visit some months later a simple code system was agreed upon, and a contract was signed for the delivery of a security system for the camp, complete with video surveillance equipment. The Agency front company in Rome provided and installed the system—with all of its secondary features.

The brilliance of the ongoing operation was in its simplicity, which came from Muhadesh and his insistence on order and routine for his students. At 9:00 each morning they would line up abreast, facing east, their feet planted square in yellow-painted footprints pointing at the camp's small armory. Atop the building one of the surveillance cameras would do its repetitive 120-degree sweep of the assembly area, displaying the image in the security center. There a single guard monitored it on one of the eight wall-mounted video monitors. On the twelfth day of each month at precisely 9:05 A.M. Captain Muhadesh Algar would address his students as they stood at attention. At the same instant a one minute portion of the image would be recorded on a special device in the captain's office, where a single, selectable monitor was installed. The sixty seconds were then condensed into a short-burst signal and transmitted the same evening at 10:00 via a low-power signal from an antenna hidden within a camera perch. A U.S. submarine in the Gulf of Sidra, waiting just below the surface with only its ESM mast breaking the water, would receive the signal. From there it was bounced twenty-two thousand miles up to a satellite and back down to the NPIC at Fort Belvoir. The pictures were enhanced and used to identify terrorists before they became dangerous. It wouldn't stop the terror movement, but it would help in the battle. Later a fax machine was installed in his office, allowing direct, same-day contact with his case officer via the bogus company, and relieving reliance on the UV ink messages on invoices and reliability assessments sent to Rome.

And so his life as a traitor began. When he was lying in his bed the reality of it seemed alien and far away. The camp was quiet and dark, dark because of jitters the air defense officers in Benghazi were feeling. American planes had come before, and very well could come again. More killing.

But Muhadesh knew that his guilt would soon end. Innocents would never die at his hands or because of his instruction again. His life would no longer be tied to a success measured in blood.

Absolution for his sins would not come automatically with his washing the blood from his hands, though. Tomorrow, he would begin to atone.

Benina

Allah will admit those who embrace the true faith and do good works to gardens watered by running streams. The unbelievers take their fill of pleasure and eat as the beasts eat: But Hell shall be their home.

Hadad let the passage repeat in his mind over and over before closing the book. The cover was still smooth from lack of use. Yes, he was devout, though that had not always been the case. The newer Koran he held was a gift from the colonel. In a way he was ashamed to think that at a time now past in his life he had been an infidel. Not in belief, but in fervor. Now his heart and soul were one with the wisdom of Allah.

There was still pain, though: the colonel. How was he now? Hadad wondered. In the solitude of the upper-deck lounge he tried to contemplate the pain his friend must be suffering, and the sacrifices that had been made. Hadad knew that their motives were different, and in a way, that was better. They were each driven by a desire for vengeance. Each had been wronged, their lives changed, and in a sense, ended by the deeds of the Americans.

The sterile ceiling he stared at from the reclined seat danced with images and faces. Places flashed; scenes of his home, that simple stone house in the land that always appeared desertlike in photographs, but was lush and rich in heritage. Palestine. He had not truly lived there with his family for many years, but it was home. The Jews and their American protectors had usurped the land from its owners, citing biblical right and the need for a Zionist homeland. Of course their money and power gave them the right to do this . . . in this life.

Hadad felt himself smile. They would all be so surprised! The Americans could not, and would not, try to understand the power of Allah. It would have to be shown to them. *You take and take and take!* Such arrogance they were capable of, believing that the little ones of the world would never strike back. If he had learned one thing, it was that the small, weak people could become one in the will of one strong protector. To the West it would seem a grandiose, wishful notion harbored by a man spurned by the world and evicted from the land of his birth. That might be enough to move some men to action, but not him. His reason was both personal and painful.

A cough came through the open cockpit door. The pilots slept, or tried to. Hadad listened for a moment before letting his head fall back in relaxation. He, too, should probably sleep, but it was impossible. Not while they sat here, waiting. The safety of their location reassured him that no one would touch them, or try to. America's hapless Delta Force would not even try anything while they were on the ground under the protection of Colonel Qaddafi. But, still, he could not rest. There was too much stored energy. He wanted to be on with the mission and leave the waiting behind.

In Paris he had tried to put thoughts of impatience aside and concentrate on what was ahead. Now that things had begun, he wanted to finish it all. The climax was the reason for all the preparations. The purpose was salvation, and vengeance, and an offering to Allah.

The pages opened once again as Hadad brought his seat upright. If he could not sleep, he could find peace in the words and wisdom that he would take with him to his grave, along with so many unbelievers.

Pope AFB

They were rested, if three hours could do that. All had slept the full one-eighty, as they called their standard three-hour nap. Some genius behaviorist somewhere had probably spent a hefty grant to figure the minimum optimum amount of sleep for the SOF.

Captain Graber was the first out of the makeshift bunk room. From ground level the 747 was a huge, winged leviathan that filled the hangar.

"Whadya think, Cap?" Buxton asked, slapping his squad leader's Kevlar-covered back.

Sean cocked his head. "I think we've got a bitch of a takedown ahead of us."

"If we go."

True. Sean wouldn't voice his realism.

McAffee appeared from the office, with Colonel Cadler and a guest. A civilian?

"Captain, get the team out here," Blackjack ordered.

"Fall in!" Graber shouted over his shoulder, bringing the remainder of the troops out and around him in a loose half oval.

Dear God. Joe Anderson thought the major, dressed in his ninja suit, had looked strange. But these guys! They looked like killers.

"Colonel."

"Thank you, Major. Men, this is Mr. Anderson. He's got some old fly-boy blood in him, so show him a little respect." Cadler glanced at the civilian. *You reciprocate*, his eyes said. "It turns out that we may have a slight problem with a nuclear weapon on board, but that's not your concern. Mr. Anderson is the specialist there." The colonel paused, seeing the exchange of looks. "You will, however, wear these."

McAffee took the bag from Cadler and gave each man, himself and Anderson included, one of the olive drab wristwatches.

"Death watches," Antonelli said as he received his.

Joe scoffed inwardly. *Dramatics.*

"Dosimeters," Cadler corrected the lieutenant. "If there is a nuke on that bird it's probably gonna be a crude one, which Mr. Anderson says means it would be dirty . . . very dirty. These'll tell us if you get a bad dose."

As opposed to a good dose. Joe concealed his comments. He hoped these guys could get him access to the device.

"Under your cuffs," McAffee directed. "Captain, warm everybody up. Aisle sprints, up and back. I want everybody loose by twenty-three-thirty for the final planning session."

"Yes, sir," Graber replied. He pulled on his helmet and respirator, as did the others, and led them into the sister ship of the *Atlantic Maiden.*

"Major, I want a workable assault plan by oh-two-hundred. I can't give Pappy our lean plan for this one."

McAffee shook his head. "I know. I know. This one is tough. If that bad guy has that vest on we can't do much except force him to blow it."

Joe shifted his look between the two officers. "What vest? What are you talking about?"

"Our hijacker friend is decked out in a self-destruct device," the colonel answered.

"With a hell of a deadman on it," McAffee added.

"Thanks for telling me earlier," Joe said. "This could have an effect on my work, you know. That thing you're talking about could very well trigger the device."

Cadler pursed his lips. "My oversight. Major," he continued without missing a beat, "I anticipate pressure from another quarter. Word has it the Bureau's Hostage Rescue Team has been working on this one, too, and that they've got a good plan."

"How did HRT get wind of the details?"

"Remember, Mike, even if there's a go to take it down, if that bird is on nonmilitary soil the Bureau gets the call—that's the law."

The major didn't like that. Cops taking down an aircraft with zero experience in the field just didn't make sense, just as the idea of Delta going in to clear a gunman out of a bank was ludicrous. The HRT was good, McAffee believed, but they were a SWAT team, pure and simple—not counterterrorists.

"Sir, can you get me some info on their plan?"

Cadler smiled wryly. "Are you thinking plagiarism, Major?"

"Not exactly, but I would like to give it a look-see. Maybe it can give us some ideas, and maybe the Bureau boys have done too favorable a job of self-evaluation this time." Blackjack set the flat-black titanium helmet on his head and cinched up the chin strap.

"I think that can be arranged," the colonel replied. "Also, I want Anderson in on the planning to give us any insight on that thing on board that might affect us doing our job."

"Yes, sir." The major tossed a salute and trotted up into the aircraft.

Cadler turned his attention to the civilian, studying him for a second. "Now, I understand what you do is classified."

"Much of it."

"Well, some of what we do is classified as well, and a hell of a lot more is highly unconventional, to put it lightly."

"I can imagine," Joe lied. He couldn't imagine, and he didn't really care about their methods. "Colonel Cadler, I know you don't like me, and that's okay: Most people don't."

"And you have the luxury of not having to worry too much about it, because *you*"—a thick finger pointed at Joe's nose—"are a precious commodity. No one does what you do."

Joe knew it wasn't flattery. "Maybe. In any case, I just want you to know that I *am* on the same side as you and I don't repeat what bears being kept quiet."

"Despite the attitude?" Cadler asked.

"What attitude?" Joe inquired, instantly aware that he had made a joke when he intended to be serious.

9
....
DESIGNS

Los Angeles

THE THIRTY-FIVE TEAMS were feeling the frustration of a zero batting average. No registration records or eyewitness accounts could place the shooters or Jackson at any of the hotels or motels close to the freeway. Frankie and Thom had finished their area, with no success, and were heading to the north side of the 10 to assist two other teams and, by their generosity, share in the frustration. They figured theirs would be a helping and a half for the day.

And that day, so far, had been sixteen hours of monotony, played out by the seventy agents as the mounting negative reports were broadcast over the radio. With the long hours taken into account it was slightly more than amazing that Frankie's senses were keen enough to notice something that no one had considered. The Bureau Chevy slowed in the right lane and glided to a smooth stop curbside. Both agents were looking to the right, Frankie leaning forward on the steering wheel.

"Thom?" she said, her smiling brown eyes studying the building and its surroundings.

"Yeah."

"Are you seeing what I am?"

"Sure am," Thom answered, unbuckling his seat belt. "It makes sense. Private. Looks like a card-access gate. It's not a motel, but it'd serve the purpose."

"Exactly my thinking." Frankie checked the traffic before opening her door. "Call it in on the cellular. I'm gonna start knocking."

Within ten minutes all those teams that had struck out on the motels were directing their efforts elsewhere, hoping against the growing odds for a success.

USS *Vinson*

The night sky was a sea of darkness rushing past the Tomcat's clear canopy. Dick Logan was riding shotgun, sitting where the radar intercept officer usually would.

"My rear ain't happy about havin' to hitch back on a COD," the pilot told Logan, the cow pies practically dripping from his staticky words. "You must be important."

Logan knew better than that. His agent was the important one.

Silence answered the pilot's question better than words. "Yep. I see." His white helmet shook with wonder. "Mister, you ever land on a carrier?"

"Vertically."

"This is a bit more violent than a helo touchdown. You cinched up?"

Logan checked his harness. "Roger." The quick preflight instructions they had given him at Sigonella were supposed to prepare him for this. Why, then, did he feel like he'd just bent over in a prison shower room?

"Ready, then?"

"Ready what?" Logan asked with surprise, craning his neck to see past the pilot's headrest and bulbous headgear. There was only blackness ahead.

"On the deck in one minute, mister."

The CIA officer felt his stomach tighten up. *These Navy birdmen are fucking crazy! Where the hell is the ship?* All he could see below was deep black, and he knew that beneath that was an even deeper ocean.

The sixty seconds evaporated quickly, ending when the thirty-ton aircraft's tail hook snagged the number one arrester wire. Logan didn't have the luxury of experience in this, and his tense body was thrown forward, testing the harness with force. Internal organs were mixed and pressed forward, nearly heaving the small base meal from his stomach into his oxygen mask.

Then, it was all over. Fast. The canopy came up and deck crewmen, dressed in different primary-colored shirts, were all over the plane, removing both men to the welcome feel of the solid, rolling ground that was the ninety-thousand-ton USS *Carl Vinson*.

A khaki-uniformed officer, peaked cap and red flashlight in hand, met Logan at the Tomcat's right wingtip and led him into the carrier's island. After a quick introduction they continued down through corridors that a stranger to the ship couldn't trace his way through on a lucky day. A knock and announcement at a door not like the steel ovals they had passed through brought him into a nicely appointed, if small, office. The lieutenant left with an informal salute, and a smile that was not for the visitor.

"Mister Logan," the man seated behind the desk began without rising or offering his hand, "I am Commander Harrold Keys."

Logan felt exposed standing before the officer, a feeling that reminded him both of his short stint in the Air Force years before, and of a firing squad scene from some movie he'd seen. "Commander."

"I run the air group aboard this ship. The *Vinson* herself belongs to Admiral Drew. The planes and their crews are mine. They're my responsibility, Logan, and mine alone. None of them are expendable. None are worth wasting. I take this all very seriously. Do you understand?"

Logan felt the tips of his ears burn. He was sure they were red. "Clearly."

Keys folded his hands on the desk, his elbows stretched straight out. He was the picture of a naval aviator. His strong, sincere brown eyes spoke volumes about courage and determination, and the wave of black hair was cropped close the way pilots preferred, not in a Marine-like flattop. The uniform, what Logan could see of it above the desk, was pressed neatly, but not impeccably, indicative of the fact that this man was a hands-on commander, one who more than likely hopped behind the stick on occasion to chase birds. On his breast were a modest few ribbons, and on his right hand he wore the ring of honor—that of an Annapolis graduate.

Logan had to respect the man, even if he was an ass at the moment.

"I do not care much for this mission," Keys explained, quite unnecessarily. He slid back from the desk and stood. "Risking good men for some raghead traitor goes against my grain. Way against it."

"He's on our side, Commander." Logan knew the words were worthless to Keys.

"Let me share something with you, Mr. Logan." Keys gestured toward two chairs at room's center, where they sat. "About twenty-five years back, not more than six months in the front seat, I caught myself some flak at six hundred knots in my good ol' F-4. And, mind you, there weren't any friendlies below. Just a slew of pissed-off gooks. Can't say I blame 'em, being that we'd just blown the crap out of a road network around their village. Anyway, my backseater didn't make it out before we hit—his seat must've screwed up or something. I hit the ground in damn good shape, which ain't supposed to happen in an eject. Nothing broken. Nothing at all." Keys's head shook slightly, almost wistfully, as the time came back. He looked up at Logan. "I was the only one to survive from the flight. Six planes. Eleven good men—dead. Thank God SAR got to me before the locals. And do you know why? Because we were getting our intel from some gook insider. He gave us lots of good stuff as a lead-in: a bridge here, and maybe some rice convoy or some other piddly shit. Just enough so our intel guys were comfortable with it all. Just enough so he could draw a bunch of us in to a grade A bushwack. We bit at it, and good." The commander looked down and then at the spy again. "He was on our side, Logan. Think about that."

Logan breathed deeply. "The orders, Commander, come . . ."

"I know, Logan." Keys waved off the reminder. "From the top. You see, that's where I differ from that candy-ass raghead of yours. *I* obey orders. *I* am loyal to my country, and to my men. You'll have everything you need to complete this mission. Everything. If you need a goddamn turkey dinner waiting here for him, you've got it. But take this advice: Don't be surprised if your beloved traitor—you know, the one on our side—don't be surprised if he's playing both sides of the fence."

"I'll keep it in mind."

"Keep this in mind, too, mister: There'll be a helo full of good men going in there with you to pull that guy out. You're not the only one who could get killed. You've got a lot of lives on your shoulders, Mr. Logan."

He was right, as much as Logan wanted to not believe it. DONNER, like any other agent, could be a pawn. *Damn!* "Message received, Commander. Loud and clear."

Keys nodded. "The lieutenant will take you to your bunk. It's small, but it's private. I assume you'll want to brief the helo crew ASAP."

"And the special ops troops," Logan added. "Who do we have?"

"A squad of recon Marines from Guam. Eight men . . . Good men."

"Point well taken, Commander."

Logan looked for some common ground that they could work from, but since he knew of the commander's distaste for DONNER, a man he had not yet met, settling for noninterference would have to do. He knew he would have all the help he needed, but he wanted more. Not approval—at least not for himself, and definitely not from this man. Maybe he was hoping for acceptance for his agent, so the man wouldn't come in from the cold and realize that home had been a hell of a lot warmer.

"Very well. Briefing in forty minutes." Keys returned to his chair, again without taking the CIA officer's hand. It was a cold signal, one that Logan heeded, immediately, picking up his escort outside the door as he left.

Los Angeles

If their average was translated into baseball terms, Agents Francine Aguirre and Thomas Daybrook would be candidates for yearly multi-million-dollar contracts. Already the word had spread that they were blessed, the Buddha whose tummy one rubbed to bring luck. That was before the immediate moment. This one, if it was a hit, would put them in the realm of legends.

Frankie heard it first. The lowered white Hyundai pulled slowly into the driveway to avoid dragging its ground-hugging underside. Its bass-heavy stereo system thumped until going silent as the headlights faded to darkness. The driver stepped out and approached. His babyish face was framed by the dark strands of his wet-curl perm, and the white Nike sweatsuit glowed, even in the dim light from the distant sodium lamp. He walked toward his boss and the two agents waiting outside the sliding night window of the storage yard.

"Daryl, come here." The owner spoke in a heavy Indian accent. His dark-haired wife watched worriedly from inside.

"Watsup?" Daryl James had almost thought the phone call from his boss was a joke, but Mr. Patel was a serious man. That he knew for sure. "You almost didn't catch me. I just walked in when the phone rang."

"Daryl," Frankie said, offering her hand. The young man, polite and calm, accepted it. "I'm Agent Aguirre and this is Agent Danbrook. We're with the L.A. FBI office."

The young man straightened up at that. "Hey, man . . . I mean lady. I don't do none of that shit that you all handle. No drugs or gang banging. Honest."

Thom was skeptical, but not Frankie. The kid wasn't a street slime, like so many others she had seen or grown up with. No expensive jewelry or flashy clothes. Even his car was sedate when compared to what other young guys who looked the part were driving. Thom, a new agent, had seen too many movies and spent too much time behind a desk.

Frankie smiled. "Don't sweat it."

Thom handed Daryl a page from the facility's register book. It was similar to that of a hotel, showing who rented each particular space. This one was for space 141, one of the small walk-in units. A picture was also passed over, which Daryl held under the light over the night window.

"Do you remember any of these men?" Frankie asked, watching Daryl for any reaction as his eyes went between the form and the strip of three photos.

"Yeah. Last week, I think."

"Which one," Frankie probed, sidestepping closer to the light as her heartbeat picked up.

"This one here. On the left."

"Jackson," Thom said to his partner, who nodded.

They had been right. It had been a simple hunch, but then that was good police work. Some of it could be taught: the investigative techniques, to an extent, and the reckoning of fact with conjecture, most notably. But that gut feeling that good cops got was inborn. Not every agent had it, but all street agents worth their salt did.

"Let's check it out," Frankie said, her manner now more serious. The time for glee was past. "Mr. Patel, the gentleman that Daryl just identified is wanted for questioning in the assassination of the president. You can imagine how serious this is. Now, we can have a search warrant here in less than an hour, if you wish, but it would be a great help if you would allow us access."

"I do not know. What if it is not the same man . . . the one you want?"

Frankie shot her partner a look, which sent him walking toward the car.

"No! No! No!" Patel said rapidly, stopping Thom after only a few steps. "I will let you in. Jira," he called to his wife, finishing the sentence in his native language. She disappeared momentarily, then returned with a key. "Come. Come."

The agents followed the diminutive man to the gate, which he opened with a card, and on to the small storage space. Daryl stayed outside near the window, still somewhat perplexed by what was happening.

The door to the space was orange, and only slightly larger, both in height and width, than an ordinary entry door.

"I'll take the key," Frankie said. "Would you wait back by the gate?"

Thom waited for the owner to get out of earshot. "Do you think it's tricked?"

Frankie shook her head. "Why would it be? These guys were interested in getting in and out, clean and quick. Jackson, too, I figure. The car they used wasn't booby-trapped. These guys had specific targets, which means that random killing just doesn't fit. Plus, what if someone had opened this up before they did their deed? It might have been enough to spook the Service." She ended with a raised-eyebrow invitation for rebuttal.

"So why have him move back?"

Frankie grinned. "What if I'm wrong?"

Thom coughed, half laughingly and half from the realization that she could be right. "It's comforting to know that you and I will be the only victims."

The key clicked upon being inserted. Without hesitation Frankie turned it, and the door swung an inch inward once released. Thom pushed it farther until it stopped against an inside wall, then he reached in, feeling for a light switch. "Here goes."

It was a single-bulb fixture on the ceiling in the room's center, but bright enough to clearly show the contents. Frankie didn't have to move any closer to see the pile of wooden boxes against the back wall. *Idiots*! she thought to herself. She looked at Thom, whose smile was that of a satisfied cop.

"Does the term *jackpot* have any meaning, pardner?" she asked, getting a congratulatory handslap in response.

Pope AFB

There should have been a share-and-share-alike attitude among those that might do the same job, but that would be in a perfect bureaucratic world. McAffee knew the realities, so the delay—a nearly three-hour one—in his getting details on the HRT plan was expected. They had it now, which was what counted. Ten copies of the ten-page assault plan were in the hands of the team, all of whom sat around a rectangular table beneath the 747's left wing.

"Interesting," Graber mumbled quietly halfway through the brief, which included operational details and several diagrams.

The HRT plan—code-named RETRIEVER—was radical in concept. Its basis was the belief by the Bureau's psychological advisers and criminal behaviorists that the terrorist could not wear and keep active the deadman's vest for the duration of the hijacking. Aside from being physically draining, the emotional trials that one would have to endure, knowing that a slip would mean death, and failure, would be degrading. Therefore, the head doctors theorized, he must take it off after takeoff and put it back on after landing.

It was during the latter when the HRT plan called for the assault to take place. As the 747 slowed on the runway, two Bureau Blackhawk helos would approach from the rear with four agents slung beneath each on STABO rigs. Before the jet stopped, the men would be deposited on each wing, where they would blow the number three doors, perform an entry, and neutralize the hijackers.

McAffee let each man finish examining the plan. "Okay, troops, tear it apart." He paused for a few seconds. "Anyone?"

"The op is good," Antonelli said halfheartedly. "At least detailwise."

Quimpo nodded. "I agree. It's doable, but tricky. Really tricky."

Sean flipped back to the second page, finding his point of reference. Joe Anderson, sitting on his right, saw this, and also the quizzical look on the captain's still boyish face.

The major did too. "Problem, Captain?"

Sean's head came up. "Sir. Sorry, what was that?"

"You seem engrossed. Is our discussion disturbing you?"

Graber laid the stapled stack down. "Maybe it's me, but this is a pile of shit." The veteran officer leaned in. His blue eyes were serious and cold against an expressionless face. "The plan for the actual takedown is good, but pretty standard. Even the entry isn't all that stunning. We considered something like it back in eighty-seven. It would have worked on smaller jets, where they'd need only four men, maybe. That's my biggest concern with the operational side of it. Those helos would have to stay out near the wingtips to make sure their rotors cleared each other, unless they came in one at a time—but there's nothing in this about that. It calls for a simultaneous insertion and entry."

"There'd be about sixty seconds of lag if they separated," Buxton figured.

"Nah!" Antonelli contradicted him. "Their helo jocks must be as good as ours, and ours could do it in half a minute easy."

"With four guys on rigs swinging below?" Buxton retorted.

Antonelli shrugged. "Maybe."

McAffee took it in. "Good call, Captain. Anything else?"

"Sure. It won't work even if they get in position perfectly. Look at the second page, at the psych profile." Graber waited until everyone had found the place. "Let me ask you this— if you were that guy on the plane, when would you be most nervous: touchdown or takeoff?"

The understanding was obvious on the major's face, while the rest of the team exchanged looks of realization.

"I sure as hell wouldn't be feeling at ease if I were about to land in a potentially hostile environment, or anywhere for that matter. I'd have that security blanket on, just in case, until I was in the air."

He was right. The team knew it. Graber's seldom used nickname was TR, for ten ring, the centermost circle on a pistol target. Sean could put round after round through practically the same hole. The moniker also lent itself to his ability to analyze a given problem or situation past the cursory and simplified look others usually gave. He saw what others did not in many instances, a sensory ability born more of an instinctive nature than of any training he had received. It was valuable to the team and, thankfully, not a sporadic talent.

McAffee gave his copy a last look. "So, is there anything usable from this?"

Graber shook his head. "They've got it backward, sir. He'll be at ease after takeoff, and their plan doesn't work in reverse."

"There's no doing that wing-walking crap when the bird's gonna fly," Antonelli said.

It was frustrating . . . damn frustrating. The Bureau plan wouldn't work, and Delta, as yet, hadn't been able to come up with anything better. McAffee pulled a breath of the cool, humid air deep into his lungs. It was representative of the weather outside, cold and becoming downright nasty. He looked up at the hangar's ceiling. Maybe the weather and their surroundings were a visual and emotional echo of the real problem. They were cut off, isolated from the bad guys. Whoever put this thing together had known their stuff. A terrorist with brains, the major thought. Perfect! Security was airtight. They couldn't be touched, but they had to be.

"We need something. Something to work with. The colonel wants an op ready to go in one hour."

Buxton's blond flattop bobbed up. "What about the lean plan?"

"Not with this one," McAffee responded. The lean plan was a sort of off-the-shelf rescue whose operational details could be tailored to make it work with most situations.

A few seconds of silence passed, feeling more like minutes.

"It's tough, sir." Graber flattened the suspect page of the report with both hands. "I just don't see any openings yet."

"Look!" McAffee shouted. "We don't have much time, if any. The word could come in a minute, or in ten, or in an hour, and we are going to have a goddamn debacle here unless we're ready to jump at the word go! Damnit! Do you think Iran was bad? You haven't seen anything. We haven't seen anything. We fucked up back then, but no innocents lost their lives. That's forgivable. But if we go in without a workable plan and slaughter a bunch of hostages like the Egyptians did, then we'll certainly be in the shit, or dead— probably both."

The team wasn't accustomed to Blackjack blowing his lid. That was a show of emotion, something that wasn't supposed to happen. But they hadn't faced anything quite like this before, a situation with two possible outcomes: bad and worse. They had seen their leader angry before, but never out of control. He, too, was at a loss for a solution.

Sean, however, heard none of the tirade past a reference the major had used. The light had gone on, instantaneously as usual. But . . . *You're nuts, Sean. It's ludicrous. It's . . . It's . . .*

"Sir."

"Captain," McAffee breathed more than spoke.

Graber was tentative beginning. "This may sound crazy,

but humor me. Triple Seven might've fucked up royally," he allowed, referring to the botched attempt by Egyptian counterterrorists to rescue passengers from a hijacked EgyptAir jet at Malta's Luqa airport in 1985, "but there may be something we can use." He went on for nearly five minutes, outlining his idea as everyone listened silently.

"This is nuts!" Joe exclaimed. "You want everyone dead? This'll do it."

The major eyed him. "Mr. Anderson, if this works will your job be affected in any way? Will you still be able to deal with whatever is in the belly of that bird?"

Anderson swallowed hard, his eyes scanning the men around the table. He knew the comment was meant to put him in his place, separate from the warriors. In real comparison, he was simply a technician, but one with enough years behind him to know when to accept a mild slap. "If it works . . . not at all."

McAffee's voice eased. "Then we'll get on with the operational details, and leave you to your preparations."

The metal legs screeched as Joe slid his chair back. The team watched the civilian move into the adjoining office. They also knew that he could be absolutely correct in his analysis of their chances.

The discussion was picked up again, and carried on for ten minutes before McAffee summoned Colonel Cadler. If they were going to offer up something this outlandish, then there would have to be a stamp on it from the GFC. The approval would be for the real brass, not for Delta. The troops knew that their word would be sufficient for the colonel. If they liked it, and wanted to go with it, then so would he.

Graber laid it out again. This time some of the team's added contributions were incorporated.

"That's a damn bold idea, Captain. It's yours, I take it."

"The basic idea, sir. Everybody fed in on the last hashing."

Cadler turned to his second. The smile was slight, but noticeable. "Major, if this is it, then it's a go from me. Pappy will go for it, too, so don't worry about any upper-echelon bull." He stopped and pulled on his baseball-style fatigue cap. "Get with the tech boys to work on those charges. The captain here's right when he says they're going to have to be right on the money. Power and placement." Cadler paused momentarily. "Maybe we better get the crew of this bird here to help on the placement end of things. They might be able to give us something on the structural side."

"That could be a factor," McAffee agreed.

"With this cockamamy plan, you'd better believe it."

"I'll get them over here."

"Good," the colonel bellowed. "Damn good work. Now . . . perfect it. Run it through, up and down, all around. I want to give Pappy the word in three hours that we're ready to go with this plan. Enough time?" The troops agreed that it was. "Damn fine work, men. Jesus, this is good work!" Cadler smiled openly, if quickly, before walking away. At the office door he looked back at the men. His men. He was proud of them and their harebrained scheme, mostly because he was sure they could make it work.

Los Angeles

Progress drove Art. It inspired him as much as frustration, only the feeling was better. His pen attacked the legal pad.

There are now two direct links between Jackson and the suspects: (1) Filings found on the floor of Jackson's bedroom have been identified as metal residue from the sanitizing of one of the two M-16A2 rifles. He looked to the technical brief from Jacobs. It was his job to paraphrase and de-techspeak the information, which would go into his report to the director. *Analysis has determined that metal samples are a perfect match.* Art decided to drop "something or other spectroanalysis" for brevity, since such terms usually took twenty or thirty words to explain in everyman's English. *(2) Packing crates for the weapons were found in a public storage facility that had been rented by Jackson, pointing to a pickup by the assassins. A melted plastic access card was found with one of the assassin's bodies, and it matches those used by the facility in composition and appearance.* To Art it was a lump of plastic, but the lab, as always, worked its miracles once it had something to compare the lump with.

The office reverberated with a loud knock.

"Come in, Ed."

Toronassi grinned his way in.

"You sound like you're serving warrants," Art joked.

"It gets me in. You got any java?" Eddie saw the almost empty pot before an answer came. There was always a pot in his boss's office, full or not. "Hey, you want something good for the director—well, maybe it's good."

Art took the two fax copies. "What do we have?"

"Relatives." Eddie leaned over the desk and pointed to the top sheet. "We found two brothers of ol' Marcus, but that's all for close blood. Once we talk to them there may be some aunts or something. Who knows."

Interesting. "The older one has quite a tail."

Eddie nodded in midsip. "That's how we found him. Ernest Jackson is a scuzzball, if only a minor one. Guess it runs in the family. GTA and ADW are the biggest, but no deaths yet."

"Didn't break into the majors."

"Lucky for a lot of folks. He's got a bunch of other stuff with the biggies, going back a long way. Most of it's violent in one way or another."

The present whereabouts box caught Art's eye. "He's in Joliet. What for?"

Eddie twisted his neck uselessly, then walked around behind the dark wood desk. "Looks like assault with intent and grand theft. Must be federal."

"He could play a part in this," Art said as he pressed hard on his tired lids. "Contacts for the weapons, maybe. At least this keeps the trail moving in the same direction."

"Huh?"

"You didn't hear?"

"Hear what? I've been hunting these guys down most of the afternoon."

It was Art's turn to share some good news. "Frankie and Thom struck pay dirt again."

"Christ! Who smiled on them." Eddie was glad it had been Francine Aguirre. She was a good agent, and had worked her ass off to shake any misgivings about female street agents. It wasn't supposed to be that way in these days of so-called equality, but old doubts died hard.

"They found the weapon stash in one of those storage places. You know, thirty bucks a month for a room or garage.

Lois and I used to keep our RV in one of them." *Until we sold it . . . had to sell it, by some damn court order.*

The Italian agent's pearly whites shone more. "Like she thought."

"Yep. The crates and all the packing stuff were still there. Markings and all. The stuff came from an Army facility in Illinois, so . . ."

"What?" Eddie jumped in.

"What's wrong?"

"The source, boss. Look at the other brother's info. PFC Samuel Jackson, currently stationed at Rock Island Army Munitions Depot . . . in Illinois."

"That's a nuke and chemical facility."

"Right," Eddie said. "Which means they'd have plenty of guards, and plenty of firepower. They've gotta store the stuff somewhere."

Art scanned the page. Samuel Jackson was just a kid, literally. In uniform for just over eighteen months. "How long has he been there?"

"A year, about."

Ed was silent as Art read over the full report. Samuel, the youngest of the Jacksons, could have been the source of the guns and LAWs, which would have put Marcus in the middleman position. It was unlikely that Marcus was behind the whole thing, even more so now that they knew of his little brother's military connection. Still, he might have been the front man in L.A. That, too, was hard to swallow completely. Nothing pointed to Marcus being either a brainy sort or one with any tangible relations to the Khaleds. There was more. Somewhere, if Art was piecing this together correctly, there would be a tie-in. A college professor had once told him that the road to certainty was paved with coincidences. That wisdom of yesteryear was now proving itself in spades.

"Ed, find out what Sam here does in the Army—what his MOS is. Then let's run down big brother Ernest's background. I'm going to call Jerry and ask him to hold the director off on this report." Art tapped the yellow pad. "Okay?"

"You got it," Eddie answered with renewed purpose. "We're getting warm, you know."

"Let's run with it then."

Georgetown

The pillows were stacked up against the headboard with his favorite down one at the top. It cradled Bud's tilting head. He wasn't tired, yet, being more engrossed in thoughts that tumbled in his head than with the preliminary report from Granger lying on his outstretched naked legs. It was neat, and bound. He wondered how it was that all reports, no matter how rushed, always came attractively packaged. Was there an undersecretary for that?

He shook the mental cobwebs away. Contentwise the report was solid. The plans, though incomplete, were thorough. The operation would hurt the Libyans, probably with few civilian casualties, though that was a minimal concern to Bud. Some still held with the belief that innocents in a hostile place were to be safeguarded at all cost. He had never been able to grasp the logic. But then he had the luxury of being a military man. It wasn't a question of playing by some unwritten set of chivalrous rules, which more often than not tied the hands of those on the righteous end of the stick. It was a question of reality, and of the future good. The greater good. A hundred enemy innocents now, or two hundred American innocents later.

Still, with all the justification and the culpability, not to speak of the moral issues of correctness, Bud couldn't come to reconcile himself with the belief that this would do much more than hurt those who stood in the light, albeit a light of "evil." It was those in the shadows who struck without warning, and it was they who would walk away with blood on their hands but little, if anything, on their conscience.

Damnit, Bud! What do you expect?

The bottle of Evian on the nightstand was less than half full, and a long draw later it was gone. Bud realized that he'd rather it were a beer. Oh well—the sacrifices of public service.

Those who had precipitated this with their surreptitious bravado filled Bud's mind before it could lock on to anything tangible. Who were they? Almost certainly the former DCI and DDI, but what about higher-ups, and what about those in lower ranks? Had the order, or even the general inference of authorization come from the president? Or, as Landau believed, were the former heads of the Agency the source of the turmoil? That would make the most sense, Bud agreed. The Iran-Contra fiasco had proven one thing: The odor of shit drifts upward rapidly. A chief executive could not expect, in the age of the media circus, to distance himself from scandal, even one that ignorance of was a truthful defense.

It was almost unfathomable. Executive underlings had done it again, only this time their actions had led to the death of a president—and not even the one they served under!

The pillows' soft bulk caught Bud's head. It bobbed backward, and then the rest of his body slid until he lay almost flat on the bed.

He could feel the coldness of the plastic report cover on his legs. A lift of his knee slid it off.

Was the military option the right one? *You're supposed to be answering questions, Bud.*

Damn! he thought. In those thirty-five pages was a plan that would work, but would it work right? It was another question, but at the moment he had little else. Certainly not any perfect answers.

In the morning he might need to recommend a strike to the president, and, he knew now, it would not be with a ready conscience. The public would support it if it became a necessity, but the long-term results would be practically nil. Maybe that's what bothered him the most. Even the experts and so-called authorities agreed that large-scale retaliation usually only fomented further acts of terror. Tit for tat was a liberal term, where our tit led to their tat. The experts, Bud reminded himself, said that negotiations were the best hope for preventing future occurrences, if they were meaningful and binding.

"But who the hell is the antagonist?" he asked aloud. Who was the protagonist and who was the antagonist? Right and wrong. Did prevention mean giving the terrorists what they wanted, if only in part? Was it good to look at an issue with irrational, evil persons and search for common ground? Was it right?

"No!"

Bud brought the backs of his hands up to his eyes, blocking out the soft light. If only the goddamn rogues had succeeded there would be no problem. Qaddafi would be gone. The source would be eliminated.

Bad analysis, Bud knew. It had been an easy out, the tainted blood option, but too slow. Too much chance of discovery, the exact nightmare they were living now.

Right target, wrong method, wrong avenue of decision. It could have been right, and legitimate, and successful, with only God being the final arbiter of its righteousness. Those involved would be called on the carpet in the hereafter. Time enough to convince oneself of absolution, Bud figured.

The last thought scared him, and enlightened him. He pulled himself up on his elbows, looking into the semidarkness of the hallway to the bathroom, and wondered if wrong could be manipulated into right.

Flight 422

Hadad's eyes opened peacefully from a dream-free sleep. His education would contradict that thought, his teachers having told him, and the other medical students, that all people dreamed during sleep. He could break from that part of his past now, too. Allah had cleared his mind. Cleansed him, actually. Completely. It had to happen so that the purpose would be achieved with purity.

He reached to his left and slid the shade up in the portholelike window. Not much like a ship's porthole, he decided, having spent weeks on a ship during his transit of the Atlantic to the medical college in Buenos Aires years before. That had been enjoyable and frightening, being on the sea the first time, especially since all that surrounded the converted freighter was endless water.

Through the thick upper-deck window he could see the first sheets of yellow coming from the sky over the buildings to the plane's left. It was still dark inside the lounge where he sat, and quietness filled the aircraft like a void. All below were asleep, or silently praying, or, if infidels, they simply were contemplating the last few hours and those still to come.

He rolled sideways in the wide seat and pulled his fatigue coat up over his neck. One of his comrades must have covered him when the chill snuck up on the desert during the night. His arm came up and twisted toward the incoming light. Almost five-thirty in the morning, or was it? Yes, he had adjusted the time. Five-thirty it was. Hadad leaned forward and tried to twist and stretch the sleep from his muscles. Soon he would need to start what would be a long journey. Not in time or distance, but in change. Every journey had a beginning and an end, a truism that Hadad knew was false for himself. Arrival at the final destination was but his first step toward a reunion.

10

. . . .

TRICKS AND TOOLS OF THE TRADE

Pope AFB

"THE PROPELLANT CHARGE is one quarter of standard," the master sergeant said. He held the 40mm grenade vertically between his thumb and forefinger. It looked like a pistol bullet enlarged by a factor of ten. "With the projectile weight being, oh, about two and a half times a normal H.E. round, the range is going to be a max of two hundred feet. We'll have to adjust the charge for the range you want." He waited for the information.

"One hundred feet," McAffee obliged. "What's the range of error?"

"Five feet either way." The master sergeant wrapped his palm around the special round.

McAffee unfolded the aircraft cabin floor plan. The forward cabin was longer than ten feet as a unit of the interior, so the margin of error was acceptable. "Okay. How many can you have in an hour?"

"How many you need?"

The major gave it a quick thought. "Eight. All the same. Two sealed in HK-69s, and six loose for practice."

The NCO nodded confidently. "You'll have 'em in thirty

minutes." He gave a few commands over his hand-held radio, instructing his crew to adjust the propellant amount in the grenades. "The frame charge is ready. You wanna see it?"

"Let's do it." McAffee turned to the aircraft behind. "Captain Graber. Outside with me . . . pronto."

The three men went to a grassy area a hundred yards from hangar 9. A row of pines hid the spot from view, but not from the electronic eyes that might be high above. To counter that a canopy was strung between four metal poles driven into the wet earth. Misty rain was settling down from the clouds hidden in the dark sky. Sunrise would be in less than an hour. By that time the weather was supposed to be back to a full-fledged rain.

A corporal stood beneath the canopy, his hand swathed in a towel to dry the aluminum panel of the moisture that was constantly condensing on its top surface. Attached to the bottom with double-sided adhesives was a single-frame charge, hastily but expertly assembled to meet the needs of the team.

"Everything ready, Geller?" the master sergeant asked, bending down to inspect the underside where his handiwork was attached.

"All set. I ran the detonator over to the berm." He motioned to the sky. "There's enough tree canopy there to cover it naturally."

McAffee and Graber inspected the charge and the aluminum. The metal was a quarter inch thick, the same as the material they would need to penetrate on the aircraft. Four concrete poles were holding the metal plate four feet off the ground. Two bolts from each pole held it securely down, the entire structure as rock-solid as a single unit.

"We have four of these, but, unfortunately, we can't adjust the power on them as easily." The master sergeant directed the Delta officer toward the mound of dirt that would shield them from the blast. "The blast won't be as loud as a door charge, and not as much backward concussion. You could probably stay three feet from it with no problem." He trotted up and over the berm, followed by the others.

"Right here." The corporal handed the detonator to his superior.

The master sergeant held it up. "Your standard setup. I will caution you: There's gonna be more smoke than usual. Remember, this thing is like a bunch of HEAT shells packaged around the blast perimeter. They're practically gonna melt the metal."

"I hope it's clean," Graber said.

The master sergeant smiled. "It will be. Guaranteed."

They were forty feet from the setup. There was no cover other than the knee-high berm, and none of the soldiers took any further cover.

It sounded like a sledgehammer coming down on a metal beam, followed by a hiss that ended the initial clang. Four sheets of whitish smoke expanded outward from each side of the new square hole in the aluminum. The piece blown free shot only a few feet straight up, with little force, and bounced off the canopy, landing just to the side. It stuck, corner first, in the damp dirt.

The master sergeant waved away a cloud of the dissipating smoke that came his way. He took a flashlight from the corporal and shone it at the center of the white cloud. "C'mon."

They walked through the artificial mist to the test setup.

"Clean." The master sergeant tentatively touched the bolted-down aluminum. It was warm at the outer edge—the center was cooling from an orange-red.

McAffee squatted under the setup, then stood through the hole. "This is fine. Good size."

Graber pointed to the blown-out section. "That could be a problem."

The master sergeant looked at it, then up at the canvas canopy. There was a four-inch tear where the square had pierced it after being blown free. "Yeah. That could cause a helluva headache. No problem. Just a minor addition on one side."

"I thought you couldn't adjust the power," Blackjack said. He rotated his body a full three hundred and sixty degrees in the opening, checking for clearance.

"We can't, but we can add a few more charges to throw the balance off."

McAffee and Graber understood. Beyond that, they trusted the NCO implicitly. His work had proven itself before, in critical situations where a misfire would have been disastrous.

The major lifted his lower body through the opening, then swung both legs back to the ground. "Captain?" He offered Graber a try at the lift. He shook the suggestion off.

"You want just the two, Major?" the master sergeant asked.

"That's all we need," Blackjack answered.

"Got it. At the hangar in twenty minutes." He turned to the corporal. "Check the wiring one more time."

"Yes, Sergeant."

A minute later McAffee and Graber were alone. Blackjack set the stubby MP5 on the metal slab. "We go with pistols."

Graber agreed. "Let's go with a double load."

"Good thinking," the major said. Each man would go into the assault with two pistols, a necessary safeguard against jamming. With the sub-machine guns left behind, a backup weapon would be the answer. "Let's get back. You get the practice going with those grenades as soon as they get here."

"Inside . . . right?"

"Absolutely, Captain." It had to be real, the major knew. The bad guys' bullets would be.

Los Angeles

Art wanted a bacon-chili-cheese dog, but Pinks was twenty minutes away. The thought had crossed his mind to send someone down to pick up a couple for him, but there were reasons not to: Each of the cholesterol bombs probably took a day off his life, and half the reason the dogs were so good was the fun of eating them at Pinks's sidewalk counter.

"Come on, Arthur," he implored himself, and a half a minute later he was at the hallway fruit vending machine. He chose a banana, peeled it, and swallowed half before walking back through the door to his office.

"Boss."

Art's head came up midbite. "Ed. I was thinking about Pinks a minute ago."

Eddie sneered at the fruit. "Great substitute. We have the stuff from Chicago."

"Great!" Art hurried over to the desk. He stood in front of Eddie, leaning over to examine the information. "Who got all of this?"

"Lomax."

"It figures," Art commented. "He's always in on the action, no matter where it is. Okay, fill me in."

The junior agent turned his head. Art's turned to meet it. "It's starting to stink, Art. Real bad."

"Go ahead." It was strange, and had to be serious, Art knew, or Eddie wouldn't have called him by name.

"PFC Sammy Jackson looks like our gunrunner. Guess what his post is at Rock Island?" Eddie didn't allow time to answer. "Armory clerk. Lomax talked with Sammy's commanding officer, and they do have all the shit used in L.A. in the armory. He has access to all of it, but the CO doesn't see how he could have gotten any of it off the base. He said it would have been near to impossible."

" 'Near to,' " Art scoffed. "Comforting."

"He's nineteen . . . just a kid. And from what his CO said he's not too big in the brains department. Kind of simpleminded and a real mousy sort. The CO added some other reason, but I think he's got it wrong on that one."

"Why?" Art turned half around, leaning on his desk.

"He said Sammy's pretty dumb because he usually volunteers for armory duty. It's pretty dull, according to him, and they almost always have to assign someone to it—except when Sammy's feeling generous."

"He's just such a nice guy," Art said mockingly.

"I asked Lomax to get the duty records from the CO."

"Yeah. Let's see just how generous our little friend has been. Those crates from the storage place had to walk out of the armory at one time or another. Some record somewhere has got to show those crates as part of the inventory, and ten to one they still show as present."

"I'll bet on that."

Art balled up the banana peel and tossed it into the wastebasket. "Two points."

"Kareem's still got a foot on you."

"So, we have our source for the weapons. What about the other brother?"

Eddie handed one of the sheets to Art. "That's Ernie's history. This stuff wasn't on his record because of some court decision, but the Chicago office had a file on him."

That was strange. No major federal record, but the FBI office in Chicago had an *individual* file on Ernest Jackson.

"Guess."

"Look, Ed, it's late and I'm dreaming of chili dogs, so spill it."

"Ernie has some affiliations that fill an interesting hole in this puzzle. He is a known member of El Rukn—remember them?"

"The street gang; the ones Qaddafi warmed up to."

"Right. He warmed up real cozy to them. Before he 'adopted' them as his own American terror group, they were just a bunch of violent, racist street thugs. They only numbered about twenty at their peak. That whittled down to fifteen when things started getting serious with the Libyans."

"I remember. He tried to ship some shoulder-fired SAMs to them."

"SA-7 Grails. Russian-made. Two of them made it over from Qaddafi's European contacts, but we intercepted both. They were planning to shoot down a big jet taking off from O'Hare. Can you imagine?"

"The airline industry would have loved that," Art said, rightly. It would have scared off thousands of travelers, some for good. TV would have played the carnage live. *Christ!*

"Lomax says Jackson's a 'passive' active member of the gang, meaning they're supposedly no longer in existence, but reality and prison scuttlebutt say otherwise."

Art smiled his first true smile in days. It was one of satisfaction. "An honest-to-God family business. The pieces come together nicely."

"I thought you'd be pleased."

The plan, as it must have sounded to the Jacksons, came together in Art's head. "First, we have a leak somewhere—probably in England—that lets on that there's going to be a meeting between the F.M. and the president. We know that the F.M.'s good friend from World War Two is the manager of the Hilton, and that he always stays there when he's on the

West Coast. That wouldn't be hard for someone to figure out and piece together. Next, someone in the terrorist infrastructure makes contact with Ernie. The resources would be well known to them, so the three brothers probably just fit into the plan by number and convenience."

"Sure," Eddie agreed. "Three bodies—anyone would do."

"I'd bet this all started some time back. How long has Sammy been in uniform?"

Eddie checked the enlistment record. "Eighteen months."

"See, Ernie gets him to enlist, and that puts him in close proximity to any weapon they'd need. It'd take some doing, but they were determined, so getting the stuff was possible. And final bro Marcus is already in L.A. That probably made the trio an attractive choice for whoever recruited them."

The Italian agent's head nodded exaggeratedly. "And with Ernie's El Rukn contacts . . ."

The silence lasted but a second. "We knew it could have been international—now it looks like that's for sure."

"This thing has tentacles, man. I don't know where it's going to stop."

Art thought about that. It could be right on the money, but there was a notable exception. "Every set of tentacles has at least one head. We've got to concern ourselves with *here's* tentacles and its head: Marcus Jackson. He was the initial contact here—everything points to that. His brothers were just tools. As for who deals with the *head* . . . I'd say it goes back through El Rukn to the Middle East, probably Libya. I don't want to get into that political crap. The director will want to know what we think, but our aim is here, and our targets are the Jacksons."

"We have two of them under watch," Eddie said, stacking the report square and neat with a few taps on the desk.

"What did you work out with Chicago?"

"Lomax is going to set up a team to move on Sammy when we give the word. The CO is aware, and he'll keep it quiet. They're also going to have Ernie segregated at Joliet."

Something sparked a thought in Art's mind. "You know, we still have to find Marcus." He paused, looking down at the gray carpet. "Ed, why do you think they did it? From the gut?"

He thought that over. "None of them seem to have any real

brains, which eliminates any ideological reasons. Ernie's a tough, Sammy's a wimpy weasel, and Marcus, he looks to me like part of the other two. Ernie's up for parole in a year; his record inside is good, so he may get out. I say he'd want something to look forward to."

"Money." It was what Art had been thinking.

"Yep. Ernie sets this up after being recruited. There's a money drop—I'd guess with Marcus—and he and Sammy take it and lie low until Ernie gets out." Eddie caught an error in his analysis. "But then we'd be focusing on Ernie for sure. Once Marcus disappeared both of the others would be under the microscope."

"True," Art said. "But if they had any brains they'd have figured that much out. So, who has the perfect alibi of all of them?"

"Ernie."

"Which means Sammy must be planning to hit the road," Art proposed. "If Ernie was the head of all this he wouldn't want his parole jeopardized. If Sammy was picked up he'd probably crack, if the profile of him is correct. That would screw Ernie."

"You think he'll run, then?"

"I would." Art knew they would either have to pick Sammy up, or let him run and hope he would lead them to Marcus. He stopped in midthought. There might be some possibilities in that. "Ed, do you think Sammy's a little skittish?"

"Probably. Why?"

"When you're nervous about something, where do you turn?"

Eddie's face showed a Gestalt realization. "The familiar."

"Exactly. Maybe we can stir young Sammy up a little."

The framework of the plan formed over the next ten minutes. Soon thereafter it was passed over to the Chicago office, who would have the responsibility and pleasure of carrying it out.

Al-'Adiyat

The sun had been up for nearly two hours. Muhadesh wiped the last of the water from his short hair and ran a hand over it, smoothing the thinning black strands flat. A shower immediately following his morning run always soothed his heated muscles. It also was a form of cleansing—and not of soil or sweat from his body. He stood under the steamy streams far beyond the time for mere bathing. There was more than that which was visible that he tried to rinse from his body. Still, it never seemed enough. By the end of the day he felt completely soiled.

He hung the towel on its hook near the door between his quarters and office. There was work to be done. Today, however, would have an agenda different from any other before.

Lieutenant Indar knocked and entered at the same instant, coming to attention a foot from his superior. "Sir! A message from Colonel Hajin."

Muhadesh took the paper, eyeing Indar, whose stare was straight ahead and solid. He read the short dispatch to himself. "An attack by the Americans is expected. Well."

Indar's mouth opened slightly, his stare changing to almost human as it found his commander's downcast eyes. "An attack, sir!"

"Do not get excited, Indar. Remember, attacks have come before. All this says is that we should prepare for any attack that might come. This is not a certainty."

"But the Americans will surely attack us." Indar's unprofessionalism showed whenever passion or emotion entered his person.

This worm. Muhadesh had things to do, and his lieutenant would be underfoot to . . . *Possibly . . . yes.* "Lieutenant," he began, as if speaking in normal conversation, "I am charging you with preparing the camp to repel any attack."

There was a wet sound from Indar's mouth as a gulp of air was pulled rapidly into his lungs. "But . . . sir, did Colonel Hajin . . ."

"Indar!" Muhadesh's voice boomed, matching his stance. He quickly calmed, perfect in the portrayal. "You will be in charge of the defenses. That is my order. Do you understand?"

Indar's body went rigid again, looking to be at a very forced state of attention.

"Lieutenant." Muhadesh put a hand on his aide's elbow. *This terrifies you: real responsibility.* "This is a challenge for you. A real opportunity to use your skills of command and strategy, and I am confident that you will perform superbly." The lie seemed to work, as the fear left Indar's eyes and his chest stopped heaving.

"I will not fail you, sir."

"Do not fail the Third. About your duties, Lieutenant."

Indar gave his usual crisp salute as he left.

Muhadesh stood motionless for a full minute after his lieutenant left, just letting the coolness of the morning that invaded his office chill him. It awakened him fully.

Things would move more smoothly now that Indar had a task to keep him occupied. Muhadesh was certain that he would attack the chore with fervor, and equally sure that he would trip over his own ineptitude at every opportunity. It would not matter. That realization saddened Muhadesh, and that surprised him.

The time for the first step had come. He went to his drawer, the one with the lock. Inside were the tools he would need. His coat was on the chair back. Muhadesh left it there, then opened the desk drawer. Two of the items were identical, and he took both, bending to put them in the left side pocket. They sounded a metallic clinging as they dropped in. The other item he took more care with.

It was black, and reflected no light in the sun gleaming through the window. He checked the magazine, ejecting it for inspection, then reinserted it. Next he checked the silencer for alignment, opening the slide to allow light through the barrel and staring through it from the business end of the silenced .22 caliber Beretta. Everything was right with it. He made sure the safety was on before placing it in the holster sewn inside of the coat.

After lunch, he decided. Indar would be well into his duties, leaving Muhadesh free to visit the airport once again.

Los Angeles

Jerry mulled over the plan silently.

"Chicago's ready to go," Art said. Eddie sat quietly.

"If they get the number, and we get the location, then how do you want to handle it?" Jerry Donovan liked things laid out fully before moving on any potential suspect.

"Full surveillance, to start," Art began. "I'll put four or five teams on Jackson. Every move he makes we'll know. Then, when he's vulnerable, we'll take him."

Donovan became the inquisitor. He considered it a part of his job. "How many total?"

"Eight or ten," Art replied. He looked to Eddie for confirmation.

"That should do it," Eddie agreed.

Again Donovan analyzed it. He noted that Art was crisp and confident, but almost too awake. The plan, however, was sound. If the Chicago end of it came through, then the West Coast part would probably come off well. "It sounds good by me." He checked the time: 3:20 A.M. There was something he had to do. "Ed, could you excuse us."

The request was heeded. It wasn't uncommon for confidential conversations to spring up with no warning. Eddie did notice something in Jerry's eyes, though. He couldn't peg it, but it worried him enough to notice.

"Art," Donovan began, sounding more businesslike than a minute before, "how are you feeling?"

The question surprised Art, visibly. "What?"

"How do you feel? I mean, you've had what? . . . three hours' sleep in the past day?"

"A little more than that. What are you getting at, Jerry?"

The senior agent wasn't known for mincing words. "Art, you've got a weak ticker—that's no secret. You've been getting help, and that's great, but . . . Art . . . I can see it in you. You're tired."

"We're all tired," Art answered, mildly scoffing at the comments.

"Not like you. I'm not talking about tired because of no sleep: It's more. It's inside, Art. I know it. You know it." Donovan sought his answer with his eyes for a moment. "Tell me I'm wrong."

"You're wrong," Art lied. He was angry, not at Jerry—he was only doing his job—but at himself. He had let it show. But he couldn't let on that it was real. Not now. He wanted this one. He wanted Jackson.

Donovan heard the words, but the feeling wasn't in them. "If that's what you say, that's what you say. I have to take it as gospel."

"You can relieve me," Art said, regretting it instantly. It was a challenge to Jerry, and it confirmed what his superior had feared.

"No, Art, I can't. I've got nothing concrete. If I did . . . I don't know." He looked away for the first time. He had tried. "Just watch it, okay? Don't push yourself . . ."

"Over the edge?" Art finished the statement.

Donovan said nothing more. Art watched him leave, trying to forget the whole exchange immediately by focusing on the matters at hand.

11
....
FIRST BLOOD

Flight 422

CAPTAIN HENDRICKSON SAT once again in the seat. It had been an upright bed for him, as well as his work chair. It was not meant to be the former. Flight seats, however comfortable during hours aloft, were not designed for sleeping. His neck ached and his shoulders had a sharp, pulsing pain running the length of each blade. Discomfort was shaping up to be the norm for this journey. Even going to the head was a luxury, considering how long his bladder had been full. The same went for Buzz, who was finally enjoying the same relief.

The quiet one, the one the leader called Abu, was with the captain. Hendrickson thought there were four of them, though only three had been seen. Another was referred to often by the others. Thoughts of overpowering the one with him were ridiculous, the captain told himself. He could plan it, though, an act that at least gave him a sense of power.

For the hijackers there would always be a feeling of fear. They would constantly have to be on guard. The captain thought that was a laugh, that this whole thing might give the hijackers ulcers.

In the end, though, he felt more helpless than anything. This was *his* aircraft, and these were his passengers. He was responsible for each and every one of them. It made him sick to know that the best he could do at the moment was nothing.

Buzz returned, looking somewhat refreshed. The water on his collar showed that he had splashed himself. With him was the big hijacker, the brute. None of them had been overtly violent yet, but this one had it in him. Hendrickson could tell by the eyes. They had a wild quality.

Abu exchanged a few words with Wael before leaving the flight deck. Buzz returned to his seat. Its cushion was still wet with perspiration.

"I think we're leaving soon." Buzz shifted in the warm seat. His back still felt prickly.

"When?"

"I don't know. I heard them talking outside the head. My Arabic is pretty damn limited!" Buzz laughed.

Wael cast an angry look at the jovial Americans. He could not understand their words. What was it that made them laugh? he was thinking. They should be afraid.

"I don't think Kong here can understand us," Buzz said in his best deadpan. The lack of reaction confirmed his suspicion.

"I think you're right." The captain checked his AC system readings. Power was still coming from the GPU, which had been changed three times so far. Each truck-mounted generator could work only so long before servicing was needed. At least they had power, and the luxuries and necessities that it allowed. Some hijackers had ruled under harsh and nearly unbearable conditions, not allowing any power to be supplied once the aircraft's built-in APU had exhausted its oil source. Maybe these "tough guys" liked their comforts, the captain thought.

"At least we'll be doing something besides just sitting here," Buzz commented.

"Earn our pay."

Buzz nodded, instinctively putting his harness on, but letting it hang loose. Both men turned when the door opened. The head terrorist, the one the others called Mohammed, came in. His clothing was different from before. He now looked the same as the others: green fatigues. The Mini-Uzi hung from his shoulder.

"Get ready to fly." Hadad motioned to the control panel. Its alien markings and devices did not interest him. "We leave in thirty minutes."

"I'll need to check the exterior of my aircraft."

Hadad brought the small submachine gun up in his right hand, pointing at the captain. It looked almost like a toy.

"You do not need to," Hadad enunciated slowly. "And you will not. Your tricks will not fool me."

Captain Hendrickson half stood, leaning awkwardly on the armrest, his body twisted to face the hijacker. "Listen, if you want this aircraft to fly safely, then either I or my first officer must inspect the undercarriage and exterior. This runway is not the best in the world, so I have no idea what was kicked up when we landed. Do you understand?"

"Do *I* understand?" Hadad smiled, his head tilting quizzically. The barrel came up roughly in the soft flesh where jaw met neck. "I think *you* do not understand, Cap-tan." He mockingly emphasized the rank. "You will fly this plane and you will do it without going outside to perform your trickery. The plane is fine."

"I am not tryi—" The Uzi pressed harder. Hendrickson was sure he could feel the barrel in the back of his mouth.

"*Shut up!* I am talking, and I am tired of your defiance!" Hadad screamed. "You have done nothing but defy my orders! You will learn to do as you are told!"

"Raghead asshole!" Buzz reached for the Uzi pointing at him, but missed, grabbing Wael's web belt instead.

Hadad saw out of the corner of his eye Wael's weapon come back in preparation to strike the co-pilot.

"Wael!" Hadad's strong grip locked on his comrade's arm, holding it back like a coiled snake.

Buzz glared at the wild eyes staring down at him. He felt the hot breath of his would-be attacker expelling from the flared nostrils. It smelled sweet and spiced, maybe from the food they brought on board. Wael lowered the Uzi cautiously. Buzz released his hold in a quick motion, holding his hands open as if gesturing surrender.

Hadad turned back to the captain. The barrel was still rammed straight up, the gun held tightly in his left hand. Hendrickson's head was tilted back by the pressure, his eyes somewhat downcast to look directly at his tormentor. "You must learn, Cap-tan. *And* your number two. I am in command . . . total command. This is *my* plane. You, your number two, all the passengers will die if I decide it is to be. You no longer have any power." His voice eased as he drew back. "Does it trouble you that a lowly Palestinian now rules over your domain? Aah! Of course it does, Cap-tan. You would kill me without a thought, so be assured that I will do the same. Now, you will learn that this is true, and when I am finished I will ask, 'Do you understand?' " The Uzi was withdrawn. "Sit and watch."

The captain sank into his seat, never letting his eyes leave Hadad. Buzz turned back to his console; he could no longer control himself while looking at the pirates.

There was a rapid burst of commands in Arabic from Hadad. Wael gave the pilots a departing look, removed a grenade from his webbing, and disappeared through the door.

Captain Hendrickson watched the head terrorist as a crooked smile came from one side of his mouth.

Below, the passenger deck instantly was filled with the noise coming from the forward cabin. Wael bounded down the stairs from the lounge and trotted down the left-side aisle, screaming in his native Arabic. The sound, a pulsing wail, was a tirade of gibberish to nearly all of the passengers, but frightening still.

Abu ran forward from the aft cabin to meet Wael. The huge terrorist was waving his Uzi in one hand and displaying a pinless grenade in the other. Those with aisle seats leaned away from the ranting Arab. The two terrorists exchanged a few sentences before Wael moved forward again, taunting the hostages. Abu followed closely. From the rear Abdul walked slowly, almost casually, chewing a mouthful of dates. He, too, pulled the pin from a grenade and held it above his head for all to see.

Abu watched as the wild man erupted from his comrade.

His sub-machine gun occasionally pointed at a single target, usually a woman, who would begin to cry. Wael thought that it was great fun to frighten the Americans. It was so easy. They cringed at the sight of the massive, dark figure standing over them. A few times he would hold the grenade inches from a terrified face and berate the person with invectives they could not understand. Some were stoic and stubborn. Wael could see those and avoided them—he was going for an effect. One elderly man protested when his wife was the recipient of Wael's furor. The metal shock of his Uzi smashed dead center on the man's face, breaking the nose and sending him backward into his seat where his wife shielded him with her body.

A few rows forward Wael stopped and called for Abu. His eyes were fixed on a man in the center seat on the left.

"You." Abu pointed to the man. "Are you alone?"

Uncertainty as to whether or not he should answer kept him silent.

"You are alone! You are! Hands on your head—now!" The hands came up, and the chosen one looked to those next to him, but they just looked away. "Get up! Get *up!*" Abu kept the Uzi leveled at the man as he slowly rose. His light blue shirt was untucked and wrinkled, and his shaggy hair was obviously only hand-combed. He still spoke nothing as he squeezed past a bespectacled young lady whose hands covered her mouth.

"Move forward. Up the stairs." The gun directed him with forceful jabs in the back. Wael followed, leaving Abdul to watch the hostages. He stood by the forward galley. It gave him a good vantage point from which to survey the front section and all the way to the rear of the aircraft, down the left aisle.

The door to the cockpit opened. Hadad held it back so the pilots could see into the lounge. Buzz saw the man standing a few feet from the door. His hands were atop his head, and his feet were slightly parted. He was young, maybe twenty-three or twenty-four. Probably one of the thousands of grad students from America who ventured to Europe each summer. Just a kid.

Captain Hendrickson looked away from the confused young

man. *A sacrifice, then. That's the lesson*. He looked up again to Hadad. "Don't." It was said as a wishful command. He knew nothing else to say.

"Watch and learn, Cap-tan." Hadad clicked the selector switch on his Uzi to single shot. The safety was already off. With one hand he aimed at the center of the man's chest and fired a single 9mm round, propelling his upper body backward. His hands came down from his head as he fell, but never made it to a position to break the fall. Unconsciousness enveloped him before his body hit the floor. He lay with his leg apart and arms outstretched to each side. Two streams of blood came from the wound, one on each side of the chest, turning the brown carpet a darker shade. The eyes were open but lifeless. They stared at the ceiling with an expression of confusion still on the face.

"Put the body on the wing." Hadad left the door open. Abu and Wael lifted the body by the arms and legs. They carried it to the stairs and dropped it with a swing onto the steps, letting gravity do the work. A few seconds later screams from below could be heard on the flight deck.

The captain felt what fingernails he had dig into the sturdy padding of the armrest. Buzz simply turned away

"Now, Cap-tan, have you learned what will happen when you defy me?" There was no answer, just a look. Hadad couldn't tell what it meant. "Get the plane ready."

Hendrickson and his first officer felt sick as they quietly began the preflight routine by reflex. It was instinct now, just a survival drive. Get the aircraft ready, up, and down again safely—wherever that might be. Their duties would take over their minds and put the ugly incident away. Not gone, just away.

Hadad had calculated this one perfectly. They would obey his commands, for they feared too much for their passengers. He smiled at their backs as they chattered and twisted dials and pressed buttons. *Tough old American soldiers, you forget too easily*.

Fort Belvoir

The watch teams were constantly monitoring Benina, as they had since the initial catch of the aircraft. It hadn't been difficult considering its stationary position. Mostly they were zooming in and out on the scene, and once Number 8601 had needed to be moved to avoid some thick cloud cover. The team at Belvoir knew the severity of the situation, at least the situation they were aware of. At CSOC in Colorado Springs the controllers were monitoring their own dilemma: Number 8601 was almost out of fuel. So desperate was it that the general at CSOC insisted on a direct order from the secretary before maneuvering his $1 billion bird.

On the seventy-inch monitor scenes were replayed over and over in real time. Soldiers would sit on or around a military vehicle. One would leave, then come back. Officers would occasionally walk into the frame to survey the aircraft or talk to the troops. One, a short, balding man— a captain, they thought—was a frequent visitor. Every second was recorded on tape and disk, to be later enlarged, enhanced, and analyzed, though "later" meant half an hour as opposed to a few weeks under usual circumstances.

"Gotcha," the senior tech exclaimed. She was former Navy out only a few years.

"Tape and VDI are nominal, Jen. What's up?"

"Starboard wing door, foreground. That's . . . what's the number?"

The junior tech looked at his notes. "Number three door." He entered something on the side keyboard. "Got it. Mark 1347 local, 1247 Zulu. Look there." A light cursor in the shape of an arrow moved across to the point. "That's a pumper; they're gonna fuel."

"Oh God." Jenny's eyes focused on the number three door. "Shit!"

"Zoom in, Matt. Just a little."

The image grew of a person stepping onto the wing. It was a man. He wore military clothing, but there was no weapon. It was obvious why.

He dragged the body by its feet out to a spot above the inboard engine. A second man emerged and walked out on the wing, holding two weapons while they stood next to the body. They reentered a minute later. The body lay faceup with its arms outstretched and above the head, as though crucified.

"They drew first blood, Jen."

"Yeah. You better call the super in."

Jenny continued to watch as the supervisor was summoned. Not long after the men left the wing the pumper truck connected its hoses to the underground pipeline and to the underside of the 747's wing. Topping off the tanks didn't take long; little fuel was used between Athens and Benghazi. When fueling was complete a tow vehicle darted under the wing and hooked up to the nosewheel.

Moments later, with the supervisor in the watch center, the big jet was pushed back from the spot it had occupied for just over a day. All the troops were gone. Just the aircraft and the tow vehicle were in frame.

The supervisor asked for the phone. "Get me a line to the White House." He held the phone to his ear, waiting for the connection.

"There she goes," Matt said. The tow unhooked and moved out of frame. He increased the field of view to include the entire tarmac just as the four turbofans came to life.

Flight 422

The four engines whined at idle, not fast enough to move her but sufficient to circulate fluids within the turbines and provide power to the other systems. Hendrickson gave the instruments a final check.

"Can I contact the tower for weather and clearance?" the captain asked.

"There is no need." The answer came from behind. "Just fly."

In front was a shimmering road of cement—the taxiway—that ran parallel to the runway. Both pilots looked over the taxiway. It was covered with a layer of dust, with drifting swirls, reminiscent of sandbars stretching the width of the thoroughfare.

"Hand me those binocs," the captain said. Buzz handed the glasses over, watching as Hendrickson dialed in and scanned the runway from left to right, leaning forward to his console for a better vantage. Its condition wasn't any better than the taxiway. "That thing hasn't been swept in days." He realized they had landed on all the crud scattered over it. "Look." The glasses were passed back to Buzz.

"So what do we do different?" Buzz asked from behind the binoculars.

"Besides pray? I don't know." The captain sat back and twisted his body into what should have been a comfortable position, but wasn't.

"Here." Buzz handed the performance calculations over. These were figured by a computer and took into account the aircraft's weight and load, altitude of the airport, and weather conditions present. They were always hand-checked by the first officer, then displayed along with other information on the displays. Still, there was an element of uncertainty. "Some of it's just a guess."

"I know."

"I allowed an extra five knots, just in case," Buzz added. His tone didn't display much confidence in his words, which got him a furrowed-brow look from the captain. "I don't have any idea what they loaded."

Hendrickson looked at the written figures. "Let's try it."

Takeoff and landing for a commercial aircraft are considered the times when the likelihood for a disastrous event is highest, necessitating procedures that assumed the worst would happen. The pilot held a firm grip on his stick, the co-pilot "backing up" the captain, ready to take over in the unlikely event that a medical problem, such as a heart attack, should strike him at a critical moment.

The worst was also planned for when considering mechanical performance. Everything assumed that the most important part of the aircraft would fail at the most crucial time during takeoff or landing. Where takeoff was concerned, the engines were the major system. Their performance, or lack of it, was the basis for calculating several variable airspeed "barriers" that aided a pilot when deciding whether to go ahead with or abort a takeoff. V-1 was the speed at which the decision to proceed had to be made and the last point at which a takeoff could be aborted by reversing the engines and applying full braking power. Beyond V-1 an abort would surely end up in a fiery slide past the runway's end. V-R indicated the speed at which the aircraft would be generating sufficient lift for a safe takeoff and climb-out, allowing the pilots to nose up—or rotate—the aircraft.

There was a gentle forward push on the back of the captain's right hand as he and Buzz advanced the numbers one and four engine throttle levers. The *Maiden* lurched up and forward, coming back down on the nose gear shocks with a pronounced bounce. Turbine compression increased in the two outboards, moving the aircraft slowly onto the taxiway, where the captain turned her to the right, lining up on the yellow center line. The ground speed crawled upward.

"Jesus, Bart. We should be rolling easy at this thrust-to-weight!"

They were an eighth of the way to the threshold area, and rolling way too slowly. Captain Hendrickson moved his aircraft to the left side of the taxiway, then to the extreme right, testing the feel of the *Maiden*. She was heavy. Sluggish was a good word, but not completely descriptive. The bird was . . . unbalanced, almost like she wanted to do a wheel stand. He touched the throttles forward a bit, then backed off, getting the same forward rise and lurch as before. Buzz looked over to him, and they both knew. Their aircraft was too heavy, and misloaded. Her center of gravity had been altered, by how much they would find out once airborne—if they got that far.

"We're damn heavy," Buzz said. "I didn't figure on *this*. Man, we feel real heavy."

"I know." The captain brought her back to center. "She's mushy on the ground, like we're steering with a flat nosewheel."

Buzz checked the overhead panels for any reds: There were none. The weight of the new cargo was going to present a big enough problem without having to worry about any minor system glitches. And just what was the weight? He wanted to ask—politely deferent, if necessary—but remembered the wrath of the hijacker. Buzz would love to get a crack at him, just a chance to snap his shit-brown neck, but not at the risk of another passenger's death. Not him. The handiwork was readily apparent on the wing, and he tried not to think about what was going to happen to the body when the aircraft accelerated down the runway.

The nose of the big Boeing came sharply left at the end of the taxiway, and a hundred yards farther came left again onto the runway. Brakes were applied and the throttles brought back to hold the *Maiden* steady. The strip before them was too short for their weight. Both pilots knew it. They would never leave pavement.

"We're beyond spec," Buzz pointed out, referring to the hot, thin air of the midday desert that would further complicate a liftoff. "What do you think?"

The captain analyzed the question. Conventional approaches could be cast aside for now. After all, the only certainty was that they were going to dig a long trench in the desert sand at the end of the ten-thousand-foot runway. He figured they would need at least twelve thousand feet to get enough speed up. Unless . . .

"Buzz, we need speed, right?"

"Yeah," he answered quizzically

It was a radical idea for a nonafterburning jet, possibly ludicrous when applied to the 747. "We're going to roll with the flaps retracted, smooth-skinned. That'll give us speed."

"But lift? We can't rotate without flaps."

The captain pointed to the console. "Look, you call out speed, like usual. Just add ten knots to rotation. We'll use up a hell of a lot of runway, I know, but we'll be fast enough. At V-R you hit the flaps—ten degrees."

"That can rip the wings off." But it might work. Buzz smiled at the runway and sighed a dry breath. In a way the thought excited him. "Just like flying a Harrier off a jump ramp."

They would trade assured lift for speed, and throw lift in at the last moment, a risky move that very well could bring the first officer's worry to reality. No one knew if the wings could take the stress, or even if the flaps would extend under the force created by the forward motion. Commercial aircraft were not designed for this.

"You ready?"

Buzz nodded.

"We firewall them on my mark."

"Okay."

Hendrickson stretched his hand around the four levers, arching his fingers to touch each of the plastic caps. His palm tensed. "Now!"

They pushed the throttles forward as quickly as the built-in resistance would allow. The cockpit rose up as before and settled down as the aircraft began moving.

Hadad heard the words from his seat behind the pilots, but he was not concerned. Everything had been prepared for. All the calculations were long since made. The plane would fly. The added load could be handled easily by the giant jet—his knowledgeable comrades had assured him of this. It would be so.

The jet blast from the *Maiden*'s four engines sent rocks and other debris flying from the runway and its edges as the aircraft gained speed.

"Damn!" The captain watched the airspeed increase slowly—too slowly.

Buzz pushed on the captain's hand, holding the throttles full open. The turbines were sucking fuel from the integral wing tanks in huge gulps as they approached 100 percent capacity, a measure of performance they would surpass. Operating beyond full capacity was possible, but not recommended for any period of time. "It's gonna be close," he said, louder than he realized. The aircraft passed the halfway point on the runway.

Those who flew did so with an instinctive ability to sense performance beyond what the mechanical indicators told them. For some it was a feeling in the gut, literally, one that told them whether the aircraft was going too slow or fast, or if some meteorological condition was affecting it. Captain Hendrickson felt the *Maiden*'s bulk beneath. It moved slowly, but there was increasing acceleration.

"V-one," Buzz called out. The 747 was already beyond the halfway marker by a thousand feet.

"We go," the captain decided, though that had been fated. He held the throttles forward.

Buzz kept his eyes on the rising speed indicator, not the ever-shortening slab of pavement which was now three quarters gone. The electronic needle crept past the first calculated V-R speed . . . less than ten knots to go.

A uneasy expression covered Michael's face. He gripped Sandy's arm with one hand, and the armrest with the other. Something felt wrong. The speed was too high. His stomach told him so. His hand squeezed, feeling his wife's soft flesh.

Silently, he willed the jet to fly.

Captain Hendrickson was invoking the same prayer when his first officer shouted, "V-R!"

"Rotate." Hendrickson pulled the stick back in a smooth motion while Buzz brought the flaps down.

The *Clipper Atlantic Maiden's* nose rose in response to the downward pressure on the elevators, which were located on the trailing edge of the horizontal stabilizers at the jet's rear. The most obvious motion, though, was the vertical jump that accompanied the lowering of the flaps. Buzz's body bent slightly forward from the force of the upward surge.

"Shit!"

"We're up!" the captain exclaimed.

Buzz retracted the gear without prompting. The aircraft responded to the reduced drag with more speed. The climb-out was on a gentle slope—no jump into the sky for noise abatement reasons. Instead, the *Maiden* skimmed above the glistening desert floor at two hundred knots, gaining speed and altitude at a mild, but acceptable rate.

"My stick," the captain announced as they passed through fifteen hundred feet. Buzz released his soft backing grip and checked the displays thoroughly.

"Number three's acting up."

"Like usual."

"It's hot." Buzz took out the performance manual. "Down four percent—no, five percent."

"We'll back all of them off twenty percent when we pass eight thousand."

"Gotcha," Buzz agreed.

They continued to take the jet up and over the water, oblivious to Hadad, who stood from his seat and now crouched behind them, looking through the thick windshield. He would rather look behind, but what was the point. Several months ago he had left his home, and now he was leaving without seeing his friend. The colonel had worked tirelessly to bring the mission, once just a concept, to reality, and the effort had weakened him further. Hadad would pray for him.

Now it was time for instructions. "Fly two-seven-oh, at thirty thousand."

Neither pilot responded verbally to the command—they simply acted upon it, banking the *Maiden* to the left in a smooth, fluid turn. The captain knew he had his hands full with the unbalanced load. Trim would be a problem, especially later as fuel was burned and the balance further changed.

They both concentrated on their flying, trying to keep thoughts of how they had left a passenger behind in the dark, quiet recesses of their minds. It was horrific. Benghazi was behind them, and what was ahead neither knew.

"Set reduced thrust."

Buzz followed the instructions, selecting reduced climb thrust on the Thrust Control Panel.

"At reduced thrust," Buzz announced. He noted the altitude. "Passing eight-five-hundred."

"Spell me?" the captain requested.

"Sure." Buzz gripped his column. "My stick."

"Slow and easy climb. The trim is lousy," Hendrickson said unenthusiastically.

The *Maiden* rose into the sky, finding the cool, thin air that made its ascent slow. It would be a full thirty-five minutes to thirty thousand feet.

The captain checked the instruments, trying to occupy his consciousness. Everything was as it should be, save number three. The mere fact that the wings were still attached could be construed as a positive. But he cared little about the technicalities at the moment. They were small, infinitesimal concerns that would not be able to hold his attention. His thoughts were elsewhere, back at Benina, somewhere along the runway.

Benina

The checkpoint was gone.

Muhadesh slowed his Range Rover, then stopped. Where the tank had been was now only a wide circle of disturbed hard sand and track marks onto the road. They had gone, by the way of the main road from the direction of the tracks. He put it back in gear and continued on.

Two minutes later he again stopped, this time at a guard shack on the north side of Benina's control tower, and was promptly waved through on recognition by the two smil-

ing guards. Muhadesh was well known to the garrison at
Benina, whose company and conversation he preferred to the
ideologues back at the camp. These soldiers were from the
rabble: common people, not very sophisticated, most from
the arid regions far from the city. They were like him, doing
their duty. Some did it reluctantly, some willingly. Few
of them understood the significance of their government's
attitude toward the Western world, or to their Arab neighbor
states. In conversation with them, topics such as goats, and
old people, and the joy of swimming in the waters of the
Mediterranean were common. It was refreshing, a welcome
and too seldom respite from everyday happenings.

Muhadesh brought the vehicle around to the front of the
tower, the bottom floor of which was the airport garrison's
command post. The implied formality of the term held little
stock here. A lone lieutenant, his shirt open to the waist,
dozed with his feet up while an old metal fan high on the
wall struggled uselessly to cool the room.

The creak of the tattered screen door awakened the disheveled junior officer.

"Captain Algar!" The lieutenant sat up, struggling against
the liberal reclining springs of the old wooden chair. He
noticed the captain's lowered stare and began buttoning his
tunic.

"Good morning, Lieutenant. Or is it afternoon? I thought
you might be waking from a good night's sleep." Muhadesh
strode from one side of the CP to the other, his hands behind
his back, eyeing the lieutenant alternately as he feigned a
cursory inspection. "Is this your usual dress at your post?"

"No," came the answer, and with it the second from the
top button.

The look was the next interrogative.

"It has been a long night, sir." He fingered some papers
on the desk, as if they were some magic explanation. "A
very long night. And today's heat . . . as always, it takes
your strength."

"Mmm." Muhadesh picked up a heavy paperweight, toss-
ing it up over and over. "Lieutenant . . . ?"

"Hafez."

"Lieutenant Hafez, where is Captain Ibrahim Sadr?"

"Sadr?" He looked to the piles of work.

A heavy, flat hand came down on a stack of files. "*I* am asking you . . . not your unfinished work. Now, again, where is Captain Sadr?"

"Sir, he left when the American plane departed."

"Where?"

A swallow, justified by fear of the captain's legendary, if seldom exhibited wrath, preceded the reply from the wide-eyed officer. "I do not know. He . . . he did not say."

Eyes bored into the junior officer. *You tell the truth.* "Did he have anything with him? A duffel, possibly?"

The lieutenant shook his head, which was enough of an answer. Muhadesh had a good idea what it meant. Sadr would not have gone directly back to Tripoli, not the prissy captain who was the "model" of a perfect officer. It was a joke, though one not funny in the least.

"Thank you, Lieutenant." Muhadesh left the CP without further discussion and departed the airport by the way he came, waving at the guards as he passed through the gate.

The drive to the camp would be short. He would go there first, and a bit later into Benghazi. Muhadesh would have preferred that it be a clean, simple job. If Sadr had been here, it might have taken less time. He could have lured the prima dona into the open spaces outside of the airport, where things would be less conspicuous. As it was, that was not to be. He would venture into the city and punctuate his departure, making life in his homeland impossible.

And it would be worthwhile. He thought for a moment as he drove. Yes, it would be, but for whom?

The White House

Was this a normal reaction? the president wondered. He was angrier than he had ever been, at the hijackers, the Libyans, even at himself, though that was caused by the frustration and helplessness he felt. Vengeance was on his mind, and he knew that wasn't right.

"Has there been any success contacting the Libyans?"

Bud shook his head.

"Sir, even their UN ambassador can't get through," Gonzales added.

The president scoffed at that. "He's falling in line."

"She, sir," the COS corrected him.

Bud felt underdressed. The president and chief of staff were dressed somberly for the viewing at eleven.

"What about the body?"

"Satellite evidence indicates it's still on the runway," Bud answered. "We'll work with the Red Cross to have it returned, as soon as the Libyans open up."

In an hour and a half he would be walking past the body of the slain president, its casket closed for obvious reasons. He would offer a silent prayer for the man, but what could he do for the other murdered American? As president he was expected to provide leadership and answers for the American people. What would he tell them? What could possibly be done to end this madness of terror against innocents? He didn't know, but he would have to. The public would want a solution. Lip service and hollow offerings, as had been the norm in the past, would not suffice. That was not his way. Whatever was decided would have to satisfy *his* sense of right as well as that of the people, and it would have to be effective.

"And some of our speculation appears to have been at least close to the mark," Bud said. "I want to show you the last part again." He rewound the tape for only a few seconds. "Now here we see the aircraft start its takeoff roll. It's going awfully slow—this is actual time, no compression or slow mo—and here"—Bud pointed to the screen with his pen, leaning in—"we have four good exhausts from the engines, so it appears to be very heavy. Moderately overweight at the least. She's passing the halfway point here."

They had watched the tape only a few minutes earlier. The scene still caused the president to grimace. The small object on the right wing slid backward and off. It disappeared out of frame as the aircraft continued on.

"And now . . ." Bud touched the remote, freezing the picture. "This is where they lift off. See, the shadow is changing horizontally under and to the side of the nose." He let the image progress, then froze it again. "And the main gear. That's only about two hundred feet from sand."

"That's one hell of a pilot," the president commented.

The COS opened his folio. "His name is Bart Hendrickson. He flew big Air Force stuff. Eight years total in uniform. He's been with the airline for about thirty years. Their home office says he's about as experienced as one can get. His co-pilot is a former Marine fighter pilot, Adam Elkins."

"The Agency is working on some weight estimates," Bud said.

"But . . . ?" The president urged a continuance.

"But so far it only adds weight to the worst-case scenario."

Gonzales's folio slapped shut. "Sir, these developments are serious. The rules have changed."

"Ellis, please." The president stood and took a few steps, then turned back to face his aides.

"What Ellis means, sir, is that the tide of events has turned. In Britain the SAS would be called in—formally. That's the way the British do it. There is no second chance for the terrorists once they've shed blood. Negotiations are used only to buy time and put the situation in the best possible position for action. We have now reached that point and the only decision we should have to make is which party is the culprit. And, what will be the best response to the situation."

He felt old, and if the president could have seen his own face with its pursing lips, he would be aghast at the gesture. "I agree. Recommendations?"

"Sir, we put Delta in a go mode and put them in the air."

The COS nodded agreement.

"To where, Bud?"

"That aircraft is going to have to set down somewhere. We can have Delta there, either ahead of them or right behind. No matter where that may be, all Delta has to do is shadow them until they show their hand. In-flight refueling can keep them up as long as we need."

"It's at least a lot more than we're doing now," Gonzales added.

The president gestured a go. "Make it happen, Bud. Any final authorization comes from me."

"Understood."

"Does Granger have the contingency plans ready?"

"I've looked over the preliminary report," Bud answered. "He's going to present a full, detailed runthrough today."

"Good. Bud, I need your review ASAP. I'll be back from the viewing about twelve-thirty."

"Yes, sir." Bud knew that ASAP did not mean whenever you can get to it—it meant now.

"I'm sorry you can't attend," the president said apologetically. Bud had admired the late president greatly. But . . .

"So am I, Mr. President."

Springer Seven-Three

The Frisbee-shaped dome above the E3 AWACS rotated continuously. Inside, a crew considerably larger than that of Hammer Two-Seven monitored the progress of the hijacked jet and the pair of swept-wing F-14s from the *Vinson* on its tail. They had arrived on station just east of Gibraltar a few moments earlier and, after clearing the airspace around them, had begun tracking Flight 422 as it headed west.

"Target, course change," the chief radar operator announced.

The commander swiveled his chair, stood, and walked down three consoles. He plugged his headset into the auxiliary jack. "Where's he going, Lieutenant?"

"Two-six-oh true, sir. Right for the Strait."

"And us. He's angels three-zero, huh?" the green-suited commander asked.

"Yes, sir."

A flip of the intercom selector switch connected him to the cockpit. "Pilot, take us up. We've got a target, angels three-zero, range one hundred, and he's coming straight on at three hundred plus. Clear us. Copy?" After the acknowledgment he switched back to cabin intercom.

"Holding two-six-oh true, sir."

"Yep. Com, get those Navy jocks back to their boat. That bird belongs to Air Force now."

"Roger that." The radar operator smiled.

Benghazi

Revolution Avenue was a row of ivory-colored low-rise buildings in the eastern section of Benghazi. They were exclusive buildings, all apartments that the "average" Libyan could never hope to live in, or enter. Government officials and ranking military officers were the privileged few who could secure an apartment there, for use as a primary residence or a second "home."

Muhadesh entered the center tower at Number 7 through the simply landscaped courtyard which continued into the structure as an atrium. The decor was sparse but attractive, something unusual in a country where niceties were often associated with the wickedness of the West, and strange when the living conditions of its people were considered. He didn't consider himself to be a socially conscious person, but it did bother him. What meager resources his country had were supposed to provide as good a life as possible for the people. Muhadesh knew better, having seen where the money went.

The sounds of the afternoon traffic faded with the closing of the elevator doors, replaced by the hum and friction sounds as he was lifted to the fourth floor. Captain Ibrahim Sadr's apartment was halfway down the magenta-carpeted hall that ran straight from the elevator. Muhadesh could see the entire corridor from the elevator. On his left were the odd-numbered rooms: 401, 403, 405, 407 . . . and 409, the one he wanted. He approached the door, removing the pistol from inside his coat and placing it in his back waistband. His toughened hand knocked for thirty seconds before the door opened fully.

Captain Sadr, wearing a white bathrobe, stood framed by the doorway. His bushy black mustache and hair showed evidence of sleep, or . . .

Of course, Muhadesh thought. *Slime, through and through.*

"Captain Ibrahim Sadr?" Muhadesh knew it was, but needed to size up his quarry. He put both hands on his hips, bringing the right one closer to the Beretta.

"Yes. Who are you?" Sadr asked impatiently, leaning on the open door and obviously annoyed at the intrusion.

"Captain Muhadesh Algar—Third Training Battalion. May I speak to you privately?" Both hands were now behind his back at an "at rest" stance, with the right hand gripping the compact pistol.

Sadr looked at Muhadesh incredulously. "I am occupied, idi—"

The last word froze in his throat. Muhadesh brought the gun up from his waistband and pointed it at Sadr's center of mass. Simultaneously, his left hand gathered at the captain's loose robe collar, pushing him inside as he quietly ordered silence. With a kick of his foot the door closed behind.

"Wha—"

The silencer touched Sadr's lips. It convinced him.

Muhadesh removed an altered pair of handcuffs from his jacket. They looked strangely like leg irons, less the chain, these being connected by a length of steel cable.

"Turn around," Muhadesh whispered. Sadr turned and reflexively brought his hands behind his back, aware of what was happening now. He was pushed firmly against the wall and cuffed. The chromed steel was cold, but worse, it was tight—very tight. Muhadesh spun him roughly to his right to face the hall. It led to an open area, a gathering room, and to another hall on the right.

"Where is she?"

Sadr gulped his spit. "The bedroom."

Muhadesh followed the directional shake of the head down the hall to the right, with his prisoner ahead. The three doors at the end were all closed.

"Which one?"

"Ibrahim." The distinctly female voice, sounding perturbed at the apparent interruption of activities, pierced the door on the right.

"Stay quiet, my friend." Muhadesh put Sadr to his front and opened the door quickly with his gun hand. Both men stepped into the Spartan bedroom, surprising the pretty woman who sat upright against the headboard. Her upper body was exposed to the intruder. She was not a very young woman, but extremely beautiful, which surprised Muhadesh. He had pegged Sadr as one who would like the fresh, youthful girls, as did he. It was not a proud self-admission.

"Ibrahim!" Her voice was pleading now. Reflexively she brought her hands up to cover her ample breasts, then set them back on the sheet at either side, clutching the white linen into bunches. She looked terrified. Sadr saw her eyes widen and wondered why. He couldn't see the slender silenced pistol come up below his right elbow, but he did hear a pair of muffled pops. Muhadesh put two hollow-point rounds into her head, one entering dead center on her forehead and the other just below the left eye. Her head was slammed back against the wooden headboard with a fleshy crack. Before it flopped forward a small fountain of blood spurted onto her face, torso, and the sheets, turning them a dark red. Death made the muscles contract, become rigid, then relax, causing the body to fall sideways onto the pillows.

"What?"

"Quiet, my friend." Muhadesh tugged the captain back into the hall and led him from behind into the gathering room. There was a prayer mat near the window, a sight that quietly angered the onetime doctor of death. For all his doubts and transgressions, he was devout in his beliefs, applying the teachings of the Koran to himself as much as possible. It disturbed him that he was not pure in his following of Islam, but it bothered him more that his prima dona was going to commit adultery and then offer himself up for forgiveness and salvation during afternoon prayers.

"On your stomach," Muhadesh commanded. Sadr fell on his front with unwanted help from his captor.

"What do you want?" Sadr turned his head from side to side, trying to see his tormentor. A boot was pressed on the small of his back, the cable between the cuffs underfoot.

"Captain Sadr, you will tell me what I require, or you will die most unpleasantly. Do you understand?"

"You will not succeed, Algar. Aaah!"

The knee pressed on the back of the struggling physicist, causing a sharp pain that was centered just above his buttocks. It was only a hint of what was to come. Muhadesh pulled the cable up to Sadr's head, twisting it halfway before looping it over and around his neck until both hands were pulled high up on the back, each nearly touching the opposite shoulder blade. There was a painful grunt, then a raspy groaning as the cable was pulled taut across Sadr's throat below the notch of his Adam's apple.

"Cahhh! Cahhh!" He couldn't scream with any force, and struggling to keep his hands high enough to relax the pull was useless; the human body's muscles didn't work to that extent. The strangle hold continued.

Muhadesh produced another set of restraints, similar to the first but with longer cables and larger cuffs. He locked one around one ankle, looped the cable over that connecting the hands, and clicked the other one around the other ankle.

Sadr's feet were pulled up to his butt by the connection. The resulting pull made the already deadly choking all the more painful and frightening.

"Now, Captain Sadr, enjoy your predicament for a moment before I come to the purpose of my visit." He watched his captive struggle to slacken the cable that was starving his lungs of oxygen. The heavy infantry boot kept him planted solidly facedown on the carpet. Soon his chest would feel the fire of asphyxiation, but first . . .

"Aagh. Cahh." The guttural gasping was wet and weak, and was followed by a strained hissing as Muhadesh released the tension pulling the wrist cuffs toward the head.

"The air is sweet, eh? Yes, yes. You are aware of my background, surely, and you must know that simply allowing you to strangle yourself would just not do. I have better ways, much better ways. But," Muhadesh said, kneeling down on the floor and putting his face close to the carpeting, "we do not have to go that route. You can tell me what I require, and . . . you go free."

The sweat beaded down from Sadr's forehead into his eyes. He tried to blink it away, unsuccessfully, and salty drops began to sting his bulging eyes.

"Now, very simply, I will ask you—what did you supervise the loading of onto the American plane?"

"Traitor!"

The raspy words of contempt and accusation elicited no emotional response.

"What was it that was loaded?"

Sadr's silence was met with a renewal of the strangling wire's tightening. As he once again fought to breathe, Muhadesh removed a small switchblade from his back pocket, clicking its three-inch double-edge blade open. He pushed the sharp point into the soft flesh and muscle where the captain's right leg joined his buttock. There was an attempted scream through the constricted throat, sounding more like a great rumbling caught high in his chest. Sadr's squirming only added to the pain of the knife, which Muhadesh continually applied pressure to.

The blade was suddenly withdrawn and wiped on the robe. The pressure of the cable was also relieved once again.

"Ah! . . . No . . . Ah."

"Now, my friend, you will answer the question. If you resist again, you will die in pain."

Muhadesh looked over the prostrate captain. The Darling of Tajoura was helpless, a victim of his own weakness. He had seen Sadr in his element while training a group of Iranian Revolutionary Guards for a possible suicide attack on the Israeli Dimona research reactor. Arrogant. Ruthless with his subordinates. A precise, calculating leader, who tolerated no lapses in performance, even in himself. He made no mistakes, except, as Muhadesh now knew, in his personal life.

When he had received the strange-looking photograph in a fax he had recognized it instantly. The profile, even with the cartoonlike enhancement, was unmistakably Captain Ibrahim Sadr. It was amazing, the technological wizardry of the Americans. Where it came from he could only guess.

"Once more, Captain, you know the question."

A click of the knife blade was all that was needed. Captain Sadr was not a hardened soldier trained in the methods of resistance. His rank was ceremonial, bestowed upon him years earlier by a grateful Colonel Qaddafi, who wanted the European-educated physicist bound by the honor of the Libyan Army uniform. Sadr enjoyed the recognition and privileges that came with the smart-looking dress greens, but that was where the charade of honor ended. Discipline and a stomach for resistance did not come with the trousers and tunic. He could not bear the thought of more pain, or the agony of oxygen deprivation. Muhadesh listened carefully for the five minutes it took his source to explain the particulars. He asked a few questions, which were promptly answered. There were some things he would need to take note of, including diagraming a device from the description. That could be sketched in his pocket notebook once he left. First . . .

Ibrahim Sadr felt the cable tighten again just as he exhaled. He wished he had inhaled first, something that made the other short stretches without air just bearable, but soon he realized that it did not matter. It did not abate this time. There was no saving breath to quench his lungs' desire. His usefulness had been exhausted. Fighting would do no good. He simply closed his eyes, his last conscious, voluntary act.

The body twitched and shook involuntarily as the captain's dying brain lost control of its host. A few minutes later the alimentary canal opened, releasing bodily refuse and fluids. It was a most unpleasant smell that followed, though it did not bother Muhadesh—he was already in the courtyard four floors below, walking casually to his vehicle. He was calm, truly. The information-gathering part of his mission was done. The rest would be easy. Confidence came with the rank.

The Pentagon

"A very thoroughly thought-out operation," Bud commented as the briefing ended. "Thank you."

The Joint Chiefs director of Operations laid the pointer on the map wall ledge before leaving. His briefing had been comprehensive and intelligent. Concentrated air strikes from B-52s and Navy Intruders, with overwhelming air cover, would decimate the Libyan military. Marines choppered into the drilling and processing sites would destroy the colonel's petroleum industry for years to come. There was no doubt in Bud's mind that the plan could accomplish what it set out to.

"General, would you walk me out to the pad?"

"Certainly," Granger answered.

The Blackhawk's rotors were still. A light rain was falling, keeping the two men under the canopy at building's edge.

"I'm going back to the White House to get ready," Bud said, pulling his overcoat collar up. "This weather is weird."

"Getting colder—in September, yet!" Granger put his cap on. "So, is it a go?"

He couldn't authorize a strike and he didn't even know if he would recommend carrying it out. "Only the president can do that."

"You can get the ball rolling."

Granger sounded impatient to Bud. "General, I asked you out here to ask you a question—will this operation have the desired effect? Honestly."

"For Christ's sake, Bud! What do you take me for? Do you think I'd put my stamp on a plan that wouldn't work?"

Bud held a hand up, palm toward the general. "Let me rephrase that. Is the effect that is anticipated the one that will *really* do the most damage?"

The general understood the line now. What *would* be most effective? "Bud . . . we can't create the perfect solution in an imperfect world. It just doesn't happen that way. The people we're trying to stop are criminals, plain and simple, and they've created their own safe haven where the only way to get them is with an operation like this. I know what you mean, Bud. It is frustrating, but what do you propose we do . . . nothing? Where would that get us?"

A whine started low and grew louder, rising steadily in volume from the near UH-60 as the rotors started to spin.

"It's the same as before: We hit them, they react. Back and forth. Back and forth."

"The eighty-six strike put a crimp in their style," Granger pointed out.

"Really?" Bud asked, semicynically. "Look where we are now. Remember when the Soviets had some diplomats kidnapped in Lebanon some years back? Right around the time we were losing people left and right there. Do you know what they did—unofficially? They let a four-man Spetsnaz team loose with carte blanche. Those responsible for the abductions soon found some of *their* family members missing, and a few showed up on the doorsteps in pieces. One guy's uncle had his balls snipped off and shoved in his mouth before they shipped his body home. Pretty, huh?"

The general's face was covered with a sour expression. "Thanks for the graphics. Are you proposing we do the same? An eye for an eye, before we lose our eye? Let me tell you, you're sounding awful contradictory considering your lack of enthusiasm for this operation."

"I am not proposing anything. But I think we could learn something from the Soviet action: They had no more problems in Beirut."

Granger turned to the helicopter, and then away. Its rotors were turning at speed now, kicking up spray off the wet ground. "Well, I wish things were that simple for us, but they're not. We're the Great Satan, remember?"

The NSA laughed. "We always get the best titles."

"So what do we do?"

"Knowing my feelings, what do you recommend?" Bud asked.

"Let's get the assets in place and ready."

One step closer, Bud thought. "All right. Have the 52s ready to launch. I'll notify the president." He tossed a polite salute before heading for the helo.

A moment later the Blackhawk jumped skyward and circled to the left, heading back to the White House. Bud looked at his watch. They would soon be paying respects to the slain chief executive. The thought that he was absent bothered him. He had to be at the center of the storm, trying to bring things safely to an end. Really, though, he was an adviser to the chess player who would move the pawns. Some of the moves would be executed soon, which was Delta's hope. Bud hoped they would get the chance to checkmate the opponent, otherwise any action would seem like vengeance. It might have been that anyway, he realized.

Whatever happened, he would be safe and secure in the nation's capital. That thought didn't bother him—it pissed him off.

Springer Seven-Three

The AWACS was now west of Gibraltar, following much the same course it had on the way into the Med, loitering slightly above a light weather system that was shrouding the North African coast on the Atlantic side for a thousand miles to the south.

Flight 422 was twenty-nine thousand feet, five thousand below that Sentry tracking it. A pair of F-16 Falcons from Spain stayed ten miles back of the hijacked jet.

"Target is changing course," the radar controller aboard the AWACS announced. "Coming left."

"Watch 'em. Give me a true. Com, let the Falcons know." The commander sat back. He was a full colonel with thirty years in the service and two wars under his belt. This, however, was an abomination in his eyes. Even wars had rules.

"Target, new course of two-zero-five. I show a slow descent."

"Cobra flight reports negative five hundred feet per minute," Com reported.

"Radar, give me a plot."

"Computing, sir."

Flight 422 was going somewhere, probably close. For a second the commander thought that it might be going down, but why the turn? No—there was a destination. *C'mon, baby, land.*

"Cobra flight on track," Com reported.

"Got it," the radar controller said. "Sir, target on a track to Tenerife."

"The Canaries. Com, alert the controllers on Tenerife, and get me a secure channel to the Pentagon."

The Capitol

Some of the most beautiful paintings ever rendered depicting events and people of early American history adorned the walls of the rotunda, beneath the classically pure Capitol dome. During the country's infancy, artists saw men and their deeds as subjects that would, and did, convey a sense of the awe felt by all at the birth of a new nation. The scenes were dark, with stem-faced people staring out to the circular room, or off into a distance not in the painting.

There was a portrait of Thomas Jefferson to the right of the entryway. It stared at the president as he walked past.

An honor guard stood at attention near the far side of the roped off area directly under the apex of the great dome. One member of each service made up the five-member guard. Their faces were frozen and emotionless. Even the blinking of their eyes seemed mechanical and precise.

The president and his aides approached the dark mahogany casket. It sat atop a riser draped with a deep red skirt, its lid closed and a single peach-colored rose lying on it. In contrast to the blank faces of the military presence, there *was* emotion visible on the president's ashen face. It was not sadness, though he felt that. Nor was it anger. It was reserved puzzlement, not really an appropriate response, but it was his way of reacting. No press was there to capture his expression, so he didn't mask his feelings. A man was in that box: a man who shortly before had been alive, respected, and loved. But now he was gone. *Why?*

How many had died? The president pondered that as he stood silently a few inches from the casket. He wanted to touch it, but was that proper? He hadn't been to a funeral since his dad's.

A hand touched his elbow. "Sir, it's time to go."

The president nodded. His chief of staff was right. He could stand and mourn, reflecting on the tragedy, the brutality, the waste. That would be easy. Or he could try to end it.

"I'm ready," the president said, ending his unceremonious visit.

12

••••••••••••

DOUBTS AND DECISIONS

Al-'Adiyat

IT WAS THE closest his soul had come to peace in years. But it was not enough. True serenity was yet to come. Soon.

Muhadesh sped past the newly placed outer guard post, manned by three lounging "regulars" who snapped to attention as their commander passed. *Indar's work.* It didn't surprise Muhadesh.

There were two other posts placed near the road into the camp, both close to the main permanent entrance. Upon nearing that, Muhadesh slowed and stopped, stepping out of the Range Rover to survey the chaos. Indar had done his usual best.

The first noticeable change was the absence of the many power poles that strung electrical and phone wires into the camp. Muhadesh looked back. The poles were missing out to five hundred yards along the entrance road. *Funny*, he thought; he hadn't noticed that until the vehicle was stopped. He climbed back in and drove on, heading for the command post.

Two work details were piling sandbags against the walls of the command post that faced the parade grounds, and a bulldozer was pushing sand into mounds against the other exposed walls. Another one must have been doing the same on the opposite side of the armory, as was apparent from the sound and clouds of fine sand rising above the low roofs.

A hand waved back and forth. The soldier ran up to the road, and Muhadesh slowed and stopped.

"Captain," the sergeant called, puffing only slightly.

Muhadesh smiled through the rolled-down window. "Sergeant Ewadi." *One of my few true soldiers.* Ewadi was actually only one of two remaining soldiers who had been with Muhadesh back in the days when the 3rd was a true military training ground

"What do you think?" the wiry sergeant asked, a knowing grin opening below the black mustache.

"It all looks interesting. You *are* advising Lieutenant Indar, correct? You must be—some of these defenses look intelligently placed." Muhadesh pointed back along the road. "The three posts?"

"Yes, that was my suggestion. The lieutenant is concerning himself with the interior defenses, as you can see."

Muhadesh could. "Obviously. Does he think that a sand berm will stop American-guided bombs?"

Ewadi laughed, careful that no one was listening. The nearest soldier was fifty feet away. "Even with good planning there are limitations."

"The soldiers at the posts?" Muhadesh offered.

Ewadi nodded. "They may be my placements, but these weakling weapons instructors of Indar's would run before they would fire."

"Speaking of the lieutenant . . ."

A finger pointed to the command center. "On the back side. He is directing the placement of the wooden poles. They are to be vehicle barriers." Ewadi's comment trailed off skeptically.

Muhadesh saluted the sergeant, then put the Range Rover back in gear. Ewadi was one of those factors that made what he did difficult, and what he was about to do painful. He was not a deterrent, however.

The sound of heavy equipment was more prevalent when Muhadesh pulled directly up to the main entrance of the command center. He ignored the soldiers scurrying about nearby and went immediately inside and upstairs to his office.

There was a smell of diesel exhaust in the room. Muhadesh walked behind his desk and slid the window down, closing and locking it, and then closed the heavy blackout shades over it. The room went dim. He switched the desk lamp on, removed his jacket, and sat down, swiveling the chair to face his older model typewriter.

He took out his notebook and several sheets of plain paper. He inserted one sheet in the typewriter and pecked out a two-sentence message. Muhadesh felt his heart sink as the last word was completed. It was really going to happen. This would seal it. The Americans would not be endeared to him for this, but he had his own battle to fight, one of higher personal importance.

The sinking feeling relaxed, and Muhadesh slipped the single sheet of paper into the fax, dialing the number from memory as he had hundreds of times before. Forty seconds later it was fed back out and the confirmation slip showed that it had been received. A few minutes after that it was automatically forwarded from the CIA front company to the Rome station, and then on to Langley.

Muhadesh sketched out the diagram as Sadr had described it, checking the picture against his notes twice before sending it off, repeating the process.

Next he typed up two more messages on separate pieces of paper, though both could have been placed on one. The Americans would prefer it that way, he knew, but this was his way: the way it had to be. The first message would tell the Americans what the objects on the hijacked plane *weren't*. The second one would shed light on what they were. Muhadesh folded the latter and tucked it in his shirt pocket.

The typewriter's hum ceased. Muhadesh laid the final sheet in the fax's feed slot and touched the repeat dial button. At the same instant the room dimmed almost to darkness. His attention immediately turned to the desk lamp, which he switched on and off. At first he thought it must have been the bulb, but then the larger problem became apparent. The fax machine was also dark, as was the surveillance control panel next to the video monitor.

Muhadesh sprang up, his legs thrusting the chair backward against the wall. The power was out. *No!* There was one more message to be sent. It had to get to the Americans. The ones already sent would not make sense, and the first, without the third, would cast doubt on his credibility. He removed it from the fax and folded it, placing it with the other in his pocket.

He was frozen for a moment, standing behind the desk. Then rage filled him. His fists clenched at his side. There could be only one cause of the outage.

The shade nearly tore when Muhadesh threw it open, and the window slammed hard against the wooden stops at the top of the frame. Neither sound matched what came from Muhadesh as he leaned through the window and screamed over the parade grounds at the top of his lungs: "Indar!"

Pope AFB

Rain fell intermittently, and when it fell the twenty-knot surface wind pushed it in bunches against the vehicles and aircraft on the expansive tarmac. Notable among them were the C-141 Starlifter, black and green in stark contrast to the misty daylight background, and two dark green Humvees nosed away from the lowered stem ramp of the jet transport.

Around the two vehicles the Delta troopers stood. They wore fresh sets of the black assault gear they would wear in the event they got a go. That they had changed gear and were milling about behind a ready-to-go transport said something. They could feel it. Something was definitely happening.

"Troops, listen up." It was Blackjack. He walked with purpose to where they stood. "Load the Humvees and follow on. We've got a go to get into position."

"Holy shit," Quimpo said.

"This is it, Major?" Jones asked.

McAffee's face was stone. "If we're there, and there's an opportunity, then we're going to take them down."

Graber read the conditions more than the words. There

were "ifs" attached to everything, it seemed, in their line of work. He also read something in the civilian's face. "You ready for some action, Captain Anderson?"

Joe nodded. It was a nervous affirmation. "Just let me at it."

"Let's get aboard," Blackjack bellowed. The Humvees, driven by two Delta troopers from the slack squad, fired up and backed up the stem ramp into the Starlifter. Each vehicle had a strange, ungainly-looking raised platform mounted on its rear.

The big Italian lieutenant did his best John Wayne: "Saddle uuup!"

Within five minutes the Starlifter's loadmaster checked the position and tie-downs of the vehicles. Delta was experienced at loading and securing their own gear. He gave it a thumbs-up, and the eleven troopers and the lone civilian settled into the suspended web seats along the inner fuselage. Five minutes later the C-141 throttled down the runway and nosed up into the late-morning storm.

Buxton leaned close to the major. "Where we headed, sir?"

"Tenerife. You ever heard of it?"

He had, but it wasn't encouraging. "Yeah. Two 747s crashed there ten or fifteen years ago. One slammed into the other when it was landing. Nothing like flying into a place with a history."

Landing wasn't what concerned McAffee. The feeling in his gut overpowered that. This one felt like it was going to happen, and experience had taught him that, unlike most human endeavors, the act surpassed the prelude in terror by far.

USS *Vinson*

The communication suite was worthy of its name compared to most areas of the giant carrier, which were comparatively small considering the ship's massive displacement. It bristled on three of four walls with communications gear which impressed even Logan, who had seen many a pretender to such a capability.

"Over here, sir." The petty officer directed Logan to a

gray door on the far side of the rectangular room. "This is our secure room."

He wasn't joking. There were two locks on the door, one a combination type with a flip-up privacy hood. Whoever operated the dial had to be able to do so by touch; the numbers were not allowed to be seen. The petty officer completed the unlocking and opened the door. "Sir."

Logan entered the five-by-five-foot room. A single chair was pushed up to a fold-down metal tray, attached to which was a normal-looking phone. Appearance was where the normalcy ended. The gear the phone was connected to was *the* most secure communications link on earth, identical to that used by the nation's strategic forces. Also hooked to it was a high-resolution facsimile printer.

The door shut behind him. He sat down and picked up the green handset. "Logan here."

"Dick . . . Greg Drummond. How are things out there?"

"I'm getting too old for this shit, sir. A fighter ride out, and then the air group commander reads me the riot act. A real a-hole."

Drummond hadn't seen the case officer in over six months. He sounded different. "He's a typical Navy man, and that makes him good at what he does. I've got some info for you. Watch the printer."

The machine was one of the quiet laser-color models, able to reproduce pictures and documents in detail unfathomable just five years before. What was more amazing was that the condensed transmission that carried the digitized data to the printer had traveled over eighty thousand miles between Langley, two ground stations, and two relay satellites, before being received and decrypted on the carrier.

Logan waited for both pages to finish printing before pulling them out of the tray.

"The drawing is something—who knows what? There was no explanation with it. We're going to have it analyzed. I wanted you to see it just in case you might be able to make some sense of it."

The CIA case officer studied it. "From DONNER?"

"Yes. Just a short time ago. Anything?"

"I've seen his writing and sketches before. This is his. I'm sure. But there's no labeling on it." *Why?*

"It was just a stab in the dark. But if you're sure it's DONNER's work, then the second sheet could be worrying."

The single sheet of paper was slick. Logan read the message. "What?"

"That's what we thought. He says he's not going to transmit the final message; he says it will come out with him."

"Christ."

Drummond could now identify the feeling behind Logan's words—apprehension. "We transmitted three requests to him. He was supposed to tell us (a) if there is a nuclear bomb on board, (b) if not, what it is, and (c) as much of the technical detail on the cargo as he was able to get. Now this diagram can only be a response to the last request, but what about the other two? He says he'll give us the last response when we extract him. That leaves one unaccounted for."

It wasn't difficult to make an inference from the situation. Donner had broken his pattern, and worse yet, he wasn't delivering as requested. Logan was instantly unnerved by it all. "This isn't good. It doesn't endear this mission to me."

"Could he have been turned?"

Logan pondered that. "I don't know. This certainly isn't like him. From what I know about him, though, it's not likely *anyone* could turn him. He'd rather die."

There was another possibility, the DDI knew. "Then maybe he's deliberately leading us into a trap."

Us? "You mean you think he might have been playing us all along?"

"Or recently," Drummond responded. "It's a consideration. Maybe part of this overall situation."

"And what would his motivation be?"

"I don't know, because I don't know him. None of us do."

That was a truism that hit Logan with force. DONNER was a mystery to them. Aside from his past performance, no one had any real sense of what the man was about, or what drove him. "So, we have a problem. What are our options?"

"We be prudent and call off the extraction, which means we don't have a chance at the other message or messages."

The DDI felt that would be the safest option. He didn't want to send a case officer and a bunch of troops into a bushwack. But then "safe" wasn't always an acceptable prime objective of his line of work. "Or we go."

That "we" stuff again. "We go. I'll just be taking in a few extra pounds of worry."

"And a flak vest."

Logan already had that ready and waiting on his bunk.

Flight 422

It was the moment after the terror, when one's body tried to recover from the physical drain that came with the aftermath of an adrenaline rush. Captain Bart Hendrickson and First Officer Buzz Elkins were feeling that now. Buzz was flopped back in the seat, his head even farther back. The captain continued his grip on the stick, his eyes focused a hundred feet in front of the *Maiden*.

"We almost bought it, Bart." Buzz still avoided looking at the runway's end just before them.

"Our brakes sure did," Hendrickson said. The antiskid brakes were thoroughly strained when stopping the overloaded aircraft. "But we're down."

"What about next time?" Buzz asked. "Are we gonna be able to stop then, with this load?"

Maybe not, the captain realized. "We may not have to worry about that, considering number three." The number three engine was down to 70 percent available power, an unacceptable limit under any circumstances.

Buzz straightened up and looked back to the pirate. He was staring, eyes wide, past both men, but not at anything. Just off somewhere. The first officer turned back forward. "So what do we do? We had a hard enough time getting off the ground with four good engines. There ain't no way we can do it with what we got in the belly, and in the way of power."

He was right. Dead right. The captain had few alternatives to deal with the problem, none of them foolproof, and one of them dangerous. That point had been proven on the ground in Libya. It was that option, though, that afforded the only real chance for a successful takeoff. It might also help with the braking if they ever got that far to need brakes again.

Hendrickson took a silent, deep breath for courage, and looked back. "Are we going to leave here?"

There was not an immediate response, but the gaze was broken. Hadad's eyes met the captain's. "Did you not learn?"

"I am not *defying* you, if that's what you think." The captain focused on the passengers; their safety was his prime concern. He had to weave this request skillfully. "If you want us to leave here, then we have to shed some weight. We have to be lighter. One of our engines, the inboard one on that side, is going down in performance. We're losing up to one fourth of our liftoff power. You saw how close it was leaving Benghazi. The simple fact is that we're too heavy with four good engines—with three we aren't going anywhere."

Hadad did remember the close call in Benghazi. Though he had since put it out of his mind, it did strike him. He had been assured that the plane would have no difficulty carrying the load, that it had powerful new engines unique to the latest version. What was wrong, then?

"Listen, I just want to get this aircraft off the ground, if that's what you intend to do. We need to get rid of some weight." Hendrickson let that hang for a moment, seeing some realization in the hijacker's face, and possibly acceptance. "We're all going to die if we try to take off."

There was acceptance, but it would come with a useful twist. Something to keep the world guessing, and to give them cause to wonder. "How many?"

The captain figured it quickly, most of it guesswork. "Everyone from the number three door back." It would be almost two hundred people.

It was something Hadad was prepared to do. The mission would continue, would go on to success. It would also give the Americans a false sense of hope. "Make it happen." And there was a surprise to add. "Contact the tower for what you need to evacuate the passengers, and to inform them of our destination."

"Which is?"

Hadad smiled and motioned to the hand-held microphone. This task he would enjoy.

Springer Seven-Three

"Sir," the com officer said, "they're talking to the tower."

The commander switched his headset over to the communications intercept net. He listened with the com officer, taking quick notes on his console. His pencil snapped halfway through, and he simply tossed it aside and finished the transcription with a pen. "Who's that?" he asked, noticing the voice change.

The message was spoken in English, though inflected with a Middle Eastern accent. It was brief, to the point, and out of the ordinary considering the play of the hijacking so far.

When the air went dead the commander tried to figure it out. "You catch that, Major?"

The Sentry's second in command was on the same net, though not visible to his boss. "Yep. So they're releasing two hundred hostages . . . why?"

"Good question. But that's small potatoes. Why announce their destination, and why did the hijacker do that himself?" The commander was playing analyst. He motioned to the com officer to send the message off to the Pentagon. "Why let one of the crew ask for a ramp, and then take the mike himself?"

"That's one for the psych boys," the major observed.

"There's plenty of those where they're heading," the commander joked.

The White House

"It doesn't surprise me," Bud said. "If they have a nuclear bomb, Chicago will give them a couple million hostages."

Meyerson's head shook in disgust. "Damn good thing the Spanish are letting us in."

"It's a shaky approval at best," Coventry said, swallowing two orange slices from the bowl on the table. A steward had refilled the Oval Office's fruit dishes just prior to the meeting. "We should still consider what they want in Chicago."

"It's our nightmare, first of all," Bud said to the other three. "They can exploit our helplessness. If they want concessions, what can we do? We have to look at it as though they have a weapon on board. If they get in, we lose. Period."

It was probably going to be the shortest discussion of any point during the crisis. Meyerson agreed completely with Bud's analysis.

Coventry still thought that something might be gained, some advantage, by knowing what the hijackers' intentions were. "But why Chicago? What is there that they see as important? Terrorists don't just pick a target for its size alone. There are tens of cities that would fit the bill. Chicago has other draws that might be as important as its population."

"Jim, the point is moot if we know that letting them in is unacceptable," Meyerson reminded the secretary of state.

"True," Bud joined in.

The secretary of state, a classic thinking intellectual, was working the obvious through several mental filters. What was left didn't necessarily add up. "Not true. If we look at how to counter what we *think* they intend to do, and we're wrong, then we may end up jeopardizing lives unnecessarily. So what I'm asking is why did they *tell* us Chicago? Why tell us anything? I don't think it's meant to scare us, or to snub us: Terrorists who behave professionally have an end in mind, and they don't muddle it with worthless trickery. They will, however, use deception if it suits them."

"So you believe this might be a trick?" the president asked.

Coventry smiled. "My logic doesn't always come with answers, Mr. President."

"I can see some of your point, Jim," Bud conceded. "If they give us a destination that we think is obvious, that should trigger something in us. Maybe they want us to believe that Chicago is a good place for them to be. They may have another objective." The NSA pondered that in the silence. "We can think on that. It may help us prepare for any response. But, prior to reacting, we have to move to prevent the worst from happening."

"You have a proposal, Bud?" The president was sure he did.

Bud explained it. The act itself was simple. The results, however, would be undeniably horrible.

The president didn't see any alternative. "Andrew?"

The secretary of defense, like the others, understood the enormity of the option. "It will work. No doubt about it."

"It's coming to this," Coventry said thoughtfully.

"I've already put the preliminary steps in motion to make this happen, sir," Bud said. "Your final word will be required to release the equipment."

There was nothing more to consider. "You have it. Andrew, draft the required papers. I'll notify the House and Senate leaders. And I want some more analysis on what their intentions might really be. Secretary Coventry, Bud . . . put some thought into that. And, Andrew, give Delta the green light to go from Tenerife."

The phone next to Meyerson preempted any reply. It was meant for him, and he listened almost entirely, saying only a few words before covering the mouthpiece. "We may have a break here, in our favor. The German ambassador contacted our military attaché in Bonn. They have four GSG-9 commandos at Tenerife airport, on their way back from Brazil. They were doing some training for the Brazilian military."

"Can they do anything for us?" the president inquired.

"They are top-notch counterterrorist troops, sir," Bud responded.

"Right," Meyerson said. "And they could be invaluable debriefing some of those hostages when they're released."

The president looked to the secretary of state. "Get in touch with the Spanish foreign minister again, and politely inform him that we consider the German troops to be *official* representatives of the United States government for the purpose of interviewing the hostages. You make that perfectly clear to him. And get someone from our embassy in Madrid out there, pronto."

Coventry went immediately to the small office he maintained in the White House. The secretary of defense relayed the American request back to the military attaché in Bonn, and it went immediately through channels to the GSG-9 troops on the ground in Tenerife. A short time later the most valuable intelligence yet received during the crisis was being extracted from the newly released hostages, though the plainclothes soldiers' thick accents were something of a mystery.

Thunder One

The aircraft's steady roar disappeared as the headset covered Blackjack's ears. "McAffee."

"Mike, I've got some good intel for you," Colonel Cadler reported from more than a thousand miles away.

"I'm listening."

"We got a damn good break. Colonel Dee had some men coming back from a South American training exercise. They were conveniently at Tenerife, and they got some good stuff out of some released hostages."

That was new to the major. "How many off?"

"It looks like about two hundred, probably just under. But the big news is that you were right about the HRT plan. It wouldn't work. No way. A number of the hostages said the guy wears that bomb *before* they land."

"That clinches it," McAffee said. Their plan was the only way now. "What about a final go?"

"We've got permission to stage from Tenerife. The chief says *go*."

"Thumbs-up on this end," Blackjack noted.

"On this end, too, Major. And thank Graber. His plan was a damn good one." The colonel released the radio circuit.

Al-'Adiyat

Muhadesh slowly scratched his chest through the shirt, feeling the folded paper inside. There were actually two, one of which he needed to get rid of . . . had to get rid of.

He paced back and forth in front of his rigid executive officer, his breath expelled in angry spurts from his nostrils. He stopped in front of Indar, looking not at him, but away, focusing on a picture of the colonel that hung on the wall. To the left and below was the fax machine, now useless. The room was lit by a pair of battery-powered lanterns, giving the faces of both men eerie lit-from-below masks.

This was the second time Indar had been summoned to explain since the power was lost.

"Now, Lieutenant, I am doing my utmost not to lose my composure with you; first, because I do not believe it is worth the effort, and, second, because I wish this entire, idiotic episode to simply be over." Muhadesh turned only his head, but Indar's eyes were fixed straight ahead, staring at nothing and avoiding his commander's gaze. "Explain, please, why you have not been able to restore power *four* hours after you so carelessly saw to its loss." Directing a bulldozer backward onto the power lines, laid on the ground after the poles were removed, was careless, if anything. "When we last spoke you were going to see to the generators. Why has this not been done?"

The lieutenant's gaze changed slightly, hinting at . . . fear? Muhadesh turned completely to face Indar. "Why?"

Indar met his commander's eyes. "The generators, sir, they are . . . gone."

"Gone!" Muhadesh exploded. His arms flailed out and up, coming to rest atop his head in disbelief.

"Yes," Indar replied in a snap, ready to shift responsibility. "Before you returned, a unit from the airfield came and confiscated our generators. Their commander was a major. I could not defy him. He said they would be better used supporting the outer defenses of the airfield."

"Both of them? And you found it so unimportant that you felt you could wait to inform me until now?" Muhadesh leaned back upon the edge of his desk. His eyes searched the ceiling for some reason, for some meaning in all this. Was Allah testing him?

"Sir—" Indar began, but was cut off by the captain's gesture.

"No, Indar. Your lies, and excuses, and your borderline treachery is over. Finished. Now, you will listen, and I will explain to *you* what will be done. You have exactly one hour, and one hour only, to restore power. Sixty minutes, and they are passing as we speak. The next thing I want to hear from you is that the power is on. No . . . I don't even want to hear from you—just turn on the power. The lights will be the signal."

The lieutenant's eyes fell, then came back up, glancing briefly into his commander's black eyes. They were frightening in the unnatural light.

"I don't even care if you understand," Muhadesh said, turning away. "Go."

He waited for the sound of the door closing before releasing his anger. It was vented in the form of a fist against the wall, connecting solidly with the plaster below the colonel's photograph.

Muhadesh held it there for what felt like minutes. He felt pain, intense pain, spread across the fingers on his right hand and it increased when contact with the wall was broken. There was no mark on the old plaster, attesting to its strength. His skin was not broken, either. He spread his fingers out, examining the trembling digits.

One hour.

He calmed himself. The anger was unproductive, he knew, but there were times when it surfaced, like it or not. In ninety minutes he would have to leave for the rendezvous. Thirty minutes would be cutting it close, but there was no choice. He had to get the other message off to the Americans.

In the meantime he would wait, alone in the semidarkness of his office. He sat at his desk and turned one of the flashlights on its side to illuminate the writing blotter. There was one last message to compose. It was actually less a message and more an explanation. A justification? Muhadesh wouldn't go that far.

He removed his writing paper and took a pen in hand, writing the words that would soothe no one, but that he was compelled to put on paper. Amazingly, they came easily.

Thunder One

Blackjack walked down the right side of the Starlifter, heading aft from the com suite, which was a generous description of the radio operator's console. He sidestepped past the Humvees, stopping at the nose of the second. "Gather round!"

The troops sensed something, but McAffee's face never belied his thoughts. Graber checked that they were all around, including the two drivers. Joe Anderson was still in his seat, fifteen feet back, staring intently at the message he had received.

"The colonel just called with the following message:

Execute Cloudburst." The major's face stayed a mask of stone, and he noticed that Graber's, unlike the rest of the team's, was also. The others let out a collective yell of relief. They were finally getting their chance to do the job the unit had been formed to do. "Settle down, troops. We're going to be on the ground in less than ninety minutes. We have to be ready to go when we land, so get your gear checked, and rechecked. Captain, you see that the buddy checks get done." Graber acknowledged the order. "Get to it. Captain, I'm going to talk to the pilot. Be back."

"Awright!" Antonelli bellowed. "We got a go!"

"Holy shit, man," Buxton said. "This isn't a game, Mikey. This is real." His tone showed some annoyance at the jubilance.

"Chris is right," Sean said, getting attention instantly. "This is it, and we better have our shit together. No fucking cheers until this all works, 'cause you'll feel like dogmeat if it doesn't." He turned specifically to Antonelli. "So save the praise and do our jobs. Buddy checks, now!"

The men broke off into pairs, going over each other's snug web gear and limited equipment.

"Captain Anderson," Antonelli yelled, his partner's hands tugging on cinch straps of his body armor. Joe looked up. "We're going in."

The Delta troopers went about their preparatory ritual. Joe watched for a second, looking over his glasses, then returned his attention to the diagram. That was a generous word, but then the CIA man he had talked to while the printout came over the aircraft's fax machine said it was obtained from someone with no knowledge of what it might be. *What might it be?* Joe asked himself. It was not a nuclear bomb, that was for sure. Even in its crudeness it could be almost anything but that.

The drone of the engines was punctuated by the chatter of the troopers. Joe heard none of it. He was in his own world, one he alone understood—most of the time. But not now. He would be dealing with this . . . thing when they got aboard, and he felt at a loss for not knowing what it was. The scary thing, though, was that it might not be anything he could deal with.

Knock that crap off, Joe.

13

••••••••••••

THE EXPECTED, THE UNEXPECTED, AND THE NECESSARY

Flight 422

"HOW MUCH DID we get?" Hendrickson asked.

Buzz checked the fuel readout again. Data on the amount of fuel in the tanks was gathered through means much different than those used in a car. Floats in each of the seven fuel tanks were operated using reverse pressure. This negated the effect of minimal sloshing while the aircraft was in motion. Readings from the floats were matched against inflow and outflow meters on each tank, and all the numbers were tracked by a computerized fuel-management system.

"Two-twenty," the first officer answered. There were 220,000 pounds of jet fuel in the *Maiden's* tanks. "I didn't pump into the outboard extenders."

"Good," Hendrickson said. The 656-gallon tanks inside the wings, right at the tips, were dry. That would keep more of the weight forward, since the wings, swept back at thirty-seven degrees, added mass behind the aircraft's center of gravity. "Is the rest spread around?" he inquired, leaving Buzz to manage the fuel while he preflighted the engines.

"The center is full. The inboards and outboard mains are splitting the rest." That still left over 130,000 pounds of free space in the tanks. "This load out and the empty seats should help."

Hendrickson came to the number three instruments right then. With a total weight reduction of 160,000 pounds, the *Maiden* was lighter than at any point since landing at Benina. But the number three turbofan was showing a marked degradation in performance, down 55 percent, even at idle. "I hope. But we're going to be dragging this one all the way," he said, pointing at the dying engine's indicators.

"What do you think's with it?" Buzz entered the final fuel numbers in the flight computer, though that would help them little without a given flight path.

"I don't know. It looked like the compressor two days ago. Now . . . ?" It was more than the compressor, he knew. It might be that, or an engine bearing. Or something else.

"Yeah."

The captain finished his checks. "She'll do it."

"Damn right."

The captain turned. Hadad was sitting, the glow of the cockpit instruments lighting his face. The eyes, like before, stared ahead. "No tower contact, correct?"

"Correct," the answer came, without a movement or a blink.

Hendrickson had won a small victory in securing the release of two hundred passengers. It still wasn't enough to make up for the death of one. *Or of another hundred and fifty*, he told himself. He had to do it. "Look, we're probably going to get off the ground all right, with the weight reduction and all. But we had to take on less fuel to get it down even more. Our number three engine is getting worse, even while we're sitting here. I don't know what's going to happen once we get up there."

The face came out of its trancelike mask. "What are you saying? If it is to release more passengers, the answer is no."

Hendrickson's head shook. "No. Let me explain. We had to take on less fuel in order to get the best possible chance at taking off. In doing that we reduced our range. With the engine not performing right, that's going to increase our fuel consumption and reduce our range further."

Hadad spoke no words in response, his eyes issuing the challenge.

"If you want to get to Chicago, then we've got a problem. With this amount of fuel, our load, and our bum engine, we'll have to stop and refuel, probably in New York."

The words did not trigger anger in Hadad. Instead, they elicited frustration, and exasperation. There was little reason for the American to lie. What would it get him? After all, his prime concern was staying alive, and keeping the passengers alive. It was another thing gone awry in the plan. "There will be no additional stop in America."

"We can't make it," the captain repeated. "We have to go a shorter route. Stop somewhere and refuel."

Why? Hadad's thumb rubbed circles on the trigger switch. He was tiring. Sleep did not help. The fatigue was deeper than mere physical exhaustion.

If they could not make it, then all was for naught. They had to have enough fuel for three hours of flying once the American coast was reached, for three hours of deception until he could leave his mark upon the Great Satan. If not, the mission would fail. The purpose would be unfulfilled. And . . . And . . .

The little face filled his mind. There had to be a way.

"Havana," Hadad said. "Can you make it there?"

Hendrickson visually checked with Buzz. They weren't sure how receptive the Cubans would be to their appearance, but then they wouldn't have much of a say. *Just like the Russians had no say with 007.* "It'll be close, but the skies should be clear. We can do that."

"Then do it. Get off the ground, now." Hadad slid back into his seat. In a minute he could remove the increasingly painful vest, and try to rest.

With a concrete destination and flight path—direct—the crew could let the flight computer and auto flight system do most of the flying. Buzz programmed in the destination, José Martí Airport.

Hendrickson checked the entered data, as was standard. A simple mistouch of a key could have serious repercussions. Each crewman backed the other . . . The captain did it almost automatically, reaching just above and to the left of the flight control computer and touching the activation button. There was no obvious sign of what he had just done, but Buzz could tell instantly from the crackle of static in his headset.

Hadad was too busy being tired, and lacked enough detailed knowledge to realize that the captain had just activated the hot mike function of the VHF radio.

Springer Seven-Three

"Break away! Break away!" The AWACS commander ˙ into his boom mike. Two seconds later the converted

Boeing 707 banked hard right as the pilot responded to the order and broke away from the KC-10 tanker replenishing the AWACS's half-empty tanks.

"Read it back, Com," the commander ordered.

"It's just chatter, sir. I've got it on tape, but the stuff sounds like preflight for their roll."

"Radar, looks like the bird's taking off." The commander checked his own display. "Anything in the way."

"Negative."

"Outstanding. Tag anything that gets within twenty miles of that bird on my scope, as well as yours, and give me a holler. Com, what's going on now?" He could hear it on his headset, but he also had to process other relative information. The com officer was dedicated to listening.

"Sir, he's got a hot mike. He's transmitting everything! Jesus H. Christ, that's one slick-thinking pilot."

"Cut the commentary. Just give me the important stuff. You're my filter, remember."

"She's up, sir," Radar reported. "Gaining altitude. Slow climb."

Okay, baby, where are you goi—"What was that?" the commander asked, interrupting his thought. He heard it, but . . .

"He said José Martí, sir," Com reported. "José Martí is their destination. Just slipped it into the old conversation."

That smart son of a bitch! "Keep off that frequency, Com. No chances. That guy in the cockpit with them might be able to hear."

"Yes, sir," Com responded, a smile evident in his voice.

"We'll just wait. Get that off to the Pentagon." It was good news, the commander felt. They had an idea where the aircraft was going, even if it contradicted their earlier announcement.

He also knew that at least one body of men would not be happy to hear the development. Their aircraft was just coming into the inner zone on his scope.

Thunder One

McAffee gave a polite "thank you, sir" to Cadler on the other end of the radio and slammed the headset down on the console in front of the startled communications officer. He stopped at the top of the stairs to the hold, letting the initial anger at the news dissipate. It took a full minute before he proceeded down.

"All right, listen up," the major shouted. The Starlifter started into a shallow bank to the left. It was obvious to the troops that something wasn't right—Tenerife was to the south, or right. "Effective now we are in a stand-down. The bird flew."

The soldiers reacted quietly. This had happened before, but not when they had been so close, in such a big operation.

Anderson looked around, catching Graber's gaze. It was downcast, but not fixed. "What happened?"

Sean noticed the diagram in Joe's hand. It had been there for over an hour. "The aircraft took off. We're heading back."

"Back? Back to where?" Joe excitedly asked.

"Pope, most likely."

Joe pulled himself up from the wraparound seat. He worked his way across the tilting cargo deck to McAffee's position in the darkness of the Humvees' side. "What the hell is this about going back? What about those things on board?"

The major looked up, almost uninterested in the civilian's protest. "Unless you think good old Fidel is going to give us landing rights, then we don't have much choice."

"What?" Joe didn't understand.

"Havana, Anderson. They're going to Havana. They announced it over the radio. Nice, safe Havana, where we can't touch them." Blackjack was pissed, and it showed.

Anderson didn't say anything else. It was just as well, since the major's eyes said, "Back the fuck off," quite clearly.

Al-ʿĀdiyat

Failure had again invaded his existence.

Muhadesh pushed the roller-mounted chair into its space the desk. It didn't go in completely, requiring him to ith more force. The jacketed arm fell into view.

Indar. He, too, had failed. An hour he had been given to restore power, and still they were without it, leaving the camp in the dark and the Americans with only a partial response to their request. Muhadesh bent down with the flashlight and shone it on the body. It was curled into an unnatural ball in the cramped space below the desk. If the diminutive lieutenant was any bigger, he would not have fit. Muhadesh lifted the arm and laid it back against the head. Still there was little blood from the bullet hole in the forehead.

The Beretta was less three bullets. Two used on the whore in the city, and one on the wormy lieutenant. It was still a waste of lead, Muhadesh thought. He tossed the still loaded weapon under the desk. "Take this with you into the hereafter, Indar. It will not help. Satan fears no gun."

He went to his wall safe. The combination was a date, one he would never forget. The date of al-Dir's disappearance. Inside the small boxlike vault were some papers, unimportant now as always, and a holstered weapon. It was a Russian-made Makarov pistol, a gift from al-Dir. Muhadesh removed it from its leather holster. The steel was cold and clean, with a slight feel of the penetrating oil he used to regularly clean it. Just enough to keep the rust away. Also in the safe were two clips, both full. He took one, inserted it into the weapon, and chambered a round. There was no need for a second magazine.

He put it back in the holster, clipping that to his belt. Next he checked his pocket; the messages were there, including the last, handwritten one. It was in Italian, his second language. If things went accordingly, someone would get it, and would have it translated in due time. It was best that those who were coming for him didn't know the entire story immediately.

He grabbed his parka, the one earned as a commando years before. The room was left behind, locked, without a second look or thought. It was now his past.

The military jeep hesitated to start in the cool night, as was usual. It turned over after a minute's trying. Muhadesh swung it around, heading south from the command center toward the camp's rear exit road. He followed that to the perimeter gate—actually a hole in the combined barbed wire–chain link fence—and drove through, getting a casual salute from the enlisted man at the rear. Within two minutes the red taillights faded to almost imperceptible dots in the distance as the vehicle headed south, and then east.

It was well past midnight. A new day, Muhadesh thought. A beginning. There was no joy to accompany that thought.

The White House

"Our choices are few, gentlemen." The president was looking for answers. "I don't like what is happening." He was mindful of the contingency plan Bud had set in motion.

Bud and Meyerson were silent. Coventry jingled the ice in his glass. The water was long gone. Outside the light was still evident, though it was tempered by the scattered gray in the sky. It cast pretty, uneven shadows on the south lawn, leaving several of the smaller trees shrouded in the shade of the larger ones.

"Can we get them to land somewhere before going on to Chicago?" Ellis asked.

"The point is to not let them in the country," Bud responded. "If we let them in, we lose."

"Then what?" Meyerson inquired of the others, not expecting a satisfactory answer.

"Sir," Coventry began, "who are the culprits in this?"

"Your point?" the president responded.

Coventry sat forward, putting his glass down. Meyerson grabbed a handful of nuts from the tray, dropping a few into his mouth.

"Leverage and diplomacy of the most delicate order," Coventry replied. "One of the causes of this crisis, one who made it possible, is sitting protected in a villa somewhere outside of Havana. The world might not know that, but we do, and a certain Communist dictator does."

Bud wasn't following the path of Coventry's words. "How does this fit in?"

"Castro is well aware of Vishkov's presence in his coun-
~v. It has been a strain on his relations with some elements
~military, our sources tell us."

true, sir," Meyerson confirmed without prompting.

"Which doesn't endear Vishkov to Castro or his inner circle. The Russian enjoys protection from Ontiveros, as you heard before, and Ontiveros is one of the political dissenters on the Defense Council. His position is even to the right of Castro."

"So you think we might be able to use this to . . . what?" the president asked.

"Not this alone. Castro won't be swayed by just the knowledge that Vishkov is peddling designs, or that one of them incarnate might be on the hijacked jet. But if we can make it clear to him that we consider *his* sheltering of Vishkov to be a major factor in this, *and* if we can back that up with some pressure, he might become receptive to our handling of the situation before something horrible happens requiring us to hold him responsible."

Bud saw another aspect of it. "And if he's really at odds with this general . . ."

"Correct," the secretary of state said, knowing what the NSA's gist was.

The president saw some hope in the idea, but the logistics would be tricky, and the communication of the message the most difficult part. He had a thought on that. But first . . . "So we need some pressure? Andrew, can we arrange for some muscle to be in place. Just enough for a credible show."

"Absolutely. We can rustle up some air power."

The president put on his business face, the one that Ellis was familiar with. He wore it when a challenge presented itself. It was time for some forceful maneuvering.

"Secretary Meyerson, get word to Delta that the go is back on. They're going to be going to some unfriendly territory. And Secretary Coventry," the president added, "get out to Andrews. You're taking a message to Havana—personally."

Flight 422

Hadad tried to rest. An hour after takeoff he still twisted in the oversize lounge seat, its back reclined fully to a bedlike position. The vest was next to him. *It* was part of the cause. His neck was now aching, the soreness having spread from the shoulders.

But the vest was not entirely at fault. He knew that in the months leading up to the mission he had become soft. Technical details of the plan that others could have handled he had delved into. Even when the colonel offered to give him more assistance, he had refused.

Hadad realized now that he had erred. He should have hardened his body to match the determination of his mind and soul. It was worthless observation now.

It could have been perfect, he told himself. *But it will still end in the same way. The purpose will be fulfilled.*

To hell with the rules.

Buzz dozed, or tried to. Captain Hendrickson had ordered his first officer to get some rest, knowing that they were both becoming physically exhausted. According to every regulation of air safety they should both be awake at the controls, but the rule writers didn't have *this* in mind when drafting those words.

The terrorist behind him was the mild one. Hendrickson wasn't sure why he classified him as that, considering his participation in the murder, but his manner was definitely different from the others.

This one also spoke English, like his leader, requiring the captain to be careful earlier while slipping information in during the surreptitious radio transmissions. Even with the constant guard he and Buzz had been able to mention, in semi-coded phrases, how many terrorists were aboard ("Did those four Indians get let off with the rest?") and the types of their weapons ("Just do what they say, Buzz. We can't take on Uzis and pistols").

And the destination. Havana. The place itself was no blessing, but just knowing their exact destination allowed the flight computer to do most of the flying. Hendrickson wasn't even touching the controls. Instead he occupied himself minding the readouts and watching the weather radar. Everything was clear as far out as the electronic eyes could see.

Buzz grunted, drawing a look from the captain and the terrorist. Hendrickson glanced back, and it was the terrorist's ʰat broke. *Interesting*.

ɪin saw his first officer settle down. A dream, he ɪt would mean that sleep was possible.

He took in and let out a full breath, straightening himself in the seat. The hot mike picked up the sound, which Hendrikson heard through his headset. All that someone on the other end would hear was air rushing past the boom mike. But why wasn't anyone answering? Someone had to be able to hear. If they would just answer, he could tell them more, maybe in a twenty-questions format.

Forget it. The thought frustrated him. At least he was getting something out. And Buzz was sleeping. With luck he could nap for hours, leaving him fresh to take over for the captain.

But luck was not theirs. The warbling tone in the cockpit confirmed that. Buzz awoke instantly.

"Number three, Buzz!"

"Damn!" The first officer gave the performance indicators a quick check, which told him all that was needed. "Down to fifteen percent. Shit! Shit! Fluid loss. We're losing the oil in it. Goddamn it, we're gonna lose the whole thing!"

"I know," Hendrickson said as he took control of the aircraft from the computers. "Has to be a bearing failure. Look there—the temp is way up. Shut it down. Shut it down!" There was urgency in the captain's voice. With no air bleeding from the compressor on the engine, hot air was building up within the turbine. In seconds the leaking lubricants would flash off and ignite, probably causing an explosion. The Atlantic was a long way down.

"Roger." Buzz cut fuel and power to the engine, which now hung uselessly beneath the starboard wing, causing increased drag. The aircraft reacted to the aerodynamic change by banking to the right. The pilots corrected the upset in attitude with left rudder trim and a reduction in power to the number two engine and an increase in number four.

The door swung open. Hadad entered to find Abu nervously pointing his Uzi at the pilots' backs. His entry was not noticed, nor was Abu's ordered departure.

"What is happening?" Hadad inquired, hiding his worry. He sounded unconcerned.

"We lost our bad engine," Buzz said. "Any other brilliant questions?"

Hadad ignored the defiance. Warning and convincing actions were no longer necessary. An aircraft could easily fly without one engine, he knew. The pilots seemed concerned, though he was confident. He stepped back and sat down.

"We're off auto for the duration," the captain said. The aircraft, sluggish already, would now require even more minute directional and altitude adjustments to remain stable and on course. It would be a constant battle. "My stick."

"Roger that. Down to three-nine-zero knots."

"Let's bring her nose up." Hendrickson made an adjustment to the throttles. "A little more power."

"Up she goes." Buzz inched the column back with the captain. The *Maiden's* nose responded, coming up fractionally. "Looks good. We're steady at twenty-nine thousand, Bart. Speed down to three-seven-zero and holding."

Hendrickson's eyes swept the panel again, a long breath of relief again amplified in his headset as before. *What if* . . . "Good. Let's see if she'll hold it. Negative flight deck audio."

Buzz caught it instantly, holding his breath while they waited for the terrorist to respond to the message the captain had slipped in. He didn't.

Anyone monitoring the frequency would now be aware that the pilots were the only ones privy to communication from the outside. Transmissions would be heard in their headsets, and not on the cockpit speaker.

"She's holding," Buzz reported, turning to the captain. The corner of his mouth twitched with mischievous glee.

The *Maiden* was responding, her dead engine now compensated for. Now, they flew, and waited . . . and listened.

"*Four-Two-Two, do you copy?*"

"Yeah. Yeah. Buzz, is our fuel okay?" the captain asked, slipping the answer into the conversation. Buzz also heard the call. *All right!*

"Looks good," the first officer answered.

"*Four-Two-Two, this is Springer Seven-Three. Confirming that you copy and transmission is secure. Do you confirm?*"

"Roger that, Buzz."

"*Four-Two-Two, that's great. We assume you have some unwelcome company with you.*"

"Uh-huh. We're holding good, even with that drag," Buzz said, trying to keep the words relevant to the situation.

"Understand, Four-Two-Two. We didn't want to spook your company with a broadcast. Good work. Understand you have a malfunction: Your number three engine is out?"

"Number three is totally down now, Cap. Down for the count. Just spinnin' in the wind."

"Good. Watch the temp on the others."

"Roger," Buzz said, straining to hold in a smile.

"We copy. Number three engine is out. Stand by on this channel. Call out any changes if you can. We're with you, Four-Two-Two. Hang in there."

The silence on the channel was disquieting after the first contact with the outside world in two days, yet they had to be optimistic. There had been contact. Someone was listening. No mention was made of who exactly was contacting the *Clipper Atlantic Maiden*, but both pilots knew that somewhere in the vicinity a United States Air Force aircraft was watching over them as best it could.

Thunder One

He had heard it all in his long Army career, but no longer. Blackjack sidestepped past the first Humvee and the miscellaneous gear stowed on both sides of it, emerging after the rearmost vehicle. Graber saw him first, noticing the look on the major's face. Something was up.

Of all the team members, Graber and McAffee were the most in sync, despite the difference in rank. It was a closeness, an understanding, that come from chasing "it." "It" was death. Knowing that a car or a bus could hit you any day, or wondering if the food you ate was so laced with chemicals that cancer was a *probability*, that was *facing* death. Chasing it was throwing yourself at the grim reaper with your teeth clenched tight and your HK hot to fire, its Streamlight beam striking all before it with the light of a coming death. Sean had chased it. So had McAffee.

Years before, in Thailand, Graber had been the second one into a hijacked aircraft, following the Thai commando leader. His job was relatively simple—throw flash-bangs as the Thai commander hit the carpet, then do the same. Two more native commandos, good men trained in the United States for precisely this type of mission, then literally ran over him and their leader, who came up from prone and cleared the front half of the aircraft. Sean brought up the rear.

The exact sequence happened at the same time, one door back on the opposite side, as the doors blew in. McAffee filled out that group. They went aft to secure the back of the airliner.

It was a picture-perfect raid. A success. The satisfaction and experience gained by the two Delta men was invaluable to the team, giving them firsthand experience to draw from. Graber was happy to share it with his peers, as was the major, but it was easier, Sean believed, for him to relate the fear they had experienced. Blackjack might have to lead them into an assault some day, and fear, though useful in many battles, was detrimental in the lightning fury of a takedown. Both, though, understood and accepted the peculiarities and advantages of each other's place in the team, and they, with unspoken agreement, did not infringe upon that domain.

This was the closeness, born from successfully chasing death, that allowed Captain Sean Graber to connect with his leader, to read his face as he returned from the flight deck of the Starlifter.

The entire team was silent, but not the aircraft. It creaked and moaned, then roared as it began a gentle bank to the left, correcting itself back to straight and level after a turn of only twenty degrees. The engines pushed harder in an obvious move to bring the huge cargo jet up to max speed. There was something going on. They had all been subdued since the stand-down order, but heads came up, looking around to each other, and the eyes of those who were napping opened to join the others.

Blackjack leaned against the port fuselage frame, across and in front of Graber. "The go order is reinstated. We go from José Martí," the major said, still not sure of the authorization himself. "If the Cubans give us a go ahead, then we go."

Joe Anderson had a hard time fathoming this. A short time ago he was in his sedate, sterile office in Washington. Now, if what he heard was correct, he was going to be part of an American military operation on Cuban soil.

Flight 422

Neither the captain nor his first officer could have seen, heard, or sensed it happening, though neither would have been surprised considering the abuse the flaps had undergone. The event was, as yet, unnoticed in any performance-affecting way.

The massive flaps, used to give the aircraft added lift during takeoff and to slow it when landing, were moved by synchronized hydraulic sliders, activated and controlled by a lever between the pilots. Normally they would be set at the beginning of a takeoff roll and retracted during the climb-out to altitude. But the added weight carried by the *Maiden*, compounded by the degraded performance of the number three engine, had necessitated their use as a rapid ascent tool, requiring them to be lowered after the aircraft had gained sufficient speed on its takeoff run. It was a radical use of the control surfaces, one not recommended for reasons obvious to any pilot or engineer. The added stresses were liable to cause catastrophic damage: the uncontrollable, instantaneous failure of the flaps, and possibly the wing as a whole.

The flaps and wings, however, were proving to be stronger than could have been hoped for, withstanding the stress of two jump takeoffs. That was not so for the primary inboard hydraulic slider, which bore the brunt of the stress when it was commanded to extend, lowering the flaps under its control. Inside the solid-cast casing a three-inch sliver of metal sheathing, which formed the smooth surface the slider arm made contact with, separated from the rest of the cylinder's interior. It came loose as the flaps were retracted during climb-out. Pressed between the slider arm and the casing, it slid out of place as the arm pulled back in, causing the casing to deform at its top. No fluid was released, as the base remained sealed and intact, and the rest of the unit was not opened by the defect.

The only effect of the mishap was yet to be felt.

14

. . . .

THE WHITE HATS AND
THE BLACK HATS

Rock Island Army Munitions Depot

SAMMY KNEW HIS big brother would take care of everything once he got to California. Three more hours. He had to remain cool. His shift ended at 2230, leaving him free for a late night on the town, but he wasn't planning for that.

"So he's alone?" the FBI agent asked. He was a huge man, reminiscent of a hockey goalie who had played too many years without a mask.

"Absolutely," the Army lieutenant answered.

The agent nodded and looked to the three others with him. They all wore the familiar blue windbreakers with the bright yellow FBI stenciled on the back, and two had their high-capacity 10mm autos in hand, locked and loaded. At the back of the Watch Office two MPs stood waiting. They wore full combat gear, flak vests and Kevlar helmets, and carried their M-16s ready to fire.

"Okay. Everybody ready?" All the parties nodded.

Their location, one building away from Private Sammy Jackson's post at the base armory, also housed the base telephone exchange, an ancient piece of equipment by standards of the day. Its antiquity would be useful, though, in the trickery they were about to attempt.

No calls had come through for the armory yet this evening, and Sammy had made none, making the operation all that much easier. One of the agents was from the Technical Services arm of the Bureau. He had with him two devices, both of which were plugged into the telephone-switching system, specifically the lines to the armory. One of the devices blocked all inbound calls, but recorded their origin.

The other suitcase-size apparatus would display any number dialed, but would not allow it to go through. "We're ready," the bespectacled agent announced, looking the part of a computer nerd.

The lieutenant waited for a go-ahead from the lead agent before buzzing the armory.

"Armory, Private Jackson."

"Jackson, you get any calls?"

"Nah. Not tonight, Lieutenant."

"Shit! Your brother called and the switchboard couldn't put it through. Goddamn ancient fucking wires! Damnit!"

"When'd he call, sir?"

"A few minutes ago. He wants you to call him back, pronto." That was a gamble. Did Sammy know where to contact his brother Marcus?

"Yeah, okay. Thanks for the message, sir."

The scar-faced agent smiled with a crooked mouth of teeth. "That was good. Get moving." The other two Bureau men and the MPs left for the armory.

"Hey," the lieutenant said. "Go easy. Nothing's been proven. He's innocent until, right?"

"Yeah, sure," one of the arrest team answered sarcastically before closing the opaque-windowed door behind himself.

"The phone's up." Attention turned to the digital readout connected to the line and the agent sitting on the floor next to it. "He took a few seconds to pick up. Maybe he's spooked."

"Or maybe he was just getting the number," the leader responded. The TS agent agreed with a look.

"Dialing."

"Whiskey One, copy?" Scar-face called on his portable.

"*Whiskey One, go.*"

"You in position?"

"*Ten seconds.*"

"Ten-four, stand by."

The phone number's eleven digits came up on the display as dialed, and the outgoing line was locked out. All Sammy Jackson heard after dialing the last number was a dial tone.

"Whiskey One, move in."

                          *   *   *

The stupid phone had to act up now! Sammy dropped the receiver into its cradle and took a deep breath. He just wanted his shift to be over so he could get to the airport.

He jumped when the door opened hard and swung back against the wall. Within a few seconds there were two men behind him with their guns pressed against his back as they pushed his nearly bald head down on the desk.

"Fucking traitor," one of the MPs mumbled, incorrectly labeling his onetime comrade.

"Stow that crap, soldier," one of the agents ordered. "Samuel J. Jackson, you are under arrest for murder, and for conspiracy to assassinate the president. Do you understand?" The handcuffs clicked shut.

"Yes," he answered in a quiet voice. The nineteen-year-old high school dropout hadn't expected this. His big brother promised him that everything was going to be fine. All he had to do was sit tight for a few days. He had done that. *What went wrong?* Sammy wondered.

"I'm going to read you your rights, Sammy."

"Go ahead," he said, with no hint of defiance in his shaking voice.

Scar-face had already transcribed the phone number onto a cipher pad for transmission to the L.A. office when the word came from the arrest team that Sammy was in custody. This had been easy, but then most busts were, contrary to popular, uninformed belief. This perp was just a stupid, scared kid, who had no idea what he had gotten himself into—wrong: what someone had gotten him into.

Los Angeles

Los Angeles is a city unlike any other, especially its weather. Seasons rarely follow a pattern of normalcy. Summer, the predominant and most miserable of all, usually began its reign in March and continued all the way into November, autumn being just a week or two of pseudo-summer with the added humidity of the coming winter.

One level above the Bureau's parking garage the city was winding down from another day of choking heat and smog.

The thermometer still read ninety-two and was expected to drop only nine degrees before midnight. It was cool in the basement lot, and in the cars. Four rows of nondescript government sedans filled the area to the right of the elevator, but Art and Eddie exited and turned left, to the row of "boss's" cars parked parallel to the gray cement wall.

"You wanna pack anything bigger for this?" Eddie asked.

Art opened the trunk. They discarded their jackets and took the dark gray flak vests from the compartment.

"Nope." Art patted his gun, as much for reassurance as for demonstration.

"It's gonna be hotter than hell in these things," Eddie observed, pulling the Kevlar one-piece vest over his head. It hung down in front to cover his groin area. Velcro straps cinched it snugly around his sides. "We'll crank up the A/C, right?"

"You bet." Art looked down into the trunk. There was a stockless semiauto shotgun and a fully automatic CAR-15 on the floor. He held his hand out and down, gesturing for Eddie to choose one.

"Me neither, boss. Too much noise," he explained, then closed the lid.

One nice thing about pursuit vehicles was their reliability. Art's car was serviced every three weeks, as were the others. The Chevy started up immediately and its tires squealed when Art cranked the wheel full to the left to pull out of his spot. On the way up and out they passed the cover cars, ones that few agents would *choose* to drive. They served the purpose of looking like ordinary cars, unlike the official sedans with their small hubcaps and dull one-tone paint jobs.

"You ever drive that old Torino?" Eddie asked. Art shook his head. "The sucker hauls. Mostly duct tape for upholstery, though."

"Yeah."

The reflected sunlight hit the car as it emerged from the underground garage. Art flipped the visor down and took his new sunglasses from the elastic holder. Eddie already had his on, but not the ones he liked. Off duty he wore his flashy rainbowed Oakleys.

* * *

Eddie checked the car clock against his watch. "The other units should be at the park."

Next to the Sheraton Townhouse was Lafayette Park, one of the urban oases that the city somehow never managed to keep free of crime, mostly drug dealing. It was appropriate that Marcus Jackson should choose the hotel next door to lie low. *Thank God for his idiot brother*, Art thought.

The drive down Wilshire to the Townhouse would be short in distance, but a fight with traffic the whole way, not to mention the dipping sun that would shine in their eyes continually. Time wasn't much of a concern, thankfully. One team was already in a room next to Jackson, after notifying the hotel manager and admonishing him to keep quiet. Three other teams would assist in the arrest.

"How do you think we should do this?" Art asked at a red light.

"Well, there's no reason to think he wouldn't be armed, so I say we kick it in—no warning."

"What if he's got someone in there? Everything points to him being a pretty scuzzy guy, and if he has any money for his part, I wouldn't be surprised if he's purchased some company."

Eddie laughed. "He's a red velvet kinda guy. Frankie said that car is pretty damn gaudy. How much you figure it set him back?"

"Who knows. We'll see how much we get for it at auction." Art accelerated away from the pack at the green. The engine whined through the gears, pushing the car through the next two lights as they went from yellow to red, before the back of a traffic wave slowed them. They were a scant seven blocks from the hotel.

"Let's you and I go through first, with King four coming behind us."

"Frankie and Thom second," Eddie suggested.

"They've done good."

"Damn straight," Eddie confirmed, playing the cheerleader.

Art weighed it quickly. No matter how equal they were, he just didn't like the thought of a female agent taking a bullet. But . . . "They deserve it. Okay."

"*Seven Sam*," the radio crackled.

Art grabbed the mike. Three blocks. "Seven Sam, go ahead."

"*Seven Sam, King Four—we have movement. Suspect is with a . . . stand by.*" The last words were hushed. Art stepped on the accelerator and swerved out into traffic, passing a group of four vehicles with only his blue and red rear lights flashing through the back window. "*Seven Sam, suspect just passed our door. He's with a young Caucasian female. Looks like a working girl. He's got no bags with him. Should we take him?*"

Damnit! Art's chest began to pound. "Negative." He let off the mike. "Ed, did the warrant get processed?"

"Yep." Eddie had his gun in hand, resting it on his lap.

"King Four, when it's clear you kick that door and secure the room. Copy?"

"*Ten-four.*"

"What's Frankie's team?" Art asked, swerving the car into the curb lane one-handed.

"King Eight." Art swung the car right and pulled across to the opposite side of the street, bringing the gray Chevy to a stop facing the wrong way on the east side of the park.

"*King Eight, go.*" It was Frankie.

"Frankie, where's Jackson's car?"

"*In the lot on the north side of the building. We're across the street in the tailor's.*"

"Are there any people in that lot?"

"*Affirmative. Ten or twelve in a group. Business types.*"

The decision was a bitch, and it had to be made fast. Jackson and his friend would be in the lot within a minute. If the agents tried to take them there, a lot of people could get hurt: Stray bullets don't care about guilt or innocence. He could have had King Four make a move up on the eighth floor, Art thought, but hindsight was worth shit now. There was only one choice.

"King Eight, where's the outlet for that lot?"

"*Right in front of us.*"

There wasn't enough time to clear the lot, and Jackson could turn right or left onto the street, complicating things further. They had to isolate him somewhat, and try to get the lady out of danger. She was just doing her job, after all.

"Frankie, get your car out there and block it so he'll turn east. Block the westbound lane on Sixth—put the hood up. And have Thom stay in the store. Copy?"

"*Copy.*"

Art looked over his shoulder before flooring the gas pedal, pulling the car back into the right-hand lane of Lafayette Park Place. "King Five."

"*Five by.*"

"King Five, set up on Commonwealth north of Sixth, and keep out of sight. Copy?"

"*Ten-four, got it.*"

"King Six." Art turned left onto Sixth.

"*King Six, go ahead.*"

"Cover Commonwealth and Wilshire, but stay away from the intersection: It's too close to the front of the hotel. Copy?"

"*Ten-four. We'll set up over on the south side of the park.*"

"All right, folks. We'll take Sixth east of Commonwealth." Art wanted to box in Jackson. Any direction he traveled could be blocked by one of the four units. Traffic was just beginning to let up on the periphery streets, but not on Wilshire. There was a steady flow westbound of late workers heading toward Santa Monica, and King Six found themselves the object of constant car horns as they turned west on Wilshire from Hoover, blocking the curb lane of traffic.

"Where the hell's he going?" Art stopped on the left again, this time on Sixth.

"Food, I'd say."

Seat belts were off now and the adrenaline was beginning its slow rise to the crescendo that would soon come.

Two minutes passed without Jackson appearing. The agent in the passenger seat of King Six had his binoculars trained on the Commonwealth and Wilshire entrances to the hotel, at times having to peer through the amazingly lush trees. He saw nothing. At the rear of the hotel Frankie had maneuvered the Bureau T-Bird at an angle so that all of the westbound lane of Sixth, and part of the eastbound one, was blocked.

She was at the right of the vehicle, trying her best to be interested in the quiet six-cylinder engine and trying equally as hard to fend off several offers of help from passing motorists, all of them male.

Another minute.

"Seven Sam, this is King Eight," Thom called. *"We've got nothing here except a crowd gathering to help Frankie."*

Art hit the steering wheel. "Where is he?"

"Maybe they're eating inside," Eddie surmised, shrugging. Art flashed him a "you would have to say that" look.

"Seven Sam, King Six. We've got him. He's on foot, with his lady friend, westbound on Wilshire. He came out the front."

"Son of a bitch!" Art cursed, throwing the car hard into gear. "We could lose him in that traffic on Wilshire. King Eight."

"King Eight, Frankie's heading for Wilshire on foot."

"Seven Sam, King Six, my partner is on foot." Two agents were now out of their vehicles, moving to cut Jackson off: one behind, and Frankie trying to head him off on Wilshire.

Art and Eddie reached the intersection of Commonwealth and Sixth as King Five did from the north. Art went south on Commonwealth, more out of fear of colliding with the other unit than desire, and King Five went west on Sixth.

"Best-laid plans, boss," Eddie commented. He was chewing his gum hard now.

Art slowed a hundred yards shy of Wilshire, and then there was the sound.

LAPD had been notified of the Bureau's presence in the area, a routine practice when one law enforcement agency was operating within the jurisdiction of another. The message was passed over the radio to the divisional units, but without having a divisional roll call to acknowledge the information. Two motor officers missed the call, having been involved in a minor altercation with a traffic offender. After all, it hadn't been an "officer needs help" call, something that would have grabbed their immediate attention.

This made it somewhat understandable, but no less damaging, when the two officers gunned their Kawasakis to catch up with the beat-up-looking Chrysler that had pulled away from the curb and across two lanes of traffic into the oncoming lanes. They were too far away to see the strangely tall radio antenna at the front of the car, but then it became inconsequential as both hit their sirens and lights simultaneously.

The sound of a wailing high-pitched siren was not unusual in L.A. at any hour, but there was enough of a ghoul factor to make anyone look.

Marcus Jackson turned to see what unfortunate soul had gotten busted. Probably someone running a light, since there were only two bursts on the siren. Kind of a "hey you, look in your rearview" sort of message. What a bitch . . .

The man was definitely out of place, both in posture and appearance. First of all, he was white, a distinctive trait in this racially mixed minority area. And he was jogging, but then stopped when he saw Jackson turn around.

No more warning was needed. "Later, babe," Marcus said, patting the lady's ass before darting out into the stop-and-go traffic on Wilshire. The .357 revolver came out from under his jacket.

Agent Dan Burlingame from King Six saw the suspect bolt. His feet began immediately propelling his slightly over-weight frame faster. "*He's running, south across Wilshire,*" he yelled into his radio.

"Who was that?" Art asked. "He didn't identify!" The accelerator hit the stops and the car lurched forward. Ahead, a wall of cars blocked the intersection.

Eddie hit the siren, but it could not *make* the cars, nose to ass, move; there was just no room. The threat of a $250 fine didn't deter people from filling the intersection. King Six worked past the jam on the opposite side of the street, but slowly. One of the LAPD motors followed him, clued in now to the Bureau car's identity, but unsure of what to do. The other motor officer pulled into traffic to clear a path in the intersection for the Chevy, its siren wailing and grille lights flashing.

Frankie, at a dead run, reached Wilshire in time to see Jackson dodging traffic in the eastbound lanes. "*This is Frankie, I'm on him. He's westbound on Wilshire. South side of the street. I see a gun. He's armed.*"

Cars were slowing at the sight of the man and his gun, making it easier for Frankie to weave her way across the street, but slowed traffic even more at the rear of the pack. She saw Dan entering lanes to her left. He was having a harder time, even having to do a half roll over the hood of a taxi.

In front of Art the motor cop threw up his hands in frustration.

"Screw it, let's go." Art pushed the door, taking the keys and a radio from the charger. Eddie followed.

The sight people were seeing was uncommon even for Los Angeles. Traffic had come to a halt on Wilshire as the agents converged on Jackson on foot and in vehicles. The lone motor officer who had stuck with King Six was in the dark as to what was going on, but he stayed close behind the Bureau Chrysler, yelling frantically into his radio for information from his dispatcher.

Jackson spun in a running circle to check his rear—he didn't like what he saw. Two of them were close!

Inside, Marc. The doorway was set into the old building. He pushed off hard up the three steps and was inside.

Frankie and Dan hit the doorway simultaneously, seconds later, one on each side. Both were puffing hard.

"*He's inside a gray-brick four-story,*" Frankie said into the radio. "Dan, check for exits."

"Gotcha." He moved east along the building's front and disappeared down a side alley.

Frankie's partner brought their car to a screeching halt fifty feet away, blocking the eastbound lanes of Wilshire. He ran toward Frankie, who directed him to the opposite side of the structure. Art and Eddie ran up, looking like half-dressed knights in their flak vests.

"Where's he at?" Art was breathing hard.

"Inside—he went up," Frankie answered. Several strands of hair had come loose from her ponytail and were hanging in her face. She threw them back with a toss of her head. "He's armed."

Art was pressed against the wall, looking alternately up and at Frankie. Eddie stood farther back by the corner, his gun trained upward covering the windows. King Five and King Six pulled up seconds apart from opposite directions.

There were now eight agents and one LAPD motor cop covering the building.

"Ed, over here." Art shouted. Another agent took up Eddie's position.

"Yeah, boss?" he panted.

"We've gotta take him. I don't want him offing himself in there. No way."

"It's probably dark in there," Eddie guessed, half joking and half not.

"You, me, and Frankie," Art decided. "Okay?"

Francine Aguirre, whose unofficial Bureau nickname was Stud, smiled and nodded. Strangely, she was not afraid, but then it might have been the high-octane chemicals her body was pumping into her bloodstream.

"Let's do it," Eddie answered, spitting his gum on the sidewalk.

"You." Art pointed to the faceless motor cop, still in his mirrored sunglasses and black-and-white helmet. The officer approached, crouching along the wall. "I'm Agent Jefferson, FBI. You cover the front. Anyone without a badge comes out, put them facedown. Got it?"

"Yeah." *What the hell is going on?* He wanted the backup he called for to be there—now!

"All units: Frankie, Eddie, and I are going in." Art tucked the radio in his back pocket. "Let's go."

Eddie led off. The front door creaked open inward—just like in the movies, Eddie thought. His gun was pointed forward, held in two hands. The Joker was deadly serious about this. Somewhere in the building was a guy who would more than likely blow a hole in him if given the chance. That didn't sound appealing.

It *was* dark inside the old building, which at one time had probably been a bustling center of professional offices, but now was a dingy brick cube full of empty offices above the ground floor. A man poked his head out of a ground-floor office. Two guns, Art's and Frankie's, automatically centered on him.

"What's u—"

"Get in-side," Frankie ordered in measured syllables. "And *stay there*." His head disappeared and the door lock clicked.

"You're sure he went up?" Art asked.

"Yeah," Frankie confirmed. "You should have seen the clodhoppers he was wearing. I heard them all the way outside."

"Okay."

Eddie looked up the stairs. "Here we go," Eddie said.

Moving upstairs was a painfully tedious process when the stairs zigzagged up to each level. Eddie found himself the point, on his back squirming up each step while training his weapon at the perch of the level above. Art and Frankie following him also concentrated their attention upward, though it was considerably more comfortable. Eddie worked his way up to the second floor with the other two a few feet behind.

"Word has it you've got a good nose," Art whispered to Frankie. "Now would be a wonderful time to demonstrate it."

Frankie was on the right side of the wide hallway, looking down its short length. There were four windowed doors on each side, and a single window at the end of the corridor. Light pierced its glazed surface, shining through the swirling dust particles and illuminating the faded hospital green left wall. She twisted her head, looking up the center of the staircase shaft.

"I'd say he's up top," she surmised. "He's gotta know he's cornered. The higher up he goes, the farther he is from us."

"I buy that," Eddie agreed.

"All right, Ed, you and I go up. Frankie, you're here. Don't let him get past if he comes."

"If he does, it means he got past us, which won't be a good sign." Eddie quietly snickered through his nose.

Frankie watched the agents begin their move up. She kept her attention focused on them; that was her job—cover. But she also shot frequent glances down the hallway, just in case.

It took a little over two minutes to make it to the fourth floor, two above Frankie. The third had looked like the second. They put it out of their minds that Jackson might be below them.

This level was like the others, but painted brown. Some real wood might have been there long ago.

Art motioned to Eddie to take the left wall. He would take the right. Each would cover the opposite side, especially the windows in each door, as they moved down the corridor. There was no light from the rooms, Eddie saw, deciding that the windows must be boarded up from the inside. *Great.* It would be dark in there, just like he had thought and feared.

This sucks, Eddie mouthed to Art.

The doorknobs were old, worn brass, probably original furnishings. Art could almost see it being the set for a movie, one of those 1930s private eye flicks. But there was no "So-and-So Bros. Investigations" stenciled on any of the doors. Behind one of them, though, would be a clue—one Marcus Jackson.

Art touched the first knob, twisting it easily with his fingertips. Locked. Eddie did the same. Also locked. Three doors left on each side.

One's heart almost becomes a separate entity during adrenaline rushes. It pounds so quickly, with a rhythm all its own, that you half expect to see it in front of you. Art's felt heavy in his chest as it thumped against the Kevlar fabric. He controlled his breathing, as was taught in the academy, or so he thought. In through the nose, deep, short breaths.

It was a bunch of crap. Whoever thought that up had never tried to clear a dingy building while wrapped in body armor. Art looked down, wondering if the vest would work at this close a range. That would depend, he knew, on what Jackson was carrying.

The second doors were clear. Maybe Jackson had done what Frankie said and gone as far away as he could—the last room. They'd see, but there were two doors to check before that.

Oh shit! Art's door swayed back at his touch. Everything was so damn silent at that instant that he heard Eddie's doorknob hit the stops—locked.

Then there was a flash, but no sound—he thought. It was so quick. Another flash, and another. And then the sound, three quick explosions—POP POP POP—followed by a trailing roar, like thunder echoing in the mountains. Art was going low, falling into the doorway, his gun coming around, pointing in and up as the room's interior came into view.

Marcus Jackson stood about five feet inside the doorway, nearest the hinge wall. He was dark, and dressed in equally dark clothes, though there was some light sneaking in from—what were those, boards?—the outside. It shone from above on his shoulders. There was a look of surprise in his white eyes, Art saw very clearly.

Two cracks reverberated off the walls. Art had fired. The man was propelled back and up from the impact, his hat jumping off to the side. He fell against the far wall, making a sick thud as his head struck the solid wood of yesteryear's construction, and there was the metallic sound of a gun hitting the tile floor.

Then all the sounds absent during the fury of the moment flooded back into Art's head—sirens, radio calls, traffic sounds from a block away, and . . .

"Eddie!"

He was slumped on his side against the door. His eyes were semi-open and fluttering, and a strange gurgling hiss came from his mouth in a broken rhythm. And the blood—it was forming in a pool at the top of Eddie's body, but Art couldn't see where from.

"Seven Sam, agent down," Art said calmly into the radio. "Suspect also down." He backed across the hall close to his partner, keeping his own gun centered on the dark form sprawled on the floor in the room.

Frankie bounded up the steps, followed by the LAPD cop. Their guns were held low, two-handed.

"Oh my God!" Frankie said as she moved down the hall.

"It's dark in there," Art said. One hand cradled Eddie's head.

The motor cop pulled his flashlight. He and Frankie entered the room with both guns aimed in a serious way at Marcus Jackson. He was lying in a heap, his head flopped to one side. Frankie slid the gun away with her foot.

"Cover him," she instructed the cop. "I'll cuff him."

It didn't appear to be necessary, but it was procedure. Dead or not, a downed suspect was cuffed. Frankie would just as soon make sure he was dead, but . . . she rolled him over and pulled him away from the wall. There was a pool of blood and a single hole in his back. When she turned him back she saw two distinct entrance wounds in his black T-shirt. Two perfect center mass hits. There was no pulse, she discovered, feeling very soiled by the blood on her hand.

"Check him for weapons and stay with him," Frankie ordered. She picked up the gun by its barrel and examined it before laying it back down and going into the hall.

"Sir, it's a .357."

Art was gently stretching Eddie out flat. He heard a siren approaching and willed it to be the paramedics. Eddie had taken three slugs, though the Kevlar had luckily absorbed two of them. They were dark indentations in the fabric covering, one at the sternum and the other a couple inches above. Jackson wasn't a trained shooter, not having compensated for the gun barrel's rise as it recoiled from each shot. They had "stitched" up the vest. The third struck Eddie in the throat, slightly below and to the left of his Adam's apple.

"Ed, you hang on," Art said loudly, hoping Ed would hear.

Dan bounded up the stairs. "Paramedics are here . . . oh Jesus!"

Damnit! Art felt the bullets, each one, as though they had struck him. His gut hurt. All the agents were there now, standing back as the paramedic firemen started working on their comrade.

"King Four," Art said into his radio.

"*King Four.*" The voice was subdued. They had heard the "agent down" broadcast.

"Get a forensics team in there and lock it down tight. Anything obvious?"

"*Only a bag of cash. Close to a million, I'd guess. Copy?*"

"Ten-four."

"*Who's down?*"

"Eddie—looks bad," Art answered, knowing he had to be honest. It did look bad.

"*Yeah. Ten-four.*"

Art looked in the room at the cuffed corpse. What was the toll now? Thirty people dead since this all started, at least that he knew of, and how many that weren't known yet. And maybe Eddie. Why? Someone at the top wanted to link this with the hijacking. *Just fucking fine.* It wasn't enough that Jackson and his brothers had gotten a cool million for helping with the slaughter at Seventh and Figueroa, and it wasn't enough that the shooters had sacrificed themselves. Hell, the whole damn thing started with the death of that little girl, an innocent. And why had it come this far? Hadn't there been enough vengeance, and wouldn't there be enough funerals? Whole families were destroyed by . . .

"Oh my God," Art said aloud. His face showed fear, and anger.

"Sir?" Frankie saw something on his face.

"Frankie, you have the scene. I've gotta get to the office."

"Okay," she answered.

Art leaned in over one of the paramedics. "Ed—hang in there. I think we figured this one out. Just hang on." He looked to one of the men working on his partner and friend.

"We don't know," the paramedic answered the look.

It didn't reassure Art, but it wasn't a death warrant. He ran down the stairs, all the way to the bottom, and sprinted past the tangle of emergency vehicles to his car a block way. The vest came off and was tossed across the front seat to the passenger side. Art checked his holster before getting in— it was secured with the snap strap. His weapon had saved his life once again, but he hoped that, unlike the time many years before, his partner would survive.

The intersection was clear now, blocked that way by the city cops. Art had no traffic to fight going east, back to the Bureau office.

It was almost seven when Art ran into his office. Carol was on her way out after a seminormal day, unlike the previous two.

"I need you, Carol," he said. "It's important."

She sensed the real urgency in his voice, like time was an important commodity right now. "Okay. What can I do?"

"Get the evidence bag from the Hilton. I think it came over earlier. There's one with a picture we took from one of the shooters—it's of a young guy and a little girl."

"Anything else?"

"Is Jerry around?"

"No."

Art wanted to bounce his thoughts off someone, but he couldn't wait. He might catch hell for going over his bosses, something he'd never done. Time. Time was a problem. "Get me a line to the director. Don't get him on, just yet," Art admonished her. Carol started back for her desk. Art grabbed her arm gently. "Carol, Eddie was shot."

"Dear God," she responded, her voice cracking. "How bad?"

Art shook his head. "I don't know. It looked bad." He rubbed her back. "I thought you should know. Now, we've got to do this, and you're my right arm. Get the evidence, and the line to the director, okay? I'll find Jerry."

"Okay." She wiped her eyes and walked away.

Jerry Donovan took the news like any man in charge of others would. He also listened as Art quickly explained a theory, but took no position on either side of it. That was all right with Art—a least he didn't shoot it down.

The senior agent thought the idea was credible. It made sense, and it came from Art. That was enough. But his subordinate had also made a major error in judgment. Jerry wasn't about to say anything at this stage, but there was going to be a change. He hated the fact that he had to make that decision.

"Go to the director with this," Jerry said.

"First I'm going to confirm something."

Jerry gave him the go-ahead and left.

Art dialed the number and waited. After it was answered he found himself waiting again while Meir Shari was tracked down by an assistant, half a world away. It would be the very early morning in Tel Aviv, just the time when someone wanted to be bombarded by questions.

The evidence bag was on his desk. In it was the picture. *So this is all about you?* Art asked the smiling girlish face. She had dark, curly hair, and big brown eyes.

"Hello."

"Mr. Shari. This is Arthur Jefferson, Los Angeles FBI."

"Good morn—well, I believe it is good evening for you."

"Yes. I'm sorry to accost you this early in the morning, but something very disturbing struck me a short time ago. The Khaled brothers have been identified as the killers of the president—your assistance was invaluable. Well, I was wondering if there was possibly a third brother?"

"I don't know. What makes you ask?"

"This picture that we found, it looks like Nahar Khaled, but then it also looks like the older one. And they look very much alike themselves. What I'm getting at is a possible link to another event. Apparently someone in our government thinks the assassination could be related to the hijacking, and that would make sense when trying to figure out a reason."

"Can you hold on while I check? We may not have a file on another brother, but there might be a notation of one in a family reference. It is a chance."

"I'll wait."

Art wondered if he was creating something where nothing was. *No.* Something was fitting together, making sense. If there was a third Khaled, he could be the link, but beyond that he would provide the reason for this all. The assassination, as strange as it might seem, might have been only a prelude to a greater attack, one that the Khaled brothers had been cajoled into. They had a true sense of vengeance, and Art really couldn't blame them for that honest emotion. Someone had used them.

"Arthur."

"Yes?"

"You are truly a psychic! There is an older brother. Saad Khaled. There is a notation that the little girl's body was released to her brother for burial. The two others were deported by this time, so it had to be another. We find that sometimes deportees sneak back in and use the names of others. That does not appear to be the case here."

"Dear God, Meir!" *Damnit!* Art had figured right, and the rest now made complete sense. He had the link, the motive, the players, and most important of all, the intent. "I have to go. Thank you so much."

"Good luck, and shalom."

Art had no time to waste. The last news he'd heard was that the aircraft had left the Canaries. He buzzed Carol and asked for the director.

What had been a murder investigation with probable international ties now was small in comparison to what he knew was going to happen. Art was relieved, but still found himself taking deep breaths to compensate for the tightness in his chest.

Chicago

He was no longer in his Army uniform. That had been stripped off him during booking and was replaced by a white jumpsuit. His left hand was cuffed to the table, which was bolted to the floor for obvious reasons. Sammy's hastily arranged attorney from the PD's office sat next to him.

"Gentlemen." His name was Bob Lomax, the special agent in charge of the Chicago field office of the FBI, and at the moment, he was one pissed agent. Word had spread that a brother agent was lying in the hospital, a bullet in his body, an event only slightly mitigated by the fact that the perp had bitten the big one. *So you're his brother. Have we got a surprise for you.* Lomax was a tough agent, but one blessed by both street and administrative finesse. There was a need here, for information. All else was secondary—he could hate this man later.

"Lomax," the attorney began, "this is highly irregular. You won't release my client to custody, instead you keep him— keep us—in here." He motioned to the cubic room. "Let's all get some sleep. How about it?"

Bob Lomax smiled at the lawyer, then shifted his happy gaze to Sammy. "Sam, guess who's here to see you. Well, actually he's here to see us, but maybe we can arrange it so he can drop by."

"Who . . . who are you talkin' 'bout?" Sammy asked. He was shooting looks between his lawyer and Lomax.

"Your brother," Lomax answered, his smile becoming cheeky.

"Marcus! He's here?"

"No, he's dead." The smile disappeared instantly. His face was flat, physically and emotionally.

"What?"

"Lomax! What the hell is this?"

"You, mister attorney, had better listen carefully, just in case your client is too grief-stricken to comprehend what is happening." He turned back to the youngest Jackson. "Your brother shot and seriously injured an FBI agent in Los Angeles before he was killed. Now, you can and will be held as an accessory to assault on a federal law enforcement officer, plus multiple counts of conspiracy to commit murder, and anything else we can find. You are had, Mr. Jackson. We have you cold. The cases that held the weapons used in the assassination were found with the stencils still on them. Marcus wasn't too bright, huh? And interestingly there was an inventory done just prior to a certain duty shift you worked, and those weapons were logged in—still in their packing crates. But," Lomax said sarcastically, bringing a finger to his lips, "some of your fellow soldiers just finished another inventory and—guess what?—the weapons are gone. Can you believe that?"

"This is unheard of!" the lawyer protested, which only earned him a wave-off.

"And you know what? Your brother Ernest is next door saying that he knows nothing about any of this. He says his El Rukn days are far behind him, and he does have a hell of an alibi. So, it looks like you're going to take this rap all alone."

"My client has not even been arraigned, Lomax!"

"He will be . . . alone."

Sammy tried to stand but was held down by the restraint. "No way! Ernie was the one, man."

"Sammy!" his attorney shouted. "Keep quiet."

"You shut up! This is my life, man. I didn't do all this alone. Ernie set it up, man—him and his Rukn bros."

"Do you want to talk, Sammy?"

"Hell yes!"

Lomax looked to the frustrated PD. "Shall I get a DA in here, and a crew?"

"Go ahead, why not?" he answered, giving his client a glance filled with pity. *Stupid kid.* "It'll get thrown out, anyway."

"You think so?" Lomax walked to the door. "I'm not so sure."

For the next thirty minutes Sammy Jackson spoke slowly and clearly into the microphone, telling all, while the video camera saved every sickening moment of it.

15
. . . .
PENANCE

East of Benghazi

HE WAS NOT of Berber descent, which meant he had spent
most of his early life in or near the city. The vast openness
of the desert was alien then. He had come to appreciate it
later as commander of the 3rd. Its location, far enough from
Benghazi to render the city lights' glow an afterthought,
made it an ideal spot to stargaze. Stars cast a light all their
own on moonless nights, of which this night was not one.
There was a small sliver of a crescent high in the sky. It
would begin to fade soon. Muhadesh looked to the east. No
trace of the coming day was yet visible.

It was quiet and cool. The engine of the jeep was off and
losing warmth. Muhadesh felt the little remaining on his butt
as he leaned against the hood. He wore his blousy dress
greens and the beloved mottled-pattern commando parka.
At his side was the World War II vintage Makarov from
al-Dir.

"My friend, what would you think of me?" He asked the
sky. Al-Dir, the warrior patriot, would shoot him, Muhadesh
knew. "You have not done what I have. You killed our
enemies." *I killed our people*, he added silently, afraid that
his friend might somehow appear in the darkness.

The Americans had given him a way to relieve his guilt,
to exorcise the ghosts that haunted him, or so he thought. He
had no particular love for the Americans, but he did love his
homeland. Why, then, had he betrayed it? *To avenge those
I have murdered*, he would answer, knowing there was a
more correct response. He had to hide his guilt. Masking his
own culpability was essential. *I am alive*! So many had died
because he had chosen life for himself. *I could have said no*!

Yes, he had saved lives with his treachery, but he wondered if the number saved was not hopelessly outweighed by those who had perished at his own hands, and those slaughtered by his students. *I am alive, while they are damned to eternal sleep.*

Muhadesh walked away from the vehicle. He faced north. The ocean was far away, yet he felt himself drowning where he stood. Again the quiet surrounded him, driving away his thoughts, and then he heard it: faint, still, and far away. It was an unmistakable sound. He slid the right side of his parka back.

It was a world of noise in the blackened cabin. Both side doors of the SH-60 Oceanhawk were fully open, with camo-clad Marines dangling their legs out, their M-16s pointing downward into the darkness. The night-vision goggles on their eight faces looked like stubby binoculars pasted on welding goggles. Each of the two pilots wore them also, as did Dick Logan.

"Pickup in two minutes," the pilot announced, though he didn't know exactly who he was picking up—a friendly, he had been told. He was flying at fifty feet in his hastily painted helicopter—he liked the "mean" look of its squat, black body—trying to pick out a man-size object, which was supposed to be there, but might not. He had flown special ops in the Gulf War, over similar terrain, and was familiar with the reality that "packages" weren't always where they were supposed to be, when they were supposed to be there.

"FLIR is showin' nothin'," the right-seater said. The Forward Looking InfraRed sensor would pick up any ambient heat, such as that generated by a man's body, on a narrow track out a few hundred meters to the helicopter's front.

"Right. Mister, is this guy supposed to signal us, or what?"

"That's not in the plan," Logan answered honestly. To either side of him the eight jarheads swept their areas of observation.

They *were* coming. Muhadesh was not certain until that moment. The pickup procedure had been laid out years before with safety and rapidity in mind, but there was no guarantee. He had ensured that they would come, however.

The final answers were tucked away securely in his breast pocket with the other note—a request.

The *whop whop* of the approaching helicopter now assured him. No longer would he fear tomorrow, or the killing. He breathed deeply. The desert air tasted sweet and dry. His soul would be safe. That was his last concern, that his body not be desecrated by his vengeful countrymen.

Muhadesh undid the buckled holster cover and brought the Makarov up close to his ear. The sound was close now, off to his left. He half expected to feel the rotor wash.

"Thank you, al-Dir," he said aloud, no longer afraid of today, or tomorrow, but still unaware that his last conscious act was motivated by the fear that was, truly, his soul's undoing.

"There!" a bulky Marine shouted, pointing with his rifle and reaching behind with his free hand to tap Logan.

"Watcha got, Sergeant?" Logan leaned over against his restraints and pulled one earphone free.

"Over there, maybe three hundred yards. Looked like a muzzle flash."

"Roger." Logan patted the flak-jacketed soldier. "Major, one of the troops saw what may be a muzzle flash to starboard. Three hundred yards off."

"Roger." The Oceanhawk banked severely to the right, making the landlubber CIA officer grab for a handhold. He was jealous of the Recon Marines who swung easily with the roll of the helicopter.

The FLIR picked it up immediately. "Two sources, Maj. Come left." The co-pilot adjusted the sensitivity of the FLIR. "One small, man-sized. The other's a truck or something, no doubt."

There would be no mistakes here. "Let's sweep the area." The pilot pulled back on the collective and brought the nose down, giving the SH-60 altitude and speed. He wanted to circle the area of the heat sources to make certain there were no surprises awaiting them. After two full sweeps the pilot brought the nose back around toward the sources.

"Dead ahead." The co-pilot now had a better vantage point with the FLIR. Altitude gave a higher aspect to the scene, making the picture more obvious, and more ominous. "Just the two sources, but I don't like it. See that one." His finger pointed to a ghostly green spot of light on the screen.

The pilot didn't like it either. "Lieutenant?"

In the cabin the Marine commander leaned farther in to escape the noise of the downwash. He pushed the boom mike almost into his mouth. "Go ahead!"

"We're showing two sources: one man, looks prone, and a vehicle about ten yards beyond him. The area looks clean. I'm gonna set you down fifty yards this side of the guy. Roger?"

"Roger." The lieutenant tapped the man to his left on the helmet, the sequence continuing around the cabin until all the Marines were alerted.

Logan felt hopelessly underarmed with his seven-shot .45, but it would have to do. Really, he hoped it wouldn't *need* to.

Suddenly everything slowed. The helicopter pitched backward and the main wheels touched the desert floor. A second later the cabin was empty, except for Logan, who felt very exposed to the night streaming in through both doors. He pulled the slide back on his Colt. At least it made him feel safer.

The thud scared the shit out of him. Everything looked surreal through the goggles. The Marines were back, six of them still around the edge, their legs hanging out as before, and two, including the lieutenant, were in the center over . . . *a body?* The helicopter threw everyone back as it rose and moved forward, banking hard to the right until it was heading due north.

"Seal it up," the lieutenant ordered. His men followed it smartly, bringing their bodies fully into the helo and closing the windowless doors on each side. One slid a heavy fabric curtain closed between the cabin and the cockpit. "Glasses off. Lights."

Where before there had been a world of dancing green specters, there was now the harshly lit tomb of the Oceanhawk's interior. The floor jumped with the turbulence of the low-altitude flight, bouncing the Marines against the walls. Some still wore their Kevlar helmets, and all looked quite emotionless in their painted faces. Young white eyes stared at the form in the center of the cabin.

Logan safed his weapon. One of the arms had fallen to the floor from where it lay against the chest, and came to rest on Logan's boot. There was blood on the arm, caked with sand, and there was blood all over the floor beneath the right side of the head. The face—the eyes were lifeless—stared toward him, and the left side of the head seemed caved in. He knelt next to the man, straddling one arm. Logan had never seen a dead person so close.

"Looks like he popped himself, mister," the lieutenant commented. "In the right, out the left." He noticed the civilian's discomfort. "Your guy made an exit, that's for sure."

Why? Logan thought silently. DONNER had made such a damn fuss about ensuring the pickup. Didn't he want to get out? Logan shook his head as he checked the man for the last message. *We pushed him.* His pockets were empty, as was the holster at his side, except for one. He pulled the three pieces of paper out, unfolding the wrong one first. It didn't speak to the questions his superiors wanted answered, but it did, at least partly, answer Logan's.

"Well," Logan said aloud, though it was drowned out by the turbine noise, "you win, DONNER."

He opened the other papers. Their messages, to his mind, were secondary to what he had just read, but still important. The singlespaced typewritten pages were in Italian, both DONNER's and Logan's second language. Translating took a moment. Logan had a sense of what the whole picture was from the discussions with his bosses back at Langley; these messages completed the picture and scared him. The little he knew about nuclear physics was enough. A goddamn butcher would shit his pants.

"Major?"

"Go ahead, Mr. Logan."

"How long to the *Vinson?*" This had to get to Langley fast. After a pause: "Thirty minutes. Tops."

Logan put the papers in his leg pocket. He could wait half an hour, but could the world? It was an overly grandiose question, he decided, one that DONNER had obviously reasoned and answered for himself. Had the man figured it all out? Probably not; the note pointed in that direction.

There could have been a great conversation when DONNER came out. Logan had looked forward to that. Case officers didn't usually get that luxury. Of course he might have been allowed to spend some time with him at a later date. That wouldn't have been good enough, though, and now it mattered not at all.

No one would ever know what Muhadesh Algar had made himself live through, least of all himself. Logan only knew that one life was over for the man known as DONNER. Such a benign code name for the man. He had lived to the extreme while trying to absolve his guilt, though no one would know that either. In the end only one person would feel some sense of relief from a life destined to end in futility, and that relief itself would somehow seem less than absolute considering the sacrifice.

16
••••••••••••

THE PUZZLE'S CENTER

Los Angeles

THE LINE WAS silent. The director wasn't known for his thoughtful pauses, leaving Art waiting uncomfortably.

"Who confirmed this?" The director's voice hinted at irritation.

"Israeli Intelligence," Art answered. "Meir Shari. He was their military liaison in D.C. when I met him. His information is solid."

Jones had no doubt about that. The theory, though, was conjecture. There could be doubts about it. The problem was that it made sense, and couldn't be confirmed or disproved. "We have a problem, then, Jefferson. If there is a third Khaled brother on that plane, and if the assassination was just meant to set things up as you think, there isn't much we can do. And if you're wrong, we might have to do something to prevent a *possibility*, something that just might kill a bunch of people."

"I know that," Art said. "But if—"

"If you're right . . ." Jones thought on that. The information didn't really change the equation in Washington, but it would end any speculation about how to respond. This would seal it, no matter what was on the plane. "Get back to your partner, Jefferson. What you just told me is going to the president. Good work."

Art didn't wait to hear the click. He hung up first. All Carol saw was her boss sprinting by, his jacket in hand.

The Chevy was speeding out of the underground garage three minutes later. The USC Medical Center was fifteen minutes away by car, ten if he drove hell-bent. Art would. It was his friend in there. He had to be with him.

There was no way he could know that the same pattern of logic, influenced by his growing emotional stress, had governed his fateful decision ninety minutes before. But the decision to deal with that improper action had already been made at one level of the Bureau, and would soon be approved by the highest level, the one whom Art had just finished with.

Langley, Va.

Landau slid the message from Logan into the DONNER file and tossed it onto the desk. It was late, and dark, but the lights from the CIA's perimeter were faintly visible through the DCI's window. The aged director reached and turned off the only light in his office, on his desk.

The outside world became instantly clearer when the office went dark. Those lights that were only specks before were now cones of light shining on the grounds. The rain had subsided hours before. Everything looked clean and fresh outside.

Why? "Why?" Landau asked the outside light.

"Herb, you in here?" Drummond asked into the office.

The DCI turned his chair. "Yep. Right here." He switched on the desk lamp.

The DDI waited at the doorway, leaning in. "Are you okay?"

"Yeah. Come on in."

Drummond came in, but didn't sit. He saw the DONNER file on the desk. "DONNER?"

"He's dead. He did it himself."

It should have surprised the DDI, but it didn't. Assets, behind the sterile name, were people, with reasons for doing things that no one would ever know. His experience had taught him that time and again, though the loss of an agent never became "acceptable," just "preferable" to some alternative. "Don't try and read too much into it."

Landau looked up, a slight smile forming. "Easier said than done, you know."

He did. "Did he get the information we needed?"

"Exactly what we needed. I'm heading over to the White House in a few. The good news is that it's not a bomb."

"And the bad?" There was always bad when a person prefaced his words that way.

"That what they've got on board is still dangerous, but it still requires the nuclear material, which we don't know if they have. There's no evidence they've removed any from Tajoura." Landau's tone conveyed the frustration in that statement.

Drummond knew he had to bring some unwanted certainty to the situation. "Herb, it looks like they do have it. One of our S&T teams doing a financial trace on this whole thing came up with some damning info. It seems the colonel was in the habit of buying scrap metal through a Tunisian front company. The kind of stuff that comes from dismantled industrial plants."

"A lot of those left around after the forties," Landau commented.

"One of those scrap shipments was particularly suspicious. Bad documentation, a money trail through PLO and other accounts." Drummond drew a breath, wishing the discovery *had* been a mistake. But it wasn't. "That scrap came from Osirak four days before the Iraqis rolled into Kuwait."

The DCI snickered. "So Qaddafi was playing the good Arab brother for Hussein, keeping the uranium safely tucked away." Landau leaned back, his fingers tapping in sequence on the desk edge. "And there wasn't supposed to be any nuclear material at Osirak anyway."

"We always suspected there was. Even the Israelis did when they bombed the reactor back in the eighties." Drummond finally sat. "We'll have to figure that one out later—a Soviet slipup, more than likely. Back in the pre-Gorby days. What's interesting is that this all appears to have been in the works before our predecessors did their dirty work on the colonel."

"Like we knew, he's wanted nuclear weapons openly for a long time," Landau said. "And now he has highly enriched uranium. Higher than Tajoura."

"It can't all be on the plane," Drummond commented.

The DCI shook his head. "No way. We'll have to check on how much could be left behind, but that could present a further problem." *Or an opportunity.*

It was quiet for a short period that seemed much longer. The misaligned wheels of the night janitor's cart were audible in the hallway. Drummond turned to check the door visually. "You know, old Harry's probably the most well informed man in this country," he said, giving the crusty old custodian of the executive level more credit than was deserved. "The things he must've heard, even in just meaningless conversations. He's been here thirty-two years."

Landau heard none of it. His mind was occupied with a thought. "Qaddafi was smart on this one, Greg."

The DDI returned to the relevant discussion. "How so?"

"He gets all this set up, the hijackers, the thing on board, all of it. The assassination, too; that's what I think. And once it's all over, if he's still alive, he has surplus uranium for whatever reasons he chooses."

"Smart and dangerous."

Landau acknowledged the correctness of the DDI's statement. "And the clever misinformation, placed just where we'd find it. The bomb design scam. They obviously didn't have the capability to build something of even its crude design."

"Just to scare us. To make us wring our hands."

"Right. And he had us, too. What's really on there may not be as frightening, but it could be just as deadly."

Drummond flashed a knowing smile. "Not-so-scary things aren't as hard to deal with."

"Neither are other things, now that we know." The DCI knew that Bud would agree with that thought.

The White House

"Sir, there's a phone call for you. It's urgent."

Bud looked at the DCI. Urgent held little meaning when a meeting with the president was about to begin. He hovered over the speakerphone for a moment. "Who is it?"

"Director Jones."

He debated the decision. "Herb, go on in without me. Tell them I'll be in in a minute."

"Where the hell is he?" the president asked. His body involuntarily paced.

"He'll be here," Ellis responded. "It must be important or Jones wouldn't have called in the first place: He knows what's going on."

The president wasn't angry at his NSA, he was angry at the shifting situation. The revelation from the DCI that *something*, though not a bomb, was on the hijacked plane had clouded an earlier decision he made. "How, tell me, *how* can I order that plane shot down with this new information? How can I do that?"

Neither Meyerson nor Gonzales had an answer. Herb Landau, however, saw little need to alter the previous course.

"Sir," the DCI began, "you still have no other option, in my mind."

"Herb, when we thought that plane was carrying an atomic bomb, then we had no choice. But now, with whatever it is, I don't know. Mass destruction is one thing, but this . . ."

"This thing can't be as destructive as a bomb," Gonzales said.

"Do you know that . . . for sure?" the DCI asked. The chief of staff signaled not. "Then until we know that, we have to assume it is."

The president checked the time. "Damnit! Bud shou—"

The NSA's entry interrupted the sentence. "We have a whole new problem," Bud spat out. He was almost breathless, and walked right to the president, who stood in rolled-up shirtsleeves by the fireplace.

"What now?" the president asked for the others.

Bud looked to Landau. "You filled them in?" The DCI nodded. "Sir, the intelligence that came out concerning what is on the plane, coupled with what the Agency discovered concerning the source of the uranium, is disturbing; it validates to a high degree what we've suspected, with only a difference in the aircraft's cargo. What we've been missing is the why. Why are they doing this?"

"Correct," Meyerson agreed. "What do they hope to gain?"

Bud nodded. His movements were quick and sharp, signaling the seriousness of the unknown to the others. "We have that now."

"Let's have it," the president said. He walked over to his desk and sat down. Meyerson and Gonzales came over, too, standing at the desk's edge. Landau followed, moving slowly and leaning forward on a chair back.

"I just got off the phone with Gordy Jones. He relayed some new information from L.A. They found the man they believe was the connection for the assassins. His name was Marcus Jackson."

"Was?" The president knew what it meant.

"They attempted to arrest him. An FBI agent was seriously wounded and Jackson was killed."

The president rubbed his upper lip with the edge of his fist. "Ellis, find out the injured agent's name." To Bud: "Go on."

Bud's breathing eased. "This is all hot, so bear with me. Some paper?" The president leaned forward and handed over a pad and pen. "We have two assassins, the Khaled brothers, with a deeply personal reason for doing what they did. You already know about their little sister. Now, they did it—there's no doubt. The FBI has positive identification on them from several sources and witnesses. The question was who helped them, and how? Well, this Jackson fellow was in the perfect position to put them in place without drawing undue attention, and since he disappeared right after the killings they went looking for him. No luck right away, but they did find the pickup point for the weapons. Jackson had stashed them there for an easy pickup by the Khaleds—that way there was no face-to-face meeting, no direct link. And for his trouble he got a million bucks, free and clean."

"More moola spread around," Landau said.

"A lot," Bud agreed. "They found the majority of it at the hotel he was hiding out in. So Jackson has his money, and he thinks the Khaleds are going to cover his tracks—wrong. They left the original weapons' crates at the pickup site after removing the stuff, *after* Jackson went to the trouble to sanitize the weapons. He just expected them to get rid of the packages."

"That's a no-brains plan," Meyerson commented, finding it hard to believe the idiocy of everything. Then again, their idiocy had been quite effective so far.

"Jackson was a no-brains guy, apparently. All he needed was a million-dollar motivation and his part was in the bag, but he just didn't put it all together. Clean up the guns and rockets, make them untraceable, and then put them back in the marked boxes. It's stupid, no doubt about it, but it happened. So the FBI traced the crates back to Rock Island, to the armory. Lo and behold, who's one of the soldiers with the armory for a duty station? Samuel Jackson, Marcus's little brother. Now we have the source of the weapons and a direction for the trail, but there is still the question of how the plan originated."

"There would have to be a connection on this side of the Atlantic, especially to show a connection to the hijacking," the president said.

"Right. The Khaleds didn't just call up Marcus Jackson and ask for his help. This thing took time to set up. Someone had connections in place."

"Who?" the chief of staff asked.

"Another Jackson."

"What?" Meyerson asked rhetorically.

"In Joliet, serving time for something or other, is Ernest Jackson, the oldest of the three boys. He's apparently one bad fellow, and smart."

"The smart ones get greedy and get caught," Landau said.

"Exactly. Plus, it gave him the perfect base of operations, and the absolute perfect alibi—almost."

"You'll explain, of course," the president said, raising a curious eyebrow.

"Ernest Jackson was, and still is, a member of a Chicago terrorist group known as El Rukn. Most people just thought of them as a street gang, but they were much more. So much more that Qaddafi 'chose' them as his American revolutionary arm."

"It didn't work out too well, I remember," Meyerson added.

"Mostly rhetoric, like we've expected from the colonel for a long time, but it got the ball rolling." Bud wrote the three Jacksons' names on one side of the paper, then drew a line down the center. He then wrote the two Khaleds' names on the other side of the line. "The Jackson brothers had the link to Libya, a semiclean one with Ernest safe behind the walls, and they had the source of the weapons with Samuel in the Army."

"And Marcus was the man on location," Gonzales completed the point.

"Exactly," Bud said. "That's the benign link."

"The benign link?" The president wondered how a conspiracy that killed so many could be termed benign. "That is definitely an interesting way to put it."

"It may not be a proper classification under normal circumstances, but it is when you compare it to the really dangerous connection."

"Which is?" Meyerson asked.

Bud put a question mark below the Khaleds. "Brother number three. There's another Khaled."

"And he fits into this how?" the president inquired.

"He is the concrete link. If this third brother is involved, his likely place is aboard the hijacked jet. I believe he is. It is the only scenario that makes complete sense: Qaddafi has a mind for revenge because of our rogue operation, maybe rightfully so in his mind. Imagine this: Qaddafi is successful in this whole thing and then dies, or is replaced by a crony who claims that the colonel acted without sanction of the people. In their twisted minds they might really believe that we'd accept that and do nothing. Of course, they're wrong, but Qaddafi has played the wide-eyed innocent many, many times before. But that's ahead of the point. The Khaleds were probably recruited by Qaddafi's terrorist apparatus, and then the two who carried out the attack in L.A. were almost certainly trained in one of the training camps. This is just about stone-cold proven when we consider the similarities between what happened and what our asset warned us of. If we then follow that the third Khaled brother is also on a suicide mission, which is a prudent bit of conjecture, we have to consider what effect he is hoping for."

"If this is the case, then there has to be greater effect desired than the obvious ones we've looked at," the DCI said.

"Right!" Bud exclaimed. "We were looking in multiples of effect, not in multiplications of effect. The two operations were not meant to be a one-two punch. The assassination was a setup. It was meant to set the stage for the real show. Think about it. We already know there is something on the aircraft meant to do damage to people other than the hostages, namely large numbers on the ground."

"But it's not a bomb, Bud," the chief of staff commented.

"It doesn't have to be. If he's on a suicide mission, why land? He can activate those things in the air over the population, and they've already secured the target: There will be over a hundred world leaders in Washington, D.C., which is on a direct path from Tenerife to Chicago. That was their original intended route. A slight course change would have put them over D.C. in a matter of minutes. Even on a Havana-to-Chicago flight path all they'd have to do is stray a few hundred miles east, or even announce a new destination—say New York. They could be on top of us with no warning."

"Oh my God." Gonzales sighed, his head sinking forward. The thought was frightening. "It's brilliant," the DCI observed. "Qaddafi must know that we know about the cargo: He's aware of our satellite capability. If the plane gets over the funeral procession and activates those things, he's probably killed thousands of people, a lot of them heads of state. If we shoot the plane down, then we've killed hundreds of our own people. Those are the only two alternatives he sees."

The president filtered the developments in his mind. "You were right, Herb. We may still have to shoot the plane down."

"But Qaddafi didn't think about Delta, or he didn't consider them to be a viable threat," Meyerson said.

"Let's damn well hope that the secretary can get them into Cuba," the president said, sounding hopeful. "That will make them viable." He saw the DCI's mindful look. "But . . . Bud, that contingency I approved you to get ready—give the go-ahead. No matter what happens, that plane gets nowhere near the States."

The president knew he had just given an order that might result in Americans killing Americans. The only hope for that not to happen was in Delta. In either eventuality, people would die. He just hoped it would be those who deserved to.

17

• • • • • • • • • • • • •

NEUTRONS

Thunder One

JOE WAS SCRIBBLING calculations and verifying them with his Hewlett-Packard calculator. The noise of the engines was finally relegating itself to background status in his ears. Those who frequently were passengers in StarLifters and other large-cargo aircraft soon became used to the continual buzzing that resonated through the fuselage. It was the same reaction that workers in machine shops experienced.

Joe could only wish. Someplace benign like a machine shop would suit him just fine . . . if only there wasn't a nuclear whatever-it-was on that plane. That was his job, and it occupied his thoughts almost completely.

The calculations so far, and all the information—hard information—proved nothing more than that he shouldn't have to be here. For all he knew the Libyans had mustard gas, or some other chemical weapon on the plane; they had plenty of those. It would be a hell of a lot more reliable and the terror factor involved was equal to, if not greater than, any threat from a nuclear weapon, especially one that might fizzle. He knew what gas could do, and the thought of his lungs being on fire was infinitely less appealing than being vaporized instantly. Most people would feel the same, he believed, but then he had lived and breathed everything radioactive for a long time now and had become somewhat desensitized to its real power. He had not, however, lost any respect for, as he called it, "the dance of the neutrons."

There were other things. The diagram, for starters. Aside from being truly rough, it was anything but a nuclear weapon. Definitely not one of Vishkov's designs because it had no chance of exploding. There was no core. There was no compression system. It resembled a semisphere, flat side down, with four short cylindrical plugs rising from its top at mild angles. No dimensions were given, and no materials identified.

What is it? he asked himself, over and over. Joe couldn't figure it out, not without more information. The world of nuclear weaponry did not work in an atmosphere of unknowns and variables. Guesses weren't his area of expertise.

A buzzer sounded in the cabin, causing Joe to look up. Nothing caught his attention, so he returned to his thoughts, examining the diagram in detail, not with his eyes, but in his mind. His eyes were shut, and the paper's edge was pressed between his fingers. One corner was bunched up already, worn and crumpled as if soon to be discarded. It might soon be, Joe thought, as it was worthless as far as he could tell.

"Anderson." Joe hadn't seen the major approach. "You're wanted in the com suite. Up forward."

There was a look in the major's eyes. Not fear. Not anger. Joe knew he had been a bastard, but that was his way and he never apologized for being himself. If the look was more of distaste it would not have surprised him, but it was not. It was one of single-mindedness, like the man he was looking through didn't matter. "Where again?" Joe stood.

"Forward. Back of the flight deck."

Joe worked his way past the Humvees and the gear, then up the ladderlike stairs.

The communications officer handed him a bulky headset, which he wiggled into more than put on. "This is Anderson."

"Anderson, this is Bud DiContino." The transmission was nearly static-free. "We just received some further information you can probably use. Ready to copy?"

"Go ahead."

The pause before the words brought static. "We've just confirmed that the Libyans took delivery of four hundred and twenty pounds of eighty-one-percent-enriched U235 just over three years ago. This is confirmed and very hot."

"Where?"

"Osirak. Some salvage company was hired by the Libyans to haul away scrap from the reactor complex. Another source inside the terrorist network gave us the numbers. That came directly from Sadr, but you are the only one to know that. Both of these things put together lead to only one thing: The Libyans bought the fuel and arranged for it to be shipped under cover back home."

"The fuel cells weren't supposed to be at the complex," Joe said. "That's the only reason the Israelis hit it, because it was cold. They wouldn't have risked irradiating Baghdad. Are you sure of this?"

"Positive. We confirmed the source of the transfer, and where the money came from." *And a lot more.*

"I still don't believe it's a bomb, DiContino."

"You're right."

What? "You lost me."

"We were able to get good answers to your questions. Each of those crates contains a thermal reactor. Make sense?"

All at once it did. "Of course! Damnit and dear God. They don't have to build a bomb out of the stuff—they just have to bring it to critical mass." Joe did some simple and quick calculations in his head. "Four hundred pounds is enough for twelve critical masses, three per device . . ."

Bud had cut the number in a third, intentionally. It was a security issue, one that he hoped they would deal with right for once. "Device?"

"Damnit, yes! That sketch is a simple catastrophic thermal reactor. Each of those four cylinders on top of each half sphere is a chute. If the division of fissile material is even and uniform among the sixteen chutes—four per device—then about twenty-five and a half pounds of U235, three fourths of a critical mass, would be in each one. It's so simple." Joe squeezed the coiled headset cord tight in his fist. "Any one of the chutes dropping its contents into the reactor core would create nothing. But two, or three, or all of them dropping would be enough for a self sustaining chain reaction. Jesus! If all four of them drop into the core there will be so many neutrons releasing that the pile will heat up and melt down in less than three minutes. And if it starts fissioning, there's not a damn thing I can do about it."

The communications officer was staring up at Joe. He couldn't hear the other side of the conversation, but this side was scary enough. Joe rotated his body away from the crewman.

"What happens if these things go critical while the aircraft is still at altitude?"

"Did you ever hear of the nuclear bomber project?" Joe asked.

"Seventies, right?"

"No, that was the earlier concept. In the early eighties there was talk of using nuclear power for long-endurance aircraft. It was supposed to use reactor power for cruising at altitude and regular jets for takeoff and penetration."

"SUMMIT," Bud said, remembering the project that eventually ended up in the concept scrap heap.

"Right. We did some studies for the Air Force on the effects of a catastrophic reactor failure in flight, fairly similar to what you're asking about. If one of those things goes critical and melts down, this is what will happen: The core of U235 will melt through the core liner first, then the cargo-hold floor, and finally the outer skin of the plane. In itself that's going to release a hell of a lot of nucleides into the atmosphere. Those are the isotopes of the different metals that will be liberated when it melts. As soon as the piles melt through and hit the air, any moisture is going to turn to steam, because all we have are four lumps of molten uranium. Anything that contacts them is instantly vaporized or reduced to its own molten state. Then we have the good news/bad news syndrome: Because the piles would be beyond red-hot they wouldn't be very cohesive as a structure, so on the way to the ground they'd break into several pieces, which would each start to cool rapidly. Without a proper mass structure the chain reaction will stop—no reaction, no heat. The fuel source may have been enriched only in a powdered form, then compressed; that's what Osirak was *supposed* to be fueled with, and it's a higher concentration than Tajoura's fuel. Once that stuff melts, cools, hits the ground, and is cooled further, you'll have a gravelly, metallic consistency with some ashlike by-products. Depending on the altitude of release the area of contamination could be as large as, say, six hundred square miles. There would be several *very* hot spots and a whole lot of widespread hot spots that would pose severe health risks. Some of the hotter areas would be putting out on the order of four hundred rems, enough to kill half the people who come in contact with the area. All in all, DiContino, it would be a major mess, way off the scale of anything we, or anyone else, have ever had to deal with."

"Well, that's precisely what the terrorists plan to do—right above Washington."

"You're crazy!"

"No, but they may be. We've pretty much confirmed it. You're the fireman on this one, just like before."

Joe had hoped never to repeat anything like that. "It was in a little different setting."

"True, but I'm certain of your adaptability," Bud said. It was a statement of fact, and a challenge.

Sure. "The hijackers are just going to lay down their guns—you've confirmed that, right? Look, that aircraft cannot be allowed over *any* populated area."

"Delta will take car—"

"No!" Joe was uncomfortable with this one. He usually dealt only with benign threats, or those caused by some mechanical glitch, but there was a madman behind this radioactive nightmare. "We don't know if this is going to work, and even if I can get at those things I can't guarantee that I can stop them from going critical."

"You have to try."

"Damnit, I will, but if I can't do anything you'll have to—"

"Mr. Anderson. We couldn't send those men up there with the knowledge that a partial failure, or even a total success on their part, might still mean death. There has to be some hope. So this stays with you: Arrangements have been made."

The inference was obvious. "That's as shitty as it gets. It's nice to have this on my shoulders." Joe pulled the headset off roughly. The com officer was facing his instruments but looked up when his phones were tossed onto the console desk. "They're all yours, junior."

Anderson made his way off the flight deck and headed back toward his seat. At the forward part of the hold he stopped, seeing the added lighting farther back where the Delta troopers were. It was a little eerie, the way the light and contents of the aircraft bounced together in the turbulence. Some thought about a "light at the end of the tunnel" popped into his head, but he quickly dismissed it for the bullshit he knew it was.

José Martí Airport

The wheels of the old 707 had stopped rolling a minute before. Already Secretary of State James Coventry, his interpreter, and the Air Force officer with the designs were farther back in the aircraft, in the conference room. Against one side of the cabin chairs were set in place, the rest of the space being used by the real oak table and the twelve chairs around it. The secretary sat at one end, near the door that led into what used to be the airborne presidential bedroom, and on his right was the interpreter, a Cuban exile for over thirty years and a twenty-five-year man at State. He seemed pensive, Coventry noticed, but then he had a right to. In this country—his homeland—he was considered a criminal. In one of the seats along the wall the captain sat. The portfolio containing Vishkov's design rested atop his lap, with one of his hands holding each short side.

There was a knock at the forward door. "Visitors, sir," the Secret Service agent said, then closed the door. His post was just aft of the cockpit, and he returned there immediately. Only he and another agent were aboard this flight, and their orders were to stay "removed" from any happenings. Officially, this meeting was not taking place.

They could not refrain from exchanging glances when "the visitor" walked through the forward cabin door. He hesitated, eyeing them up and down, before following two of his entourage toward the back of the jet. Five men in all came aboard. Both agents decided quietly that they had not seen them, a move that would have pleased their boss to no end.

It was the captain who saw him first. He thought he looked huge, much larger than television seemed to portray him. And where were the olive drab fatigues?

Secretary Coventry stood. He was in shirtsleeves, partly because he felt it would make him look like he meant business, and partly due to the inadequate air-conditioning in the old executive jet. His counterpart—at least on this aircraft—wore a sand-colored military-style jacket with a modest plate of ribbons and medals over his left breast. There was no fatigue cap, once a trademark of the man, only a headful of thick gray hair. Even the beard was graying, its short, curly hairs trimmed neatly so his mouth was clearly visible. The man, after all, was a performer of sorts, and the way he said his words was sometimes as important as their meaning.

The men did not shake hands. President Fidel Castro took a seat at the opposite end of the conference table. He dismissed all but his interpreter, who sat next to him.

Castro looked around the room and smiled. "A present, perhaps, from your president?"

Coventry returned the smile for a second. "I will ask, Mr. President."

"So, it is early in the morning—why now does your government desire such a high level of contact?" He gestured grandly. "It has been many, many years."

Poker face and no bluffing, Coventry reminded himself. "Sir, we have a very big problem, one that your government has unknowingly allowed to happen. You obviously are aware of the hijacked *American* civilian airliner. It is on its way to Havana to refuel."

"Yes. Yes. It will come, we will refuel it, and it will go. We have no desire to endanger innocent lives. And your comment did not go unnoticed." A wagging finger pointed across the table. "Your charges are old and tired, my good Mr. Secretary. Never has your government been able to prove any of its accusations. Why would a small country, a poor country, such as mine sponsor such terrorist acts? How could we?"

A master. No wonder he's still in power. Coventry nodded to the captain, who opened the case and set the drawings before Castro. "President Castro, I'm certain that you are very familiar with a Mr. Anatoly Vishkov." The Cuban leader looked up from the pages as he leafed through them, folding them back toward the table's center. "That is one of his designs—a nuclear weapon. Our Central Intelligence

Agency purchased it at an auction of sorts in the Netherlands. Unfortunately, another of the designs got past us and was obtained by Colonel Qaddafi. It's of similar dimensions and capabilities. We believe that it is on the aircraft, and that the hijackers plan to detonate it over Washington."

Castro closed the case. His face was without emotion while his lips twisted in thought.

"Your government has allowed Vishkov to live without fear of accountability for—"

"Mr. Secretary, you—"

"No, President Castro! This will not drag out into an exchange of ideologies; there is no time. We have ample corroboration of our beliefs, and that is that. What must happen now is an agreement between our governments to cooperate in ending this matter. Our Delta Force has devised a plan to secure the aircraft, but they must stage it from this airfield."

"Attack an aircraft with a nuclear weapon on board? On Cuban soil? *American* military forces?" Castro let out a grunting laugh which ended in a series of coughs. "And we are responsible? Hah! I suggest you take up the question of responsible with those you have oppressed for so long. Now *they* have the upper hand. And you," Castro spit the words out, "you, a representative of the American government, come here to beg for my help, for the help of the Cuban people! I have heard all that can be heard! How soon we forget your country's aggression against mine."

The secretary laid out his hand before his interpreter. The man smiled ever so slightly as he drew an envelope from the inside pocket of his jacket.

"President Castro." Coventry waited for the interpreter to slide the envelope across the table. "That is a list of targets in your country. Yes, targets. If our rescue forces are not allowed to do their job, your country, by way of its sheltering of a known peddler of nuclear terror, will be held responsible with others for this act, and the military forces of the United States *will* completely dismantle your military forces . . . all of them. Right now we have massive air forces positioning themselves in the Southern states. It will be massive, President Castro. And devastating."

"You are out of your mind," the Cuban interpreter said without prompting.

"No." Coventry stood and walked to the row of windows on the starboard cabin wall. There were several military vehicles around the blue-and-white 707. "Not in the least. We've had experience with this, as you are fully aware of. When the American people learn of what your refusal to allow our forces to stage from here has caused, you will be lucky to escape this affair with your life. I think I can be honest if I say that any action will not stop with air strikes; it may become necessary to invade and occupy your country. Similar to what happened in southern Iraq, and in Panama. You do remember Panama?"

The verbal jab was effective, as evidenced by Castro's trembling cheeks. "Your threats are just that! Our forces are not the weak peasants you think they are. They are committed! They will stop you!" He slammed a fist down hard. His eyes met those of the American interpreter, and they were his match. The man had a cold stare, one of hate. Yes, he had seen that before. That look. But he would never understand the reasoning.

"They will not," the secretary retorted, in his laid-back Midwest monotone. "Your words are very similar to a Middle Eastern dictator of the past, one whom we dispatched of in a fashion similar to what you are facing. So don't consider it a threat, President Castro—consider it an ultimatum. Your General Ontiveros has locked you into this position." Coventry had to congratulate himself for adding that.

Castro fumed within himself. *Ontiveros! You have been a sore in my leadership for too long.*

It was time to offer an out. "We can solve this problem, and begin an era of new and better relations. My government does not wish to take any action against the Cuban people. We do, however, want the chance to save our people—that is all." *Now, the fly.* "I am certain that you can deal with Mr. Vishkov in your own way. We have no claim to him; only the Russians do, I believe. The decision is yours."

Secretary Coventry took his seat again. He thought his words sounded scripted, as official exchanges often did. He was fitting in just fine, he realized, which, in a way, was a bit disappointing.

Castro fidgeted back in the chair, rising up against its back, then standing. His surprised interpreter, a ranking member of Cuban Intelligence, followed the lead. "Of course, Mr. Secretary, you will remain until your Delta Force completes its mission."

The secretary did not want to disclose the somewhat unorthodox plan, but there would need to be some exchange of information. "Yes, I will. Our forces should land shortly before the hijacked plane does, and then, I presume, they will set up. The force commander can discuss specific details with your officers via radio."

"That would be best." Castro casually saluted the American. He was a crafty player, somewhat blunt, but then he had the muscle to back up the threats. Alone, the ultimatum would not have swayed him; his forces could have dealt the Americans a serious, if small defeat, and the Americans seemed to neglect the fact that Cuban MiGs could also reach the Gulf Coast of the United States. Ontiveros, on the other hand, was a problem. No matter what would have come from an American assault, Castro was sure the arrogant general would seize the opportunity to advance his position in the government. Well, he would be in for a surprise, a very unpleasant surprise, as would Anatoly Vishkov. The physicist and his protector would no longer be a bother to the Cuban leader. As soon as the sun rose, a man would fall.

"You did good," Coventry told his interpreter when the door closed behind the visitors.

"I would rather have shot him," came the reply. The man remembered the Cuban jails of the sixties.

The secretary thought he understood the man's commitment to some ideological, nationalist cause, but he didn't. He truly would have shot him.

Several minutes later the 707 taxied behind a guide vehicle to a darkened section of José Martí airport where maintenance was normally performed. For the next few hours no maintenance would be occurring, and no flights would be arriving. To the contrary, before Air Force Three stopped rolling, the word had gone out for all the commercial aircraft to leave the airport. Though it had not yet been agreed upon, many of them, including several Aeroflot jumbo jets, would disperse to airfields in south Florida, much to the surprise of American controllers. Also before the jet stopped its move, a call was made to the White House from a quietly gloating secretary of state.

New Orleans Naval Air Station

By the time the call made its way to Dr. Ralph Cooper it had passed through several high-ranking officers of the Louisiana Air National Guard, and was subsequently relayed to him by his wing commander. Driving through the gate he flashed his ID at the guard and mentally shed his hospital greens. Soon he would change nameplates, step into his dark green flight suit, and become Major Ralph "Snoopy" Cooper, weekend aerial warrior.

It had been a while since he had been pulled out of bed for a deployment exercise, but it was something he prepared himself for. It was better than his old Air Force days in Korea, where it was way too dangerous and too damn cold.

Flight ops was all lit up, and several security guards stood solidly outside, gauging Cooper's maroon Volvo as it approached. Colonel Brown, the fighter squadron's commander, was with them.

"Major, glad you could make it. C'mon." The colonel led off around the flight ops building.

Major? Cooper noticed the serious formality. Weekend flyers usually had a somewhat relaxed hierarchical rank structure, one that was ruled by first names or pilot call signs. "Hold on, don't I get to change?"

Brown halted. "Sorry, not today. You can change over by the bird. We've got a van there."

This was different. Something was up. Hell, usually he would show up for a two-day activation, shoot the bull with the guys, and fly for as long as they'd let him. He made all the money he'd ever need working four days a week teaching internal medicine at the university, so getting to "play" in an F-15C was sometimes hard to believe. They *let him* have fun in a multimillion-dollar jet!

"So what *is* going on, Colonel?" Cooper asked.

"I'll fill you in while you suit up."

They were at the aircraft in under ten minutes. It sat outside one of the old metal hangars, not the concrete blast boxes that housed the twin-engine Eagle. Cooper knew instantly that *different* was not an adequate description of the statement. The bird was not a sleek F-15C Eagle—before him was a relic from his past.

"What the . . ." Cooper said aloud as he walked, hands on his chute webbing, toward the delta wing, sky-gray fighter. It was nosed toward the hangar. "An F-106? What gives?" he asked, stopping to eye the aircraft from nose to tail.

"You flew these a few years back."

"A few years? More like twenty. Christ! I haven't even seen one of these babies in . . . must be ten years."

"It's mission-capable," the colonel commented. He was right. It looked to be in almost perfect condition. The nearly forty-year-old aircraft's skin was smooth under the glow of the outside lights, no wrinkles or mars being visible. Every detail was crisp. Lettering and the old squadron flash were impeccably done.

"For what mission?"

"Look," Colonel Brown answered, pointing to the underside of the Delta Dart.

And there it was, just like Major Cooper remembered, except for one important difference. He had flown with the Air-2A Genie nuclear-tipped air-to-air missile long before in Korea, and had participated in "live" practice-fire exercises using inert warheads in the deserts of the west. It hung from the center bay hoist like a stubby cartoon bomb, ready to be pulled fully into the weapons bay. This one didn't have the distinctive blue-colored warhead section in the missile's center, which would have identified it as an inert practice round. This missile was entirely white.

18

·············

FRIENDS FALLEN

Flight 422

HADAD LISTENED TO only a few moments of their words before turning his attention and thoughts elsewhere.

"North of a town called Ojai," Buzz said. "You ever hear of it?"

"Somewhere," Hendrickson responded. "But I haven't the foggiest idea where it is."

Buzz shook his head with assurance. "Doesn't matter. What does is that there's a place north of there called the Smith Wilderness Area. It starts at the base of what's known as Pine Mountain, right across the road. There's actually a bunch of peaks there, but Pine's the biggest of them. Anyway, most guys that try and hunt that area come away empty-handed with their tags just aching for a rack of antlers to be tied to. You know why?"

The captain was more of a fisherman than a hunter, but he'd taken a few whitetails in his time. No muleys, though, like his first officer, the California native, was talking about. They were practically mountain goats to most eastern hunters, a fact that added to the captain's innate curiosity. "I'll bite: why?"

Buzz feigned panting, mimicking someone out of breath. "They all get pooped out in there. Some just from sitting around and waiting. Some from stalking the muleys only from convenient spots. There's only two roads that head back in, and the one with highway access is restricted by Fish and Game. Only about five folks a week get to drive on back. But even they come out with nothing. Nothing, Cap, I swear!"

The performance indicators got a glance. Everything was

as good as it could be, and there was no traffic anywhere near them, a knowledge made possible by the shadowing Air Force jet. "So people just burn themselves out chasing the beasts?"

"Exactly. These deer are conditioned, and a good bunch of them are prime, and I mean *prime*. They migrate back and forth between the Los Padres Forest to the west—there's a protected condor sanctuary there—and the Smith Wilderness to the east. When the pressure's on they move west, where they can't be hunted. Fish and Game is pretty damn strict about the condor sanctuary rules. No firearms, strung bows, or anything. Then, after the season, they move back. People might get a glance every now and then during the season in Smith, but it's usually just a doe or two browsing."

"And your secret?" Hendrickson's interest was coming alive.

A grin appeared. "You gonna sell my surefire method to *Field & Stream?* Course not! Well, I head in the night before archery season opens in that zone, just pack my bow and enough gear for two or three days—real light traveling, if you know what I mean. Then, by sunrise on opening day, I'm sitting just a mile east of the sanctuary border in my choice of juniper patches, just waiting for the herd to browse on by. It never fails. I've bagged my limit there every year for twelve years running."

The captain laughed with a soundless smile. "You do that bow stuff, though. That is not fair. The animals think all the Indians are dead, Buzz. You're cheating them."

Hadad shifted in the jump seat. Why did the Americans talk of such trivial things? They were in danger, about to die, yet their thoughts were of pleasure and the past.

It was not so in Hadad's mind. He saw only the future, martyrdom. Like those before who had given their lives in the cause of Arab unity and preservation, he, too, would be in glory's bright light before long.

For the first time in days a true smile came to his lips. Not one of power, but one of joy. The words of the pilots faded again to a mindless hum. Through the windshield ahead he could see stars flash briefly as the jet pierced the scattered clouds. He took it as a sign. Allah was smiling back, giving one final blessing to the mission.

Hadad sat straight up, a steady stream of joy filling his heart and soul. The purpose would be achieved.

Springer Seven-Three

"I've been where he's talkin' about, Colonel," the com officer said.

The colonel slid the earphones off and checked his watch. "An hour and a half," he said aloud, though no one heard the comment. The headset went back on. "Com, keep listening and have radio backup work it through with you. If they're trying to slip us something in that talk, I want to know."

"Yes, sir."

The colonel didn't think that was the case. It was more than that, something older than spies, or terrorism, or senseless killing. *Just two guys talking.* So his com officer had hunted the place the right-seater was describing. "Maybe you'll get to hunt there with him sometime, Lieutenant."

"I hope, so. I ain't got nothing there in the six or seven times I tried."

Los Angeles

The doctor shifted the chart toward the overhead light, scrunching his nose as he looked past the half-size bifocals at the drawing of the human neck. "It isn't good, but it could be a lot worse."

Art fumed at the imprecision of the comment. "And what the hell does that mean?"

Maria Toronassi snapped her head toward Art. His hand reached out and pulled her to him. "Sorry," he said, to her and the doctor.

The apology was accepted with a smile. "I mean good things by that."

"My fault, Doc. I'm all cranked up over this."

The hand on her shoulder tightened, and . . . "Art, are you okay?"

She was asking *him*! Art knew what she meant and let his hand close into a tight fist on her shoulder, where it rested. The rest he just held in. *A while longer, Arthur. Just a while.* "I'm okay."

"Here, let me show you." The doctor, a neurosurgeon, pulled a pen from his lab coat pocket. "The bullet entered here, just about a centimeter from the trachea. It progressed back through muscle and nerve fiber—no significant damage there—then impacted with this: the third cervical vertebra. Now in a lot of cases that would mean the end, but your man was very lucky. He must participate in some kind of sport to develop his neck muscles to the extent they are."

"Wrestling," Maria said. "He coaches at our son's high school, but I think he gets into the demonstration part of it a little too much sometimes." She wiped a single tear with the back of her hand, catching it high on the cheek.

"Well, it probably saved his life. That muscle fiber took most of the shock, which slowed the bullet down appreciably. When it struck the vertebra it bounced off, and came back about an inch. Right here." His pen circled a spot on the chart. "We're going to go after it in a little while. Our only concern, though, is a big one. There is a bone fragment that chipped off the vertebra and entered the spinal canal. It's right in with bundles of nerves. The spinal cord at this level is extremely delicate, and fairly inaccessible to us, so we'll have to just leave the fragment there and hope that it stays put."

"Is he going to be paralyzed?"

"No, Mrs. Toronassi. There has been no damage to the spinal cord that we can see, but with that bone fragment in there a chance will exist for some time that damage could be done."

"Which means?"

"Your husband will have to curtail his activities somewhat. The more sedate he is, the better his chances are for a normal life. No wrestling, no more gunplay in dark alleys . . ."

Art swallowed hard, though not noticeably. "Just the kind of stuff a street agent does, right, Doc?"

The doctor thought it easier to pronounce death to people at times, rather than limitations. "That will have to be looked at. But let's remember something: He is alive. He is breathing, his brain is fine, and in a week or so he'll probably walk out of this hospital on his own, God willing."

Maria nodded, thanked the doctor, then buried her head

in Art's chest, her hands pulled up between her face and his shirtfront.

"Hey, hey. Come on, little lady. He's going to be okay." Art waited for the sobs to stop, then for the sniffling. "Here." He pulled two folded pieces of tissue from a pocket.

"It's like, I don't know." Her tear-streaked face pulled back slightly and looked up to the ceiling. "You always hear about this stuff when your husband's a cop, but it's just TV. It's never really real. He goes away in the morning, and he comes home later, just like a regular job." Her eyes began to fill again. "But people don't shoot at other people in a regular job."

Art guided her head down again, this time sideways to rest against his chest. He was a full twelve inches taller than her and could see clearly into the rest of the lobby. It was filled with agents and cops from everywhere. He caught Frankie's glance and motioned for her to come over.

"Maria, this is Frankie. She works with Ed and me."

The women looked alike, though Frankie was an even ten years younger than Maria. "Mrs. Toronassi, why don't you come with me. We'll get something to drink, and just talk. Okay?"

They walked off down the hall and disappeared to the right, a roomful of caring eyes looking at their backs.

Art turned away, looking the opposite direction. The flood of emotions was too much. He had ruined a marriage, his own life, and now . . .

His hand tensed up involuntarily. He looked down at it as it came up closer to his chest. Tears were in his eyes as he tried to open the hand, but couldn't. *Ed, I'm sorry. This didn't have to happen.*

A voice came from behind, but it sounded strange. Very loud, yet far away. He knew it. It was Jerry, but it was strange. The words were stretched out into almost unintelligible lengths, none making complete sense. One side of his body became very warm. Not hot, and not painful, but warm. A kind of moist warmth.

Art tried to turn to greet the voice, but his body became a corkscrew of sorts, spiraling down to the floor, where everything became very dark, and very quiet. Next, it was as black as a dream with no dreamer.

Thunder One

"Half an hour!" Blackjack announced.

Sean noted the time. They would do final checks first, then land. Land in Cuba! If someone had told him that, he'd have taken any odds against it. Strange was always able to outdo itself, though. Sean had learned that from experience.

The Delta captain leaned forward and scanned the hold from side to side, checking his squad. They were all quiet, spending the last few moments with themselves. Buxton was checking his backup SIG meticulously one final time. The sergeants were all eyes closed, except for Makowski: He had his pocket-size Bible open and was focused on one page. The only Delta member not in some kind of quiet reflective state was Antonelli, which was par for the course. One ear was covered by the headphones of his personal cassette player, his head moving from side to side as he paged through a newer edition *Superman* from his collection of comics.

Blackjack was semihidden in the shadows of the lead Humvee. His eyes were open, Sean could see, and staring ahead at nothing. It was his way.

Sean turned to Anderson, sitting one seat to his left. His upper body was contorting, bringing his neck down into his shoulders. Then his head would rotate halfway to the left, then back to center, then to the right. Graber watched the process repeated twice.

"Limbering exercises?"

Joe was in his own kind of trance, but snapped out instantly at the question, shaking his shoulders and arms loose. "You got it." He still didn't face the captain. "I can get into some tight spots sometimes, literally."

"So you've got to wriggle in wherever, right?" Sean asked.

Joe nodded. "Wherever it is, whatever it takes." He paused and got up, then sat one seat closer to the captain. "Listen, I don't want you to take this wrong, but have you ever done this before? I don't mean exactly what you're going to do in a while, but anything similar?"

"Sure. A couple of times. One time I went in with the forces of another country on a 'lend-lease' kind of arrangement. The major did, too."

"Can you say where?"

"Sure. It was in the papers and even in a few texts since it happened. Thailand. There were a bunch of 'separatist who-knows.' Communist guerrillas they later figured out. Three guys and one girl took over a 707 at the airport in Bangkok. The Thais asked us for assistance with the entry since we'd trained their commandos. Basically we just tossed the flash-bangs and brought up the rear. We nailed them all cold." Sean's words ended for a moment. "But we didn't get there fast enough, at least not for the three folks the bad guys killed before we got in."

Joe noted sincere regret in the captain's voice, not the voice box utterings of an automaton he might have expected. "But you did your job?"

"Sure, that's what the powers that be can claim. But to us any life lost is a loss. We can't work on the assumption that there will be an acceptable number of casualties, simply because no one can give you a good, moral answer as to what that is. Is one percent okay? What about ten percent, or twenty percent? At what point does 'success' become failure? No, Mr. Anderson, we don't go in thinking that we can lose one or two people. That just doesn't work."

"I see." Joe understood a little better the troops' motivation for doing what they did, and it wasn't even close to his preconceived notion. Gung ho might be a description of their determination, but not of their motivation.

"This may be the first real shot we've ever had at doing our job," Sean said. "It would be nice to earn our pay for once."

Joe, you can be such a thick skull. The civilian felt somehow humbled. His mission was to defeat a machine. Theirs was to defeat men to save men. "What about Iran? Were you there?"

"Yes," Sean answered, the memory coming back. It was manageable now. "I was a sergeant back then, a gun-toting rescuer of innocents." The captain released a wistful sigh. "We all thought it was going to happen, that we were going to go in and snatch those folks out all safe and secure. When everything got fucked up, we cried. Every goddamn one of us whimpered like a baby. Except the major. He dealt with it his way. The rest of us, though, we were hurting. It's not an easy thing to watch men die because of screwy-ass operational details, none of which we even knew about until after the fact. Hell, we set down at the desert rendezvous and the next thing we knew was we were going to be short choppers. The rest . . ."

"You know, back there in the States, it was Vietnam all over again. The military fucks up!" Joe leaned forward on his knees.

"Yeah. But you learn from it. We did." The old memories were part of the past, but at times they still could sting. "What about your end of it, Anderson?"

"You mean have I done this before?"

"Or something similar."

He was about to go into a tricky situation with some homemade nuclear reactors ready to melt down, but it wasn't like anything he'd done before. It might turn out to be easier, and though most people would consider it unlikely, it bore less of a devastating potential than Joe's shining moment. "Something like it, though not up here."

"Need to know?" Sean asked, sensing the reluctance to discuss whatever it was.

"You know the game," Joe responded. There were always those who "wanted" to know some bit of restricted information, but very few who had a "need" to know. It was the foundation of the government's compartmentalized security policy toward information, and it worked. Still . . . "Let's just say I've dealt with some of our own big guns when things went awry."

Sean smiled. "I get the picture. Those things can go haywire?"

"They're mechanical. Things go wrong," Joe explained, not giving the whole picture. He knew the limit.

Sean went wide-eyed at the thought. A nuclear-tipped ICBM gone wrong! "They must have hushed that up real good."

"They did." Joe didn't say that a local newspaper in the Great Plains had nearly picked up on the "real" story, and would have, had it not been for some fancy footwork by the DOD. It was just as well. The country, or the world for that matter, didn't need to know the real story. Neither did the Delta captain.

Sean felt more comfortable with Anderson, even with the knowledge that he, at times, could be a real ass. What counted was ability, and he had that, Sean reasoned, or he wouldn't be among them. "Guess you'll earn your pay on this one, too."

"Just doing my job," Joe responded. "Like you."

19
••••••••••••
THINE ENEMY

Thunder One

BLACKJACK HELD HIS SIG up for the troops to see. "I want no mistakes here. No screwups. So watch me close." He slid the receiver back until it emitted an audible click. "No rounds in the chamber and no magazines inserted."

"Isn't that being a little less than careful?" Quimpo asked. "I mean, the Cubans, no matter what anyone says, they're not our friends."

"Precisely why we're doing this." McAffee released the slide back to forward, giving the pistol its normal shape, and tucked it into the holster high on his thigh. "If there's any antagonism I want our weapons safed. There will be no reactionaries in this group . . . on this team. Mr. Anderson, would you please verify that everyone's weapon is empty and safe?"

Joe made the rounds of the eight team members, two drivers, and the major, taking each weapon in hand personally.

McAffee continued, "The word we have is that the Cubans will cooperate, but keep this in mind. First, we're only going to be on their soil a short time, God willing, and second, if we do anything to prevent our chance to take that bird down, then we've screwed ourselves and a whole lot of innocents."

Everyone was quiet now. Their weapons were checked and holstered. Soon they would remove them and load the magazines with 9mm Glaser ammunition, a round designed for use by counterterrorist troops who might find themselves firing at targets among tens or hundreds of hostages. Special equipment, the latest available, was at their disposal, but the lowest common denominator was each man and his weapon, the SIG in this case. Each man, isolated from his conscience for the duration of the mission, was a killer. It was a sobering and sometimes horrid thought to those not connected with such antiterrorist efforts that men could have such a cold and calculated purpose. To kill. It was their only function. Kill the bad guys. Kill them at the first opportunity so that they would never again be able to wreak terror upon innocents. Kill them. One and all. Dead. Leave no chance of retaliation or retribution, and take no prisoners. If a terrorist tried to surrender, he or she was dead. No second thought. A shot, preferably just above the bridge of the nose, would be fired, giving a long last look at life through the blast of a muzzle flash. Every man knew his job, trained for it, hoped for a chance to do it, and prayed that he never would. Their existence was a dichotomy of desires, but one that they were uniquely able to live with, for they knew that, at the moment of truth, they were as close to death as their adversaries.

The Starlifter's co-pilot loosened his harness a bit and leaned forward, looking out the side window to the right and behind the aircraft.

They were there, though he could see only one. There would be another on the left side, symmetrical with its wingman, about a hundred feet off and fifty feet behind the wingtip, slightly above the big jet.

"I got one on this side," he said. "Friendlies, right?"

The pilot, a thirty-year Air Force veteran, liked the sarcasm in the lieutenant's voice. "You got it. Compliments of Fidel himself."

Another look satisfied the lieutenant's curiosity. All he could make out in the darkness were the anticollision strobes underneath the much smaller aircraft. "The light pattern looks like a twenty-nine," the rightseater commented, referring to the MiG-29 Fulcrum, a compact Soviet-built fighter.

"Well, the Cubans have a bunch of those, for sure. You can bet whatever's under the wings doesn't hold extra avgas."

"Right, sir."

It was a good guess. If the light had been better they would have been able to clearly make out the AA-10 Alamo air-to-air missiles on each wing.

The navigator swung his mask over his mouth. "We've got glideslope in two minutes. Suggest descend to eight thousand and come left to two-five-zero."

The pilot acknowledged the recommendation and began nosing the Starlifter down toward the waters south of the Florida Keys and turning it toward Havana. He made the adjustments slowly, giving his somewhat unwelcome wingmen ample time to come clear and modify their flight profile.

"We're cleared straight in, right?" the airman operating the com console asked, for verification only.

"That's a roge," the lieutenant answered. "No tower contact required."

"Let's take her in," the captain said. "Everything by the numbers. Com, let the major know we'll be on the ground in fifteen."

The time evaporated rapidly. McAffee felt his web seat shift slightly to the left as the pilot flared the aircraft for touchdown, then, five seconds later, the main gear, just forward of the team, grabbed the runway. The nosewheel came down a few seconds later, and with no fanfare, the Americans had come to Havana.

Thunder One rolled to the end of the runway and turned left on the last taxiway, following a decidedly military-looking aircraft-service vehicle. Atop it was a rack of rotating amber strobe lights and in its bed were two soldiers in Cuban Army smocks and carrying the unmistakable Kalashnikovs familiar to all American military men.

As the aircraft's roll slowed, the team went through their final checks. Graber checked each Humvee, paying particular attention to the stowed equipment.

"One is loaded," he announced loudly. "Charges are present." Sean moved back—actually forward—and looked over the number two vehicle. Everything was ready in this one, too, though there were no charges. That had been decided during the final planning stage. It was better, they figured, to have the two very special frame charges together, ready to be used when needed, considering that one would be useless. "Two is ready."

"Fire them up!" the major ordered. The Humvees rumbled, belching a short spurt of smoke which was vented out through the Starlifter's filtering system. "Okay, listen up. When the ramp goes down we're going to move to cover. Where that is I don't know. The word is that we'll be directed somewhere. I want everyone in the buggies when they roll out. I'll be on foot. Do not pass me. Understood?" The drivers gave a thumbs-up in reply. "Mr. Anderson, you're with Captain Graber's section. Keep track of your gear."

"Got it," Joe answered, trying not to sound nervous.

"All right. We'll do a final talk-through once we have a spot to lay up. Remember, the bird's going to be here in about twenty minutes, and we don't know how long the turnaround is going to be, so everyone is ready to go now— right?"

"Right!"

Joe looked around, embarrassed almost that he was feeling a twinge of nerves. This was really going to happen!

"Mount up!"

The vehicles filled quickly. McAffee walked the few yards to the hinge of the stern ramp and waited for the aircraft to stop completely. A minute later it did with a last forward lurch. Immediately the outer part of the rear opening swung upward, allowing streams of light from numerous vehicles to bathe the inside of the aircraft. The ramp dropped next. It touched the tarmac with a metallic clang.

The Cuban major saw the first American trot down the incline from the airplane's interior. He was black, as were many of the security troops around the area, but much darker. Direct African descent, thought Major Sifuentes. Not much like his own troops, who were a motley mix of Caribbean blood.

McAffee stopped short of his Cuban counterpart and saluted. "Major," he began in flawless Spanish, "on behalf of my troops and my government, thank you for your much needed assistance in this terrible, terrible incident."

Sifuentes recognized the content as gracious. Behind the words and thankful tone, though, the American must have been gloating at his being here. *What is happening? Why would the general secretary allow this?*

"Yes, yes. It is a terrible thing that some would deny others liberty." The hand came down from its return salute and rested atop his pistol holster. "Major Orlando Sifuentes, and you?"

"Major Mike McAffee, United States Army." The major did not offer his hand, as it was silently understood that a military salute would be the boundary of their shows of mutual respect.

"Yes. Army." Sifuentes turned his head, breathed, then looked back to his onetime nemesis. "You may ride in my car. I understand you have your own vehicles, no?"

"Two. I'll have them follow."

The Cuban nodded. His own men were all over the tarmac, a good portion of them forming a widely spaced human gauntlet to the service hangar where he would lead the Americans.

McAffee returned down the ramp, the lights of the Humvees coming on and backlighting him from inside. "We're ready, Major Sifuentes."

"Good. Let us hurry, then. I understand your quarry is not far behind."

As the open-back truck pulled away with Sifuentes and McAffee, the two Delta vehicles rolled down the stem ramp. Graber radioed the pilot of Thunder One that they were clear. The Starlifter would have under five minutes to get airborne and clear of the area.

In the lead vehicle, Joe held his black duffel on one knee while watching the right-side guardrail of gun-toting soldiers. Their white eyes showed no love of the guests, leaving Joe with a realization that there truly was an adversary of some determination very close to home, a thought even more sobering considering that this adversary was now a very unwilling bedfellow.

Springer Seven-Eight

Springer Seven-Eight loitered twenty-five thousand feet above the billowing tempest that usually was the peaceful watery paradise of the Florida Keys. The cloud system was playing havoc with shipping far from land, and closer in to shore the oil rigs off the Gulf Coast were battening down for the storm. It wasn't a hurricane yet, just a strengthening tropical storm, named Aldo. It was moving almost directly west after lashing Nassau with sixty-mile-an-hour winds, and there was no telling which direction would be next.

"This thing's a bitch," one of the radar operators commented with a shake of his head. He was on weather watch, his set using special Doppler techniques to track and analyze the storm system.

"A bastard, Airman."

"Sir?" The young white kid from Coeur D'Alene, Idaho, was taken by surprise. The louie had heard him.

"Bastard, Wickham. Aldo is a male name. It's all gender-respective now."

"Gender what, sir?" The talk was above him. He could handle twenty million dollars' worth of radar equipment, but fancy talk soared right over him.

"You're on the weather scope, son—you should know this. Severe tropical weather systems, like tropical storms and hurricanes, they used to all be named after women. Nowadays they alternate between male and female. The last one was Zelda, so Aldo got the call on this one."

"Yeah. I see." He didn't really. Hell, they were clouds after all, right? Clouds were clouds. Sure, they did different things, but why name them. Blizzards and tornadoes didn't get names.

"What's south Florida saying on the winds?" the lieutenant asked.

The airman looked to his last report from the land stations on the tip of the panhandle. "The cape's showing sixty-five knots, and Fort Meyers got a straight sixty, sir."

That meant Aldo was probably going to go north. Before getting AWACS duty the lieutenant had spent two tours in Central America, mostly in Panama and Guatemala. His MOS was meteorology, a pseudo art form he had perfected forecasting Pacific weather. The East Coast stuff wasn't so different he had discovered in his two years on the Atlantic side.

"What were the readings at Fort Meyers thirty minutes and ninety minutes ago?"

"Uh . . . just a minute, sir." He folded back two pages of the printout. "Forty knots ninety minutes ago, and fifty-eight thirty minutes ago."

It was the pattern, and the history. Aldo was going to follow the warm coastal waters of the Florida Gulf Coast almost directly north. His was a little conjecture mixed with the scientific, the lieutenant knew, but tropical disturbances moving due west had proven easier to forecast over the years. The nature of the beast, he figured. Aldo would never make it to hurricane strength. It'd try too hard to suck up that nice, warm Gulf water and then run aground still thirsty. There'd be some nasty thunderstorms for a day or so, not much more than Aldo's peripheral systems had given to the Atlantic coast all the way up to Norfolk.

"Keep an eye on the direction, Wickham. He'll probably go north."

"Yes, sir."

Farther forward, two operators were sweeping the sea's surface and the nearby air corridors for traffic. Aside from two unlucky Aeroflot jets heading north to New Orleans there was no traffic between Havana and Miami. Only flight 422 and its tail, Springer Seven-Three, were visible, moving west by southwest, twenty miles south and far below Springer Seven-Eight.

"Commander, this is Radar One."

"Go ahead."

"Air traffic is clear, and surface traffic is moving out."

"Good. Okay, clear Seven-Three: We've got the bird now. How many surface contacts?"

"Two, sir. Looks like the weather did most of the work."

It had. An exaggerated National Weather Service forecast had sent those in the area scurrying for the shelter of the coast. The commander wondered what story the higher-ups would have concocted if Aldo hadn't conveniently shown.

"Com, send to Snowman: *The weather is clear.*"

Almost directly below the AWACS the USS *Chandler*, a Kidd-class destroyer, was ending her own search of the area. Even with the weather churning the sea surface and playing noise games with her sonar there was no mistaking the sound of nuclear-powered steam turbines pushing two submarines out of the area at flank speed. The rush of superheated coolant through their pumps sent waves of sound through the ocean, the easily distinguishable high-frequency whirring in stark contrast to the staticky low harmonics of the surface disturbance.

Both of the subs would soon be out of the exclusion zone. One was American. The other was as yet unidentified.

Fifty miles to the east the USS *John Young*, a Spruance-class destroyer, was moving north at full speed through heavy seas, her own area now sanitized.

The stage was now clear for the players to be engaged.

Flight 422

Hours after wearing the vest, the soreness turned to a sharper pain as Hadad donned the explosive-laden garment before landing. Two wide lanes of fire ran front to back over each shoulder, exactly where the metal support straps were. Comfort hadn't been a priority when designing the weapon, and, he reminded himself, it shouldn't cloud his determination now. *Others have suffered much more than this minuscule discomfort.* He could see the faces of them in his mind, and every time he slept. They were the force behind the purpose.

Hadad entered the cockpit, relieving Wael once more. He, in turn, would go below and allow Abu a rest. The door clicked shut without either of the pilots turning to acknowledge or challenge their new guard. Again Hadad wriggled into the jump seat and let the Uzi lie across his lap.

Through the windshield a light glow was visible coming from below, but no discernible feature emitting it. Hadad raised himself up until he had a higher vantage than either of the pilots. There were a cluster of lights visible to the left through what must have been a cloud cover, and almost straight on, but farther off, there was a short line of parallel lights. A runway.

"How long until we land?"

Hendrickson stretched his neck and half turned. "A few minutes."

And a few after that you'll be Swiss cheese! Buzz thought. The radio message hadn't been specific, but it assured them something would be happening.

Hendrickson asked for a last check of José Martí's runways. Buzz pulled the information up on the flight computer.

"That's two-three ahead," the co-pilot said.

"Do you think they *want* us to use it?" Hendrickson asked rhetorically. The Cubans—or whoever was running the show—had only one runway lit amid the blackness: number 23, identified by its compass heading in tens of degrees. "All right. I figure we're cleared right in. How about you?"

"Maybe we should check it out with our leader here." Buzz was trying for a little antagonism, just to keep the pirate off-balance. "How about it, Mr. Big? Have we got your permission to land, or do you want us to do a low pass just for show?"

Hadad barely heard the crack and gave it no mind. The time had passed for an iron hand. The end was almost within sight.

"Guess so."

"Let's set her down," the captain said, mostly to himself, his thumb rubbing the control column tenderly. Almost a caress for the *Maiden*. "Approach checklist."

The two officers ran through the landing checks in under a minute. They were eight minutes from touchdown. Ahead, the rows of lights were becoming more defined. Hopefully the *Maiden* would touch down dead center between them, just past the patchwork of red threshold lights. That would give her ample room to stop.

Without tower contact they had no exact word on wind conditions at ground level. Fortunately their surreptitious shadow had fed them enough information to allow for some plans for the landing.

"I show a marker," Buzz called out. "Don't know what kind. They don't use the North American system, do they?"

"Good question. Did you see any others?"

"Nah. It must've been an outer." Or there might have been none at all, Buzz knew. The Cubans had never faithfully bought into any of the conventions of air travel in the Western hemisphere, their main customers being carriers who didn't fly into U.S. airports, but seemingly minor things such as airport distance markers were ultraimportant to 422.

"Okay." The captain thought quickly. "Let's ignore it just to be safe. It's pretty damn close in for an outer. We should have passed a middle."

"We're doing it by dead reckoning, then."

"Right," Hendrickson confirmed.

Intensity of the lights grew, as did their definition into separate specks. The Cubans did have visual referencing, split-colored lights near the runway's end to give pilots cues as to their position on the glide slope. The *Maiden* was right on.

"Ten degrees," Hendrickson ordered. His hands were secure on the column, leaving the flap adjustment to his first officer.

"Ten degrees . . ."

The bright red flashing square caught their attention more than the extraloud warning buzzer. A major system had failed. The flaps!

"Damnit!" Buzz yelled. "Locked at zero degrees." He typed a quick command one-handed for a system readout. "Pressure is at one hundred and ten percent!"

Shit! Captain Bart Hendrickson had to now think faster than he ever had in his life. The *Clipper Atlantic Maiden* was a minute from touchdown, with minimal brakes remaining, and a malfunctioning flap system.

"What is it?" Hadad asked excitedly, leaning forward.

"Shut up!"

Hydraulic pressure at 110 percent could only mean that there was some sort of system blockage at the extenders. The pumps were trying to move the big control surfaces to slow the jumbo jet before landing, but something was preventing it. They'd gone into a nonplanned overdrive, pumping harder to free the stuck system, and raising the operating pressure to above max. If 110 didn't free it, nothing would.

Hendrickson released his death grip on the twin upright column handles. He was going to be calm about this. Calm and determined. "Cut number two, all the way."

Buzz hit the emergency engine shutoff for the inboard left-side engine, in effect cutting off fuel and oxygen flow to the turbine. That would add some drag to slow the plane.

The runway was coming up at them rapidly. Hendrickson brought the column back farther than would be normal to compensate for the reduced lift. The flaps, at this point during landing, would be providing lift and drag, keeping the aircraft in the air while the drag slowed the airspeed and thus its ability to stay airborne.

"When we hit, reverse one and four, and stand on the brakes."

"Gotcha." Buzz had both feet ready to stamp on the pedals as soon as the nosewheel was down; any sooner would lock the main gear and bring the aircraft's nose down hard—maybe too hard. Nose gears had collapsed before when inexperienced pilots had hit the brakes too soon.

"And push your stick full forward. Let's see if we can make her real heavy." The captain wanted to use downward force, created by simulating a dive, to artificially raise the weight of the *Maiden*, creating more drag. Maybe, just maybe, everything in combination would work. But, his experience told him, probably not.

Behind the pilots Hadad could sense the trouble, though he knew little of specifics. His physical senses also told him that the plane was going very fast—faster than he had ever felt a plane go during landing. It would be a final test of the righteousness of his mission. Allah, in His great wisdom, was granting the purpose one final sanction. Hadad sat back, his eyes wide open to watch his prisoners, but his mind free and drifting.

Sitting four full stories above what would soon be the ground, the captain had to aim farther down the runway than pilots of other craft would. It was an artificial point, some fifteen hundred feet past the threshold under normal circumstances. The *Maiden* needed all the room she could get, so Hendrickson focused only a thousand feet past the beginning of pavement.

"This is too fast!" Buzz watched the speed gauge drop way too slowly. It was only down to 230 knots, and with only fifteen seconds until—impact?—it wasn't going down much farther. "Jesus, Bart, we're gonna hit hard."

The forward motion was terrific, and as frightening was the stonelike rate of descent now that the *Maiden* was forcing her way to the earth. She was going to land fast, the only way under the circumstances, and she was going to come down with millions of pounds of force on the runway.

"Let's hope they laid good concrete," the captain blurted out just as he pulled the column into his gut to slow the *Maiden's* descent. The big jet crossed the point where grass met the runway at 210 knots—40 knots faster than normal. Prayers, silent and personal, filled the flight deck.

With her nose ten degrees up, the *Maiden's* multiple-carriage main landing gear screeched when the rearmost wheels caught the runway at 206 knots. Like giant shock absorbers the struts on the main carriages compressed under the massive weight, but not enough to compensate. Two tires on the right mains blew a fraction of a second after hitting, but it was barely noticeable as an occurrence, entirely because of the violent metal-scraping-stone sound that came as the contoured rear of the 747 made contact and dragged along the runway. Sparks shot sideways and backward, then the nose eased forward, setting the dual front wheels on the ground.

The jolt inside the aircraft was tremendous. Below, several passengers went frantic, a reaction unnoticed by the hijackers, who were themselves frightened by the noise and violent vibrations. Wael hadn't settled into a seat and fell awkwardly into the aisle, forward of a group of male passengers. He recovered quickly, grabbing the arm of an empty seat and pointing the submachine gun at the startled men. One, he noticed, was smiling, an expression he could not comprehend at the moment.

Hadad, too, was surprised, even in his enforced serenity. His free hand found the fold-down armrest and dug into it instinctively. *In the name of Allah, the compassionate, the merciful . . .*

Instantly upon feeling the nosewheel touch, Buzz reversed the remaining two turbofans and stood on the brakes. Hendrickson also brought both his feet down on the pedals, full force. There was barely anything left of the brakes, and less than seven thousand feet of cement in front of them.

"Push the stick!"

Buzz heeded the shouted command, joining the captain in holding the control column all the way to the panel. The front end of the *Maiden* dropped noticeably as upward force on the rear elevators caused an opposite reaction on the nose.

It was working. Though the big Boeing was still moving down the runway way too fast, she was slowing. Whether it would be enough would become apparent very soon.

"Halfway," Buzz called out.

Hendrickson broke protocol and took his eyes off the direction of travel, glancing at the speed gauge. "One-ten."

"It's too damn fast. We're not gonna make it." Buzz looked left. The captain was staring through the thick Lexan with an icy gaze.

"Weave!"

"What? At one hundred plus? We'll . . ."

"Do it, with me, or we're going to fire-ball regardless."

Again the pilots broke the rules. Not those of behavior or standards—though several of those were notably excepted in their unorthodox techniques—but those of mechanics and accepted physics. By all common sense and engineering logic the nosewheel, barely enabled to steer at a hundred knots, should break off when forced to turn at the high rate of speed they were traveling.

It didn't, not even emitting a groan or squeal. The captain, backed up on the rudder pedals by Buzz's strong pressure, played the *Maiden* left and right, close to one side of the runway then back to the other. He was creating all kinds of forces to slow the aircraft, and now added severe friction to the list. It was similar to a near skid, only the rear never jackknifed—thankfully.

Eighty. Seventy. Sixty.

"One quarter! She's doing it!"

"C'mon, girl," Hendrickson coaxed and cajoled his big baby.

Fifty. The steering was more responsive now, but the brakes were practically nonexistent. On the floor, the pedals felt like steel slabs on a weak spring.

Forty. Thirty. The runway end was upon them.

"Left! Hard!"

Buzz followed the lead, instinctively leaning toward the center console as the *Maiden* heeled over to the right, opposite the direction of her turn. The tires screeched, and for the first time the blown right-side tires were apparent as the aircraft slid slightly. They were turning hard onto the last taxiway at the end of two-three. It wasn't even lighted. The aircraft's own landing beams provided illumination, sweeping across the grassy edge of the strip and painting the fronts of several buildings with a passing glow. Then she slowed in midturn onto the sweeping taxiway, her brakes letting out a final, abrupt moan as the massive discs ground metal into the contact surfaces, and finally, stopped cold.

Hangar 3C, José Martí

The 747's right side was displayed perfectly to the center hangar which her lights had passed over only seconds before. Behind a line of metal-framed windows a group of men in black stood watching.

"Hell if she didn't make it down," Antonelli said, genuinely surprised after the show of sparks they had seen at the far end of the airport.

"Damn," someone said. The team was realizing it now. They were going to go.

McAffee nodded to Graber.

"Okay, troops," the captain began. "This is your only good look at the bird. Look at the rear—where the cargo door is." He was standing behind the others, trying to prep them based on his own experience. "Remember what it looks like now, because you're going to be up close and personal real soon."

Less than ten minutes later their pistols were loaded and their faces blackened with antiflash cream. Then, with two Cubans at the slightly parted hangar door, they boarded the Humvees, which nosed close to the exit.

Flight 422

Hadad refused to allow the aircraft to be towed to the refueling point nearer the service area, and also nearer the terminal. Four fuel trucks, ancient in comparison to those in the "real" world, approached, along with a dispensing pumper. Their antiquity, in this instance, was an asset, allowing the four big tankers to feed fuel to the dispenser truck, basically a big piston-type pump on wheels. Hendrickson gave the tower—and whoever else was there—credit. With only a short radio refusal to come to the normal fueling station, he hadn't been able to give them much. But someone had figured this solution out, and it would work. Within twenty minutes her not quite depleted tanks should be back up to just beyond two hundred thousand pounds, a little more than half full. It would be plenty to get them to New York, though all three men in the cockpit knew that there was no intention of going there.

"There's nothing left of the brakes. Zippo."

Hendrickson knew his first officer was right. The pedals barely sprang up from fully depressed, and the metal-on-metal sound near the end of their roll could only have been the retaining pins of the brake pads digging into the discs. There would be several concentric circles of gouges in the hard metal surfaces, caused by the tens of thousands of foot-pounds of pressure applied. When the brakes were released after the roll, they were frozen open. The captain thought there might have been some further damage caused by the heat generated during braking, possibly to the hydraulics on the struts. That was of little consequence now. Other problems and happenings would soon be in the forefront, namely that if they had to land again, an act their captor had no intention of allowing, they wouldn't be able to stop.

"Wherever we go from here, I hope they have a net big enough to stop us," Captain Hendrickson joked, knowing that the hot mike was still engaged, and hoping that those listening were appreciating the seriousness of their situation. If someone tried a rescue they might be dead, and if they had to take off—with no flaps and less one engine—they might be dead. And landing—though both pilots had figured that this guy had no intention of setting the *Maiden* down anywhere in one piece—was potentially the most dangerous of all the possible outcomes.

Things weren't looking good, an understatement the captain was frightened to surpass.

Romeo Flight

Major Ralph Cooper felt the connection separate a few yards behind his head. The KC-10's refueling boom rose above the F-106, the light on its nozzle end shining through the cockpit's angular canopy onto Snoopy's white helmet.

Several individual vapor streams, the remnants of the tricky nighttime refueling maneuver, trailed off of the rubbery connector fitting which was retracting farther into the flying boom of the dark green Air Force tanker. Her refueling and anticollision lights both dazzled Cooper's vision and lit up the underside of the flying behemoth against the star-flecked blackness.

"Romeo, you took about seven-zero-zero gallons," the boom operator reported. That brought the Delta Dart up to her max internal load of 1,514 gallons, or 9,841 pounds in more correct aerial terms.

"Roger, Tiger Flight. Thanks for the drink." Cooper watched the military version of the venerable DC-10 gain altitude and bank left, heading north to the States.

His heading was 120. In ten minutes he'd be in Cuban airspace. The controllers aboard the AWACS informed him that his escorts would pick him up two minutes out. From there they all would circle and wait almost directly north of Havana, just five miles off and fifteen thousand feet above the Cuban coast.

It didn't seem too strange, other than the geography of the matter, until one thought about the nuclear-tipped missile in the Delta Dart's belly. Cooper tried not to think about it, but the fact that he was sitting atop a thirty-year-old nuclear weapon had frequently slipped past his mental defenses since takeoff.

20
....

CLOSER TO PARADISE

The White House

MEYERSON WAS THERE, as were Bud, Landau, and the president. The secretary of defense sat away from the others, talking via phone to General Granger in the NMCC. He hung up a moment later.

"Granger says the B-52 flights are meeting up with their tankers west of Gibraltar right now."

"And the rest of the forces?" the president asked.

"All in position. From your word, they can execute the first strikes in just twenty minutes."

Bud listened, passively on the exterior, but . . .

"What about the bombers? How long can they hold before we have to send them in or recall?" The president was a detail man on the military specifics. After hearing his NSA's recommendations, he had read the entire brief from the CJCOS himself.

"The F-111s are orbiting as we speak. They can tank once, but after that we'll have to do something." Meyerson saw the need for a more definitive answer on the president's face. "About three hours, sir. The stateside bombers are a bit more tricky. It's such a large flight that we just can't manage another tanking of the whole force and still have enough to get them back across the Atlantic." The European allies didn't mind a few F-111s staging from NATO bases—unlike the eighty-six raid—but a hundred and fifty big U.S. bombers would be political dynamite in most of the nations. Everyone, it seemed, was full speed ahead on the demilitarization policies, an economic necessity for them, and most of the world as well. "It's a little over three hours for them, also. The 52s will have to head for home first.

"It's all timing, sir. We have to match our resources—especially the in-flight–refueling ones—to our needs really carefully here. To pull something off this soon after the initial go is a tremendous undertaking."

"I know, Drew. The military deserves a major attaboy on this one. Bud, how long until Delta will need the final word?" He already knew what it would be. What other choice was there? It was the hostages' only chance.

"Within thirty minutes," the NSA replied after checking the clock. The time was approaching fast for action, and the time was already here for a very different kind of the same. Bud knew it was time.

"Mr. President, I'd like to toss something out here."

Landau smiled with one corner of his crotchety mouth. He could tell what was coming. *The man's got balls.*

"Go ahead." The president lowered himself into the single seat at the coffee table's end.

"There's no doubt that this is the time for decisions. I think we already know what the one concerning Delta and the hostages will be, barring any unforeseen happenings. What I'm talking about is an entirely different decision. A big one."

The secretary of defense joined the three others, taking a seat on the couch and filling his empty mug from the tureen of coffee.

"Remember how General Granger described that missile the aircraft is carrying down in the Gulf right now? He said shooting that at a plane was like killing a flea with a sledgehammer. Well, I think we might be doing something very similar in Libya, except that we might be missing the flea—so to speak—all together."

"You think?"

Shit or get off the pot, Bud thought. He remembered. The president wanted commitment, not conjecture. "I believe this, sir. We should not go ahead with the full-scale strike."

"For Christ's sake, why not?" Meyerson challenged.

Bud leaned in. "Look. Think back to the eighty-six raid. Did it work? Obviously not. It's a damn cycle of act and react. Someone blows up a plane, or hijacks a ship, and what do we do—react to their action. Our policy has been no negotiation with terrorists, and swift retribution when someone is killed. Unfortunately, neither has been practiced faithfully or regularly by past administrations. And the latter, not at all."

"Explain." The president was interested.

"Take the Achille Lauro. We were able to apprehend all of the terrorists who carried it out, and the man who planned it—Abu Abbas. Then what happened? Because we vacillated, the Italians let Abbas off scot-free. And the Germans are so damn afraid of retaliation that we can't get the trigger man they hold, Hamadi, out of their hands for trial. We're castrated in our effort to deal with these barbarians."

"So what do you suggest, Bud? That we bomb Rome and Berlin to punish our allies for impeding the judicial process? C'mon. Your logic is going nowhere." Meyerson exhaled an exasperated breath and finally undid his tie. "We've got the force off Qaddafi's coast to shut down his military and his economy. Two very viable, and very reachable, targets."

"Sure. And they're easy. Don't you see? That's what I'm getting at. We had this Abbas guy nailed for what he was a hell of a long time before he pulled the Achille Lauro thing, but we just waited. It was easier to react, and to take swipes at a pushover of a country."

"A major supporter of international terrorism!" Meyerson bellowed.

Bud paused before continuing. "And, nonetheless, a pushover, as I said."

"What he's saying, Mr. President, is that we should save the bombs and use just a few bullets." Landau's analysis, in its cryptic simplicity, was sufficient to drive the point home.

Bud looked to each of his counterparts, but they were looking at the chief executive.

"Might I remind you, Bud, that what you're proposing is similar, if not identical, to the events that started this whole mess." The president's analysis was not completely right.

"Not correct, sir." Contradicting any president, even one as young as this, was risky. Bud realized this entirely, and also that he was in the right. "The events that precipitated this situation were planned and executed by men in high places operating outside the bounds of our own law. We can't say that they abrogated any international agreements since there never has been a comprehensive treaty or convention that dealt with real, hard issues on terrorism. Not one. Only half measures and resolutions of so-called solidarity have been enacted—no, correction: adopted. Enacted implies at least some sort of action, of which there's been none.

"Our laws, however, do specifically address the matter. Laws were broken, and—Director Landau will back me up on this—their choice of targets and methodology was wrong. Not because it wouldn't work, or because Qaddafi doesn't shoulder some of the blame for the state of terrorist activities, but because its impact and results are going to be fruitless. Even detrimental."

"Herb?" the president asked, seeking an explanation.

"It's obvious, Mr. President. We knew from the start that

Qaddafi's motivation to undertake this act is vengeance. My predecessors failed to realize that their brilliant plan, however deniable it might have been, had a lag time for full effect. Qaddafi had time to figure it out, and time to set this all up. A more immediate resolution of his activities would have been more appropriate."

"Assassination in the classical sense." The president rubbed the furrows on his brow.

Meyerson's head shook. "There's a hell of a difference between a flat-out assassination, by gun, knife, poison, or whatever, and a retaliatory strike to punish. We can't just kill every head of state that supports terrorism. Hell, there would be few Middle East governments left if we'd done that."

"You missed the full point, Drew," Bud pointed out. "The method was wrong because it allowed a response. The target was also wrong."

"I thought you agreed that Qaddafi was culpable?"

"Yes, Mr. President—culpable. But not fully responsible. The reality of any war on terrorism, because it's an undeclared conflict, is that we can't take the easy way out and go after the backers. There will always be more where they came from. We're learning that in spades with the drug cartels now that our policies and interdictions have some meat and are hurting them. The same applies here. We have to go after the idea men and the foot soldiers. We have to send a message that just because you call yourself a freedom fighter, that doesn't mean you're immune from retribution. And I emphasize the word *retribution*. It's a scary word, one that I'd hope every would-be terrorist would think about."

"So you're suggesting that we hit only those terrorists who've pulled a trigger?" Meyerson still couldn't grasp the whole picture. "How the hell are we supposed to identify them if they haven't done anything? There are a hell of a lot of first timers in this game. Kids, women, old folks—the whole gamut of society. How do you expect our people—whichever ones you'd charge with the responsibility to carry out this policy—how would you expect them to predict who was going to be a terrorist before they actually were?"

Bud had the answer ready. "Guilt by affiliation and profession."

The president looked perplexed, and the secretary of defense was obviously incredulous.

"Bud. Are you hearing yourself? I mean, listen to what you just said. It goes against our own legal definitions of guilt supposition. Guilt by association is not—"

"Again"—Bud held up his hand—"you didn't hear me. Not guilt by association: guilt by affiliation. There's a big difference. If you go around saying that you are affiliated with a known group of murderers, and that you are going to follow their lead and kill Americans because they're Americans, then by God you better believe that they deserve the label of guilty, long before they get behind the trigger.

"It's just a more defined form of what we are ready to do with our fleet and our bombers. Ninety percent of those *freedom fighters* in the targeted training camps have never fired a shot at an American, much less even looked at one. But we're still going to blast them to their maker, am I right? Well, if that's not guilt by affiliation and profession, then I don't know what is."

The ending of Bud's soliloquy hit home. It was precisely what they had been planning to do, only it was sure to stir further resentment elsewhere in the Arab world. And would it send a message other than that America had the biggest guns in town? It rang back to Teddy Roosevelt's *speak softly and carry a big stick*. The stick was no question, but the words were thunderous.

"So you think we should forgo the strike and concentrate on quieter means?"

"Within the law, Mr. President. Following the guidelines for covert action."

"There are still laws against what you are proposing," Meyerson commented. The wind seemed to be out of his opposition.

"Again, not entirely. There are laws that allow personnel of government agencies to use necessary force to protect civilian lives. You can look it up. I have."

Obviously, the president thought.

The phone rang, and Landau picked it up. "It's Secretary Coventry, Mr. President."

He took the receiver and listened for only half a minute before handing it to Meyerson. "The secretary has informed me that the plane will be refueled very soon."

It was approaching decision time, and now the president had a second, and more difficult decision to make.

Flight 422

"What do you think, Bart?" It was their first open, unheard question in many hours.

Hendrickson glanced back. The door was shut. "There's enough noise from the engines. He won't hear."

The head terrorist had left them unattended, unexpectedly and without notice. It was their chance for some real information.

Buzz nodded. "Do it. Hurry."

"Four-Two-Two heavy to any United States aircraft; come in."

There was a short pause of static, then the reply. "*Four-Two-Two, what is your situation?*"

Hendrickson could sense the worry in the caller's voice. "Don't worry. The head guy left us alone. He's the killer, but I don't know his real whole name. Just his first: Mohammed."

"*Right, Four-Two-Two. We have good IDs on your friends. Now listen carefully. You were just about to hear from us. Help is there, at the airport, and they're going to join you real soon. Do you understand?*"

Hendrickson looked to his first officer and mouthed the word *what*? "A rescue? But how are . . . never mind. Go on."

"*All right. You're gonna play a big part in this. How's your acting?*"

Huh?

Without waiting for an audible reply the caller went on, explaining the plan in just under a minute. "*You've gotta deliver some kind of diversion and keep Mr. Big in the cockpit as long as possible. Something believable. Can you handle it?*"

The pilots were still trying to swallow the idea of what was going to happen. "Yeah. That's a roger, but are you sure about this?"

"*Army says it'll work, and I hear they get things right sometimes. Hey. They're good. They'll get you out of this.*"

Right. Okay, I guess I've got to believe this. The captain realized he'd forgotten something. "Air Force, if this works we're going to need a hell of a long runway."

"*Your brakes are gone, then. We monitored your engine and flap trouble. Hell of a job flying there, Four-Two-Two. Okay, we'll get that figured out, and good luck on your takeoff. Weather informs me that you've got a twenty-five-knot surface wind coming straight down that runway you came in on if you go out the reciprocal.*"

That might not be enough, but it would definitely help. "Thanks again, Air Force." Hendrickson hoped it would be enough. It was time for some curiosity satisfaction. "Air Force—what the hell is weighing us down?"

Again, a pause preceded a terse reply. "*Four-Two-Two, you don't want to know.*"

First they had started fueling on the left side, and then they switched to the right, necessitating moving the tankers and the pumper. Hadad wondered at first if they were not really workers, rather commandos in disguise. But, after all, this was friendly territory. The Cubans would simply want them to land and be on their way, and the closest American commando was across the Florida straits.

Why, then, am I nervous? he asked himself, instantly realizing that he was exerting extra pressure on the small round button that kept him alive. *Possibly because I am so close to victory. Yes.* The two brother fighters he took his name from, Mohammed Boudia and Wadi Hadad, had tasted victory. *And they, too, are in paradise.* That thought calmed him.

His seat on the right side of the lounge allowed him to watch the entire process: the scissorlike lift on wheels lifting two blue-clad workmen up to the underside of the wing, where they attached the thick gray hose. The rumbling of the vehicles' motors was distinct above the steady whine of the jet engines. Hadad wondered when they would be done.

"Mohammed." It was Abu. Wael was beside him, looking perplexed. Hadad knew why.

"Go, Wael," he said in his native Arabic. "You watch the Americans."

The big terrorist looked at Abu, who still stared at their leader, then entered the cockpit. Hadad turned back to the window.

"I can feel your words, Abu, so do not hold them in on my account."

The younger of the two ran his hand through the black waves atop his head, his eyes searching the floor for words before coming back up to his leader. Hadad had turned to face him. His eyes were sullen, and very, very tired.

"We are in trouble, Mohammed?"

Hadad shook his head. It leaned slightly right, giving him an angular perspective of his comrade. He looked up and down at him.

"You are lying."

"And you are too soft."

"Soft!" Abu shouted, the word coming out in an Arabic shriek. "You leave the Americans alone at the controls, for how long now, so you can sit in here and . . . what? . . . pray for good fortune! And you say that I am soft?"

Hadad did not match Abu's furious tone. "And who did you leave to watch all those below?" The rhetorical inquiry broke Abu's gaze, sending his eyes back to the floor, but leaving his teeth visibly clenched. "Abdul."

"He is—"

"—is alone with hundreds of our prisoners right below your feet. When there should be no fewer than two of you watching them, you leave only one. And as for good fortune, my friend, my brother, it is assured. Would Allah not have blessed us with life to this point if He had not wanted us to succeed?"

Abu breathed out his wrath. "Then we are in trouble."

"Allah has protected us."

"Against what? Why do you try to deceive me, and the others? We are not blind. The aircraft acts as if it is dying all around us." Abu's tone was a mix of cynicism and pleading. "Why are you pushing us so hard? Why are you pushing yourself? We are safe here. If there are problems with the aircraft we can stay and have repairs done before going on. The Cubans would not deny us that. What would a short delay—"

"No delay!" Hadad responded in a burst of determination.

"But—"

"No!" He stood up and stepped closer to Abu, leaving their faces only inches apart. "We are on a mission, one charged by Allah, and we will not delay its conclusion. If you choose to be weak and soft, then I have erred in my judgment of you. I believed that you were a soldier of Allah, a true one, who would accept his fate willingly." Hadad knew the last words had slipped out.

Abu's suspicions, which had grown in the last twelve hours, were confirmed. This was never meant to be a mission to humiliate and win concessions from the Americans. The reasons and intentions now became crystal clear. It was a personal mission they were on, not of their choosing, but of their leader's. A grand drama of deception, indeed. One most effective on the integral parties.

"And the weapons in the hold?" Abu remembered being assured by Hadad that they were just for the Americans' benefit, and were totally harmless.

"Gifts from Allah and our Arab brethren."

Insh Allah, Abu said to no one. "You are going to use them on the Americans . . . in their own land."

"We are," Hadad corrected him. "At the very heart of their infidel government. It will be more than appropriate, and convenient for them. The mourning will already be in progress."

"I see." It was all Abu could think to say. His wife and his child would be living without him. The solace was that, if his leader was right, he would soon be in paradise, awaiting a glorious reunion.

That thought, however comforting, was short-lived. Abu had to admit that there were doubts now in his thoughts. Would he be with Allah, and the prophets of Islam? He wondered. He truly wondered.

Hadad slid back and sat on the arm of the aisle seat, leaning on the back with his free arm. "Accept your fate, my friend. Go below and help Abdul. I will have Wael rest up here. He has been awake much of the journey, yes?"

"Yes."

Hadad smiled. It was meant to reassure his comrade. Abu turned his head first, his body following a split second later, and headed down below, his soul not yet at peace, but his mind having accepted his fate as a martyr.

* * *

Sandy was still sleeping, thank God. Michael could feel her chest rise and fall against his left arm, and occasionally her nose would rub against his neck as she nestled closer. The shouting from above had not awakened her as it had a few others. A man and woman across the aisle exchanged worried looks with Michael, and the terrorist forward of where they sat had nervously looked up sporadically during the verbal match. None of what was said—or yelled—had been heard with any clarity, but could displays of bellicosity mean anything good? Michael thought not.

The muffled thud of hard shoes on the carpeted stairway started, then stopped. One of the hijackers had come down. That left two upstairs. Michael had found himself increasingly keeping track of where the terrorists were, and how many were anywhere at any one time. Their situation, he felt, was not getting any better, and the fight or whatever upstairs didn't lend comfort in the least. Something was wrong, in spades, and he was determined that if they started shooting, he was going to know where the nearest gun was, and he was going to take it—or die trying. For Sandy's sake.

The thoughts that would have been more familiar in his military days abruptly faded. One of the terrorists, the one who had just come down, was walking aft. He was approaching Michael's row.

For whatever reason, their eyes met, and the visual exchange seemed to slow time. The shared, silent exchange was brief, yet telling. Michael had seen something, more in the terrorist's eyes than on his face. It was . . . what—futility? No. Resignation. That was it.

Michael was scared. For both of them. He was doubly grateful that his wife was sleeping, and he consciously listened to the sound of the footsteps retreating aft. He figured, after they had stopped, that the man was past the middle bulkhead of the nearly silent aircraft.

The rhythmic thrumping of the piston-driven pumper stopped with a sputter. Hadad moved to the window quickly. They were done. The last of the tank trucks was pulling away and the scissor lift was coming down next to the pumper. He carefully shifted the thumb switch to his left hand and took the Uzi in his right. Its barrel tapped rapidly on the cockpit door, and Wael opened it inward without taking his eyes off the pilots.

"Wael. Go rest." Hadad added a head toss to the words.

Silently the huge terrorist slid between the half-open door and its frame, which Hadad closed and locked.

"They are done with refueling, correct?"

Genius! "Just now," Buzz answered.

"Then we are leaving." Hadad pressed the gun to the back of Buzz's neck and leaned far forward, looking out the right-side window. The last two pieces of equipment were just clearing the area. "Get moving."

"No way," Hendrickson responded to the order.

With the barrel still embedded in the co-pilot, Hadad held the thumb switch out toward the captain. "You defied me before. This time your number two dies. Now move."

"Listen. We have no brakes. None. How do you expect us to get in position for a takeoff if we roll into the mud beside the runway trying? If you want this aircraft to get off the ground, then we're going to need a tug to position us. Got it?"

Hadad eased up the pressure of the Uzi. Buzz wanted to laugh, but just continued smiling and looking straight ahead. The cap was playing this guy hard.

"Get it," Hadad ordered, stepping back. He held his left hand and the switch out in front until reaching the jump seat. It was just a minor delay, he kept telling himself. Just a minor delay.

Hangar 3C, José Martí

"Did you see him?" McAffee asked.

"Twice. It was the same guy, I'm sure." Sean handed the binoculars back. The vantage point was almost perfect through the six-inch opening between the hangar doors. "He was just looking out the cockpit window, and a minute ago he was looking out from one of the upper-deck windows."

They had never had a picture of the head terrorist, but it was a sure bet he was the one in the cockpit. Past experience had shown that these guys liked to be in control.

"Captain, remember the face: He's ours."

Control Tower, José Martí

Secretary Coventry was flanked by one aide and two gun-toting Cuban security troops, neither of whom seemed to be officers. It looked as though Castro wanted as little official contact with the United States as possible. All the better, the lanky Minnesotan thought, as he watched events unfolding from the blacked-out glass box a hundred feet above the ground.

The setup was entirely modern, to his surprise. He was a pilot, schooled completely in small, private craft, and had visited many a tower in his adult life—and in his early life, he reminded himself. His father was a farmer, then and now, though at almost eighty years of age he had largely turned over the operation to his youngest son, the secretary's little brother. In his prime, though, he had flown the crop duster personally out of the airport near the four hundred acres, often taking his children up with him.

He had expected old analogue instruments and sweep lights on circular radar displays, but instead there were modern Japanese sets. They couldn't have been more than two years old. The controllers spoke in hushed Spanish, more quietly the longer he had been among them.

One of the operators looked up, speaking directly to the State Department interpreter. The balding Cuban American listened to the full message. "Mr. Secretary, the aircraft has just asked for a tug. Apparently they have no brakes."

"That's no surprise." Coventry held out his hand. The interpreter removed the handset from the portable unit slung on his shoulder and gave it to his boss.

The White House

The president answered the phone himself. "Yes."

"The aircraft is about to leave, sir." Secretary Coventry sounded cool. Maybe it was easier being close to the action, the president surmised.

He looked around at the other three. "Any last-minute concerns?" There weren't. The situation had practically dictated the responses to it, a truism that the president was now well aware of, and determined to prevent from recurring. "Jim, I'm giving Delta the authorization to rescue the hostages as per the plan."

Not ten feet away Secretary of Defense Meyerson picked up a tan-colored phone on the president's desk. It rang immediately in the NMCC.

"Granger here."

"General Granger, inform Delta to execute CLOUD-BURST."

There were no other words. Both the president and Meyerson hung up simultaneously.

"Here we go," the NSA said. "People are going to die."

"The right people, Bud." Landau massaged the wooden arm of the chair. It was smooth and hard, and the grooves made by colonial workmen were impeccable still, after two centuries of wear. "That may seem wrong, I know. We're raised to fear God, and to believe that every life is precious. Jesus, you know, we've got to believe that, even in this business when we're talking about death . . . about causing death. It's just that somewhere, for whatever reasons, some folks turn bad. They take a wrong turn. God knows some of them really believe they're in the right, but they can't preach their own divinity. My wife always says that a man can believe what he wants to believe, that he can convince himself of anything—anything!—but there is one force in the universe"—Landau's wiry finger pointed upward—"that knows." He paused, letting the words sink in. "We may be the great pretenders, but if so, then we're the pretenders on the side of right. I can look inside my heart each night and see that. We all can."

Wisdom, fortunately, spoke eloquently when aged in human form. Landau told the others all that they needed to hear, for their silent doubts were surfacing at the moment of truth. He had known such moments before, and again he had shared of himself.

"Bud," the president started, then held his words for a long moment. He stood, digging his hands deep in his pockets. "I've thought about your idea, or proposal, whatever it is. It may be your thinking, but if I agree with it and decide to execute it then I am the final arbiter. You are an adviser."

"Mr. President?" Meyerson sensed that one military operation was all that was going to happen.

The president faced his defense chief. "Stand down the strike, Drew."

"Yes, sir," he answered, without visible disappointment, and picked up the same phone as before.

"Mr. President, are you going to approve the proactive plan?" Bud asked.

"Tentatively, yes. But I want this to be legal, accepted by those in Congress who need to know, and covert as hell. About the only thing the Agency's previous residents did that was even semi-intelligent was trying to keep their actions secret." To most those words would be deceitful, almost sinister, but the practice of "need to know" was meant to protect. In a utopian society everyone could know about everything—maybe. But not in the twentieth century. Some deeds of leaders were best left to follow those in the know to their graves.

"We'll need a time line for Congress," Landau noted. Only eight members of Congress would ever know about it, the absolute minimum allowed by law.

"I'd like Bud and you to put that together. Drew, your office will work with Bud and the CIA to get the operational details down." He looked at his national security adviser. "I want complete security on this, Bud. Your responsibility."

"Absolutely."

The president went behind his desk and sat down. Except for the darkness through the window behind him he looked as though he had just sat down to start work. He dialed the office of his chief of staff. "Ellis. I just gave the go to Delta, so your work is going to pick up in an hour or so." Gonzales was working with the presidential press secretary to ensure that the right word went out when the time came. "And, Ellis, I want you to call the Speaker and Majority Leader right away. Inform them of what's going on, and set them up to be in my office at seven tomorrow evening. Yes, evening. There's no time before the funeral, and the rest of the afternoon is shot. I don't want to break any routine on scheduling this . . . capishe? Good. Right, it's quiet. And, one more thing. I want the

attorney general in here in one hour. Quietly, also. Thanks."
He set the receiver down and looked at the wall clock. "How
long, Drew?"

"Fifteen or twenty minutes. We'll know in a half an hour."

Many times before, presidents and their advisers had sat in
that very room under similar circumstances. The Mayagüez
incident. The Iran rescue mission. Son Tay. None had been
completely successful, and one had been labeled a grand
tragedy of failure. However, they would all pale in comparison to the success or failure of the present attempt to wrest
American innocents from a willing and able foe. Success
would bring jubilation and a major boost in the approval
rating for the fledgling administration, an accepted measure
of a chief executive's ability to govern, like it or not. Failure,
aside from the obvious loss of life, would shake the new
government, and no one in the Oval Office had any illusions
about the survivability of the new president if that should
happen.

Romeo Flight

His "escorts" were waiting exactly where the AWACS
had told him they would be. He tracked them on radar,
and they him, until their separation was minimal. Now their
anticollision lights outlined their frames, in unmistakable
detail. Fulcrums.

Cooper's usual ride, the F-15C, would be more of a comfort right now. It was damn hard to shake the sense of
helplessness he felt just floating along, ten thousand feet
up, with MiGs on each wing. Some other Air Force plane
had been graced with their presence. The radio told all.

Radio, he remembered. It was just about time. He dialed
in 243.0 on his radio, the military emergency frequency. The
procedures for contact had been established hastily, leaving
the weekend warrior wondering if the Cubans would be listening. And if they were, would they understand English?

"Romeo Flight to Springer Seven-Eight." With only minutes to go, Cooper wanted to make damn sure no one else
was near, especially in his blind spot.

"*Romeo, go ahead.*"

"Request traffic check."

"Romeo, you're clear out to two hundred miles. Just your two friends close in on you."

The AWACS wouldn't even have a defined radar picture of the MiGs. They were too close. It was their lack of proper Interrogator, Friend or Foe response that gave them away. When search radar emissions from the AWACS painted the three fighters, small transponders in each, if turned on, would add a "biography" to the energy reflected back to the sending unit. If the unit was friendly, a coded response would identify it as such on the display. If not, it would be tagged a bandit—hostile. The MiGs were as concerned as the F-106 about being mistaken by their own radar, and, wisely, had their own IFFs turned on.

"Roger, Springer." Now it was time to contact the Cubans. "United States aircraft, Romeo, to Revolution Flight." They were obviously prone to ideological theatrics, even in their coding!

"Romeo, Romeo, go ahead." The reply was in an amazingly accent-free English. Cooper had heard about something like this in recent years. The Cubans were using pilots well-versed in the language of the *norte-americanos.* Their linguistic skill had come from actually working and going to school in the States, a feat made possible by the much lamented DGI, the Cuban intelligence service. It had been one of their few successes in recent years, until the CIA had turned an overseas DGI agent, who had gladly told all. Operation *Hermano Grande,* as it was known in ironically Orwellian Spanish, soon came to a halt, though not until two dozen or more Cuban agents had been cycled through training north of the Rio Grande. Mexico, Guatemala, and Honduras, all friendly nations to the United States, were unwittingly used as back doors into the country for the agents, who then were free to roam, with their forged visas, and become proficient in the language.

"Revolution Flight, I am climbing to angels"—he had to correct himself—"to twenty thousand." The Cubans might know English, but he hoped they were still ignorant of military terms. *God! What if one of them's in the Air Force?*

"Understood. We will follow and break away at—" the Cuban pilot watched as the Delta Dart nosed up and went to afterburner. Obviously the *yanqui* wasn't going to wait. But,

their orders were specific: escort and protect. That made the pilots, both alumni of *Hermano Grande*, want to spit. The Alamo missiles under each wing were meant to be targeted at Americans, not . . .

Cooper felt the familiar old kick in the butt as the J75 engine's afterburner lit up, adding a crude form of rocket propulsion to the jet's normal thrust. The F-106 pulled away from the Russian-built fighters, though there was no question that they could, if desired, fly circles around it. That was the blessing of modern aircraft.

There was one thing the old bird could do that its younger bastard cousins couldn't, and that knowledge scared the hell out of Snoopy. The Russians couldn't see his helmet shake slightly as he pondered just what he was supposed to do.

Flight 422

The three men in the cockpit lost sight of the squat-looking tug as it went beneath the nose of the Maiden. A minute later the big jet bucked backward a bit.

"She's hooked." Buzz noted the positive lock light go on, and also moved his gaze to the left a few inches. Another light would be going on soon, and with it a subtle buzzer.

Hendrickson sensed that the terrorist had again sat down. Did that mean he was relaxing? The whole crazy plan hinged on that. He had to make sure the killer felt safe.

"That's it, Buzz. We're rolling, and next stop is New York." *Nice* try, the captain thought, knowing that he was neither a hypnotist nor a psychologist. He decided that he'd better just let things be, and hope for the best.

They were moving forward, Hadad felt. Very slowly. He let his eyes close for a moment, and his head tilt back. It was a moment of relaxation, his whole body feeling the release, with the notable exception of his thumb.

When his eyes again opened Hadad could see motion through the windshield. Faint lights moved from left to right as the aircraft swung slowly to the left.

As the *Maiden* finished her turn off of the curving crossway she had stopped on, and her rear aligned itself with the long taxiway along the runway, a set of double sliding doors came open in the darkness three hundred yards behind.

The Humvees sped across the narrow grass median between the hangar and the crossway in ten seconds, and powered up to 40 mph on the taxiway in eight seconds. They were blacked out, their drivers relying on the sidelights along the pavement and the glow of the 747's underside strobe. Their target was on the right rear, aft of the pulsing light and in the cockpit's blind spot.

Graber rose from his sitting position on the platform at the lead vehicle's rear. There was an identical one on the following Humvee. Eight feet off the ground and moving at speed the captain knelt upright. McAffee had his left ankle from below. The wind was cold, and Sean figured it would even feel that way without the speed-induced gusts.

The *Maiden* was coming up quickly, and the drivers adjusted speed, expertly slowing without using the brakes. It was one time a sensitive accelerator and the governor worked well in an Army vehicle, requiring only a lifting of the foot off the pedal to slow the green-and-black vehicles.

Graber was astride his target now: the starboard rear cargo door. He rose up on his feet, holding on to the crude rail they had installed. Still, he was only at eye level with the metallic circle on the rectangular door's lower side. He removed the four-inch key from around his neck, keeping it on the long lanyard that would catch it if a slip happened.

They all saw the captain's foot stomp the metal grate platform. It was time for the light. Quimpo held up the Streamlight, aiming at the point that Graber's outstretched arm was reaching for. The driver slid closer to the slow-moving jet, just . . . close . . . enough . . .

There it was. A one-inch vertical slit, dead center in the circle. It came closer, or the Humvee slid left—Sean couldn't tell. But it was close enough. The toollike key was gripped solidly in his right hand, and he moved it toward the slit, aiming and hitting the solid door the first time, and connecting perfectly on the second try.

"What is it?" Hadad stood at the buzzing sound.
Show time. "Son of a bitch!" Hendrickson reached across the console. He and Buzz were tapping and playing with the same switch. A light was flashing near it.
"What?" Hadad's tone was calmer. He had almost become

accustomed to setbacks, and for a second he wondered if Abu had been right. Maybe they should have waited for . . . *No*! The timing would be completely off. The purpose would not be achieved, and his brothers would have died in vain.

"Don't worry, don't worry." Buzz turned his head as the captain continued to fiddle with the control. "Just our ram air turbine. It gives us power if the engines cut out on us." He turned away then quickly back. "It ain't surprising, considering what she's been through."

"Will it fly?"

It was Hendrickson's turn. "She'll fly, but if we need the RAT we're going to be out of luck, unless it resets."

Hadad sat back. *Allah. Allah. Not now, when I am so close.*

Graber waited until two of his teammates clambered up onto the platform before pulling on the key. Once turned it functioned as a handle, allowing the cargo door to be hefted upward. This was the manual method, of course, the usual way being to use the built-in hydraulic lifters. The necessary equipment to do that was a luxury in this case, requiring brute force to be used.

"Ready?" Graber shouted above the engine noise, getting nods from Antonelli and Quimpo.

He made sure the handle was turned fully, then pulled. The door cracked, then came outward and up giving an eighteen-inch clearance for entry. Sean maneuvered his head under the big door and felt for a handhold on the floor of the cargo deck. The perforated floor provided many, and he hefted himself up through the opening, which Antonelli had made even larger.

He was in. The viewpoint looking down was impressive. The driver of the Humvee looked straight ahead, gauging his speed perfectly against that of the aircraft. "Let's go! Move! Move!"

Quimpo came next, and by the time he was fully in, McAffee and Anderson were atop the platform.

"Don't drop that thing," the major joked to Antonelli as Joe was pulled into the hold. McAffee followed the civilian in immediately. Two of the team then held the door from the inside as the biggest Delta trooper slid through the opening.

Joe slid back, away from the door to give the soldiers room, and came up against something solid with his back. His quarry.

The first vehicle pulled away and the second spurted forward into the precise spot. It took under two minutes to get the remaining Delta men aboard, then the Humvee slowed, turned abruptly, and joined its partner in a dash to the darkness of the taxiway behind.

Graber, Antonelli, and Quimpo found handholds on the door and pulled it down to the closed position. "There's supposed to be an inner handle here," Sean yelled above the rumbling.

"There." Quimpo had the light on the black twist handle.

"Got it." Antonelli gripped it and turned it back to vertical. That would release the outer key they had used. It would be lying on the pavement now.

"We're in." McAffee said, then gave the order to get ready.

The *Maiden* had to travel a near complete squared oval, much like the Indianapolis speedway, before she would be back in position to take off. First she crossed the runway on which she had landed, and then a parallel runway before coming left on the far taxiway. Then another left brought her back to her takeoff point, a spot she had traversed in the opposite direction a while before. The tug swung left one final time and positioned the 747 at her start point.

"This is it," Buzz commented. The tug pulled away forward and turned off the runway at the first crossway.

"Fire-wall it and forget, I guess," Hendrickson suggested. There was no procedure for anything like this. Taking off with three engines, overloaded, and with no flaps; they'd either write the aviation history books or fire-ball into a cane field.

"One, two, and four all show nominal." Buzz looked at the overhead console. "Safety systems are ready."

The captain looked up too. Right above was the switch that, when thrown, would require the greatest acting job by any pilot since Jimmy Stewart.

And the tires. Hendrickson remembered about those. The

four blown right mains would mean even more difficulty. "We're going to need to compensate for the tires."

"Rudder and nosewheel, as long as she holds." Buzz didn't know if it would. The flat tires would add friction on the right side, making the aircraft want to steer in that direction. Rudder to the left and manual steering would have to work, otherwise they would find mud and grass less than halfway down the runway.

"You know, Buzz, in my craziest dreams I could have never thought this up. Never."

The old Marine smiled. "Something to tell the grandkids about."

The captain looked around the cockpit, for no real reason he realized. It just seemed the thing to do. "As ready as we'll ever be." *Ever? Now or never.*

Once again the throttle hand of each pilot held the lever, Buzz backing up the captain. In one quick motion they pressed the handles forward against the built-in resistance. It was a quicker acceleration than normal, which bounced the 747's nose up and then down as she gained speed.

"Fifty."

Hendrickson had only one plan to get his baby airborne: pull the stick into his crotch at the end of the runway. It would be close. Without the flaps they would need to be going in the neighborhood of 200 knots to get up with just the elevators to point the nose skyward. With a 25-knot head wind—if it was still blowing—they could do it with 180 knots, their normal takeoff speed with systems functioning fully.

Buzz tweaked his column left with taps to keep the *Maiden* straight. It was working, even without using the nosewheel.

"One-twenty." They were passing the halfway point, gaining speed. The faster they went, the more lift the wings generated. As that happened there was less pressure on the main gear, which allowed the blown tires to actually rise up off the pavement and spin somewhat freely. That reduced the friction and allowed for more speed and less worry about keeping on the centerline.

"One-fifty. She's doing it! She's doing it!"

Hadad heard the number two's excitement, but he already knew they would make it. It had been difficult. More difficult than he had imagined, but he had been successful. He laid the Uzi on his lap and reached into the left breast pocket. The click came first, and then he let his thumb rise for the last time. He massaged it on his forefinger, and set about clearing his mind for the journey that would begin at the end of this one.

The three-quarter mark shot by as Buzz called out 170 knots. The captain brought the stick fully back into his gut as fast as the built-in resistors would allow. The nose came up around them.

"One-ninety!"

If he had calculated correctly the end would be right . . .

Now! The feeling of air enveloping a plane was unmistakable. It was like suddenly being suspended in smoothness, with the vibrations of the earth lying far behind.

"Shit." Buzz kept his hands ready to back up on the stick and the throttles. "She's up! We're up!"

They were at one hundred, then two, then three, and slowly gaining altitude and speed as the captain brought the nose down a bit. He looked across the console to his first officer.

"You're sweatin', Bart." Buzz smiled like a kid in a go-cart.

"Slow climb. Real gentle." Hendrickson would keep the *Maiden* right where the powers that be wanted her. The rest was up to them. Almost.

21

....

IN THE BELLY OF THE BEAST

Flight 422

"HOLD TIGHT TILL he levels it out," McAffee said. Once off the ground the noise abated.

The team had placed and activated several small magnetic

lights, each one spreading a wide beam of high-intensity light. Some of the men were squeezed nervously in the spaces between the four big boxes, their arms pressing to the sides to steady them.

Joe, however, was already prying at one of the wood coverings. It was all cosmetic, he was sure. Whatever was in there was heavy, and, with the amount of shielding necessary to make the crude reactors feasible, the wood wouldn't support any of it.

"Shouldn't you wait, Anderson?"

Joe ignored the major and kept working at the box. By the time the aircraft leveled somewhat he had one side almost off.

Delta had its own job to do.

"Lewis." Graber led the sergeant forward. He shone his flashlight on the curved right side as they walked. Red numbers stenciled on white backgrounds proceeded in ascending order as they moved. Each one was a location number, identifying the support section at that point. The 747, like other large aircraft, was made up of many parallel circular frames which were held together by long metallic stringers that ran the length of the fuselage. Around the skeletal cylinder a thin skin of aluminum was stretched, giving the aircraft structure and most of its load-bearing capability. Graber was looking for a specific section—or ring—that would put them below their desired entry point.

But first things first. Before going in they had to see what was there. Debriefing of released hostages had told them that the passengers were all forward now. That would lead one to believe that the terrorists were also. But they had to know for sure. If they went in aft, and there was a bad guy standing over them, it would be beneficial to know that first so he could be taken out.

Sixteen C. Sixteen C. "Where are—here." Graber stopped and cocked his head to the right to get a look at the ceiling. They were all walking hunched over in the five-foot-five-inch cargo hold. He ran his hand from right to left on the smooth aluminum panel. Above that would be a flame-resistant plastic floor liner that acted as a sound and climate insulator, and above that an eighth of an inch of padding, and then the carpeting. The center floor stringer was his guidepost. Six inches to the right was the spot. He looked forward at the solid metal bulkhead three feet away, then behind three feet at the forwardmost crate. The rest of the team was readying the charges near the door.

"Do it, Lewis."

The sergeant was the team's tech specialist, which meant that he handled the high-tech—expensive—gear. In this case an ultra-high-speed lithium-powered drill and the fiber-optic viewing device that would be inserted through a hole into the cabin above.

Lewis scratched the spot with an etching pen, just to give the carborundum bit a starting point. There was only one speed on the specially built instrument: fast, or fucking fast as its users said. The sergeant held the penlike tip and tucked the flexible drive cable under his arm. It led to the actual motor unit, hooked to his belt.

It whirred first, then went almost silent. He touched it to the aluminum. Only a slight hum was heard. That was the beauty of the instrument. Unless you were drilling through granite or marble, the high rotational speed of the bit simply pulverized its target, allowing no room for resistance. The high heat tolerance of the carborundum bit aided in the silencing of the work. Friction caused great deals of heat, which expanded traditional bits of steel or light alloys. As it expanded it would contact the sides of the hole it was boring, causing sound. A foot away the captain could barely hear it.

Lewis sensed the breakthrough and continued with little pressure on the instrument, cutting right through the plastic and padding. Dyed guide marks on the bit told him the penetration and when to stop. "Through." He switched it off and let it dangle to the floor. Next he undid the instrument and set it down.

"Let's take a look." The captain checked the time. *Six minutes.*

Lewis retrieved another instrument. It looked like a camera lens, or a sniper scope, with an eyepiece at one end and a thin black tube at the other. Barely visible extending from the tube was a thin monofilament wire, much like fishing line. At the end was a micromanufactured lens.

Graber slid the fiber-optic lens through the hole after

spraying it with an aerosol coolant. His left hand maneuvered the filament housing while his right held the viewer to his eye.

The picture was bluish at first as the lens penetrated the carpet's fibrous clumps, then absolutely clear except for the slight fish-eye distortion of the wide-angle lens. Graber had practiced this often, and he found that the stress of a real takedown wasn't affecting his performance. He moved the lens to the left and right with simple twists of the housing, his head instinctively twisting to mimic the motion.

"Clear," he announced after twenty seconds.

"Nothing at all?" Lewis inquired. McAffee approached.

"Both sides." Sean pointed to the bulkhead. "There's a wall right above that."

"Aftmost galley," the major said, remembering the layout. He touched the ceiling just aft of the hole. "Row forty-five, troops."

Lewis nodded. "Right on."

McAffee and Graber started marking the precise points for the entry holes. Each would be just forward of seats 45D and 45G, the inner aisle seats at the front of the rearmost cabin section. They measured out the twenty-four by twenty-inch space needed. It was close. The longer dimension was laid out parallel to the bulkhead.

"Charges. C'mon." Jones and Buxton brought the frame charges to the spot and test-positioned them first.

"It's tight, but a good fit." Jones did some crude hand measuring. "Move them back an inch, okay? There's plenty of room back to the seat." He pointed to the metal plates eight inches behind that marked the tie-down point where the seats were bolted to movable runners.

"They could be a little forward, remember." Graber remembered the pilots of the practice aircraft showing them how the rows of recliners could be slid up and back to a desired position, then wrenched down and locked.

"Not here," Jones contradicted. "It's the forward row, so, like that pilot said, they've got to have thirty-six inches."

"You're right." It came back to Sean. "So if we move back a bit we'll have more pull-up room." It would make it easier for the troopers to get out of the hold, not having the galley wall in their faces.

Jones did a quick position check, then peeled off the strong adhesive covers on the business side of the frame charge and placed it on the aluminum overhead. Lieutenant Buxton did the same.

Joe had no interest in the military side of things. He was at work. A form of obsessive tunnel vision focused him on the task at hand.

Once the covering was off he could see the first device. The sketches didn't do it justice, either in description of ugliness or bulk. It was squat, and massive, resembling a newly picked garden vegetable, upside down, with four short roots poking out at equal angles toward the sky. And it was as black as coal.

The roots were the chutes, each containing the nuclear material—if the information was correct. It was time to verify one part of it. He removed a neutron analyzer from his bag. It, itself, was a short black object, with an LCD display at the bottom. The top held the actual instrument. Radioactive material, because of its constantly unstable nuclear state, was a voracious neutron emitter. That was the quality that made it so powerful. Neutrons racing away from their source struck the nuclei of other atoms and, in simple terms, sliced them open, sending even more neutrons out toward other atoms. In subcritical nuclear assemblies the reaction would never reach the stage where neutrons were continuously bombarding and attaching themselves, only because the mass of nuclear material needed was insufficient. When a precise amount or more was present, the reaction would become self-sustaining—a chain reaction—or, without proper controls, supercritical: the point when physical temperatures overcame subatomic bonds and the critical mass melted.

Joe switched the instrument on and placed it over the bulbous center of the object—the core, if he was correct. There was an increased amount of neutron "travel" as he called it. But not exceedingly abnormal. He slowly rotated the instrument on its side, and saw an instant and steady increase in activity.

The neutron analyzer used by NEST was an expensive and miniature model of larger instruments that measured activity in nuclear power plants. Its added feature was that it was directional: It could detect not only the amount of neutrons transiting through two-inch-square gold filaments, but also, by measuring the time between transits through the parallel sensors, it could determine the angle of penetration, and thus the direction.

He kept the analyzer's body touching the curved top of the device and slid it up to one of the chutes. It was sure, as the readout showed. There was nuclear material in the chute, and not just a small pellet or a depleted slug from a waste site.

"The real thing," Joe said aloud, though the others were too involved to notice. He moved the instrument to the center between two of the chutes. The readings weakened, then rose again. That meant there was an equal amount of material in each chute. "Damn it, they were right." It was a thermal reactor, probably with three fourths of a critical mass in each of the chutes.

So if that were the case, how was the thing going to be triggered. Joe examined the reactor—it was that, now— above and below. He crawled around the base of it, and felt with his hands over every exposed portion. Nothing. Just a greasy black exterior. It had to be in the chutes. There appeared to be no obvious work on the cylindrical tubes: They were as smooth as the rest of the thing. *The tops!*

And there it was. There had been some work done there, and then patched with something: lead and oakum, maybe, or possibly filled with a molten lead. Joe picked at the surface of it with his nails. It was solid, with no signs that it had ever been intended to be opened once constructed.

Son of a bitch! He knew what that meant. It confirmed what everybody had told him—what everybody believed.

What would the trigger be, then? A radio signal? Maybe barometric, set to go off when there was a sudden change in pressure. *Like when a bomb goes off at altitude*, Joe thought. No, that had too many variables. Whoever had planned this part knew his stuff, so he had to figure for maximum effect. That would mean letting the material come to reaction in a semisteady environment. The reactors would have to be level, or—he checked the lower shape once more—possibly within five degrees of level. A radio signal seemed the most logical, but not reliable. Even a coded signal could be set off by a fluke, or the transmitter might be screwed up. And what if the chutes didn't all go off? Of course the reactors needed only two to drop for a critical mass, but the waste didn't make sense. They were going for effect. It had to be a reliable system to trigger it, one that was reliable and consistent.

A timer. *A timer.* That had to be it! Uniformity in release. Reliability. A system with little chance of interference or false triggers. And . . . and the time factor. That's why the guy with the bomb was taking all these chances with the aircraft. It had to be in position on time, or there would be no point in hurrying.

Joe had to smile. *Sadr, you brilliant bastard. But now your toy is on my turf!* Time to think. Time to—

"Ready your weapons!" McAffee hollered. All the men pulled back the slides on their SIGs, chambering the first round, then did the same to their identical backup weapons which were then reholstered. Antonelli and Quimpo readied their special grenade launchers. They were based on the HK-69 pistol-shaped launcher, a weapon designed for firing 40mm grenades of various types. The round they inserted, though, was quite special and had never been tried in the situation they were going to use it in. But then, they had never even anticipated something like this happening. Not again, though.

The major did a final check of his troops, then went aft.

"You better brace, Anderson." The civilian's face was black from something, and so were his hands. "Mask and helmet on until we secure the aircraft."

Joe nodded. "It's for real, Major."

McAffee gave the ugly thing a look, with real distaste in his eyes. "Yeah. I thought it would have to be. You can do your thing?"

"I'll try. It's on a timer, I figure, but there could be some backup trigger up there. A radio if there is one. So don't give anybody with a transmitter a second look."

"Anybody up there with a gun gets only one look."

Again, Joe nodded, and the major went back forward. He was a civilian, and these were soldiers, Joe realized. But had they killed before? Had they? he wondered, knowing that some of them might be getting their first taste of death. He just hoped they were all on the right side of the bullet.

Hadad was nervous, but telling himself not to be. The plane was damaged; hurt like a dying whale. And it was climbing so slowly. They were already ten minutes out of the airport, with the coast fading behind them in the darkness, yet the altitude had risen only modestly. Was there something more wrong with the aircraft? Sadr had said that they would need to be at twenty thousand feet for maximum effect, but would they be able to go that high?

The worry must end, Hadad decided. Allah had seen to it that he had come this far, through the small trials of the mission so far. It would all work. He left his seat and exited the cockpit.

"Jesus. It's almost time." Buzz checked over his shoulder.

Hendrickson knew that, and also that the terrorist hadn't removed that bomb like the other times after takeoff. "Four-Two-Two to U.S. military aircraft."

There was added silence, then a reply. *"What is going on, Four-Two-Two? Why are you on the air?"*

The cockpit door opened again before the captain could answer. He looked back. The hijacker was there, as he had been for most of the ordeal, and as before, he had removed the bomb. Hendrickson noticed him sucking on the end of his thumb.

"Why are you watching me, American?" Hadad plopped down into the seat.

Hendrickson turned back around, not bothering to answer.

"You are flying low. Why?"

The first act, Buzz thought.

"With no flaps we have to rely solely on the elevators, and with reduced power we can't overdo our nose-up attitude. It's something called a stall condition, if you care." *Take that*. The captain thought it was convincing.

"How long until we reach twenty thousand feet?"

"An hour."

So they would reach the desired altitude. Good. Hadad wanted nothing more to hinder him beyond then. "When we reach that altitude . . . stay there."

"Whatever you say," Hendrickson replied with just a hint of sarcasm.

Hadad ignored the pilot's tone. Instead he kept a finger outside the Uzi's trigger guard, just in case. The Americans were getting arrogant. He might have to sacrifice another passenger in the air, if the pushing did not stop. He cradled the gun on his lap and hoped that they would behave. Then he said a silent prayer to Allah.

He had no way of knowing that it fell on deaf ears.

Romeo Flight

The MiGs turned left and right, away from the F-106, and headed for the haven of their base.

Cooper didn't notice. "Repeat, Springer Seven-Eight."

"Your target has broken protocol. There was a transmission, then no response to our inquiry. I don't know if it means anything, but mission parameters dictate informing you."

It wasn't good. It couldn't be. Major Cooper bore the burden of his mission, to an extent the controllers on the AWACS couldn't imagine at this point. The pilot of the hijacked jet had broken the instructions given to him less than an hour ago. With that the major knew that he had an authorization to fire.

He could move in and fire immediately.

The 747 was six miles ahead, its position marked by its bright anticollision lights. Was something going wrong on board? If the pilot were trying to contact him he couldn't hear it. Only the AWACS was dialed in on the plane's frequency: the civil emergency air net. The F-106 was on military. The AWACS was his only direct link to the jet.

Positioning himself was a simple matter. He throttled up and brought the F-106 level with and three miles behind 422. The old visual sight for the Genie swung down into position at his touch. It was an old one, but then none had been used in twenty years, just as the Genie itself had been relegated to curious relic status. He took his first look through the sight, the eyepiece and first-stage magnifier of which resembled a modern starlight sniper scope. It was nothing so fancy, and had no light-amplification property at all.

Fortunately the target—*the target?*—was lit. Cooper adjusted the Delta Dart's heading and pitch slightly to bring the 747 into the aiming reticle. In the sixties he had been one of the first pilots to fly operational missions with a "hot" Genie in the racks, and had even fired three training rounds. That was a luxury given to few pilots of the era. It had made him the prime candidate for this mission. He felt comfortable in the old bird, and the layout, at first foreign, was completely familiar again. Everything was where it was so long ago. He was the right man for this, and it made him angry to believe that.

Should he fire? Now? It wasn't time. Whatever was going to happen onboard shouldn't have gone down by now. But the radio call?

"What is going on!" Cooper added a silent curse in the name of compartmentalization. Need to know. *Shit*! His orders were brief. Four minutes past 0900 Zulu—0400 local—he was supposed to open his bay doors and fire the Genie at flight 422 and the couple hundred people who just happened to be on her. Only the proper code phrase broadcast from the hijacked aircraft would belay the shoot-down order.

That was cut-and-dry enough, Cooper figured. He wasn't going to kill hundreds of people just because some pilot forgot his instructions. If the time came, he would do his duty as ordered. He was a soldier, and he was a doctor. It was an uncomfortable and wholly incompatible combination of ideologies, one that he had to live with.

His left hand moved to the side console and moved the Genie's arm switch from safe to fire. The bay doors opened behind and below him. Only a touch on the stick-mounted fire button was required now.

Flight 422

Antonelli and Quimpo were closest to the charges, and they would be the first through. Not much of the blast should hit them. There was, however, always some shock factor when shaped charges were used, even in the low power they were employing.

McAffee and Graber were behind the big Italian, just five feet from where the left-side entry hole would be. The major checked the time.

"Weapons ready." Everybody had their SIGs in hand,

pointed upward with their fingers off the trigger. The two point men held the HK-69s two-handed.

Graber had his free hand on the frame charge detonator taped to the cargo hold floor.

"This is a go, troops," McAffee yelled. "Everybody on your toes. Let's smoke some bad guys."

"Right on," Buxton said back.

A last look at the watch. McAffee's free left hand reached back. Three. Two. "Cover!" One.

His hand slapped Graber's knee at the count of zero.

22

....

EXECUTION

Flight 422

THE EGYPTIANS HAD tried something similar during their attempt to rescue hostages from an EgyptAir flight on the ground in Malta, though the type and amount of explosives used were totally inappropriate. The charges were so overpowered that when one of the Unit 777 commandos detonated them, in much the same way Delta was going to, an entire row of seats above was blown into the roof and six passengers were instantly killed. It was a lesson of the past. One well learned.

Over six hundred tiny-shaped charges on each of the frames detonated simultaneously upon receipt of the electrical firing command. Each one sent a tiny jet of white-hot explosive gas upward into the aluminum. The result was quite similar to an instantaneous rupture of the cabin floor in perfect squared sections, as if a blowtorch had cut symmetrically identical openings to the hold below. A millisecond after the first detonation a second row of charges, aligned inward of the cutting charges, fired. These were pure blast, and they worked perfectly. Each panel of ruptured aluminum, along with the insulation and carpeting, was blown upward. A slight increase on the blast charges at the center of the frames tilted the panels as they were blown clear, sending them to one side in addition to upward.

The door was now open.

Hendrickson's hand was already moving upward to the overhead panel when the shudder hit the cockpit. There was an accompanying pop, like distant firecrackers, and the lights on the flight deck dimmed for just a second. His finger found the safety latch and the switch in one quick flick.

"Wha—" Hadad's hasty word was cut off.

The claxonlike buzzer was very loud, and red and amber lights started flashing all over the panel in front of and over the pilots.

"Blowout! We have emergency depressurization!" Buzz feigned worry, grabbing onto a harmless small lever overhead and working it back and forth furiously.

"On oxygen!" The captain took his mask from the lower left panel and slid it over his face. "What's wrong? What did we lose?"

"I don't know!"

Hadad stood. He pointed the Uzi at the pilots and screamed at them for an answer. The noise was too much, he thought. They couldn't hear him. Or were they ignoring him. He caught the co-pilot as a glance came his way. That wasn't right. That wasn't right!

Buzz knew he had been seen. A worried pilot wouldn't care about some raghead pirate if the plane was going down. The jig was up.

A second later it mattered not at all.

The charges had worked perfectly. Two openings led upward, into the smoky light of the cabin.

Antonelli was through first, just a second ahead of Quimpo. Four troopers below boosted the pair and held them. Once the upper halves of their bodies were through, each leaned toward their respective aisle—Quimpo left and Antonelli right.

It was a straight, unobstructed shot down each aisle. The plan was to fire two flash-bang grenades into the forward cabin, where the stairs led to the upper deck. These would disable any bad guys there and, unfortunately, any hostages. They had fired several inert practice rounds in the 747 back at Pope, trying mainly to get the trajectory right. Grenade launchers were ballistic weapons, much like mortars. The projectiles—40mm grenades in this case—when fired arched through the air to their target. This necessitated a certain amount of vertical space to allow for the distance to the nose of the aircraft. It was close, as they had found in practice.

The initial *pop!* of the firing was followed by a *whoosh* as the bullet-shaped projectiles shot toward the front. Seven meters from the muzzle the false nose cones of each broke away, leaving a barrellike object not much bigger than a plastic film can. They began to tumble just past apogee, three inches from the interior ceiling.

Both of the grenades hit and detonated within a split second of each other. The forward section first filled with a blinding light that seemed strangely long in duration to those who could see. Abu and Abdul were not among them.

The initial flash blinded both of the terrorists. Four other multiple flashes, each thousands of times more powerful than the brightest camera strobe, followed within a hundredth of a second. None were seen by those they were intended for, though two passengers on the left side also felt the effect.

Abu was closest to one of the explosives. After the magnesium flashes had finished, eight small military firecrackers burst outward from the casing. Three went straight up and fired four feet off the floor, just a foot from Abu's left ear. The immediate effect was a thunderous cracking in the range of 180 decibels. As the sound reached his eardrums they ruptured fully, unable to absorb the audible punishment. He recoiled against the bulkhead, his hands pressing hard against his ears, elbows out, and the Uzi lying uselessly at his feet. Miraculously he hadn't fallen, and just rolled back and forth against the partition.

Abdul was luckier in that none of the noisemakers had fired so close to his ears. He was, however, thrown to the floor, partly by reflex and partly from exaggerated force of the blasts.

The flash-bangs had done their job.

* * *

The explosions in rapid succession almost beneath him sent Hadad's eyes wide.

Both pilots went silent as their heads swung instantly back to the hijacker. He appeared to be confused. His eyes darted back and forth in his downcast face. Then, with a jerk, his head came up and his eyes locked on the captain's. Hendrickson thought he saw a slight shake of the terrorist's head, but maybe not. Was he truly surprised?

"No." It was said firmly, yet without much emotion. Hadad brought the gun up, training back and forth between the pilots. His free hand felt for the door behind as his feet inched backward. "I will still win."

McAffee and Graber were through the left-side hole before the last pop of the flash-bangs. Buxton and Jones were the first through the right side. Both pairs ran forward at a dead run.

There was little residual smoke from the blasts. Graber was in the lead, his SIG held two-handed and pointed forward. His eyes were already searching for targets past the tritium post sights as they entered the forward cabin. There was no hesitation.

McAffee heard the shots first, to his right. Buxton and Jones were firing. Both were. The four shots were in too rapid a succession to be from a single weapon. Graber was three feet ahead and turning to the right. The major turned, too. There was a bad guy down in front of Buxton, and . . .

Graber fired almost straight back at the major, but to his right. Three quick shots, and the gun came at McAffee, following the body down to the floor. The head brushed Blackjack's leg as it hit.

Shit. McAffee only had time for a split-second look, but it said all that was needed to the captain. *Thanks for my ass!*

There were two down. The other two had to be upstairs, and there was no room for hesitation. McAffee and Graber moved toward the straight stairs that went aft and up, unlike the spiral staircase on older 747s. They got within two feet when several bullets stitched down the risers from above. The major fell left out of the way. Then there was the scream in combination with the bullets. It was actually more of a wail, and it got louder. Then everything came toward them.

Neither had to say anything. Both of the senior Delta troopers leaned into the staircase—into the path of the bullets—and fired at the massive hulk of olive drab coming down at them. Two rounds connected, both in the head. The huge terrorist went instantly limp to his knees, and then hard down on his face. He was dead.

Let's go! The words were internal. McAffee led off up the stairs. He stepped right on the body without a second thought.

Buzz knew he was just seconds away from death, but then he was a Marine, and that thought had never brought him fear. His legs moved automatically, and his left hand pushed off the armrest as he catapulted his body up and back. Two feet away was death. The murderer. Buzz's right hand was outstretched, reaching for the Uzi as it came closer by inches and rotated toward him a bit faster.

Hadad pulled the trigger in three rapid taps. The co-pilot's body went down, his legs stuck awkwardly between the seat and armrest. Six of the nine bullets connected, all in the dead man's face, which no longer resembled anything human and, fortunately, lay against the dark carpet and out of view.

For a second Hadad froze. Then he felt the stare of another. The captain. His eyes were full of fire. Hadad could feel the hate, but there was no time to respond. He had to get to the vest. Of course, he could kill the pilot here and they would all die, but the devices would never be used. He might not get his chance to irradiate the American capital, but he could contaminate a hundred square miles of ocean.

Hendrickson had to fly. His anger, seething and ready to drive him to kill, would have to be checked. His friend was dead, though the body continued to spasm and gurgle about the head. He swallowed hard as the terrorist left the flight deck, then he turned back to the controls.

Jesus Christ!

McAffee, with Graber on his rear, reached the top as Hadad turned back from the cockpit door. There was no hesitation on the Delta major's part, but he had to swing his body and weapon a hundred and eighty degrees as he cleared the railing. Hadad's Uzi was already pointing in the right direction, but his reactions were slowed by fatigue and confusion. He moved to his left and brought the submachine gun up at the crouching and spinning black figure twenty feet away. The vest was eight feet from him, and he continued to move at it. His finger came down on the trigger at the same time McAffee's did.

Blackjack was moving right, almost falling. Two rounds caught him square in the chest, and another two farther to the left, in the upper arm. The firestorm of pain was instant and intense, but he kept the SIG trained on his target with his right hand.

Hadad saw only a brilliant white-and-yellow flame, like a candle growing in intensity uncontrollably. There was also a sound of sorts, but he couldn't tell what it was. Then he felt cold, and his body seemed to tumble in the air. Was he floating? He didn't know. Everything was strange, and quiet, and then, very suddenly, the last of his consciousness faded away.

Graber, too, had fired. Twice to the major's four. Two of McAffee's shots had missed and were embedded in the seats to the right. He didn't miss like—

"Medic!" Graber yelled at the top of his lungs, then reflex overcame emotion and he checked the rest of the lounge. Buxton and Antonelli were behind him and they went straight for the cockpit. Everything was clear in the lounge.

"Downstairs is secure, Cap." Buxton said, coming out of the cockpit. "There's one down in—" He saw the major. He thought Sean had wanted a medic for the co-pilot. "Oh shit!"

"Get Goldfarb up here," Sean ordered. "And keep guns on everybody until you're sure all the bad guys are down."

Buxton headed down.

The major was half-conscious. His vest had taken two of the slugs, but two others had nailed him between the shoulder and the bicep. Graber tore away at the wet black material. The wound was bleeding like an open valve.

"Oh Christ! Get back, Cap." Goldfarb put a firm hand on Graber's shoulder and pushed him aside.

"It looks like two, Jeff." Sean steadied the major's head between his hands.

"It's a bleeder. There's no way I can pack this this close to the joint. I'm gonna have to tie it off. Shit!" The Delta medic pulled a piece of surgical tubing from his bag and looped it under the major's shattered arm, above the wound and almost in his armpit. He pulled it tight with both hands, then tied a single knot. The blood flow slowed instantly and stopped almost completely a second later.

Graber was now in command. *The signal!* "Jeff, take care of him." Only McAffee and Sean were privy to knowledge of the fighter tailing them.

"Gotcha."

Graber bolted up and into the cockpit. Antonelli was there, moving a body with only a pinkish mass for a face out of the way. He arm-dragged it into the lounge area.

"Captain Hendrickson."

"Yeah. Yeah. That's me."

"We . . ." Graber stopped. Something was wrong. "What happened?"

Hendrickson pointed to the center of the dark console, just above the throttle levers. "The bastard was a lousy shot," he said with as much agonized humor as he could muster.

Sean already had his light on. He trained it on the console. Three holes, spaced close to each other, ran diagonally up the instruments. At least one of them had hit something vital, as there wasn't an instrument lit in the entire cockpit.

Hendrickson leaned in and stuck the tip of his forefinger into the middle hole. "Right back in here is an electrical trunk line. It's a one-inch insulated cable that goes right into two separate transformers. I'll bet if you pulled the panel cover off the cable would be sliced in two. That's the only way all this would have gone out."

"What about the radio?" Graber asked.

"No good. Out."

Holy shit! "What about a backup radio?"

"Look, I'm just glad that she's even responding. She'll fly—landing's another story. And you want a radio? No. There's no backup. We don't plan on bullets getting loose in here. The transformers for all our radios—HF and VHF— get their power from these cables the bullet cut. The only other transmitters are in the survival rafts, and those won't do a damn bit of good in here."

Graber eased himself into the dead pilot's seat. His light swept across the wet red liquid on the center console. "Well we're in trouble, then."

"Why?"

Sean checked his watch. "In about a minute a fighter a couple of miles back is gonna splash us."

"Shoot us down? For God's sake, why?"

It hadn't occurred to the Delta captain that the crew was in the dark. Then he decided that it had probably been for the best . . . at the time. That time was past. "You've got some kind of nuclear shit in the cargo hold. There's a guy from DOE down there working on it."

"A bomb?"

"No. Not exactly." Sean knew there wasn't time to explain. "Look if we don't get the right signal to that fighter we're going swimming." *Damnit, Blackjack, what would you do?*

Hendrickson fought the feelings that could very well have overwhelmed him. Buzz was gone. Gone. *Murdered.*

He had to think. The soldier was looking to *him* for some kind of answer. No radio, and they had to let the fighter know that shooting them down wasn't necessary. The thoughts of what had to be done—or attempted—lost out to emotions for a second, and the old Air Force pilot found himself blinking away the tears that welled up. *Wait . . .* The idea came instantly. "What's the signal?"

"Why?" Graber asked.

"Never mind. You want to live? Then tell me."

Romeo Flight

His thumb was rigid. A quarter of an inch of downward force would push the firing button far enough to make contact and complete the firing circuit. Flying straight and level, as the F-106 was, the G compensator wouldn't even add any reverse pressure on the button. It would be easy. Hardly a physical act at all.

There was more to the act than the twitch of a muscle, though. A man with a mind and a conscience was in the cockpit.

Cooper checked the fighter's old timepiece. Everything should have happened by now, he thought. He had a three-minute window of opportunity. During that time, which began at the moment of the scheduled assault, he could fire or wait. After 180 seconds, however, the decision was taken away. He had to fire. That decision was not his, but he would carry it out.

The Genie's 1.5-kiloton warhead was armed, and the bay doors were open. Power was already flowing to the weapon's firing circuits, and was allowed through to the two-phase detonator. The loop would be complete after the missile was fired, when, two miles from the fighter, the stored energy would be released from the shaving-cream-can-size capacitor. The high explosives would fire, triggering the nuclear explosion.

From Major Cooper's vantage the 747 was cast in an eerie pulsing glow. The huge jet looked small from three miles away, and the moist air enveloped it, diffusing the external lights into a sphere brighter than the surrounding night.

He again checked the frequency setting. This was the third time in two minutes. It was right. "Come on. Come on," he coaxed the silent radio.

The M.D. from Louisiana waited until only ten seconds were left. Twenty years before he would have removed his bulky glove, but flight garments had come as far as his usual ride. His fingers moved easily, finding the fire button, mounted at a slight upward angle on the stick. He breathed heavily, hearing it through the mask-mounted microphone that carried sound like an intercom.

What . . . At first he thought an unseen wave of heavy air had swept in from the side, blocking the 747 from view. But then it was back, but without its anticollision lights. A stream of moonlight penetrating the cloud cover above glinted off the white body of the aircraft. Cooper stretched his thumb upward. It was time. His neck craned upward slightly to sight in on the target. The magnification made the jet fill the reticle.

"Sweet Jesus . . . forgive me—"

His eye caught it through the sight first, then he backed his face away. It was visible to the naked eye.

The bright landing lights on the 747 came on, then went off. On again, and off. One more time the sequence repeated. Cooper's thumb hovered over the fire button. After a brief pause the lights came back on, shining distinct cones of light from the xenon lamps into the clouds ahead. They went off quickly and back on for a longer period. It was Morse!

"You lucky bastard," Cooper said. His thumb went back to the side of the stick. "We've got an S and an A, fellas. C'mon with the rest."

The *F* and the *E* followed, but Snoopy wasn't going to shoot down anybody for a misblink if there had been one. He allowed himself a breath before closing the bay doors and safing the Genie.

"Springer Seven-Eight, we have a Sierra—Alpha—Foxtrot—Echo. Copy?"

"That's a big a-affirmative Romeo. We didn't catch it on our radio. What gives?"

"Something's wrong with the aircraft's radio." It was no longer a target. "I can't figure it, though. I'm gonna move up and check it out. My Morse ain't too awful bad."

Flight 422

Graber watched the seconds tick past the time limit until a full minute was gone. "I wish you guys had a rearview in these big birds. I'd give my right nut to see what that fighter's doing right now."

Buxton came in. "Cap."

Hendrickson and the Delta captain both looked back. The pilot turned back to his work upon realizing his reflex reaction. The kid sounded like Buzz.

"Yeah."

"Four bad guys down—all dead. One"—he thought of the right word to use—"American dead. There's a couple of wounded passengers, all from the flash-bangs. Lewis is with them. They'll be okay. Goldfarb says Blackjack's pretty bad. He can't tie the wound off all the way. Well, you saw the blood."

"Right." Graber thought about where he was sitting. "Hey, Captain Hendrickson, do you need someone to sit here and help with anything?"

"You a pilot?"

"Nah, but maybe there's someone on board who is." To

the lieutenant: "Bux, check it out below. See if there are any pilots on board. Small plane, commercial, hell, even any helo jocks would do." Nam had bred a whole generation of whirlybird fliers.

"We'll get you someone," Sean said, turning back to the captain. His face, he saw, was flat and passionless. The guy must have been a good friend. He stared down at the blood. McAffee suddenly filled his every thought. No matter how much training there was, it never prepared a man to lose a friend in combat. This was combat, after all. Blackjack wasn't dead, Sean reminded himself, erasing the morbid *yet* from the sentence in his mind.

"You wanted to see the fighter?"

The words startled Graber. "What?"

Hendrickson tossed his head to the left. Sean bent forward and looked past the pilot out the side window. The fighter was there, off the left front. It was lit by its own lights. "What the hell's that?"

Hendrickson looked. "A relic, son."

"What do you fly?" The black-clad soldier seemed to tower over him.

"Helicopters," Michael Alton answered. "Crop dusting, mostly. We spray pesticides in the San Joaquin Valley."

"Where?" Buxton asked.

Michael shifted. "California. Ever hear of the Medfly?"

"Yeah. Yeah. Okay, where'd you learn to fly? Army?" The question was natural.

"Air Force," Michael replied, feeling that slight rise in interagency rivalry and pride. The old military BS did stick.

"C'mon, we need your help."

Michael turned to his wife. She looked scared, still, but in a different way. "I'll be back, okay? I'm just gonna help out."

Joe had the location of the U235 pegged in each chute. It was near the top of each, yet still left enough room for whatever release mechanism was there. It was a timer, he was convinced, which gave him some time to work.

A thud came from forward. Quimpo dropped through the right-side entry hole. "Anderson, you need some help?"

"Stick close: I might."

"Captain said to tell you that everything topside is under control. All the bad guys are dead." The Filipino soldier flashed a "we told you so" smile.

Joe turned back to the reactor. "See those boxes: Tear the wood off and shove it back there."

"Yes, sir."

The logical thing to do came next. He had to secure each of the U235 plugs in their respective chutes, blocking them from falling into the core. But how? There were some options that were risky, and he discarded those without second thoughts. The best way, he decided, was to simply put something in the way of the plugs.

He took the neutron analyzer again and checked the position in the chutes another time. When the lowest point of the U235's location was found, he removed a drill and long bit from his equipment bag. His plan was to drill into each chute below the mark and insert a rod through the hole on both sides to act as a "stop" for the plugs. It should work.

The bit slid into the holder and he set to work, boring into the soft lead housing.

"It's not good," Goldfarb said. "The bleeding stopped, then started up again. It's deep in his arm, Cap. I can't do much about it."

"Sergeant, you're a combat medic! For Christ's sake, what would you do in combat?" Sean yelled.

"I'd take the arm off and tie the arteries," Goldfarb answered. It wasn't the response he wanted to give.

Graber didn't hesitate. "Then do it! Save his life."

The Delta captain walked over to the seat where the bomb lay. Just two feet from it was a bloodstain, marking the spot where the head terrorist had fallen. The body was gone, moved to one side of the downstairs lounge with the other three corpses, but the image was fresh in Sean's mind. There was the body, facedown, lying on the Uzi, and one hand outstretched toward the . . .

Wait. That didn't make sense. If the terrorist had wanted to knock the aircraft out of the sky, all he would have needed to do was shoot up the cockpit. He killed one pilot, so why not finish it? That would be a sure kill. Trying to get to the bomb to blow up the jet might be a notion of grandeur, but quite unnecessary, and equally likely to fail. *And it did!*

Sean knelt down by the vest. "Antonelli!"

The big trooper trotted over from his spot by the cockpit door. "Yeah?"

"Give me a hand." Graber lifted the vest and laid it out on the carpet, the inside of it down, exposing all the pockets. "It's safed, don't worry."

"Yeah, sure," Antonelli answered warily.

"I've got a bad feeling. Let's check the pockets." The captain's body lay flat next to the thing. "You got your mini-lite? Good. I'm going to lift each flap to get a look inside the pockets. You give me the light."

"Cap, are you sure this is a good idea?"

"Listen, this guy went for this thing instead of just smoking the pilots to make us crash. Now, maybe he was into big bangs, or maybe this thing has a connection to that shit in the hold. Capishe?"

"*Si.*"

Sean began working his way through the pockets. The intelligence from the British described what he was seeing, three-by-one-by-four blocks of wrapped whatever, probably explosives. He moved his body around the vest, leaving it still. The pocket with the safe mechanism showed up. "More light." There were the four rocker switches, set in a sequence that must interrupt the firing circuit from the thumb switch. "Okay, next one—" *Just a minute.*

The lieutenant saw his captain recoil an inch or so. "What is it?"

"The Brits said there were three rocker switches on the safety—this has four." Sean maneuvered his head up, down, and side to side, examining the box closer. "Holy shit!"

"What?" Antonelli asked, his tone pushing for an answer.

Graber snapped up to a crouch. "He wasn't going for this thing to blow it; he was going to set those things in the hold off. This thing has an extra switch!"

"That's a guess, Cap."

Sean stood, his breaths now coming heavy. "You're right, and I might be, too." He spun and ran to the stairs, disappearing to the main level.

Michael gave the soldier running past him a long look before continuing up, following Lieutenant Buxton to the cockpit.

"Captain, we've got someone for you."

Hendrickson noticed the panicked look on the man's face. It was visible even in the flashlight-lit cockpit. "Sit there," he directed. Michael took the right seat, and the Delta trooper left them.

"The name's Michael." He looked around, not even bothering to belt himself in. The captain wasn't either, he noticed. "What can I do?"

"I'm Bart. What have you flown?"

"Helicopter. UH-60s and Kiowas mostly."

Hendrickson knew it wasn't ideal, but the guy *was* someone with experience. "Okay, this is what we've got: The number three engine, over there, is out; no flaps, so we're pretty nonresponsive when landing and taking off; no brakes; our trim is lousy because of the stuff they loaded on our hold; and, as you can see, no power on the flight deck. She does respond, though."

The civilian in Michael tried to fall back on his long-ago military training, but all he could do was stare at the blackness of the cockpit. "No instruments or radio?"

"None. Are you ready?"

Michael's head snapped to the left. "Ready for what?"

"Your first flying lesson in a 747." The captain leaned just slightly over the center console. "I'm retiring after this flight, so I plan to make it down. It's going to take two of us, so I need you to help me make it to retirement. Now, take the stick. We're going to give you a feel for the *Maiden*."

His hands wrapped around the column handles. "The who?"

Hendrickson's full smile was apparent, and would have been without any illumination.

"Anderson!"

Both Joe and Sergeant Quimpo were startled by the yell. Graber dropped through the hole a second later.

"What?" Joe sensed the urgency. He lowered the drill, removing the bit as the captain approached.

"I think these things might be triggered by a signal from

that vest the head guy was wearing," Sean said. He was crouched over, panting, his hands resting on one knee.

Joe didn't see the need to question the captain's word. "If that's true, and my theory is true, then there are two ways to set these off; timer and signal."

Sean nodded. "That would make sense. The guy was going for the thing, and there was an extra switch on the safety. It has to be it."

There wasn't time to be too delicate. "Sergeant, get those wire rods from the tray supports." To Graber: "Your man here thinks quick."

"How so?"

"I drilled holes completely through each of these chutes." Joe pointed to the three-sixteenths hole. "We need to stop any of the fuel plugs from dropping into the core. Sergeant Quimpo thought the wire supports on the fold-down trays upstairs would work to fit through. Quick thinking."

There was a change in Anderson's attitude, Sean noticed. Subtle, but still there. "So does this affect anything?"

"It could. If the plugs just drop in, the wires should hold. But if there's a charge of sorts to release them, then the force could push them right through the wires."

"Which would screw us all," Sean observed.

"Precisely. As it is now, with these little holes here, there's an increase in radiation down here." Joe saw the captain's head straighten up. "Don't worry. It's not enough to do any harm."

Quimpo came back down with two handfuls of the chromed wires. "I got twenty." He handed them to Joe.

"Tie off one end in a big knot so it can't slip through the hole, then insert them all the way through." Joe motioned to the devices. Sean was observing. "Take your time. I'll do some, and you do the others."

The sergeant nodded. They went about the task. Five minutes later they had the wires through both sides of each chute. Then came the tricky part: tying off the loose ends. There wasn't much room at the free ends, and the stiff wire didn't lend itself to effective knotting. But there was little else to do. Joe and the sergeant went to each together, checking each as best they could.

"Cap, you wanna take a look?" Quimpo asked.

Graber shook off the question. "Nah. I'll keep my gonads away from that shit."

Romeo Flight

Cooper had his landing lights on, and was a quarter mile ahead and to the left of the 747. The pilot seemed to be following his lead, which was the first hurdle. With no instruments the big jet would be entirely dependent on him for guidance.

"Springer Seven-Eight, this is Romeo. Where should I lead this guy?"

The controller aboard the AWACS signaled him to stand by. Major Cooper flashed out a question to the 747, asking about their ability to keep him in visual contact. An immediate reply told him that the line of sight was good.

"Seven-Eight, let's give me a vector," Cooper implored to no one.

Flight 422

"What's that?" Michael asked as the tremor shook through his hand and wrist.

Hendrickson felt it, too. "Heavy air. We can't get above this weather, so we're going to have some turbulence."

A jolt shook the *Maiden*, almost on cue, as the captain's last word was uttered.

Antonelli was standing from a kneeling position as the reverberation of unstable air shook the aircraft. He was naturally off-balance from the stance, and the movement ensured a fall, wanting to push him forward. But that would have landed him right on the major. To avoid that he tossed his arms back, realizing too late that he was falling right on top of the vest.

The strange buzz came next, but no explosion. He was relieved, but only for a second. "Oh my God!"

The sound was that of metal sliding against greasy metal, then of wire twanging as the fuel plugs dropped toward the four cores. One sound, though, was different, coming a split second after the others. Joe knew what had happened. The plugs were all loose, and one of the sixteen had made it past its wire restraint and was in the core . . . in the reactor right next to him.

"You, out!" Joe ordered Sean. To Quimpo: "Check the wires on those three, and then get out, too! Hurry."

Neither man argued. The Delta captain was through the hole into the cabin within three seconds, while Sergeant Quimpo circled each of the other three reactors, checking the tautness of the restraints.

"Everything's fine. They're stretched, but holding." Then he, too, was gone. Both Quimpo and Graber waited near the hole, looking down into the hold and listening to silence.

Joe slid the neutron analyzer onto the suspect reactor. As it passed the hole in the nearest chute, the readout went into the danger zone. A quick calculation confirmed what Joe had feared: He was getting almost a direct shot of two hundred rems from the near chute, and Lord knew how much background radiation from the others.

He checked the four chutes. One wire hung limp on the inner hole, and was not visible on the outer side. One slug, three quarters of a critical mass, was in the core; another would send it into a critical state. Joe wasn't going to let that happen.

"Stay out of here!" Joe yelled, just as a reminder. He checked the other three chutes on the reactor. Two were holding good, but the third . . .

Shit! Joe took a pair of needle-nose pliers from his belt pack and grabbed the outer wire end as it was about to slip in, releasing the second plug. "Ahhh!" The weight of the plug was more than he'd expected, and it strained on his hand muscles as they squeezed the pliers closed on the wire. He was now holding one end, as the knot had come completely undone.

He was also receiving a consistent, deadly dose of radiation through the seemingly small hole. The pliers were nonlocking, requiring him to stand in place to hold the wire. "Captain!"

Sean lowered his head into the hold. "I hear you."

"Tell that pilot to get this thing down, fast. I can't hold this forever."

"We'll help."

"No!" Joe said, adamantly. "No one else needs to be contaminated. Just get this plane on the ground! And," Joe continued, "find out what happened."

Antonelli caught Sean on his way up the aisle and explained what had occurred. Graber heard, but ignored it. There was something more important to do.

The captain's head sank, then bobbed up. "What is it?"

"The things in the hold, one of them started to go off, or whatever they do. Our DOE guy says to set this aircraft down fast!"

Hendrickson found the landing light switch and began flashing out the newest problem.

Romeo Flight

Jesus Christ!

"Seven-Eight, Seven-Eight. I need an immediate vector, now! Four-Two-Two is declaring an in-flight emergency. They have a problem with something in the hold." Cooper purposely didn't mention the reactor comment in the Morse message, for both security reasons and because he technically wasn't supposed to know the particulars.

"Romeo, turn left to heading two-seven-five. We're going to set you down on a long one. Copy?"

"Roger." Cooper signaled the 747, then banked gently to the left, sideslipping at the same time to keep position with his follower. The *Clipper Atlantic Maiden* turned with him, but took a longer time to settle into the new course.

Cape Canaveral

The shuttle *Endeavour* was bathed in the white lights on her launchpad five miles from the Launch Control Center. She was ready for a launch in forty-eight hours.

The morning senior watch officer yawned at the phone before picking it up. "LCC."

His tired face became instantly awake as the voice on the other end gave the orders and offered only a brief explanation.

"Right." He straightened up in his chair, pushing the center wide alarm next. The intercom switch was flipped to open. "Attention. Attention. Emergency alert, condition orange. This is not a drill. Clear the shuttle-landing runway of all non-emergency personnel. Crash crews set up at the far end. All other personnel immediately go to your assigned shelters."

He turned to see his three fellow watch officers stand, unsure of what to do. His expression convinced them, and they left for their bunkerlike shelter, leaving the senior watch officer to direct the coming unorthodox happening. It wasn't surprising. An orange alert was intended to be used only in the event of a problem with the shuttle while it had a nuclear payload onboard, such as a reactor-powered satellite.

Whatever was coming in would be met by crews trained to deal with a radioactive situation, though not in a manner they were accustomed to.

Flight 422

Joe shifted one hand off of the pliers. His position allowed no room to maneuver into a place for shelter from the deadly radiation bombarding his body. Most of the damage was being done in his hands as the rays penetrated and did their work on his blood cells.

The results would be obvious, he knew. There was nothing left to do but hold on. He could, after all, save some lives.

"Sorry."

Sean saw the true regret in the lieutenant's eyes. "Hey. I should have moved it." The Delta captain blamed himself as much.

"Cap," Goldfarb said. Something was wrong.

Graber took two steps over. The carpeted area was awash with blood, the sound coming up from the soaked material in wet squishes. The medic was on his knees, but not hovering over Blackjack as before.

"I lost him," Sergeant Goldfarb said. "I just couldn't stop it."

The scene should have been revolting, with the major's amputated left arm lying a foot from his head, but it wasn't. Sean only saw Blackjack's face. It was tilted back, its eyes open with only the whites showing.

"Hey, I . . ."

"Don't beat yourself up, Sergeant," Sean suggested. *Men die in a war*. And this was a war, he believed.

The captain walked to the stairs, paused, then descended. Perfection, so he was learning, came rarely in any action.

Hendrickson followed the fighter directly on now. They were lining up on the long shuttle runway at Cape Canaveral. Fifteen thousand feet-plus of beautiful concrete was awaiting them.

"How much visual referencing have you done on landings?" The captain asked his assistant.

"Plenty," Michael answered automatically.

"Then that's your job. That runway has the standard red-green split circulars at the threshold. I'll fly her in, but you've got to call me out as high or low. Just remember, you're sitting four stories off the ground."

Michael flexed his hands on the column. "Okay. What about the stick?"

"I'll give you the word when it's time to shove it forward, all the way." Hendrickson adjusted the *Maiden*'s position behind the glowing blob ahead. "It worked once before; it might again. Maybe we'll be able to stop this girl one more time." He quieted for a second. "Ain't that right, girl. You're going to do it once more . . . once more for this old fart."

"Did you get all that?" Joe asked, yelling.

"I got it," Sean replied. When the aircraft stopped—if it stopped—he had clear instructions from someone who should know.

"Cap," Quimpo began, "that crap's gonna kill him, ain't it?"

Sean didn't answer. There were already two good guys dead. That was too many. But Anderson . . . he had no control over it.

Romeo Flight

Major Cooper flashed off a final "good luck" to the *Clipper Atlantic Maiden* before peeling off to the left, clearing the way for the 747 to come right in on the row of lights dead ahead. He wanted to stay overhead, acting as a chase plane of sorts, but knew better. His cargo was as dangerous as that on the big jet, and they would be anxious to get it into safe storage once again.

He threw a salute as the jet passed him on the right. "God speed, folks." A minute later he was heading south at speed, careful to stay over water all the way back to Louisiana.

Flight 422

"Everyone's belted in," Antonelli told the pilot.

"You do the same," Hendrickson instructed.

Michael craned his neck, trying to compensate for the thinning clouds. "I see the lights. We're low, just a little."

"Good. I want to bring her up right at the end. We've only got elevators." Hendrickson put his right hand on the throttle levers.

The pattern changed from red on the bottom to green. "On slope. It's steady."

The captain cut the number two engine completely. The *Maiden* responded with a noticeable slowing and a falling sensation. He pulled back on the stick and throttled numbers one and four up. The speed stayed lower, but the falling sensation ceased, replaced by the familiar gentle gliding.

Michael practically had to stand in his seat to see over the abnormally high nose. "Still good. On slope. We're close."

The triple rows of referencing lights came at them fast, and the 747 came *down* toward them equally as fast.

"On slope!" Michael's voice rose with the excitement. He was operating now as a pilot, forgetting completely the fear. "Slope! Slope! Threshold!"

The lights disappeared beneath the *Maiden*. She was now over concrete.

Hendrickson kept his eyes forward. He pulled back on the throttles, reducing engine power. His aircraft responded accordingly, her body dropping hard onto the runway below. When the mains contacted, the remaining right-side tires and two left-side blew out with a forceful *bang!*

The rear of the jet scraped the runway for the first hundred yards, sending a fountain of sparks behind her. Hendrickson smoothly pushed the stick forward until the nosewheel touched with a screech. They were forty knots over speed when he reversed the two engines.

"Now!" Both men pushed the sticks forward, to the console. The *Maiden's* nose drooped toward the runway.

With no speed indicator, Captain Hendrickson had to go by dead reckoning when judging if he could weave the 747 to each side of the runway as he had before. He tapped the brakes, just to check, but they were nonexistent.

"It looks like they're waiting for us," Michael said, seeing the rotating strobes at the far end of the runway.

"Let's oblige by not creaming them."

The sensation of speed was diminishing. A terrible screeching roar was coming from below the aircraft, signaling that the blown tires had disintegrated, leaving the metal wheels to drag along the pavement. The friction was welcome, as it slowed the *Maiden*, but it required compensation as it also pulled the jet to the right.

They passed the halfway point at about a hundred knots. Hendrickson started weaving about then, when his "aviator's stomach" said it was okay. "Help with the rudder." It was getting harder to weave and compensate for the right-pulling drag.

Michael touched the pedal. It was down and stiff.

"Now some right," Hendrickson said. They worked it together, going left to the edge of the pavement, and back right, though not as close to that side. Back and forth, and back and forth. On the fourth weave the *Maiden's* nosewheels blew.

"Jesus!" Michael yelled. The violent contact of metal to pavement vibrated through the rudder pedals, jabbing an invisible spear into his heel. Instantly the aircraft slowed considerably.

"Easy left. Easy left." The captain wanted to bring the *Maiden* back onto the centerline, but her steering system, crippled by the last blowout, followed the right-leaning groove into the grass at the runway's edge. Rain had soaked the earth. The nose gear dug in and sank a full two feet into the ground, and a second later the right mains did the same.

Then, it was over. The *Clipper Atlantic Maiden* came to a full stop.

Captain Hendrickson killed the remaining two engines. His body leaned forward, his head resting on the dark instrument panel. A few breaths came rapidly and deep, then he sat back up.

Michael let go of the column and examined his hands. They trembled, but were dry as his mouth.

"Come on."

The reluctant co-pilot looked up.

"Michael, let's get out of here." Hendrickson reached for his arm. "You did good. We're down. Now, we need to get out. You have a little lady back there, right?"

That struck home. "Right. Let's go."

The Delta troopers and the flight attendants opened only the forward doors, deploying the yellow evacuation slides with them.

"Lewis.. Makowski." Sean looked to them both. "You go out first, one on each side, and direct everybody forward. Anderson says not to let anybody near the rear of the aircraft." The two sergeants slid out before the rows of passengers lined up to follow, directed by the flight attendants.

Sean ran aft one final time, rubbing the deathwatch under his cuff. "Anderson. Anderson!" It was quiet finally.

"Who the hell landed this thing?" Joe cringed. His fingers were cramping badly. "Get somebody in a nuke suit to bring me locking pliers. Hurry."

"You got it." The Delta captain went forward, just as the last of the passengers were evacuated.

"Cap." It was Antonelli.

"Where's Bux?"

"Upstairs with . . ."

Sean nodded. He knew what was meant. "The crew off?"

"Everybody," Antonelli replied. A crash truck pulled up, its red and yellow lights sweeping across the field outside.

"Tell Bux and Goldfarb to take Blackjack off. Then you, Jones, and Quimpo get the other bodies down—the co-pilot first." There was a hierarchy even in death.

"Got it."

Sean leaned out the open portside door. A lift-equipped fire truck pulled up. Two crewmen were in its basket, but they weren't wearing the standard crash suits. Of course. A minute later they stepped off the lift and into the cabin.

"There's a guy back in the hold. He needs some help."

The bubble-helmeted crewman nodded, then pulled a heavy visor over the face mask, leaving only a slit for viewing. His partner signaled for Graber to get off the aircraft immediately.

"Cap," Antonelli called from the starboard door. "You and me are the last."

Sean looked aft, wondering if he would ever see Anderson again. It was a question that would have to wait to be answered. He walked to the starboard door and followed Antonelli down the inflatable slide.

The White House

Bud set the phone down. "They're down. The passengers are safe."

"Whew!" the president said, slapping one knee.

Herb Landau smiled and looked to the floor. "They did it."

The president left little time for glee. "We can celebrate more later, gentlemen. There's a funeral in a few hours."

"I think some sleep is in order," Gonzales suggested, directing it specifically at his boss.

"Yes. Everybody." The president gave a mock "out" signal with his thumb. "Bud, I want to speak to you for a moment."

The door closed last behind the chief of staff.

There were no words for a few seconds. "We stopped them, Bud. Probably for the first time we fought them on their own ground and won."

Bud agreed, nodding. "Yes. We did that."

The president, in addition to being a bold young man, was keenly observant. "How many, Bud?"

"Two. The commander of the assault force, and the co-pilot of the 747."

What words there were would not be sufficient, the president knew. "Two more funerals, then."

"The last from this affair, God willing," Bud said. It might be a hope, but . . .

"Maybe, though, we can prevent some," the president said.

"If your policy idea goes through, we might just be able to deal some preemptive justice."

"We can do that, but it's going to have the same tainted feel to it." Bud knew that killing, by any standards, was what its name said it was.

The president thought about that for a moment. "That may be so, but I'll suffer with that if it saves some innocents."

EPILOGUE
•••••••••••••

BETWEEN THE DARK AND THE LIGHT

Nellis AFB

FROM THE SLIGHT rise of the mesa three miles away, Joe Anderson was watching the burial of the would-be destroyer. His eyes strained without their glasses to see the scene through the binoculars, a task made more difficult by the late-morning heat shimmer rising from the desert sand.

He had been to this part of the Nevada desert many times during his career. Most of those times he had observed underground nuclear tests, and the other times things not far removed from those detonations. The DOE did all of its testing here, as it had for twenty years, for reasons of safety and security. Treaty restrictions on aboveground testing were the primary reasons, though.

Joe pulled the binoculars away and rubbed the sweat away from his eyes, then put his glasses back on. With the naked eye the huge white jet, whiter than the desert around her, was visible almost fifteen thousand feet away, her nose pointed toward the dark area before her. Two solid months it had taken to dig the mammoth grave, and another three weeks to line it properly. Nothing could be allowed to leak or escape from the tomb once sealed. Joe had seen to the details and planning himself, a thought that he had chuckled at numerous times in the previous month. He was going to bury his killer, and he would soon join her, though his grave would be in a shady spot somewhere in the Minnesota backwaters. Only three months after his exposure he was already in stage-one leukemia. The president had offered a full military ceremony and burial at Arlington, but Joe had decided to leave that place for the real heroes.

The radio on his escort's hip announced that the crew was ready. Joe acknowledged the Air Force major's repeat of the transmission and gave the final go-ahead.

He let the binoculars hang from his neck as he watched the process begin. It had actually begun long before, when the *Clipper Atlantic Maiden* made her circuitous final flight from the Cape to the isolated Air Force runway at Nellis. From there she had been slowly wheeled across fifteen miles of desert, over a movable steel mesh whose designed use was as a temporary airstrip liner. By the time the 747 had reached the spot of her burial two weeks before, the tomb had almost been finished, and there she sat. At night she was bathed in the glow of bright floodlights, and at all times there were no fewer than two hundred security troops guarding her. The material aboard the jet was unstable, and priceless to some nutcakes.

Word came that the *Maiden* was rolling. It was obvious when she reached the long, sloping ramp that had been graded to afford access to the hundred-foot-deep pit. The nose of the blue-and-white bird slowly dipped as she began her last descent. When the tail pitched forward Joe pushed the glasses back atop his head and raised the binoculars. All looked good. The *Maiden* was now almost completely within the tomb, and for the first time the huge mounds of the reddish clay-boron mixture that would fill the pit were visible close beyond the hole. If the unthinkable happened, and the U235 aboard the aircraft combined and melted down, the compound would help slow the reaction, but not stop it.

Something else was said on the radio. "The aircraft is in position, Captain Anderson," the major announced.

Captain. They must've briefed everybody, Joe thought. It shouldn't bother him. After all, they were just showing respect. His rank was long gone, though. He was just Joe Anderson. Mr. Anderson to some. *And not even that for long*.

"Good." Joe let the binoculars drop. The strap tugged at the back of his neck, reminding him that he was already sunburned. Some half-funny thought about skin cancer ran through his mind. "Tell the foam trucks to get in there, but have them wait for the dozers to move into position."

The officer relayed the instructions. As soon as the bulldozers were ready to start burial they would begin pumping liquid foam into the interior of the *Maiden*, both cargo hold and cabin. This would harden within the hour, giving added crush resistance to the big jet so that the weight of the earth soon to cover her would not deform the outer skin or structure. When that was complete the clay-boron mixture would be pushed in, filling from the bottom up. The entire process would take two days, but Joe would be done there in a few minutes.

He watched for a long minute before realizing that he couldn't see anything of interest or importance. Even the desert around the site, which would be eternally off-limits, was naked and unappealing. It was too dry here, Joe thought.

The sun was too damn much, he decided. "Shall we, Major?"

"Certainly, sir."

Joe wanted to laugh at that, a major calling a captain "sir." Would wonders never cease?

They walked toward the blue Air Force Humvee parked a few yards away. *Blue*, Joe thought, letting his mind picture a place where he would spend the time he had left.

"So tell me, sir," Joe began, "do you do much fishing around here?"

Los Angeles

"Two bags only, huh?" Art commented awkwardly. He didn't know what to say. Things were changing too fast in his world.

But hell, Eddie looked good, and things were going to go good for him.

"Hey, boss, you know the routine." The smiling agent pulled both of the small bags from the trunk and set them curbside in front of the terminal. "Check it, and you lose it. Carry-on's the only way to fly."

Art forced a smile. He closed the trunk lid, leaving his hand on its warm surface. The two men stood still among the diesel exhaust and noise that pervaded the upper level at Los Angeles International Airport. Buses and vans, along with private autos, darted along the white cement roadway searching for the choicest spots for unloading.

"So, it's the academy for you?"

Eddie nodded, tight-lipped. "Can you imagine that?"

Art could. Eduardo Giuliano Toronassi was a damn good agent, a true Bureau man. Maybe not the exact type old J. Edgar would have imagined, but so what. The FBI Academy was getting a fine addition. It was just a shame that his street career had to be at an end, thanks to that one bullet. The only visible remnant was a simple Band-Aid just below and to the left of his Adam's apple, but less obvious results were very real. The effects were slight, but enough to disqualify him from street duty. Now he would teach other young agents, using his unique insight and talents.

"You'll do good, Ed," Art said sincerely.

Eddie's mouth dropped slightly. "C'mon, boss. You want me to cry or something?"

Art didn't, and let a laugh out. At least it wasn't forced.

Eddie saw his old boss look slightly away. "And what about you? What's next?"

Good question. "Hmm. If only I knew." His eyes went back to his friend. "There's no place in the academy for an old dog like me, you can bet on that."

Eddie smiled, knowing that Art was right, but for the wrong reasons. He wasn't too old, but in many people's eyes, many of the people in power, that was, Art Jefferson was too close to the edge. His personal life was a mess, and the Bureau doctors said his health wasn't far behind. A ticker could only take so much in the form of physical and emotional abuse, as the heart attack had proven.

"I don't know," Art said, his words coming from distant thoughts. "It's all so damn much right now. Lois and all the other crap. Man, I've been doing every damn thing that shrink says, even the weird stuff. Lying down and visualizing all sorts of things. It's supposed to relax you, you know, but all it seems to do is clear my mind so all the bullshit can fit. All sorts of negative shit, Ed."

"Art, listen. You gotta go easy. Take a load off. Get rid of some of the stuff that's bothering you."

Easier done than accepted, Art knew. "That was done for me."

"What do you mean?" Eddie asked, perplexed.

"Jerry talked to me a couple days ago." Art paused. "They want me to resign from command. Go back to field stuff. Be a street agent again."

Eddie didn't have to think long about it. "It sounds good. Do it."

The smile was almost automatic. "I thought the same thing after the initial shock of it."

"Why not? You'll be out of the bureaucratic end of it and back where the action is . . . where you know the score."

"Where the action is?" Art commented. "Like where you were when that slug found you? Unh-unh."

"So I duck worth shit, what about it?"

Art slapped the shorter agent's face gently. "It's good they're sticking you behind a desk. Even I can nail you."

Eddie mocked pain and rubbed it off his cheek. "So where are you gonna be, boss?"

"Working for Cam."

"Homicides? Dead bodies and all?"

Art nodded. "The whole schmear."

The Italian's puffy cheeks jiggled as he shook his head.

The time had gone quickly, and too much so. They would see each other again. Art was certain of that.

"You want me to walk you in?"

Again Eddie's cheeks shook. "I can get it." He stuck out a hand, and Art took it firmly. "We'll be seein' you, boss."

"You, too, Ed." Art watched him take the bags and head for the terminal door. He stopped just short of entering and turned.

"And get yourself a lady, you big black love god!"

Art almost choked on his laughter as all heads within earshot turned. And then his friend was gone.

He adjusted his jacket with a roll of the shoulders and slipped back into his car, a brand-spanking-new Acura. The heater came on with the engine, which was nice. L.A. was in the midst of a cold snap, and rain was almost certain by nightfall. The local ski resorts were in heaven, with the best snow in almost ten years thick on their slopes. People were finally staying local to ski, instead of heading north to Tahoe or Mammoth.

That sounded fun, Art thought. He did have a week left on his medical leave. Why not? In an hour he could be home and packed, and a few hours later on the slopes.

He had to remind himself that he hadn't skied an inch in his life. But then he'd never tried, which, so far, hadn't stopped him from doing much harder or more stupid things.

Near Tripoli, Libya

The city lights were a glowing half oval on the horizon, growing from only luminescence to defined structures lit from inside as the Mercedes truck drew nearer.

Both men in the cab were intent on their duty. The driver had a Walther pistol sandwiched between his legs, barrel forward, and the passenger kept his weapon, a stockless AK-74, in hand but below the window line. Their job was twofold: get the precious cargo in back to its newest hiding place, and do it without drawing attention.

The driver tapped the brake hard, then released, throwing himself and his partner forward with a jerk.

"Watch it!" the passenger screamed. Both men were equal in rank, lieutenants, but the one riding shotgun was easily the leader.

"There was an animal of some kind. It darted across the road." The driver geared down, the engine whining as it pushed the truck back to speed.

A quick look behind eased the passenger's worry: Both barrels were there, and still upright under the tarp. Inside each one was one hundred pounds of highly enriched uranium, enough weapons-grade material for several crude atomic bombs. This was the third move in a week for the barrels, as the Libyan Army tried to stay one step ahead of the American spies and satellites that were certainly watching.

"Damn!" the driver swore.

"What?" the question came, along with a reflexive tightening of his grip on the Kalashnikov.

"Another truck, with goats in it." The gear was dropped again as they reached the grade that would leave them on the plateau of the city, though still ten miles from it.

Both vehicles were heading up, each beginning to struggle with the angle of the road. The lead truck, heavily laden with its cargo of livestock, was old, at least ten years older than the one that followed it.

"This road should have been closed, or cleared," the driver said, the nerves obvious in his voice and the sweat already heavy on his forehead.

His passenger looked over. "And that would please the Americans greatly, wouldn't it? Think, idiot! They are probably already here, in our country, and they would easily notice such blatant security measures." He shook his head.

The driver's stomach tightened. He had been with his precious cargo constantly for three weeks, eating and sleeping with it, and he had grown to hate it.

Both trucks rounded a right turn at the base of a flat spot on the grade, just below the final climb to the plateau. Neither the driver nor the passenger had noticed anything out of the ordinary, an oversight that was about to prove very costly. The five-ton truck ahead fishtailed intentionally as it braked just short of the incline, forcing the Mercedes to slow quickly and hard, but not skid. It stopped fully three feet from the left rear of the truck. Immediately the driver reached for the gearshift lever, ready to back up hard.

There simply wasn't enough time. The Mercedes was a regular model, with no armor or bulletproof glass to protect the occupants. The first volley of fire from the truck impacted the window at an angle from the right. No fewer than thirty 5.56mm rounds hit, shattering the glass into tiny shards of shrapnel, and tearing a zipperlike row of holes across the front of the vehicle from the right door to the hood just forward of the steering wheel. The truck, thrown hastily into reverse, rolled backward off the roadside, sticking in the soft sand only twenty feet away.

Buxton knew that his first burst had been enough. Through the night-vision goggles he could see that the cramped cab of the truck was demolished, his stream of fire missing the bed entirely. Nothing in the front could have lived. He kept the M-249 Squad Automatic Weapon trained on the now quiet vehicle, his finger off the trigger, as three forms approached the truck from each side. Antonelli, lying prone next to him, brought the Galil assault rifle close to his cheek.

The team approached quickly and cautiously. Graber led the three from the right side. On the left, Makowski, Jones, and Lewis stopped twenty feet short of the side. Sean and Quimpo moved in, leaving Goldfarb back. It took only a rapid check of the truck's cab to see that no resistance would be met. Quimpo hopped down from the running board. "Clear."

Sean did a circular scan of the area. "Let's do it."

Antonelli saw the hand motion and stood up in the middle of the baaing goats. He moved to the front of the bed and pounded on the back of the cab. The native CIA agent put the truck back in gear and swung it around, driving back fifty feet before stopping and reversing to the rear of the other vehicle.

The men of Charlie Squad were up on the truck, removing the tarps. Sean walked close to the two black barrels. He removed an instrument from his equipment bag and checked the readings of the containers. "They're hot, but safe."

"Just like the spooks promised," Antonelli said, his toothy smile appearing cartoonlike in the night-vision world.

"Okay, let's move them," Sean directed. The barrels were edgerolled onto the friendly truck in just a few minutes.

The captain hopped down while the transfer was being done and walked to the bullet-riddled cab. Everything had gone perfectly. The disinformation campaign done by the Agency was masterful, keeping the Libyans concerned about "snatch teams" that never existed. Their reaction, a continuous series of moves that U.S. satellites were able to follow precisely, was predicted and planned for. The result was a perfect example of "spook and follow," and it had given Delta its radioactive quarry. Sean was glad the mission was successful, but there was something else to do.

He stepped onto the running board on the passenger side and looked in. The bodies were both slumped to the left, away from the force of the fire that had shredded them into a tangle of skin, bone, and muscle. Sean couldn't discern any colors in the permanent green environment created by the goggles, but the sight was unmistakably grotesque. He reached into his breast pocket and removed a card, then tossed it onto the seat to the right of both bodies. It landed faceup. The face of the Jack of Spades was stoic, Sean thought, as it stared straight up.

He jumped down and returned to the other truck. The loading was done.

"Ready," Buxton reported.

"Let's get out of here," recently promoted Major Sean Graber directed his squad. The last ones climbed into the truck bed. The driver started back the way they had come. Two miles down the road he turned right, to the south, onto a roughly graded dirt road. In a few minutes they would stop, dismount, and take their "prize" a few hundred meters to the waiting Blackhawk.

Then the eight Delta troopers and the native CIA agent would be gone, absent from a place they had never officially been.

The message left, however, was very real.

STUART WOODS

The *New York Times* Bestselling Author

GRASS ROOTS
71169-9/$5.99 US/$6.99 Can

When the nation's most influential senator
succumbs to a stroke, his brilliant chief aide
runs in his stead, tackling scandal, the governor
of Georgia and a white supremacist
organization that would rather see him
dead than in office.

Don't miss these other page-turners from
Stuart Woods

WHITE CARGO   70783-7/$5.99 US/$6.99 Can
A father searches for his kidnapped daughter in the
drug-soaked Colombian underworld.

DEEP LIE   70266-5/$5.99 US/$6.99 Can
At a secret Baltic submarine base, a renegade Soviet
commander prepares a plan so outrageous that it just
might work.

UNDER THE LAKE   70519-2/$5.99 US/$6.99 Can
CHIEFS   70347-5/$5.99 US/$6.99 Can
RUN BEFORE THE WIND
                     70507-9/$5.99 US/$6.99 Can